CHAMELEON

*To Dany,
Enjoy the read!
Elain Duguay 2014*

Chameleon

Book I of
The Chameleon Sagas

Edain Duguay

Wp

Wyrdwood Publications
Canada

THIS BOOK IS PUBLISHED BY WYRDWOOD
PUBLICATIONS, OTTAWA, ON, CANADA

This is a work of fiction. Names, characters, places, and incidents either are the product of the author's imagination or are used fictitiously. Any resemblance to actual persons, living or dead, events, or locales is entirely coincidental.

Text copyright © 2013 by Edain Duguay
Cover art copyright © 2013 by Wyrdwood Publications
All rights reserved.
Printed in the United States of America
Visit us on the web! www.wyrdwoodpublications.com

Library and Archives Canada Cataloguing in Publication

Duguay, Edain, 1966-, author Chameleon / Edain Duguay.
(Book I of The Chameleon Sagas)

ISBN 978-0-9879980-7-1

I. Title. II. Series: Duguay, Edain, 1966- . Chameleon Sagas ; bk. 1.

PS8607.U37623C52 2013   jC813'.6   C2013-907031-1

First trade paperback edition December 2013

DEDICATION

This book is dedicated to my family, who are the rocks in the sea of my life.

Special mention goes out to Marc for his patience, and to Lee Ann and Heidi for their support and advice on this crazy journey

Memory

My eyes were closed.

They felt so tired, so heavy.

My body just did not want to move, it felt pulled down under an enormous weight. My mind vaguely wondered why that was.

Then I remembered.

"MUM!" I screamed as I sat bolt upright and my eyes shot open. Panic hit me hard like I'd run into a brick wall, taking the air from my lungs. I instantly burst into tears and let them fall unchecked down my cheeks. I looked around me in a confused panic at the white, and entirely too bright, strange room.

The door burst open and a young nurse rushed across the room to me.

"Kate?" She said.

I just stared at her not understanding what she was saying watching her lips move as the tears continued to drip off my chin; her face was a blur through them.

"Kate?" She took me by the arms and gently lay me back down on the bed. "Everything is alright Kate, you were in an accident, but you're okay. You are in Chipping Norton Hospital. Do you understand me, Kate?" She asked.

I nodded blindly as I lay my head back down on the soft pillow, which crinkled strangely as if it were covered with plastic. Closing my eyes, I could still see my mum's lifeless face, her head leaning against the steering wheel at an odd angle. Her dead eyes stared directly at me. Deep inside I felt a hole open where my heart should be and shoot out pain like lightning. The bone deep sadness and pain must have shown on my face.

"You're alright, dear. Just a few broken bones, a bump to the head with some nasty bruising, but you're going to be just fine." She said. A bright and cheery smile appeared on her face.

How could she not know? I would never be fine again. I had lost the only person who loved me, my mum. How could anything ever be fine again? My mind raced with panic.

"What is it Kate? Are you in pain?"

"Mum. My mum." I said. My dry, horror stricken throat making the sound come out as a cracked whisper.

"What? Your mum?" She leaned closer, "Don't worry, your mum just went to get a coffee. She'll be back in a minute." She said as she checked my pulse and wrote it on the chart.

"No. My mum is dead. I saw her. Dead...in the car." The words made a ragged hole inside me grow, like wind tearing a hole in a cobweb.

"Of course she's not dead, young lady. I just spoke to her. You got a bit of a bump to your head and got things mixed up is all." She smiled down at me.

"She is dead. I saw her. I saw her face." I sat bolt upright clutching at my side as a sharp pain burst through me, making me gasp.

"Now, now...relax, dear, she's just fine. Lay down before you hurt yourself more. You must have dreamt it, lots of people have nightmares after accidents. It's all quite normal. Your mum will be right back and very happy to see you're awake, I know she will." She reached over and plumped my pillow. "Are you thirsty? I can fetch you some water."

I just nodded and she quietly left the room.

Not dead? Could it be true? But I saw...what I saw...why

would she lie? Of course, she wouldn't, it must have been a dream. Was it? My brain couldn't take it all in.

I could feel I had several broken ribs; they had shot pain through me when I sat up. I tried to relax and breathe gently, however, that was only one of my injuries. I must have also broken my left wrist, which was now encased in a heavy white cast. I could feel a bandage on my forehead and remembered the warm sensation of sticky blood running down my face probably caused by the flying glass from the car's windscreen.

Looking up at the square white tiles on the ceiling and wondered if I'd been dreaming. I tried to remember some of the details, when, without warning and with an incredible force, the last month's events flooded back into my mind, leaving me breathless and terrified. It felt as though someone had turned on ten TV's at once, all of them on different channels, with bright images and loud sound. The truth of how I came to be lying in a hospital room, if my memory was to be trusted, was even more bizarre and frightening than anyone would believe. I closed my eyes as my head began to spin, it felt increasingly like I was going to vomit.

The door opened again.

"Nurse, I think I'm going to be sick." I mumbled through clenched teeth and squeezed my eyes tightly shut trying to fight it. I breathed hard through my nose and clenched desperately at the bed sheets. Vomiting is the one thing I really hate and would avoid no matter what, if I could.

"Katy, you're awake!" The sound of mum's excited voice burst through my concentration.

My eyes shot open as sat up too quickly to look at her and vomited everywhere.

It took two nurses several minutes and a few gasps of pain from me, before they had me cleaned up. All the while, mum anxiously hovered in the background, obviously wanting to help. Soon the nurses left and mum placed her cool hand on against my cheek and soothed my hair away from my forehead, just like she always does when I'm ill. It felt great to feel it again now.

"They said you had a concussion and may feel a bit nauseous when you came to. How do you feel?" She said.

"Oh mum, I'm so happy to see you...I...thought..." The relief welled in me to the point where I burst into uncontrollable sobs and I couldn't finish the sentence.

Mum sat on the bed and hugged me very gently, trying not to hurt me. She was a small woman but I felt completely covered by the warmth of her loving arms. I had never been so happy to see her in my life.

"I love you, mum." I hugged her back with everything I had.

"I love you too, hun. Everything is all right now." She gently stroked my hair again.

"I thought you were dead, I saw your face." I looked up into her face seeing only the dead eyes again. I shuddered and closed my eyes to block out the horrible image.

"I'm fine, sweetie. Honest. Look, not even a bruise, which I admit is odd, considering how badly you got bashed about. The car is a complete write off." She pulled back, tucked her hair behind her ear, "Mind you, I can't really remember what happened. Dr. Davis thinks I hit my head too and that's why I can't remember, but I feel fine and have no bumps or stitches to show for it, unlike you. Poor thing." She gently touched my forehead.

"I have stitches?" I reached up and then changed my mind, perhaps poking new stitches wasn't such a good idea. "Wait, you can't remember the accident?" I said.

"Nope, not a thing after leaving the pub. I remember us getting in the car and leaving the car park, then nothing until I woke up on stretcher in the ambulance. That's it. I also remember being worried about you when I was being checked over by the doctor and waiting to hear how badly you were injured, but nothing more about the accident." A shadow of something, perhaps fear or maybe doubt, flicked across her eyes, "I'm sure it will come back to me, eventually." She said as she looked away and straightened my covers.

I could tell she was bothered about not remembering.

"What do you remember?" She looked up at me, speaking quietly.

"Erm...not much and what I do remember is obviously wrong, because you're alive." I said, hating to lie to her.

Mum laughed uneasily, "The doctors said that a bang on the head can sometimes mix things up, perhaps we'll both remember more soon. What's important now, is for you to get better." She gently kissed my cheek and stood up. "I'd better go and ring your dad, he's very worried about you."

"Do you have to?" My anger began to burn in a familiar way. "I'm sure he is too busy with his new family to care."

"Of course I do, Kate." She said as she looked at me sternly, "No matter what he's done, he is still your father and deserves to know how you're doing." She looked down at herself with dismay, "I should also pop home and get cleaned up. I'll come back as soon as I can, okay?"

I realised she still wore the same clothes from the accident, which were gruesomely covered with dried blood. The blood stain had darkened the entire front of her favourite blue sweater.

My eyes widened with amazement. "Have you been here since the accident? The nurse said I had been unconscious for hours."

"Of course, I have, silly." Mum's face showed a gentle worried smile, "I couldn't go home until I knew you were okay." She reached over and gave me another hug.

"Ow!"

Mum cringed, "Sorry, Katy. Did I hurt your ribs, your head or your arm?"

"It was my ribs, but it's worth it for a hug." I grinned, "Okay, go home and change, you like look an escapee from a zombie movie with all that blood."

Mum left, promising to be back soon and at last I was left to my own thoughts. The relief that my mum was still alive had vanished in the light of the memory of the last few weeks. I could now fully remember what happened. I could remember it all very clearly and the last thing I could do was tell my mum the truth or anyone else for that matter.

Things had changed.

Changed forever.

I closed my eyes and took a careful breath. The last few weeks had been such a whirlwind I wasn't even sure I actually understood it all, and since I had nothing better to do than think, I was going to try to make sense of it.

If I could.

SHAKESPEARE

One Month Earlier

Monday started just like any Monday should.

The alarm had awoken me at 6.45am. Groggily, I slapped the alarm, threw back the covers and slowly climbed out of my warm, cozy bed. I stumbled, bare footed, out of my small room and headed down the hall to the bathroom with bleary eyes and a not completely awake brain. I glanced in the mirror at my wild shoulder length hair and my fringe, which always wanted to stick up at the front in the morning, no matter how I slept. Yawning loudly, I stretched and climbed into the shower. I stood there letting the hot water massage me awake. I love morning showers, they're the best way to wake me up and, seeing as I'm allergic to caffeine, the healthiest way.

By 7.30am I was running out of the door, having kissed mum goodbye and grabbed some toast off my plate. I ran for the school bus at the end of our lane, I just made it in time and climbed aboard. The bus driver, a round happy woman whose name I can never remember, nodded good morning to me, pulled away from the curb. Walking carefully down the bus as it lurched, I sat in the empty seat next to Ally, the nearest thing I had to a best friend. Well, okay not exactly best friend but a friend...I had only known her for a short time.

"Mornin', Ally." I said with all the enthusiasm I could muster, which was very little at this time of the morning.

Ally looked up from the textbook and pushed her glasses up her long thin nose. "Morning, Kate." She said and went directly back to reading a book on what looked like, cell division.

"Crap! Do we have a test today I've forgotten about?" I said, peering at her book.

"Nope, tomorrow but I just wanted to make sure I grasped the concept." Ally replied without looking up. Ally was the type of student that permanently has her head in a book and always did well on tests.

Sickening, really.

I'd met Ally on my first day when I was in the school office, getting all my class information from the Secretary. Ally had come out of the nurse's office holding her nose after a nosebleed; apparently, she had actually walked into a door while reading. A subject that was not to be laughed at, decided Ally upon our introduction. As Ally had several of my science classes, she suggested I should tag along with her until I'd found my way around. Well, that was last Monday and a week later, I was still following Ally about.

Unfortunately, I'd moved to the school two weeks into the start of the September term, which meant the other new students had already meshed together, leaving me the odd one out. Some of the students in my year had also been together through the local comprehensive school and had firmly established friendship groups when they moved here. I, on the other hand, had just moved to the school as it specialized in the sciences and performing arts. Both of which were the subjects I wanted to be qualified in. I had decided that my grand plan was to become an actress but if that failed and I couldn't get work, well, then, the science was something to fall back on.

"So how was your first week?" Ally said.

"Not bad, too many rich kids for my liking but the school is

Chameleon

pretty cool. Thanks again for letting me follow you around."

"You're welcome. It's nice to have someone like me to talk to." Ally looked up over her glasses and smiled.

"Like you, you mean someone not spending daddy's trust fund?"

She grinned. "Yep." With that, her attention was back in the book.

I settled back in my seat and, over Ally's head, I watched the village houses pass by.

Mum and I had only recently moved from London to Shipton-under-Wychwood, in Oxfordshire. It's a small town in the middle of nowhere, which sits between the River Evenlode and the Forrest of Wychwood. The town has a pub, a couple of supermarkets, a small public library and Marston Court. An Elizabethan Manor House, which was, apparently, according to the school brochure, 'the jewel of the Marston Estate'. The only reason mum and I came to such a small town, was for me to attend The Marston School of Performing Arts and Sciences, named after Mathers Danforth Marston III, the son of a rich peer who wanted nothing more than to study the performing arts and the sciences. The brochure said that, 'he persuaded his father to build the school in 1899 and create a financial legacy that enabled the school to be free to all students. Mathers' father, Lord Mathers Danforth Marston II, invested in the school so heavily; the school can boast that it's the only public school that has the resources and facilities of the best private schools anywhere in England'. Well, I didn't know about all that but I liked it.

It still amazed me that I'd been given the chance to study here. Not being an exceptional student nor had I any special talents, I could only think it must have been a fluke. My mum, being the 'always think positive' person she is, had filled out the application form and posted it before telling me. She wasn't even surprised when we received the confirmation of a place,

Edain Duguay

even though it came right at the end of the summer holidays when I'd given up all hope of ever getting in anywhere. Within the hour, she had given notice at the solicitor's office, where she worked as a Law Clerk and had found us a small semi-detached cottage to rent in Shipton-under-Wychwood, however, she had to work her two weeks notice, hence why I missed the start of the term.

Within a couple of weeks, we'd moved into a rented cottage in a new town, far away from everything and everyone we knew. I didn't have chance to be nervous about the new start, new school, new home and hopefully new friends because I was doing it before anything had sunk in.

I realised my mind had wandered for the entire bus journey and I'd not spoken another word to Ally. Ally didn't seem to mind though; she usually had her head stuck in a science book and rarely spoke anyway, which gave me plenty of time to daydream about my future as an Oscar winning actress. Like my mum said, 'If you don't have a dream, how can you make it happen?'

The bus slowed as it went up the gravel drive of the Marston School. The reception building is all you can see from the drive, it's an impressive gothic building; full of windows and ornate brickwork. The school is surrounded by several hundred acres of parkland and forest, which housed The Marston Theatre, The Mathers Danforth Science Building and The Marston Family Library. Each building was gorgeous, but compared to the reception, they definitely took second place. The bus pulled to a stop just outside the massive wooden doors of the reception building, above which sat the school crest carved in stone, with the motto 'Semper Vivendus' beneath it. I glanced up at the crest as I climbed down the steps and onto the gravel drive, I liked going to a school that had its own motto.

Walking through the main doors and we passed the massive

Chameleon

reception desk, which looked like it had come from an old hotel in the movies, and followed the crowd of noisy students up the massive oak grand staircase to our Form room. The Form room looked more like a lounge than a classroom, except for the desk, where our Form Tutor sat. The room had several comfy sofas and there were a few tables with chairs scattered around. Form was a 15 min prep class where our Form Tutor took the register each morning and afternoon, it was also where everyone had chance to finish last minute homework, cram for exams or chat with friends before the lessons started. Form room was the place where we were allowed to come during class breaks and at lunchtimes, if we weren't in the dining hall or outside.

Form was usually noisy and relaxed; today was no different, students laughed and talked, some had music playing in their earphones and I, as usual, watched them nod their heads in time to the beat, while they studied. I always found Form interesting, it was the one place where everyone seemed relaxed, happy to be themselves. People watching had become one of my favourite things, you could learn so much from it.

Sitting down next to Ally at one of the tables at the back, I munched on an apple and half read the text book over Ally's shoulder, which looked, not surprisingly for Ally, to be about cancerous cells and how they mutate.

Through the crowd I noticed a new student walk in, he had his back to us while talking to our Form Tutor, Mr. Hitchins. I hadn't seen the new student's face and nudged Ally.

"Hey, look, I think we have a newbie." I said.

Ally peered over the top of her glasses and through her blond curly fringe at me as I nodded towards the front of the room. We looked over as the new student turned round. My blood instantly rushed to my face when he looked directly at me with the most amazing blue eyes I'd ever seen. He immediately looked away, as if he hadn't seen me and walked over to an empty chair by the window. I blushed furiously and my heart beat against my ribs like it was trying to break them and escape. I became momentarily speechless, he was possibly, no definitely, the most handsome guy, I'd ever seen. My mouth became so dry I had to tear my eyes away from him, just to be able to swallow.

"Wow."

"What?" Ally's head shot up.

"Him, I mean...well....wow."

"You said that Kate, what about him?" She sighed and frowned as she peered over towards the window.

"What about him?" I said incredulously. "Are ya kidding? I mean just look at him."

"Just another good looking bloke, who looks like a Goth, vampire wannabe to me. He looks well off too, judging by his clothes and attitude." Ally said as she turned her head back towards her book, having already lost interest.

"He's gorgeous and looks like he doesn't know it." I couldn't take my eyes off him, "Now that is rare." I said.

"Yeah right, no one that good looking doesn't know it. He looks like one of the rich kids and it's not like we don't have enough of them around here, is it?" Ally asked sarcastically without even raising her head.

"I know this school brings them in droves but...I dunno...he looks...different to me...I wonder who he is." I looked at his clothes, "Anyway, don't Goths only wear black clothes with lots of make-up, jewellery and paint their finger nails black?" I tried to remember the ones I'd seen in London. I secretly watched him as he sat waiting for the class bell to ring. He had the blackest hair I'd ever seen, a real raven black that shone in the light of the September sun as almost blue, which in turn made his skin look pale by comparison. His hair was styled sort of softly spiky but, thankfully, not plastered solid with gel. He seemed so relaxed as he stretched out his long legs, with his hands calmly placed on his lap as he waited. For a new student he did not seem worried or nervous at all.

"Whatever, I dunno, don't really care." Said Ally bringing my attention back to her just as the first bell went and the Form room erupted into chaos.

Within seconds he had vanished into the crowd in the hall. Ally and I packed up our things and made our way out of the main building and across the courtyard to Physics in the Daniel Mathers Science Building. The day was warm and we soaked up the September sun as we walked between the buildings. Several students seemed to be excited and there was a growing crowd ahead of us.

"What's going on?" I ask a girl I recognised from class, as she rushed by.

"Oh." She squealed, "One of the Marston boys is here." She vanished into the crowd.

"Yeah, I know that. Wil is in the year up from us." I called after her. "But what's the crowd about, is someone hurt?"

"Don't bother, she's already gone." Ally said.

The crowd became so large we walked on the grass to get round it and we still couldn't see what was happening. Eventually, we gave up, knowing full well that the gossip would catch up with us.

Sitting at our usual table we noticed there were very few people in class, probably due to the craziness outside. Mrs. Rutherford, our Physics teacher, waited impatiently at the door for everyone to rush by her in an excited babble.

"Alright everyone, settle down." She called through the influx of students. "Find your seats quickly; we have a lot to cover today."

I'd already lost interest in the crowd and became engrossed in the process of emptying my books and pens out of my bag as my mind started to wander off thinking about the afternoon's

Theatre Studies class, which I loved.

"Ah, Mr Marston, I thought that might be the problem, oh well, what's done is done. Everyone? As you now know we have a new member of the Marston family here with us in school and he will be in our class. Please make sure you welcome Joshua, when you get the chance." Mrs. Rutherford said. "Joshua, there is a spare seat over on Ally and Kate's table at the back, on the right, please join them quickly, the class has been delayed enough for one day."

My breath caught in my throat at the mention of my name and my heart sunk as I realised what she had said. Now I would have to sit next to some stuck up rich kid with no brains, just family money. "Ugh! Why me? Damn it."

"What's up?" Ally asked looking up at me.

"We get the new spoiled rich brat at our table. How is that fair?" I complained and the crowd thinned out as the students sat down.

"Thanks a lot. I didn't mean to ruin your day." The angry words were spoken right next to me.

I jumped at the voice so close to my ear and turned to see who had spoken; it was him, the gorgeous guy from Form with the fabulous blue eyes that were now staring angrily down at me from his scowling face. Damn he is too much of a babe to look that angry, I thought. Blushing instantly, I mumbled "Sorry" and quickly looked away, trying not to think about his unusual accent or his lovely eyes.

I could hear him unpacking his bag and taking off his coat but I didn't dare to look at him again. He might be a babe, but who wants to get to know a spoiled brat? I turned my body half away from him towards Ally and prepared for some serious Physics. For the rest of the class, I ignored his very presence and concentrated on the course work.

By lunch, I'd discovered that not only was 'The Brat' - as my

Chameleon

brain had now nicknamed the Marston guy - in my Physics class, but also in my Chemistry and Biology classes. Luckily, there was no room for him to sit anywhere near us in those classes and he had been claimed by some of the other rich kids in the lessons. A huge relief had washed over me. He may be very good looking but he's rich and I don't date rich guys, which was a very good thing seeing as I don't handle rich kids very well. I'd decided I'd drool from afar and nothing more.

Later, enjoying the warmth of the autumn day, Ally and I sat outside to eat our lunch on one of the low walls surrounding the gardens.

"So what have you got this afternoon?" Ally asked, "Do you have Theatre Studies, Property Making and Theatrical Makeup or Scenic Arts & Production Class? I thought I had your timetable nailed but Monday afternoon is a loss to me."

"I've Theatre Studies and Swimming, actually. Are you memorizing my schedule?" I laughed, looking at her.

"Yup, once it's in..." She pointed to her temple, "it'll be one thing less to worry about." She grinned and bit into another sandwich.

"You know you're a bit crazy...right?"

"Yup, my Grandma thinks so too but she believes I'll cure Cancer one day, so she is quiet happy to have a crazy Granddaughter." Ally laughed.

"Well, as long as she is happy about it." I grinned and looked at Ally as she finished her last sandwich and rummaged in her multi-coloured, over-sized lunch box for fruit.

Ally's parents had been killed in a car accident when she was only three years old and her Grandmother had brought her up. She had told me about it on the first day we met, she had simply stated these terrible facts like she was reciting a list. Her personality took a little getting used to, but Ally was never one for small talk, which suited me just fine, it gave me the chance to

Edain Duguay

daydream more. I guessed that's why I was still following her around a week later.

"What classes do you have?" I said.

"I have Medical Histories and then Swimming like you. I hope I can keep Mr Jeffries talking, so I'm too late to swim. Why do I need to swim when I want to be a doctor?"

"I dunno, perhaps you could be a ship's doctor." I joked.

"Don't be daft, Kate." Ally looked shocked at my reply. "Anyway, I can swim already, so who needs to practice? Such a waste of my time." Ally sighed.

"I don't mind swimming, I actually quiet like it." I packed away my lunch box in my bag and threw it on the ground at my feet. "Really looking forward to Theatre Studies though, I think it's my favourite subject so far. Finding out about the history of Theatre and getting the chance to play some of the roles in the classics...wonderful." I grinned knowing full well that Ally didn't share my interest.

"Sounds so boring, full of people who like showing off. Don't know what you see in it, give me bits of anatomy and microscope slides anytime." She said.

"Yup, crazy." I laughed shaking my head just as the bell rang for afternoon Form.

"Come on." I said as I jumped off the wall. "Let's see if we can get a sofa in Form, so I can let this boring cheese sandwich go down before I'm onstage with my adoring fans." I said throwing my arms open wide, posing and looking serious about it.

"Oh please, and you say I'm the crazy one. Yeah, right." Ally grabbed my arm and laughingly started to drag me back to the main building.

I laughed too as I fell in step beside her; perhaps friend maybe the right word for Ally, after all. It felt comfortable being around her, I could be myself and she didn't care if I wanted peace and quiet, she enjoyed it too.

Chameleon

We made our way back up the grand staircase to our Form room for the afternoon register and luckily found an empty sofa. Crashing on it and we relaxed while Mr Hitchins read out everyone's name and made a mark in the register. He called The Brat's name but there came no sound, Mr Hitchins didn't even look up at the lack of reply he just continued onto the next name. There was no sign of The Brat at all; perhaps he had decided to change Form to be near some of his new rich friends. Shame, I wouldn't be able to drool over him but I could live with that. All too soon the class bell rang and we grabbed our bags ready to head out.

"I'll see you on the bus later, Kate" Ally smiled a smug grin.

"Not at swimming? Are you ditching class?" I asked faking shock.

"Oh no, not me." She pretended to be horrified, "I have an important library assignment to do for Mr Jeffries." She smiled and added, "One he doesn't know about yet, of course." She winked at me.

"You are so bad. Swimming really isn't that bad, ya know. I'd understand if we had gym or track...ugh." I said.

"Well, I find that I'm unfortunately otherwise engaged." Ally grinned as she placed her bag over her shoulder and we both headed for the door.

"Alright then, I guess I'll see you on the bus. Hopefully, I won't miss it like last week and have to walk home again."

"Hmm...another good reason not to swim, it takes ages to get dried and dressed again hence potentially missing the bus then having to walk home. See, so many reasons not to swim." Ally reasoned as we walked back down the grand stairs.

Ally and I parted ways and I headed for Theatre Studies. As I walked along the bricked path, through the small rose garden towards the theatre, I could hear the shrill voice of Rebecca Stirling coming from behind me, it sounded like she was walking with a silent companion and obviously trying to impress them. She was telling all that would listen, how her daddy had made his money by designing some cool app and how he had promised to buy her a Porsche and driving lessons for her seventeenth birthday, on Saturday. Her voice made my skin crawl, all high pitched and nasal. It suited her though; she was unbelievably skinny and always in the latest 'fashion', she was also, amazingly, a natural blond. Sometimes I just had to thank Mother Nature for her sense of humour.

I felt sorry for her companions, whoever they were, and I bet they didn't deserve this treatment...or maybe they did, maybe they loved hearing about her pointless, self absorbed 'rich' pursuits. They were probably also 'rich kids' with a padded bank account from 'daddy'. Rich kids always made me shudder, so false and full of themselves. The only problem was that there was a plague of them in the Theatre orientated classes, I guess the academic classes were a bit too hard for such an inbred bunch. So, okay...I can be bitchy too.

The Theatre Studies classes were held in two places, some of the lessons each week were in a classroom and the others were held on the stage in The Marston Theatre. Today's lesson happened to be held in the theatre. A gloriously old fashioned Victorian theatre, complete with thick velvet curtains, elegant boxes on each side of the stage and an orchestra pit. The acoustics were excellent, of course.

Finding a seat in the front row, I sat down and began taking out my note pad and pen from my bag. I could hear Rebecca still chattering away like some demented crow a few seats behind me and I tried to tune her out but failed. I imagined myself leaping over the seat and throttling her scrawny little neck. Calm. Breathe. Calm...I mentally ordered myself and tried to focus, this was my favourite class and I wasn't going to let anyone stop me from enjoying it.

"Good afternoon, class." Miss Claremont announced as she walked out from behind the stage curtains. A small, rounded lady with very curly grey hair and the type of wild curls that could only be natural. She smiled and adjusted her glasses, "As discussed during last Friday's lesson, this week we shall be studying two scenes from William Shakespeare's classic 'Much Ado About Nothing'. Today, we will be having a read through on stage and then a discussion." She moved to the front of the stage and looked directly at me, "Kate, on the chair near you are the scripts, could you possibly hand them out, please?" She pointed to the seat two up from me, where the pile of papers sat.

Willing to help I leapt up, accidentally causing my bag to fall from my lap onto the floor, pitching books, pens and my personal stuff everywhere. Rebecca burst out laughing with her hideous high-pitched laugh. Horrified and blushing furiously, I quickly bent down to retrieve my belongings, crawling around on my hands and knees, in front of everyone.

"Oh dear. Christina, can you hand out the papers, since Kate is otherwise engaged?" Miss Claremont said.

Christina, a small American girl with short spiky hair and a kind face, walked past me and picked up the papers. She handed me a copy, which I took furtively and sat back down quickly, clutching my bag against me. I slouched in my chair, with my face glowing bright red, I was hideously mortified.

Miss Claremont glanced at the scripts in her hand, "Right, let's look at the first scene Act I, Scene 1. We shall start from the entrance of Don Pedro, Don John, Claudio, Benedick, and Balthasar. Remember, we already have Leonato, Hero, and Beatrice discussing their arrival." She looked out at her audience, "When I call out your name please come up on the stage, bringing your scripts with you."

I slunk deeper into my chair, hoping I wouldn't be picked, at least not until I'd stopped blushing and had regained some composure.

Miss Claremont glanced at her notes, looked out at the students again and called out our fates, "Michael you can be Don Pedro, Robert you're Don John, Billy you're Claudio, Joshua you're Benedick..."

My head snapped up at the mention of his name. Damn, he was in this class too? I couldn't escape him.

Miss Claremont continued through her list, "Marcus, you're playing Balthasar and Matthew you're Leonato, Rebecca you will be Hero and Kate you will play Beatrice."

I groaned inside.

"You all have five minutes to have a quick read through your lines and then we shall go through them together."

I hung my head horrified. Not only was I still bright red from throwing the contents of my bag to the four winds but I was also going to have to face Rebecca and her new buddy, which, I now realised had probably been Joshua Marston. I quickly dumped my bag on my chair and headed towards the aisle, keeping my eyes cast downwards while I begged for my cheeks to stop burning.

I cringed as I picked my way past the other students and climbed up on the stage. Sadly, my blush had only deepened as I remembered what was coming. Much Ado About Nothing is one of my favourite plays and I could often be found watching Kenneth Branagh's version of it. Why me? Why do I have to be Beatrice and Joshua, Benedick? A deep dread started to build inside, I felt, on instinct, that this would not turn out well. The more I thought about the wording of the play, the more the dread turned to inner glee. I may actually enjoy this. I thought, as a sly, wicked smile crept onto my face.

"Everyone ready?" Asked Miss Claremont, who was rewarded with various noises of ascent. "Okay, ladies and gentlemen let's see what you make of it and....action."

Chameleon

A brief pause as we all moved nearer to the front of the stage, Rebecca stood almost attached to Joshua's elbow. Well, that definitely solves whom she was smothering earlier, I thought, slightly shaking my head.

The class began to read the lines and all too quickly it was The Brats turn...

Joshua/BENEDICK: *"Were you in doubt, sir, that you asked her?"*

Joshua smiled accordingly as he delivered his line, a perfect smile that literally transformed his face and made my heart leap and skip a beat in my chest. I could feel the tingling of blood as it rushed to my face and my stomach lurched downwards like someone had just pulled a plug out.

Damn it!

His voice was so honeyed and warm, with an accent that sounded both English and American, it felt like it reached out and caressed my skin. I quickly realised I'd missed a few lines, luckily not my own and scrambled with the script pages to catch up. Annoyed he had managed to distract and fluster me.

Joshua/BENEDICK: *"If Signior Leonato be her father, she would not have his head on her shoulders for all Messina, as like him as she is."*

I took a quick, deep breath and I swallowed hard.

BEATRICE: *"I wonder that you will still be talking, Signior Benedick: nobody marks you."* I said it with a suitably superior expression.

Joshua turned to look at me with the full blaze of his gorgeous blue eyes.

Joshua/BENEDICK: *"What, my dear Lady Disdain! Are you yet living?"* He gloated.

The lines of the script flowed quickly now.

I replied, *"Is it possible disdain should die while she hath such meet food to feed it as Signior Benedick? Courtesy itself must convert to disdain, if you come in her presence."* I began to enjoy the insults of the script.

"Then is courtesy a turncoat. But it is certain I am loved of all ladies, only you excepted: and I would I could find in my heart that I had not a hard heart; for, truly, I love none." Joshua grinned.

A sly smiled appeared on my lips, *"A dear happiness to women: they would else have been troubled with a pernicious suitor. I thank God and my cold blood, I am of your humour for that: I had rather hear my dog bark at a crow than a man swear he loves me."* I said.

Joshua took a step backwards and held up his hands, *"God keep your ladyship still in that mind! So some gentleman or other shall 'scape a predestinate scratched face."* He smiled, seemingly enjoying this too much.

All other cast members said the required "Ooo's" and "Ahhh's"s.

I waited for them to finish and said, *"Scratching could not make it worse, an 'twere such a face as yours were."* I inserted venom into my words that came from deep down and bubbled outwards as angry tears filled my eyes. Damn, why do I well up when I get angry, it makes me look so weak.

"Well, you are a rare parrot-teacher." Joshua looked surprised at my anger.

"A bird of my tongue is better than a beast of yours." I said through gritted teeth. It had become very hard to stick to the play's script now, as memories of my father leaving, with his new, rich girlfriend and her stuck up son, flashed through my mind. I knew it wasn't Joshua's fault but my anger and frustration just craved to be vented.

"I would my horse had the speed of your tongue, and so good a continuer. But keep your way, I' God's name; I have done." He replied.

Chameleon

He took another small step back but this time stunned at my reaction, which only fuelled it and made everything worse, I could feel my face burning and tears over flowing, as I became incensed. All my hate for rich people just taking what they wanted, no matter the consequences, exploded. *"You always end with a jade's trick: I know you of old."* I spat out. I directed it at Joshua and had not spoken it in the true mood of the script.

"What the hells wrong with her?" Rebecca obviously couldn't stand it any longer. She thrust her angry face in front of mine. "Are you crazy? It's a play."

"Shut up, Rebecca." Joshua growled at her and moved forward quickly.

My hate exploded. "I don't need your help." I raged at him, "In fact, I don't need anything from someone like you." Tears streamed down my face as I shouted.

Several things happened at once, Joshua stood in front of Rebecca before she could comment again and he had the audacity to look surprised, the other members of the cast gasped in shock.

Miss Claremont stood up quickly, "Now that is quite enough of that, Kate." She bellowed, "Get off the stage and calm yourself young lady."

I threw my scripts at Joshua, stormed off the stage, grabbed my bag and headed for the nearest exit. I was incensed at him, at every rich kid and at myself. My legs had turned to jelly and they couldn't get me out fast enough. I left in a flurry of tears and seething rage. I ran into the calming embrace of the cool air in the foyer.

I stood outside the door to the theatre panting, I breathed in the September air and slowly tried to calm myself, what the hell was I doing? I wondered. I started walking, shakily, towards the gardens, where I knew I could chill out. There had been a light rainfall while I was in class so I put my jacket on the damp bench and sat with my face lifted up to the sunlight with my eyes closed, listening to the birds and the rustle of the leaves. I could smell the last of the roses, their faint smell mixed with the earthy smell of the soil and the sweet smell of recent rain.

Well, what an idiot I'd made of myself, I thought, everyone in school would know about it, damn it. I felt stupid; this was the worse day ever. I'd have to apologise to Miss Claremont, of course, for ruining the lesson and acting like a real diva.

By the time the bell rang for swimming, I was waiting calmly outside the changing room, my face a normal colour and all traces of the rage and tears had vanished. Did I mention that I was a good actress?

Once in the pool, I took all my frustrations out on the act of swimming and completed several more laps than I did last week. My only drowning sensation, if you could call it that, came when I spotted Joshua over in the dive area, waiting for his turn. I discretely appeared to be resting between lengths as I peered out of the corner of my eye at him. He seemed no worse for wear, considering my outburst and stood laughing and joking with the other guys, as they waited their turn. He had not spotted me, but then we girls all look the same in the water with swimming caps and goggles on.

Why did I care if he noticed me at all? I wondered shaking my head.

As I watched him, I was able to get a good view of his body, which was nicely muscular, a surprise, as he'd not look so well toned when dressed. How could I like what I see, when I hate what he is? I shook my head again and reminded myself to only drool from afar, then I did the only thing I could, I threw myself back into the mind calming monotony of more lengths.

I hung back when everyone got out at the end of the lesson to avoid the stupid and yet inevitable questions from students who had already heard of my outburst. I eventually walked out

Chameleon

of the changing rooms into the late afternoon sunlight, it had begun to rain again but heavily this time with a cold wind. Pulling up my hood, I made a dash through the puddles, heading for the bus stop at the front of the main building. I reached the stop just in time to see the bus disappear out of the drive and speed away.

"Damn it." I said and glanced round to see if anyone else had missed the bus but everyone from swimming had either got out earlier and caught the bus or were heading to the dorms or the car park. Seeing as I had very few friends, and none who had passed their driving test yet, I swore and started to walk down the long gravel driveway. I headed towards the main road with a heavy heart, I knew it would eventually lead me home but it was a long walk in the rain and it was cold too. I would arrive soaked and frozen. Great, I thought, gloomily, as I kept on walking.

The main road was narrow with no footpaths but at least it was still light as I trudged along. There were several large puddles along the way and not much traffic; it was too early for the commuter traffic. I pulled my hood closer and walked with my head down so the bitter wind couldn't whip the hood back.

I could hear a car coming from behind me and I tried to stay closer to the grass verge to give them plenty of room as they passed. A deep midnight blue Audi rush past, narrowly missing a puddle, which would have soaked me. As I watched the car drive away, I saw the brake lights come on. It came to a stop ahead of me, I couldn't see who the driver was from this distance. I suddenly felt somewhat isolated and vulnerable, alone in the middle of nowhere.

The car backed toward me and stopped again.

My brain feverishly tried to work out what I could do when the psycho got out of the car, to do God-knows-what to me. I tried to remember some survival tips we were taught at my last school, which had been in a poor area in London. Keys. That was it; hold your keys in your hand making sure the keys stick out between each of your fingers when you make a fist. I quickly grabbed my house keys from my pocket and spread them between my fingers. If nothing else, I thought, I could kick him in the groin and run like hell. I felt happier knowing I had a plan, it made me feel more brave. The car door opened and I held my breath.

Was this it?

Was this the end of my short life...maybe they would make a film of my life...maybe they would call it 'Rain Killer.' I thought crazily and laughed nervously to myself as I glared at the opening car door and tried to swallow but my throat had dried up from fear.

OPINIONS

The stranger walked directly towards me, seemingly not bothered by the heavy rain or wind that happened to be whisking raindrops violently around him.

As he drew closer I recognised him. Joshua stood just three feet away from me. He seemed oblivious to being instantly soaked through and did not seem to even acknowledge it, nor shelter himself against it. He was unbearably handsome even as the rain dripped off his hair and the end of his nose.

"Hello." He said and smiled.

"Err...Hi." My voice shook. I was not sure if it was my previous fear of an attack or because it was it him stood before me.

"If you don't hate me too much, could I give you a lift so you don't catch pneumonia?"

I stared at him, feeling both shock at seeing him and sheer relief. "I...erm well, okay." I mumbled, embarrassed at feeling shy.

"Good." He turned, headed back to the car and opened the passenger door for me without another word.

I rushed round to the passenger side wondering what the hell I was doing, wasn't I just ranting at him only a couple of hours ago? He'll think I'm the psycho. I climbed in the plush interior and fastened the seat belt as I watched him calmly walk back around the car to his side and climb in.

"This is kind of you..." I said, looking for more words, my brain having stopped.

"I couldn't leave you walking home in the rain, all alone in the middle of nowhere. There might be psychos around. Apart from you that is." He grinned and glanced at me as he brushed back his wet hair with his hand. He restarted the car and pulled away from the verge.

I stifled a nervous laugh. "I thought you were a psycho when you pulled up."

He laughed, a deep and attractive sound.

"I don't hate you." I whispered as I sat looking out of the passenger side window, utterly embarrassed by my outburst this afternoon. I bit my lip unsure of what to say next.

He didn't say anything either and continued to keep he eyes on the road.

"I'm sorry about...earlier." I said as I turned to look at him.

"Don't worry about it." He glanced at me quickly and smiled.

"What? You're not angry at me?" I was astonished and didn't wait for him to reply, "I made a complete ass of myself and you, in front of the whole class, including your new friends."

"There are far more important things in life than being angry about your explosion. As for Rebecca, which I presume you meant, I would not call her my friend." His lips turned down in a show of disgust.

"Oh, I thought she was."

"No. She's not."

"Oh, well...that's good..." I said, unsure of how to go on. "Thank you."

"What for?" He pulled over to the verge just before a T-junction, letting the car idle and turned in his seat towards me.

"For the lift." I pushed a damp strand of hair away from my eyes, "And for the record, today wasn't really about you, things just...came out."

Chameleon

"Glad to hear it, I'd wondered what I'd done to annoy you. Seeing as we only just met." He grinned.

"You have a strange accent, where are you from? I said.

He smiled at me and I could feel a strange excitement build inside of me as I looked at his smile.

"I was born here, in the UK, but I spend half my time in Canada. My mother is Canadian and we have a place there."

"Oh, I thought it was American. Canada, huh? It's supposed to be nice there." I turned in my seat to face him.

"I like the wilderness." Suddenly a flicker of worry flashed across his face. He almost looked like he had said something wrong. He turned back in his seat to stare coldly out of the front windscreen.

I frowned at his odd reaction and felt instinctively that there was a mystery about him. "Is that why you started three weeks into the term? Sorry, I can be nosey...you don't have to answer."

His mood instantly changed again. "Actually yes, I flew back last Saturday. Left or right?"

"What?"

He gestured to the road junction ahead, "Left or right? I have no idea where you live."

"Oh right.... I mean, go left and follow the road into town, do you know where Blackberry Lane is? Down the side of the Greenman pub?"

He nodded.

"I live down that lane." I settled back in to my seat. I could smell the leather and wet clothes but I could also smell an earthy woodsy smell. It was very pleasant, like taking a walk in the woods on a sunny day. I wasn't sure if it was an air freshener in the car or some sort of cologne that Joshua was wearing. Either way I liked it, I liked it a lot.

All too quickly we were driving down the lane beside the pub, heading to the row of cottages at the bottom.

Edain Duguay

"Which one?" He asked.

"Number thirteen, it's the one with the apple tree in the front." I said.

He pulled over outside my house and stopped the car without switching the engine off. The silence became instantly awkward.

"I guess I will see you tomorrow." He said and grinned.

"I...erm...yes, I guess so." I said. "Thanks again for the lift." I quickly undid my seat belt, grabbed my bag and leapt out of the car, closing the door behind me. I didn't look back, but I heard him drive off quickly, like he couldn't get away quick enough. Perhaps his mood had changed again. Perhaps he was a psycho after all.

Later that night, as I lay in bed waiting for sleep to creep up on me and I couldn't stop thinking about Joshua. Funny, how he had gone from being the 'The Brat', to being Joshua in my mind. Admittedly, he was very good looking and even seemed nice, if a little moody; after all, he didn't have to give me a lift today, especially after the way I'd treated him. Maybe he was nicer than I first thought but, and this was a big but, he was still one of the rich kids and I'd had some experience of how selfish they can be. I mused over him and his reactions to me as I snuggled down, I hated feeling interested in him when I hardly knew him. How could I ever get to know him when he lives in a different world? Did I really want to, knowing how selfish children of rich parents are? My mind whirled until I finally I felt my eyes become heavy and thankful sleep slowly took over my confused brain. The last image I saw was his beautiful blue eyes looking into mine.

It felt like I had just closed my eyes when I heard a noise.

"Katy? Breakfast is ready, hun." Mum called as she knocked on my bedroom door.

I glanced at my alarm clock just as it went off, making me

jump. Odd, I wasn't normally so edgy. I turned the buzzer off and jumped out of bed. Unusually, I was wide-awake this morning and not even slightly blurry eyed. I quickly showered, dressed and rushed downstairs to the smell of bacon.

"Mornin' mum." I walked over to the counter as she put the last of the bacon into our sandwiches and I kissed her on the cheek.

My mum, Caroline, was exactly the same height and build as me, at 5ft 5 inches and medium weight, which meant to not too skinny nor too plump, just nice and curvy. She didn't share my love for shoulder length hair though, hers had been cut in a short bob and was a little lighter in colour than mine, a lovely nut-brown colour. Her eyes are blue grey while mine are brown. My eye colour, I got from my dad.

"Good morning hun, you're in a good mood for this time of the morning." She smiled sweetly and passed me my bacon sandwich. "Is there something I should know?"

"Thanks." I sat at the table and poured some orange juice "Nope, just feeling alive today, I guess."

Sitting down, she stirred her coffee and bit into her sandwich enthusiastically. "There is something I have been meaning to talk to you about, Kate." She said between bites. "I have to go away for a few of days to a training course at head office. Do you think you would be okay here, on your own?

"Oh, yeah. No problem, mum. I'm sure I can stay out of trouble for a few days."

"I have to leave Thursday morning but I'll be back on Sunday night; can you keep yourself entertained for four days?"

"Maybe I'll have a couple of wild parties." I laughed.

"Yeah right, like that would happen. You hate parties." She said, grinning.

"Darn, foiled again."

Mum chuckled. "Seriously though hun, will you be okay?"

"No problem, mum. I could paint my bedroom seeing as you've bought me the paint. That should keep me busy."

"What a good idea; perhaps you could ask a friend round to help you. What about that nice girl at school, Ally was it?"

"Yes, but somehow I don't think painting is Ally's thing, I can ask though." I glanced at my watch. "Oh no. I've got to go or I'll be late for the bus again." I quickly finished off my sandwich and OJ.

At school, in the Form room, I suddenly realised I was looking for Joshua and couldn't help glancing at the door every time someone came in. As usual Ally was reading, but unusually this time it was a newspaper.

"Have you seen this?" She asked not looking up.

"What?" I leaned closer pretending to look at the paper, whilst keeping my eyes on the Form room door.

"There has been a rash of unusual deaths in Oxford."

"Unusual how?" That got my attention and my eyes flicked to the newspaper.

"It says here that...'Five people, three women and two men, all in their early twenties, have died in the last two weeks. They died of natural deaths according to the Coroner, who also confirmed he'd 'never seen anything like it in his twenty five years of service, five young and healthy people do not suddenly drop dead'. Thames Valley Police are investigating the strange circumstances surround their deaths.'"

"That's weird, how can someone who is 'young and healthy' die of natural causes?" I wondered.

"I don't know." Ally's forehead creased. "I remember the same thing happening before, in Scotland last year. I believe there were six people that time. I think they were in their early twenties too, in fact, I think some were younger. They also all died of 'natural causes', even their Coroner was confused. Hmmm..." Ally sat deep in thought.

Chameleon

"Bloody hell, Ally, what are you? A walking crime encyclopaedia?" My eyebrows shot up.

"What can I say? I just soak up information, especially about true crimes." She finished reading the article, "There's nothing else, the cops think there's more to it but there is no explanation of what they think. Now, what happened between you and the new rich boy yesterday?" She looked me straight in the eye.

The sudden change of subject caught me off guard, "What do you mean?" I wondered if she meant the outburst in the lesson or the lift home after school.

"I heard you ripped him a new one on stage. What did he do?" She looked over her glasses at me.

"Ah...I just flipped out, it wasn't his fault." I tried not to drag the conversation out, not wanting to relive it.

"Well, he hasn't shown up yet...so maybe you scared him away." Ally said, while trying to keep a straight face.

"Oh, very funny." I laughed despite myself just as Joshua walked in.

The laughter died in my throat as it squeezed shut, I felt inexplicably excited to see him and my breath became faster with nerves. I sat gapping at him. He glanced over towards me, smiled a full and indeed very sexy smile and nodded. He continued to an empty chair on the other side of the room.

"Well, well. Won't this be fun to watch?" Ally said.

"Shut up, Ally. Why don't we get back to those dead people...the newspaper said 'natural' causes, what does that mean...exactly?" I dragged my eyes away from the Joshua to see Ally chuckling darkly to herself.

"Oh dear, you do have it bad...it's going be a bumpy ride." She smirked, "You're so bad, trying to distract me with something medical, but, of course, you knew it would work. Well, 'natural causes' are, and I've just Googled it on my phone, is when the cause of death is a naturally occurring disease process,

Edain Duguay

or is not apparent given medical history or circumstances."

"So basically, they have no clue how they died then?" I glanced up at Joshua who seemed to be sitting completely still, like he was thinking on a problem. I sighed like some silly girl in a romance story, I wanted to kick myself...but then again, he did look even more handsome today, if that was possible. I tried really hard to concentrate on what Ally was saying.

"Exactly. There's definitely something going on in Oxford, which is like the cases in Scotland, if not the same. Something very odd indeed." Ally's brows creased again deep in thought.

The bell rang for the first lesson, which today was double Biology. Within minutes we had walked to the Science building and found our usual seats in the classroom. Ally and I were on the second row of desks, while Joshua went to join Mat, from our Theatre Studies lesson, on one of the back tables. Not that I was watching, of course.

Ally snickered.

"Shut up." I said. "I'm not really that obvious, am I?" I looked hopefully at her.

"Sorry, Kate...but yeah, you are. To me, anyway." She smiled kindly and put her hand on my arm. "I won't tell a soul."

"Thanks."

"No problem." She turned her attention back to the lesson.

After class, while we were packing up, Ally approached the Biology teacher with the newspaper in her hand.

"Mr. Rightman, can I ask your advice about something?" She said.

"Of course, Alison. What can I do for you?" Mr Rightman stopped packing his briefcase.

"Have you seen this article in the Oxford Times? I just wondered what your opinion would be on it." Ally passed him the newspaper.

Mr Rightman took his seat again and put his reading glasses

back on. "Ah...yes, the mysterious deaths in Oxford. It's all very odd, isn't it? Like something out of those crime novels I lent you." He said as he passed the newspaper back.

"Well, Sir, I was wondering...aren't unexplained, sudden deaths frequently recorded as 'death due to natural causes'?"

I looked at Ally, wondering what she was trying to get at.

"That's right, they are. Do you have some theory on this, Alison? I can see something is happening in that criminologists brain of yours." He said and leaned back in his chair.

"Well, at first I thought perhaps it was an infection, or some sort of pollution in the water, that had killed them. But as the Coroner didn't find anything like that and I began to think it might be a serial killer, it would explain how similar the deaths are to the ones in Scotland last year."

Ally had obviously put a lot of thought into her theory.

"Who's a serial killer?" Mat asked as he and Joshua walked past the desk just at that moment and stopped near us.

"Alison thinks the deaths in Oxford are the product of a serial killer and, following her train of thought, is the same person responsible for the deaths in Scotland last year." Mr Rightman said and turned his attention back to Ally. "One problem, how is the 'supposed' serial killer actually killing them? If the Coroner in both places can only record the deaths as 'natural causes'?"

"That's the part I haven't figured out yet, but I will, I just need a bit more time." Ally replied with confidence and smiled brightly.

I glanced at everyone in turn to see if they all thought Ally had gone mad, how could she possibly 'out think' the whole of the Thames Valley Police Force? When I glanced at Joshua he seemed strangely wound up, angry almost. Perhaps he did think she was nuts.

"Thanks, Mr Rightman." Ally smiled and we left the classroom with Mat and Joshua following behind us.

"Do you really think it's a serial killer?" Mat asked excitedly. We all stopped in the hall.

"Actually...yes, I just don't how he did it." Ally said.

"How do you know it's a he?" Joshua asked.

Ally turned towards him. "You must be Joshua Marston, nice to meet you, I'm Alison and this...is Kate." Ally thrust out her hand, "But of course, you two have already met." She smiled sweetly.

At that moment, I could see the doctor in her that she would eventually become and it gave me a proud thrill.

Joshua smiled at Ally, but the smile did not reach his eyes. He looked cautious and didn't extend his hand.

"Don't take it personally, but I don't shake hands. It's nice to meet you, Alison." He turned to me, "Nice to see you've dried off, Kate." He said as he unleashed his smile again.

Alison and Mat glanced at me quickly as I blushed; they were obviously wondering what he was talking about and why I was blushing. I was having difficulty getting past the smile and trying to make words come out again.

Withdrawing her hand, Ally rescued me, "In answer to your question, Joshua, you do have a point. I don't know whether it's a male or female and there are no signs of struggle. We really can't assume either sex."

"Nor can you assume it's only one person. It could easily be more than one." He replied. Joshua appeared calm and had replied in a calm manner, but I could not shake the feeling that underneath he was anything but calm, like a smooth lake of ice with a person drowning under the surface.

"That's very true. I can't say what sex the perpetrator is, or how many of them there are." Ally was getting excited talking about the case and seemed to be warming to Joshua, after their initially frosty start. "Kate, are you okay?"

"What?" I look round at her as everyone else looked at me.

"Yup, I'm fine." I frowned and shot a quick look at Joshua. Something was definitely amiss; I was sure of it but I couldn't grasp what it was.

"You look pale. Maybe you did catch a cold, despite my efforts." Joshua said.

Ally and Mat looked at us both again.

"Honestly I'm fine, all this talk of serial killers is making me edgy. We'd better get to class. I think the bell will go any second now."

As if by magic, the bell rang and everyone burst out laughing. The feeling of unease vanished and Ally gave me a very meaningful look, as if to say 'you will tell me everything later'.

We said goodbye to Ally while Mat, Joshua and I headed to Scenic Arts & Production. We walked together across the courtyard towards the Marston Theatre, sometimes in silence and sometimes making small talk. For some silly reason, I felt nervous around Joshua so nervous that a small whispered giggle escaped my lips. Joshua's head spun round to look at me as if he heard it, which was impossible as it was so quiet I barely heard it myself. He quickly looked back to Mat as he continued talking with him.

Has he got the hearing of a bat? I wondered, careful not to make a sound this time, no matter how quiet. I wasn't sure I liked this new discovery, it made me feel a little defensive and so I tried to keep my thoughts on the lesson ahead of me and not on him.

At lunch, Ally and I met up in the entrance to the main building and she forced me into telling her about the lift I'd gotten from Joshua the night before. Finally happy with my explanation, we walked towards the Dining Hall.

The dinning hall is a long room and filled with tables that ran down the middle of the room. At the far end there were the serving counters, where the kitchen staff dished up hot and cold foods, which were usually excellent. There's also a serve yourself area with salad, chilled yoghurts, drinks and fruits. Because of the rain, the hall was full and the line up for the food was long but we'd brought packed lunches, so were able to look for a table straight away.

We managed to find room on a table of senior students. I didn't know any of them but Ally knew the girl she sat next to. On the table opposite sat Joshua's brother and his friends, I recognised him from my first day at school when he had been called up in assembly for an award in some sport or other. I took the opportunity to study him this time to see if the good looks ran in the family.

William Marston, or Wil as he was known to his friends, was taller than his brother at over six foot. He looked well built and muscular like Joshua, with the same jet-black hair, only his was a lot shorter and heavily gelled. His face and eyes were very different; he was handsome, yes, but in an angular way. His eyes were a very dark colour unlike the bright blue of his brothers, although, I couldn't make out the actual colour from this distance but I presumed they were dark brown like mine. He too had a smile that lit up his face and eyes, but not is the same way as his brother.

I sat watching Wil for a while, when I felt someone's eyes on me and my skin prickled. I looked around me and finally realised it was Joshua, watching me, watching Wil. An odd look passed over his face, but he quickly concealed it. Again, he looked like he knew a secret but was not saying it. I looked back at Wil and at Joshua again, he continued to watch me like he was looking for something. Looking back at Wil once more I realised what I'd been watching, what had drawn my attention without me realising it.

Wil didn't touch people, not a single person.

Others touched him in a friendly way like a pat on the back

Chameleon

or a nudge, but he never actually touched anyone and I realised I'd never seen Joshua touch anyone either. I thought back over the times I'd seen him in Form, at swimming, in class and in his car. No, I was positive. I'd never seen him touch anyone. I remembered when Ally tried to shake his hand and he refused. Now that is odd, one of them I could kind of understand, perhaps a germaphobe, but both of them? Was it a religious thing? I couldn't help but feel it was very weird. I continued to watch them both for as long as lunch lasted, testing my theory.

By the time the bell went for Physics, I'd mulled over my theory trying to make some sense of it and failing, but I headed to Physics with determination to crack the mystery and to put my theory into practise somehow and see what happened. I felt a little nervous about what I intended to do, although I couldn't explain why. I knew that Joshua had to sit next to me in Physics, there were no other seats free in this class.

I was surprised to see that Joshua had already arrived, with his books out on the table, waiting for the lesson to start. I glanced at him and he returned a smile but it seemed to be a cautious one, almost as if he knew what I was about to do.

"Hi." I said as I slide into the seat next to him.

"Hello." He replied, almost stiffly.

There was not much chance for small talk during class: the first part of the double lesson turned out to be the test that Ally had warned me about yesterday, it was a good job I'd listened to her and studied. In the second part of class, Mrs. Rutherford talked about how we were going to investigate the terminal velocity of steel ball bearings as they passed through glycerol.

Thrilling.

Sitting so close to Joshua made me both nervous and excited; I couldn't help it. He seemed to affect me in odd ways whether I liked it or not. Ally sat with a smug look on her face, having heard from me over lunch about our encounter in the rain and she was convinced there was no hope for me. I could have kicked her but thought better of it.

I had planned my experiment carefully. It was a simple but clever plan, I thought.

I would ask if I could borrow his red pen to underline something in my notes, pretending to not have mine with me and, when he passed it over, I would quickly grasp it in the same place where he held it. That way, I would force him to touch me and see how he would react to it. I noticed his red pen was on left side of his note pad while I sat on his right. Perfect. He would have to pass it to me, rather than offer for me to take it. Here goes nothing, I thought.

"Can I borrow your red pen please, Joshua? I seem to have lost mine." I smiled sweetly hoping he would not see the deception.

"Yeah, sure." He picked up the pen.

Here it comes, I thought. I was becoming breathless with excitement. He paused, holding the pen just above the desk, still on his left side and looked directly into my eyes. He tilted his head slightly, like he was listening. Bloody hell, could he hear my breathing? Could he hear that it was faster? That my heart was racing?

Before I could move, or even see, he had placed the pen on my notepad, so quick that his hand seemed to have become a blur. I blinked, now my eyesight was going too, he is making me crazy. I've never had these crazy thoughts or a belief in 'bat hearing' before I knew him.

He made a sly half grin and returned to his own note taking.

I sat stunned and stared at the red pen. Well, that didn't work. I'd have to think of something else, but there's no way he could really hear my heart beating in my chest. Could he?

Finally, class was over, although for me, it had ended long before, thanks to my lack of concentration. With Joshua sitting next to me, I was so full of questions that I didn't know where to start.

"Are you okay, Kate?" Ally asked as we packed up our books.

I couldn't help but feel that Joshua was listening. "Yeah, I'm fine. Just a bit tired, I think. I'll be okay, honest. Meet you at the bus after last lesson?"

"Actually, my Grandma is picking me up after school today. Tuesday is shopping day, remember?" Ally rolled her eyes; she hated shopping about as much as some girls loved it.

"Okay." I laughed at her expression. "I'll see you tomorrow then?"

"Yup, see you on the bus in the morning. Have fun." She winked at me meaningfully, knowing full well I had Theatre Costume with Joshua for the last lesson of the day. She smiled wickedly and left the classroom.

"Do you want to walk over to Costume class together?" Asked a voice behind me.

My breath caught in my throat and my heart raced like a wild horse. I finished fastening my bag without looking up, not wanting to see his lovely eyes. If he could really hear my heart beat, I was in big trouble. "Sure." I tried to sound nonchalant but my voice only came out thin and wobbly. Damn it. I discreetly glanced out of the corner of my eye at him, only to be rewarded with a smug expression and a smile, just as I'd expected. I took a deep breath and drew on my inner strength I use for acting, this seemed a perfect time to practice. I lifted my head and clicked into character.

"Okay, I'm ready when you are." I smiled and looked him straight in the eye, cool as a cucumber.

He raised an eyebrow very slightly, threw his bag over his shoulder and gestured for me to lead the way out of the classroom. I took the lead, keeping my head up and walking confidently, I can do this, this is my world. He's in my territory now, I thought. I could feel a deep sense of smugness building within me, it was nice to turn the tables on him for a change. We walked down the corridor that led out of the science building and headed out in the light rain, back towards the theatre. I allowed him to open the door for me and I thanked him in a very calm way. I could tell it was amusing him and he was willing to play his part.

Costume class passed without incident. We were split into teams to work on the design of the costumes for the senior's Yule play. The lesson flew by so quickly, that before long we were putting away our notebooks and packing up for the day. I hastily grabbed my coat, threw my bag over my shoulder and headed for the exit, ready to catch the bus home.

"I see it's still raining. Would you like a lift home?" His voice came from very close behind me, I hadn't heard him approach.

I swallowed hard. "Erm...thanks, but I can't. I have to pick something up on the way home." I tried not to show the disappointment I was feeling as I turned towards him. He stood very close to me but was not touching, of course. I could smell him, a wonderful mix of musk, the outdoors and wood smoke.

"That's no problem. I can take you where you need to go and drop you off home afterwards." He said and smiled.

I battled pointlessly with my inner workings as my bones melted. Damn it. Would it ever end? And honestly, did I really want it too? I thought, even though the excitement was exhausting.

He led the way out of the building, I followed him down the steps from the door of the theatre, splashing in the puddles and giggling to myself at the pure childish joy of it as I went. Joshua turned to watch me having fun, with a look of happiness on his unguarded face. Looking into his eyes and seeing that look, I lost the plot completely. Instantly, my feet and brain disconnected and I slipped down the wet stone steps. Immediately his

Chameleon

hands shot out, one grabbed my arm, the other my hand. I became frozen to the spot by an electrical shock running up my arm from my hand. It was an intense and almost painful static shock. For a split second we froze in place, then he quickly let go of my hand, like it was something distasteful. I rubbed my fingers as if they were tingling with pin and needles even though they weren't. The feeling was just the memory of the electric shock. I looked directly at him in amazement.

His face looked angry and closed in. "I'm sorry, are you okay?" He said.

"I, um...yes, I'm fine. My hand feels odd though. What the hell was that?"

"I'm sorry, I didn't mean to...err...it...it must have been static." He whispered and cleared his throat, "Are you sure you're okay?"

"I'm fine, honestly." I said, as I looked him in the eye. My mind felt stunned by the shock.

Joshua lowered his eyes and said, "I'll fetch the car." He quickly spun round and walked over to the car park with his head hung low. Within a minute he pulled up outside the theatre, climbed out of the car and held the passenger door open for me. His face betrayed a strange mixture of emotions, worried and yet very angry. We drove in a strained silence for several minutes.

"Where do you need to go to?" He asked in a tight voice.

"I have to go to the ReMix music store to collect a CD I ordered." I glanced at him; his face looked angry and closed in again, like a glass window with a concrete wall behind it.

I sighed, "What just happened, Joshua?" I said.

"Nothing, just static." He replied as if through gritted teeth and drove faster.

"Rubbish. That was not just static and you said that you 'didn't mean to'. Didn't mean to what? Where did that electricity come from?" I turned towards him.

"I told you, it was static. Now can we drop this, please?" His voice had become a mixture of anger and pleading.

The car came to a stop. I looked around to find that we were outside the ReMix store.

"Thanks for the lift." I said in a flat tone and undid my seat belt. "Bye."

"I'll wait here for you, I did promise you a lift home." He continued to stare angrily ahead at the traffic.

"Oh...okay. If you're sure?"

He nodded without looking at me. His lips were squeezed together in a thin line.

I sigh and said, "I'll be back in a minute." Jumping out of the car, I rushed into the store. I didn't want to inconvenience him any longer than I had to. Thankfully, I walked back to the car with my CD in five minutes, which was all the time it took for Joshua's mood to have changed again.

"Did you get what you wanted?" He asked with a cheery voice and smiled as he restarted the engine.

So another change of mood and subject is it? I thought. I will come back to it, I promised myself. "Yes, thanks." I tried to sound cheery but his mood swings were beginning to annoy me. I tried to think of a neutral conversation starter. "This is a nice car, how long have you been driving?"

"The car was a present from my parents for my seventeenth birthday." He answered proudly.

"Wow, nice pressie." I looked around, appreciating the car, "You passed your test quick."

"I'm a fast learner. Besides, my father let's me drive on our property all the time."

And again the conversation had run out.

We finally turned the corner onto Blackberry Lane and headed towards my home.

Chameleon

"Well, here we are...home as promised." He smiled.

I looked at him, it was almost as if he'd never been anything other than this relaxed, happy person. Almost. "Right. Thanks for the lift." I gathered my things, "See you tomorrow." I said as I got out of the car.

"Yes, you will." He smiled as he leaned over the passenger seat to look me in the eye, "Have a good evening, Kate."

"I will...and you." I walked toward my front door in the rain. Unlocking the door, I pushed it open realising that he hadn't driven off straight away this time, instead he waited for me to go safely inside and then pulled away. That was a gentlemanly thing to do, at least, I thought. As I watched his car vanish into the distance, I sighed in confusion and closed the door behind me.

That night, I had a very disturbing dream about Joshua and the shock that ran through me when I held his hand. I could see me on the steps falling and his hands saving me again. Suddenly, he was kissing me and holding me tightly against him, an enormous shock burst through my chest and into my body. It felt like searing heat was burning its way through my flesh, fear and panic made me scream as it reached my heart making it beat out of rhythm and stop. Joshua was laughing at me as I clutched my chest and died in his arms. He let my body slip to the ground and stood over me with an evil and triumphant look on his face.

I woke up with a start, my heart beating madly in my chest and the sheet sticking to my sweating, terrified body. I lay gasping for breath too terrified to even reach over and put the light on. My mind was a jumble of the dream images and the pain and fear I'd felt. Time slowly ticked by as I tried to calm myself and steady my breathing. Eventually, I managed to switch the light on and lay there blinking in its brightness staring up at the ceiling. I knew I wouldn't be able to go back to sleep straight away, I never could after nightmares. I sat up and picked up the book from my side table, it was a new book I'd borrowed from the library, a fantasy about the Norse Gods and, grateful for the distraction, I began reading.

Slowly, as I read and time ticked by, I began to feel drowsy again and finally gave up as I was reading the same line over and over again. Snuggling back in my covers, I switched off the light once more and drifted back into a fitful sleep full of confusing scenes from my book that, strangely, included Joshua holding bolts of lightening like a Norse God.

LIGHT

The young woman looked at herself in the bathroom mirror and ruthlessly examined her naked body. She smiled. Her flesh was firm, her body was trim. She was in the prime of her life and deep down she knew it. She gave her long blond hair one last brush, touched a little perfume behind her ears, between her breasts and at the back of her knees, just as those women's magazines say. She took a deep breath; it was a big step she was taking. She just knew he was the right one and she would allow him to be her first sexual partner. She could feel it in her bones.

He was so handsome and charming in such an old fashioned way, holding open doors for her. Even now he was opening some wine in the bedroom that he had insisted on buying. She had fallen head over heels in love with him instantly, in fact the very second he had started talking to her with that sexy voice and smile. With her heart beating wildly, she opened the bathroom door and stepped out, trying, a little too hard maybe, to be as sexy on the outside as she felt on the inside.

He had lit every candle she owned, making the room glow in soft muted colours. It was warm and inviting.

"You are a Goddess." He said as she walked towards the bed, where he lay naked and muscular.

"And you are a God." She said boldly. Her eyes roamed over his body, taking in every inch. In their whirlwind romance, she *had not seen him naked before and she was enjoying the view.*

He smiled that deeply sexy smile that made her want to take matters into her own hands, and reached out his hand to offer her a glass of wine. Taking a sip, she put it on the bedside table.

She was surprised by her lack of nervousness, she drew near to him, needing to feel his lips on hers again, he responded in kind. He held her closer than they had ever been, flesh touching flesh, her breath came quickly as she closed her eyes, she could hear her heart beating faster and harder. She felt the touch of his lips, the soft and warm touch sending a tingle through her body. She groaned gently and kissed him more firmly as his hand came up to her cheek caressing her, while his other arm pulled her closer. The kiss became more passionate and breathless. She began to feel strangely drawn into him, she began let go of all her control and let herself be taken by the flow of the moment.

He became more insistent, kissing her greedily, crushing her lips almost painfully. She felt the pain, but seemed to be at a distance, as if watching her body from deep within. She sensed he was enjoying her but the longer he touched her, the further inwards she went from her flesh. The sense of floating away was intense; she had one final view of him as he took his fill of her. His image was strange to her blurry eyesight. He became a dark shadow with the soft light of the candles behind him, she saw a strange red misty light coming off her and surrounding him, pouring into his body making the building darkness throb with the colour of blood.

Beautiful, she thought as her vision faded and the red light grew dim. The beating of her heart slowed dramatically until finally there was nothing but silence.

Silence, blackness and cold.

Meeting

Wednesday began brightly with the Sun streaming through my window, it was beautiful but I was too tired to enjoy it. The strange dreams I had just woken up from left me tired, listless. Most of the night I'd spent half awake, impatiently rolling around in my bed. I sat up and was struck by giant wall of pain, first in my head then I realised it was all over, as if my body had been crushed in the night. Every joint ached and I could feel the muzzy-headedness of a cold virus taking over. I groaned and dragged myself out of bed, bursting into a fit of sneezes.

"Katy? Wake up. The power must have flashed off in the storm last night and we slept through the alarms." Mum called urgently through the door.

"Come in mum." My voice sounded odd in my ears, croaky and weak.

The door opened quickly, "Oh, you sound bad, hun and you look worse." Mum stood, shocked, in the doorway looking at me as I stood in the middle of my room like a zombie.

"I feel like crap." I tried to blow my nose and groaned.

"Get back in bed, love. I'll call the school and tell them you aren't coming in today. Do you want me to bring you some breakfast?" Mum said as she tucked me back in bed and felt my forehead for a high temperature.

Edain Duguay

"Nah...I'll get something later. I just want to sleep." I said as I snuggled down.

"Okay, hun. I have to go or I'll be late. Give me a ring at work if you need anything, okay?" She smiled and kissed me on the forehead.

"Okay."

"Take care and I'll see you tonight." She rushed out of the room to get ready for work.

I dozed off and on and barely heard mum leave. My mind wandered off into the strange images of last nights dreams as I floated back off to sleep. Suddenly, I sneezed myself fully awake and glanced at my clock, I was surprised to find it was already lunchtime. Weird, it felt like I'd just closed my eyes. I sneezed again and decided to look for something that would make me feel less deathly. I threw my spare blanket around me and staggered sleepily to the bathroom cabinet in search of medication. I'd just swallowed some blue gel pills, which promised to remove all my symptoms for twelve hours, when the doorbell rang.

Snuggled up in my blanket, with my cosiest PJ's underneath, I made my way down to the front door. It was probably just another training manual for mum, she had been getting a lot of parcels delivered lately, with her new job. I unlocked and opened the front door and stood motionless. My brain was unable to take in what stood before my eyes.

"Hello." He smiled, casually.

Here I was, my hair sticking out in all directions, in my PJ's, with fluffy purple slippers on and a head full of an ugly cold virus, looking at the most gorgeous person I'd ever seen.

Life is cruel, kill me now.

"I came to see if you're okay. You weren't at school this morning and I was worried." Joshua looked at my, obviously, shocked expression, "Can I come inside? I don't think you need to stand

Chameleon

in this cold wind, you look ill enough."

Without a reply he headed through the doorway. I backed up and let him in as if I was on automatic pilot. What are you doing, Kate? I demanded in my head. What is he doing? My head replied.

He stood only one foot away from me, "Which way is the kitchen? I brought you soup and some lemon balm for tea." He looked at me expecting an answer.

All I could do was dumbly point down the hallway towards the kitchen. He headed off, leaving me standing in the hall. I shook myself out of my shock-induced stupor, rewrapped the blanket around me and made my way towards the kitchen. Within seconds the soup was in the microwave and the kettle was on for the tea.

"I wasn't expecting company." Especially you, I added in my head.

"Obviously. Don't worry, you still look good." He gave me that smile again. It was beginning to be a habit, one smile from him and a wonderful reaction of fire coursed through me. The excitement and fear he created in me were annoying and yet I was beginning to like it too.

"Oh yeah, I'm sure I'm gorgeous." I said sarcastically just as an explosive sneeze erupted.

"Excuse me." I blew my nose. "You really shouldn't be here, you know. I'm probably very contagious. How did you know I was off ill, anyway?" I sat down at the kitchen table and waited for his answer.

"I asked at the office." He replied.

"Oh...right. You mean you charmed the ladies in the office." I rested my now hot forehead on my hand and watched him lean against the sink waiting for the water to boil.

"Why don't you go up to bed and I'll bring you lunch?"

"I don't mean to sound ungrateful, but why are you being so

51

nice, today?" I asked, wondering what had brought on this 'best buds' attitude.

"Do I need a reason to be nice to you?"

I raised an eyebrow.

"Actually, I was hoping to make up for yesterday...I was a little..."

"Snappy? Grumpy? Grouchy?" I offered.

"I was going to go with sharp but any of those will do too." He said, "Now go and get warm, lunch is almost ready."

"Okay, okay." I got up and headed for the door.

"Now I know you are really ill...you're actually doing as you're told." He laughed.

"Hush or I shall breathe these germs on you." I threatened as I climbed the stairs. I could hear him chuckling to himself.

I resisted the urge to check myself in a mirror. Nothing I could do, in the small amount of time I had before he came upstairs, would make any difference. But I did use the next few moments to quickly tidy the worst of my room. By the time I had climbed back under my thick quilt with my head spinning, I could hear Joshua climbing the stairs and I knew he could see into my room from the top step. He walked to the door and knock on it even though it stood open.

"You can come in, I'm decent." I chuckled to myself. I guess he really was trying to be nice.

He confidently walked into my room, placed the tray carefully on my lap and sat down on the chair at the end of the bed.

"Thank you. This is such a surprise. Umm...aren't you having any?" I felt somewhat exposed and awkward, unsure of what to do.

"Nope, I've already eaten."

He looked round the room, seeming, at last, a little out of his element.

"Not been in many girls bedrooms have you?"

Chameleon

"This is a first."

"So to what do I own this honour?" I grinned.

"Isn't this what friends are supposed to do?"

"Is that what we are now? Friends?"

"Yes, we are. New friends admittedly, but yes, friends." He said in a firm voice.

I couldn't help feel the firmness of his voice was an act, his face and eyes looked almost vulnerable as if he was unsure of our friendship.

"Friends it is." I said, "One thing though, aren't friends supposed to trust each other completely and not have secrets?" I knew I was being rude and pushy but I just couldn't help it. I felt that there was something I needed to know about him, my instincts were just too alert around him. "I...erm...don't be angry...but I still want to know what happened yesterday."

"Yes...we are friends...." He paused, seeming to choose his words carefully, his face showed a conflict of emotion. Joshua sighed, a deeply unhappy sound, "Trust me, you need to let it go, there are things you do not want to know. It is safer for you just to forget about it." He looked vulnerable and tired. "Please try to forget it."

"I'm sorry but I can't forget it, at least until I understand it, it's like a loud question in my head, being asked over and over." I tried not to look at him again, I didn't want to be swayed by how sad he looked.

"I can't talk about it. You have to let it go." His voice had grown urgent.

"But why? Why can't you tell me? What's so important?"

"It just is. Please, Kate." He said.

"Okay, okay...but promise me you will tell me one day...if not today." I said.

"I promise I will tell you what I can, when I can...how's that?" He said, seemingly relieved.

"Okay, fair enough." I said, glad the tension between us had vanished again.

Slowly, his face recovered to its former friendly appearance.

I sneezed again and instinctively my knees came up, tipping the tray, threatening to throw hot soup everywhere. Joshua's hand shot out very quickly and caught it before even one drop had spilt. I chose to ignore that his movement was too fast, I was in no state to deal with his strangeness now. "Sorry." I lay back on the pillows, exhausted, "Actually, I'm not sure I'm that hungry."

"Just have a little and some tea. It will make you feel much better, I promise."

I did as he'd suggested because, it was easier that way. I was even more confused than usual around him. In silence, I ate half the soup and then sat back drinking the tea. Eventually, Joshua took the tray far away from me and my explosive sneezes.

"I'm finding you difficult to figure out, Joshua. Sometimes you are so sensitive and closed in and other times you're just nice and thoughtful, like when you open doors for me or bring me lunch." I gestured to the lunch tray.

He looked away from me and glanced around the room. "I know." He said solemnly. "I would like to know more about you." He added, changing the conversation back round to me.

"And I want to know more about you, if only you would let me in." I said.

"You are persistent, aren't you?" He grinned.

"Sometimes, when I want something badly enough." I blushed realising what I had just said and took a quick sip of the tea as a distraction, "Hmm...this is actually quite nice."

"Mother gives it to the staff whenever they're ill. She has an interest in herbs."

"The staff?"

Chameleon

"Ah...yeah, we have staff at the house. You know gardener, grounds keeper, cleaners... the house is, rather large and we need them." Joshua looked uncomfortable.

"Oh...yeah." I tried not to show my distaste, "I knew you were...erm...rich...I mean, from a well off family but I'd not actually thought about it..." I could feel my face glow as I desperately searched for words. I was feeling the usual rage against rich people but this time it was mixed with my attraction to Joshua. I just didn't know what to think or feel anymore.

"Could I sit there and ask you something?" He gestured to the end of the bed.

"Sure." I leaned back and pulled the covers up a little, trying to ignore the butterflies that had set up residence in my stomach.

"What is your problem with rich people?" His big blue eyes looked up at me.

I took a sip of the tea to stall a little, was I ready to admit everything? To him...him, of all people?

"You don't have to tell me. Or not right now. I thought I said or did something to upset you in the rehearsal but the more I think about it, the more I come up empty and you said it wasn't me."

"Don't take this personally but I have a problem with rich kids." I glanced at him to see his reaction; I didn't want him to get defensive because then I would never get this out. I was pleased to see he sat calmly waiting for me to finish, I took a deep breath, "Last year my mum found out my dad was having an affair with a woman from his work. Actually, she was the boss's daughter and heiress to his fortune. Mum threw him out, of course." I fiddled with the corner of the quilt not looking at him. I paused wondering how to continue.

"Go on." He said gently.

"We bumped into him this summer, on my mum's birthday

55

of all the days. He was with the woman and her teenage son, the worst part was... she was pregnant. Things just went wrong from there and it turned into a shouting match. Her son, a rich brat, started in on me saying my dad was his father now, so I should mind my own business...and much nastier stuff, that I'm not going repeat." I could feel the tears running freely down my cheeks as I drew a breath. "That, coupled with the rich kids I knew on a farm my dad and I used to visit...who used to bully me for being poor, make me dislike rich kids. Now I feel so wound up every time I see a rich kid, the way they talk, their attitude, it just makes me angry. I know it's wrong and unfair, but it's just how I feel."

"Is that why you moved here?"

"No, we came here because I got a place at the school. Can you see the irony there? I hate rich kids and end up at a school full of them." I laughed weakly through my tears.

"Yeah, I can see why you would find it hard. You know, we aren't all like that, some of us are actually half decent." He grinned wickedly.

"Only half? I guess I'll have to keep an eye on you, then." With a half-laugh I wiped away the tears, feeling a lot lighter inside myself than before.

Joshua suddenly looked apprehensive and rose slowly, like he was unsure if he should stay or go. Then, seemingly decided, he quickly closed the gap between us and reached out, his fingers gently caressing my hot, wet cheek.

I froze, expecting to feel that terrifying shock from him to hit again. This time it didn't happen. Instead it was just a warm gentle buzz under the skin. I could see that he was trying really hard to focus on something, his features were pulled tight in concentration, was he struggling with his feelings too? I began to feel tired and sleepy, his face started to blur a little, as I re-laxed. I could faintly see a look of triumph across his face, as if he had just managed something very difficult. Then the world receded as I floated gently down into a deep dreamless sleep.

I awoke alone, the late afternoon sunshine coming in through the curtain. I felt terrific. I could breathe in easily, there was no sign of the cold virus at all. In fact, I felt very healthy and full of life. I leapt out of bed realising that Joshua must have gone back to school. Presumably, he had taken the lunch tray back to the kitchen on his way out, as it was no longer on the floor.

"Wow that soup and tea really did work, he was right, I do feel better." I said to myself as I often did when alone.

By the time Mum got home, I had showered, dressed and was making dinner. She was as amazed as I, at how I had made such a speedy recovery and we decided it must have been a twelve hour bug and that my system must have fought it off while I slept.

"These fajitas are great, hun." Mum smiled at me across the table. "Thanks for starting dinner early. Do you fancy a DVD tonight? Your choice."

"How about a girly movie? We could even make some popcorn."

"That's a great idea. After dinner, I'll get cleaned up and pack my bag for the course this weekend, then we can watch it. Are you sure that you are well enough for me to go away? You're not just being brave, are you?

"No, really mum, I feel great. In fact, better than I did before I had the cold. I guess I just needed to catch up on some sleep."

I washed the dinner pots while mum showered and packed for her trip. We spent the next couple of hours snuggled up on the sofa under a blanket, eating popcorn and watching a movie.

Later, I lay in bed thinking about Joshua and how easily it was to talk to him when he opened up. More importantly, I knew I was attracted to him and already had feelings for him. I shook my head, knowing it was ridiculous after such a short time. It surprised me to realise I'd only known him for three days, even though it felt like longer and I'd already told him my most painful memories. There was just something about him, something that was different from the other guys I'd met. I tried to understand him but the more I thought about the mystery of him not touching people, the strange electric shock and the 'bat' hearing, the harder it became. Nothing made any sense, of course I could not forget about his quick reflexes and movements. There was just something weird going on, something not normal about him. All these things couldn't be a coincidence, could they? All night, I tossed and turned, my brain full of images, mostly of Joshua and, in particular, the strange electricity of his touch.

Mum left for her training course very early the next morning, before my alarm had gone off. When it did, I practically bounced out of bed full of energy. The thoughts that had been brewing in my head for most of last night had galvanized me into action and at breakfast I spent some time doing research on my laptop. I became convinced I had the correct analysis of the situation.

Go me.

Later that morning though, I was unsure I wanted to face my theory, if it was true. I didn't get much chance to see Joshua for most of the morning, except from a distance; he sat with Mat in Chemistry and was in another group for Property Making in the theatre workshop. In the afternoon, though, all four of us, Ally, Mat, Joshua and I had double Library Studies, during which we were allowed to study any subject, so long as we worked quietly. The studying sessions were held in the Marston Family Library.

It was the most amazing library I'd ever seen. Not only was it beautiful in terms of architecture and design, but inside it was full of thousands and thousands of books, all of which lay on the richly coloured mahogany shelves that stretched up from the floor to the vaulted ceiling. Some of these books were only accessible with the rolling mahogany ladders or via the gallery walks. There was also a gallery floor with brass railings. From the arched wooden ceiling hung several Victorian-looking gas lamps. Although they still looked original, they had been converted to electricity presumably many years ago. In a few select places, were portraits of several generations of the Marston family, some dating back to the 1600's.

Before settling down at one of the study tables with Ally, I walked around the library looking at the family portraits, everyone in them was incredibly good looking. They all had dark hair, although some were darker than others and a few had the magnificent blue-black that Wil and Joshua have. Most had beautiful pale skin, almost luminescent, many of them had Joshua's stunning blue eyes. The Marston family definitely had good genes, but still, the sheer beauty of them all just seemed wrong somehow. Almost...creepy. I was reminded of a vampire movie I'd recently watched where no one aged.

These family portraits had become the second part of my theory. I was convinced that he was probably not the only 'strange' person in his family. There was an eeriness to his entire family history. I'd planned on taking a look at his parents to see how they fitted into this jigsaw puzzle of a theory. Unfortunately, there were no images of them here, I even checked twice to be sure. I also hoped that the library would have some helpful information on the Marston family, perhaps newspapers, microfilm or something in the vast array of books before me. I started my search, not really sure what I was looking for, except that I would know it when I saw it. I used the family estate indexes but nothing 'unusual' popped out at me. No mention of odd happenings in or around the Marston family, in fact nothing out of the ordinary. I was very disappointed but should have realised that it would not be that easy, if my theory was indeed right. How could it be, though? My mind was still not willing to accept the connections it had made.

I moved over to the local newspaper archives that were stored on microfilm and fiche, but I found only the usual births, marriages, deaths and high society parties were listed in the indexes. Nothing out of the ordinary, nothing helpful for my curious mind. Again, I felt disappointed and yet at the same time relieved, perhaps I was just imagining things. Perhaps Joshua was just as normal as everyone else.

Perhaps.

Eventually, I gave up looking and sat trying to study Theatre Architecture from a large leather bound book, which I supported on a book cushion to help protect the spine. Nothing from the pages of the book was sinking in. I had to see Joshua again privately. I needed answers and I needed them now...before I went crazy. I glanced up and looked across the room over to where Joshua and Mat were sat reading in the big, red leather chairs in the lounge area of the library. They were about thirty metres away, ideal for what I was about to attempt. I knew he'd not seen me yet as I'd kept an eye on him and he seemed engrossed in the book he was reading. I wanted to test something out. I wanted to prove that his hearing other day wasn't a fluke.

"Joshua." I whispered, so low that Ally couldn't hear me and she was sat only six inches away.

Joshua's head snapped up instantly like someone had shouted at him and he looked round. I looked down quickly and waited for a good five minutes, pretending to read. For the reasons of wanting to ensure that my experiment was valid and the result was not a coincidence, I decided to try again.

"Joshua." I whispered so low that I could barely hear my voice.

Again a reaction, only this time when his head shot up he looked directly at me and glared, obviously furious. I looked away quickly, not wanting to be on the receiving end of that look any longer than necessary. His reaction had sealed his fate, I would confront him with my theory and force him to admit to me that my suspicions were right. I had to do it, today. This afternoon, I decided. The questions in my head were driving me nuts. Although, the thought of confronting him made me nervous, the fact I'd made my decision gave me a sense of calm and strength of purpose that I hadn't felt in days.

Time seemed to drag as I put together a plan. I could hear the big clock on the library wall ticking, the only sound in the huge library. I grew impatient and sighed. I'd lost what little interest I had in the book that lay before me.

"What's the matter?" Ally quietly asked without looking up from her book at me.

"I dunno, I just can't concentrate today."

"Here, look at this." She slid a newspaper off the top of her book placing it in front of me. On the front page the bold headline read:

Sixth Naked 'Victim', Police Baffled!

I read down the article quickly. Every one of the 'victims' were of similar age but not race, with no other connecting factors except they were all found naked in their bedrooms. I shuddered. There was something about it that was so scary, but I didn't know what. I was glad that mum had gone in the opposite direction to Oxford, I couldn't bear it if she had gone there. Admittedly, she was older than the average age of the dead people, but still, the thought scared me silly. I would definitely be glad when she got home safe and sound on Sunday.

"Do you still think it's a serial killer?" I whispered to Ally.

"Even more so now they've said all the victims were naked and in their bedrooms. That's too much of a coincidence."

"But how are they being killed?" I glanced up at Joshua across the room and realised not only was he looking our way but I was sure he was listening to our conversation.

"I'm still unsure, there are a few ways to kill someone with hardly any traces, but still after six you would think there would be something to say how they died. Unless..."

"Unless what?" I looked back at Ally.

"Unless they do know more than they are saying and just aren't releasing the details. You know, the details that only the cops and the killer would know. It helps to stop the loonies from confessing, if they can't get the story right but also they can trip up the suspects with the information. I wonder if they have any suspects yet?" She said.

"Wouldn't they say something like 'we have a man in custody who is helping with our enquires' like they do on the TV or something?"

"Maybe, maybe not." Ally sighed, "I hate it when I don't have enough information to understand a whole situation, it's so frustrating."

"Tell me about it." I whispered under my breath and look pointedly at Joshua who smiled that half grin and went back to reading.

Damn him.

The bell for the next lesson rang, I said goodbye to Ally as she headed off to the science building for her lesson. Joshua and I, on the other hand, had Property Making again. I held my head high as I walked past him, not saying a word or looking at him directly. I moved ahead of the crowd as I made my way to the exit. He stood with a few other guys talking but I felt his eyes on me, watching my every move.

Once outside of the Library, I became separated from Joshua

Chameleon

by many of the other students, who were all heading in different directions. I walked away from the Library towards the Marston Theatre but instead of going to class, I had decided to get some answers. I walked towards the large gardens that surrounded the school. Once in the ornate gardens and hidden from view, I whispered quietly to myself, "I know you can hear me. Meet me at the waterfall in the school garden, near the old oak." I smiled to myself knowing that Joshua had heard me. It was handy, but still very weird and I wanted answers.

I walked through the ornate gardens to the wilder area behind them, which was full of paths and trails, and even had some nice places for picnics. The pathway had become sheltered by a leafy canopy over the years, many trees overlapping each other on both sides and the ground was full of wild mushrooms. The air had an earthy damp scent and I breathed in deeply while enjoying the short walk to my destination. I sat on my jacket, on a damp rock by the top of the waterfall, listening to the rush of water, watching the force of it rush downwards and hit the pool below. There were several places along the path that had benches but I liked sitting at the top, on the edge, looking down. Heights had never bothered me. Students weren't supposed to come here, since there was no fencing and, as we were in lesson time, I knew that Joshua and I would be alone.

I hadn't heard him walk up behind me but instinctively I could feel him, standing only a foot or so away. I had butterflies at the thought of what I was about to do and say. What if I was wrong? Would he think me insane? More importantly, what if I was right? Would I still like him this much? Yes, I really did like him a lot, possibly too much already, no matter what the outcome was going to be. I knew I was completely head over heels in love with him, after only knowing him for four days. I shook my head in disbelief, talk about love at first sight. Ally was right, there really was no hope for me.

Edain Duguay

"Thank you for coming." I said without getting up or turning round.

"Thank you for calling me." A gruff voice replied, not the honeyed one I expected.

I jumped up and spun round, instantly terrified. My instincts crying out, telling me I was in serious danger. I backed away a couple of steps but could go no more. I had become trapped between this unknown, and dangerous looking man, and the edge of the waterfall with a twenty-foot drop.

"Who are you? Want do you want? My boyfriend will be here in a minute." I babbled, my voice rising in pitch as terror sank in.

The man just stood looking me up and down with a sly grin on his face. He was tall with dark auburn hair and very pale green eyes. He was handsome but in a feral, aggressive way. His pale eyes were startling in an unkind way, the way you'd expect a serial killers to be. My mind remembered Ally's theory and I began to shake. He was wearing jeans and a t-shirt with trainers, no coat and definitely, not a student.

I tried to be brave and said, "What do you mean I called you?" I failed miserably, my voice shook and wavered like a frightened child.

He took a step closer, then another, until he was just inches away from me, I could smell the sweat on him and something other, something rancid and sweet. My stomach churned and bile rose in my throat. I swallowed hard and tried desperately to control my breathing.

"Whispers are invites, didn't you know?" He grinned. The grin made him look even more like a predator, primal almost.

"W...What?"

"Your little friend has not told you the rules, has he? Too bad. He will pay for that mistake. No rules, no foul. I can claim you and what a lovely prize you are." He licked his lips suggestively.

My throat dried instantly, I had no idea what he was talking about, but his intent was very clear. I glanced behind me to see if I could step back but there was no room left, no escape at all.

"Now we can do this two ways. The easy way, you won't feel much or the hard way...well, you won't like it much. Which would you prefer?" He put his head on one side as if listening and suddenly grabbed me by my arms.

His hot fingers were digging into my skin, I screamed and kicked him but nothing seemed to work. Suddenly, I could feel fire on my skin, a burning sensation that travelled up my arms from his hands and I began to scream.

He laughed, "I guess it will have to be the hard way, seeing as your 'boyfriend' will be here soon." He held me close against his foul smelling body and kissed me roughly, crush my body against his.

I struggled hard but the burning sensation spread from every place his body touched mine, his lips, face, arms, chest, groin, legs - everywhere. My vision began to go hazy, I knew I'd begun to lose consciousness and all my strength was leaving me. I felt like I was floating away from my body.

The last thing I saw, as I fell backwards over the cliff, was the face of my murderer and the blur that was Joshua running up to us inhumanly fast. Then all I could see was the peaceful, cloudy sky as I went backwards and downwards.

I felt my heart slow and finally stop as I was swallowed into the darkness that is death.

KNOWLEDGE

I could hear sounds in the blackness, faint sounds off in the distance. It sounded like people talking but I couldn't be sure. It was too faint for me to make out the words. I struggled to understand where I was. Was I in Heaven? Where was the bright light everyone said you should see when you die? I knew with absolute certainty that I had died. I'd felt it take over my body and shut down my heart and breathing, but this darkness and the sounds just didn't make sense. I tried to move but I seemed to have no body.

I concentrated on the words; they were the only thing I had. After a short while, they seemed to get louder or closer maybe. There were definitely two voices, one male and one female. Neither of voices I could recognise, but I soon lost interest in the voices not being able to distinguish the words, they both seemed to be mumbling. I tried to get a sense of my own body, anything, but nothing came. I tried again and again, determined to feel me. Slowly, very slowly, a sense of self started to return to me. I became instantly elated and encouraged, the joy of finding me was glorious. I started to feel like I was inside a heavy weight; I presumed and hoped it was my body.

I had no clue if I was standing, sitting, lying down or flying. There was nothing that I was attached to, that could give my any information. Gradually, as time passed - well, I thought time passed, it was hard to tell - the weight of my body seemed lighter. I managed to make a muscle twitch, it exhausted me but the euphoria I got from that tiny movement blew my mind. Did I have a mind? How about a head? I couldn't feel it, so how would I know?

I kept twitching the same muscle I had before, each time it got easier and easier. I tried another and then another until I realised I'd been working on the muscles in a finger and was now able to move it very slightly. A finger meant I had a body but did it mean I was alive? Don't you still feel you have a body when you are dead? Didn't I see some film about mentally allowing yourself to have a body when you died, as a way to comfort yourself?

Oh boy, was I in trouble now. My mum would kill me if I died.

When moving the finger a fraction became easier, I moved onto the other fingers. Soon I could feel the entire hand, the air around it feeling warm and dry. There was something next to my hand, something soft, material of some sort. I worked on my arm trying to make it work; slowly and surely it came back to life. Almost like when you sleep on your arm and it feels dead and then life comes back into it again, but without the pins and needles. I worked hard on getting the sense back in my body. I felt I was either leaning up against something or lying down because I could feel the back of my body pressed was against something soft.

I tried hard to not think about what happened before the blackness, as I worked even harder to pull myself out of it, bring life back into me and make parts of me come alive again, I hoped quiet literally. The few times that my mind returned to the scene of my death, I saw the auburn haired man again and felt the burn of his skin against mine. The thought sent a tremor through me and I felt my body shudder. All at once, I noticed there was no sound, no talking. I felt a heavy pressure on the soft material against my skin.

"Kate?" Asked the male voice softly. "Kate? Can you hear me?"

Kate. That's my name, I remembered. I could hear the man but I couldn't answer, I hadn't been working on my face or throat. How could I let him know that I had heard him?

"Kate, try to squeeze my hand if you can hear me." The man put his fingers in the palm of my hand.

I concentrated hard and managed to squeeze his fingers very slightly. I heard a collective sigh exhaled from both of them. It seemed that my movement meant something important, but who were they?

"Excellent, Kate. Excellent." He sounded excited.

Who was it? His voice sounded almost familiar but not quite. I forced myself away from the thought and returned to reviving the rest of my body. I realised I was in fact lying down, the weight of gravity pushing down on me from above, I could actually feel the weight of it.

I worked on my eyes, knowing it would give me the most information as to where I was and who they were. It was so hard feeling for control of eyes when you couldn't actually feel them. Finally, the sensation of eyelids came back to me and I knew that the darkness was now due to my eyes being shut. Slowly, I tried to open them, but not slowly enough as excruciating white light burst in and I had to quickly slam them shut again.

"Helena, close the curtains please. I think Kate is trying to open her eyes." He said.

I could hear the woman walk cross the room, her heels tapped on the presumably wooden floor from the sound of it. The light went away with a curious sense of relief on my part.

"Kate, try again. It's darker now."

I tried, like he asked and my eyes fluttered open and blinked

Chameleon

a few times. All I could see was an ornately carved piece of wood above me, it confused me even more, I closed my eyes and opened them again. It was still there, I had expected a face at least.

"Look her eyes are open." A woman's voice was soft, sensual and husky, and strangely accented.

I closed my eyes again and concentrated on my neck muscles and spine. I was gaining control of my body more quickly now. I opened my eyes again and looked at the wood above me, was I in a coffin? Since when do coffins have curtains that 'Helena' could draw? My mind obviously wasn't working fully yet. I turned my head to the right slightly and saw a handsome man seated on a chair with a stunning woman standing behind him.

I knew neither of them, nor recognised where I was.

They were both so very beautiful with strong high cheek bones, their faces looked like they were carved in the palest marble. Both had luxurious dark hair and the man had the most amazing blue eyes, they reminded me of someone. Suddenly, in a flash I saw they were the same eyes as Joshua's. My mind instantly jumped to the last time I'd seen him, he had moved so fast he'd become a blur, running up behind the green-eyed man who was hurting me. Then I remembered the burning and looked down at my hands, expecting blackened skin. My skin was white and perfect, not a mark on it. I tried to move my mouth to make a word but nothing came out.

"Kate, are you trying to speak?" The man asked, leaning closer.

I squeezed his finger again and heard the feet of the woman approaching.

"Here, drink some water. It may help." She lifted my head and held the cup to my lips, letting some water dribble into my mouth. I concentrated hard and managed to swallow it. The next sip was easier to swallow. The cool liquid slid down my throat quenching the feeling of the burning, which was stuck in my mind. She laid my head back down on the pillow and I noticed she smelled nice, of flowers and green things.

I tried to speak again, this time it was easier, "Josh...ua?" It came out in a faint whisper.

"He is asleep in the next room." The man answered simply, although his tone suggesting something wasn't right.

"Is...he...o...kay?" I croaked out. I looked at them both as they exchanged a strange look. "What's...wrong...with...him?" A deep panic started to set in. If he was hurt because he rushed in to save me, I would never be able to live with it.

"He is...exhausted." The woman – Helena – said, clasping her hands before her. "What he did...what happened...he's very tired."

"Where...am I?" I could move a little now and turned my head to look around the large room. It was filled with antique furniture and I realized that the carved wood I had seen earlier, was the huge wooden canopy of a four-poster bed that I lay beneath. There was a huge unlit fireplace on the right hand wall and opposite the bed were large curtains obviously covering a very large window.

"You are at Marston Court, Joshua's home." The man replied.

"I am? How did I...get here?" My voice had begun to return fully and I could feel my back aching from lying down for what must have been a long time. "How long have I been...here?" I tried to sit up but was still too weak. Helena instantly stepped in and helped me into a sitting position. "Thank you." I managed a small smile for her.

She smiled a lovely sincere smile back, "You have been here since last night, since..." She glanced at the man with a worried expression.

"Joshua managed to bring you here last night." He said. "I am Daniel Marston, Joshua's father and this..." He held out his

Chameleon

hand toward the woman, "is Helena, my wife and Joshua's mother."

Oh my God! I blushed and must have looked worried. This was not the best way to meet his parents.

Helena saw my face and moved to my side, "It's alright dear, don't worry. Everything will be alright." She smiled again. Joshua was very much like her except for the eye colour.

"What about the man that...killed me?" I suddenly asked.

Daniel cleared his throat, "He has been dealt with and you do not have to worry about him anymore. All you have to do is concentrate on getting better."

"How come I'm alive? I know I died, I'd felt it. I felt everything stop. So how come...I'm not dead still?" I asked, my brow wrinkling in confusion.

They looked at each other again. "That is a very long story and one you will need to hear...but not now." Daniel said.

"I understand your mother is away, is that correct?" Helena asked.

"Yes, she's out of town on a course, she'll be back on Sunday night. Why?"

"In that case, you can convalesce here for the next two days, without a worry. We weren't sure when she was due back." Helena put her hand on her husbands shoulder and smiled as she spoke. "Joshua managed to tell us before he...before he went to sleep." She stammered.

Shakily, I reached out and managed to pick up the glass of water from the side table, I enjoyed being able to make my body work again. I glanced at her worried face.

"What's wrong with him?" I asked quietly, worried about what they weren't telling me.

She glanced at her husband again and then looked back at me with a worried expression on her face.

"You have to tell me what is wrong with him." I said, impatient anger beginning to flare in my voice.

"Please don't exert yourself, he is just asleep." Daniel looked sternly at me and then his face softened, "I see you care deeply for him."

I blushed but pressed on, "I do. Tell me, how long has he been asleep?"

There was an awkward silence.

It was Helena who spoke first, "He's been asleep since he brought you home last night. We got a few words out of him, about what had happened, before he collapsed and fell into a very deep sleep...we can't wake him up. We have tried everything." She tried to look brave but I could see she was terribly worried.

My head spun, 'Collapsed after he brought me home' were the only words that kept going round my mind as I looked at her in amazement. Was this my fault? Had he put himself in danger because of me? Me and my silly plan? The need to see him, to know he was just asleep and not worse, was unbearable.

"I need to see him." I said.

"I don't think that is a good idea." Daniel said.

"Probably not, but I'd like to make up my own mind, if that's okay." I started to move the covers off my legs and looked down to see that I was dressed in an old fashioned sleeping gown. It was made of long white cotton with long sleeves and a button up front with a row of lace across the chest and round the cuffs. It was somewhat crumpled but covered me from head to toe.

Daniel burst out laughing, it was a lovely deep rich sound. "Joshua has mentioned you a couple of times over the past few days and indeed, I think he may have met his match in you, Kate." He said as his face erupted into a broad, handsome smile.

Helena gave a reassuring smile and came to help me out of bed. My legs were wobbly at first but were much stronger than I'd expected. I was able to walk reasonably well, while leaning on

Chameleon

Helena's arm.

Daniel led the way and opened the doors for us. He led us down a wood panelled hallway with thick rugs, past several doors and until finally he opened the last door on the right. I stepped into the quiet room and saw that it was very similar to the one I woke up in. I glanced round to the right and saw Wil, Joshua's brother, sitting on a large and ornate wooden bed with Joshua asleep behind him.

To say Joshua looked paler than usual, was an understatement. He literally looked dead. His face was white as the sheets on his bed, his sunken eyes were rimmed with dark shadows and his cheeks were drawn inwards, which made him look gaunt. The only reason I knew he wasn't dead was the fact that I could hear and see him breathing. It was the only sound in the very quiet room. With Helena's help, I moved closer to the bed, where Wil solemnly moved off the bed allowing me to sit next to Joshua.

"I'm glad you are back with us, Kate." Wil said, his voice was rough with emotion, his face looked tired and haggard.

He'd never spoken to me before but he seemed to know who I was, I guessed Joshua must have mentioned my name at some point. I nodded to him and said, "Thanks."

For some reason, I felt the urge to talk to Joshua, like he'd still hear me. I looked back to his parents, "Look, I don't know everything yet but I do know Joshua can hear me when I whisper from several hundred yards away, maybe more. I have a feeling he will hear me now. I just wanted to warn you before you think I'm crazy." Again his parents looked meaningfully at each other but said nothing.

I moved up the bed closer to Joshua's head and took a deep breath, my hands were clammy with nerves. I was edgy from everything that had happened and being in a roomful of people I didn't know. I leaned in a little and looked closely at Joshua's lovely face. It looked perfect, even in this deathly pose. He almost looked like a marble statue, pale, almost translucent. I reached out my hand to touch his face.

"Don't touch him!" Daniel said. He quickly stepped forward and grasped my wrist. "I mean...he won't awaken just by touch, we have tried everything." He said looking a little sheepish at his outburst.

Without looking at him I replied, "He won't hurt me, we have touched before." I could almost hear the three of them looking at each other in amazement behind my back. I pulled away from Daniel's grasp and gently laid my palm against his Joshua's cheek. I could hear everyone in the room breathe out, like they'd collectively been holding their breath.

I could feel the strange buzz under my fingers, almost like if you put your tongue on a battery but it seemed much less intense than it had been before. "Joshua? Joshua can you hear me? It's Kate."

Nothing, not even a flicker or a twitch of an eye.

"Joshua." I said in a more forceful voice. "It's me, Kate. I'm okay, you saved me. I don't know how but I know you did. Listen to me, you have to wake up, you have to come back to me. Joshua."

Nothing.

I took a deep breath and tried again, keeping my hand against his cheek, "Joshua, damn it. Don't you give up, I need you. Please come back, listen to my voice and feel my hand on your cheek, use them to find your way back. Please, Joshua." I could feel the tears running down my cheeks and I realised that my feelings for him really were as intense as I'd first thought. A gentle, warm hand rested on my shoulder.

"Try again, Kate." Helena said.

"Joshua, listen to me. I'm well and I'm waiting here for you. Hear my voice, feel my hand on your face...follow it back to me.

Chameleon

We are all here, your parents and Wil. Please Joshua, try..." The tears flowed freely down my face, I didn't even bother to brush them away. Then, I became aware of the slight vibration under my hand, I was sure it was increasing. I could definitely feel it much more than a few moments ago. "Yes, Joshua!" My voice echoed my excitement. "That's it, follow my voice, feel my hand."

"What's happening?" Daniel asked urgently as both he and Wil moved round to my side of the bed.

"I can feel him coming back, I can feel the buzz more." Tears and a smile mixed on my face. "Joshua, come on, you can do it, listen to my voice."

"What do you mean you can feel the 'buzz'?" Daniel's perfect eyebrow rose in astonishment.

"It can wait, Daniel." Helena told him, in no uncertain terms.

I didn't care. I could feel every part of Joshua 'waking up', like I had. "That's it Joshua, you can do it." I said but I was beginning to feel tired, drained almost and started to slump off the side of the bed. Helena swiftly caught me and held me but my link with Joshua was broken the instant I let my hand drop from his face.

I sat motionless looking at Joshua, still he did not move.

Slowly, I began to feel better and was able to sit up again on my own. I looked at Joshua and realised I could see small movements or twitches around his eyes. The longer I watched the bigger the movements got, until finally I saw his eyes were trying to open. It took a few goes but then they popped open and the sheer beauty of them pierced my heart with joy.

Many things happened at once. Helena rushed to him and kissed his forehead, whispering to him. Daniel rushed in closer. Wil cheered loudly and began laughing with relief. Joshua now started to move, first his hands and then his feet. Finally, he moved his neck and looked around the room, he tried to speak.

He touched his throat and Helena quickly gave him some water.

"Kate?" Was the first word Joshua spoke.

His parents stepped back so he could see me.

"I'm here, Joshua." I moved closer and could see the worry in his eyes. "It's alright, I'm okay."

"Thank...God. I didn't think...I had...managed it." He took my hand.

I felt the gentle buzz and smiled, speaking softly I said, "I guess ya can't get rid of me that easily, huh?"

He laughed, even if it was croaky sound and not his normal laugh, it was wondrous to hear.

"I guess you...will demand...to know...what is going on, now?" He asked.

"I'll wait."

He looked stunned and looked at me as if he didn't believe a word of it.

"I'll wait until you can walk again, which should be in about five minutes." I grinned.

He laughed again, which was comforting and he sounded more like himself.

"Come, let's leave these two to talk." Helena ushered both Wil and Daniel out of the room, "They have much to discuss." She smiled at us as she left, closing the door behind her.

"I guess that's your cue." I grinned at him, rubbing my arms through the long sleeved nightie.

He looked a little uncertain and then asked, "If you are cold, you could...come under the covers." His strength was returning in leaps and bounds now, just as mine had.

I looked at the king size bed and decided there was enough room for me to get warm and still be far away from him, far from temptation. "I am a bit chilly out here." I could feel my cheeks warming with a blush. After a moment's hesitation, I climbed in the huge bed beside him and snuggled down. The

Chameleon

bed was so large that we weren't even touching and it was much warmer than outside of the covers.

He smiled at me, "You just want to have...your evil way with me...while I'm weak." He pretended to be shocked.

"You should be so lucky." I joked, "Actually, I don't think either of us are in any state for fooling around."

"True."

I fiddled with the covers, trying to decide how to ask what I so desperately needed to know.

"So, what are you?" I asked.

"What do you mean, what am I?" He laughed.

"You know damn well what I mean. I have theories of what you are but I'm not sure about them now." I bit my lip, wondering if I should have started this conversation after all.

"Theories? Like what? He grinned and managed to propped himself up on the pillows so that he was looking directly at me.

His normal healthy colour had returned, his hair was bed rumpled and he was handsome as ever, and, in bed with me. I swallowed hard trying to keep my mind focused on the words that were coming out of his mouth.

"...whatever the theory is, you really shouldn't look like that because it's asking for trouble."

"Look like what?" I asked while trying to look innocent. Instead, I was feeling guiltily excited by him and the heat of a blush rushed over my skin. My inner struggle had vanished from within me now, I knew what I wanted and it was him.

"You look like you're about to pounce and devour me."

"Shut up." I snapped, blushing even more.

"Okay, I won't wind you up. Come on, I really want to know about your theories."

"Well...at first I was convinced you were something, but I didn't know which type and now I'm not so sure."

"That's incredibly helpful. Thanks for clearing it up." He

laughed, "A few more details, perhaps?"

I took a deep breath...he would either laugh at me or have me committed, personally, I wasn't sure which I preferred. "Okay, let me get it all out and then you can comment. Deal?"

"Deal." He managed to look serious.

"Right...okay, here goes nothing. I've decided, after much in depth study and observation, that you are not what you appear." I could feel myself becoming more nervous as the moment neared. I looked down at my hands; they were already shaking. "You don't like being touched. You are very pale, extremely charismatic and I've never seen you eat. You have amazing hearing because I know you can hear me from a long distance away and you can move very fast, so fast you just become a blur. You also have a strange energy current coming off you." I looked up into his lovely eyes and paused trying to get the courage to continue.

He looked serious and his eyebrows had formed a small frown. He nodded, as if to tell me to go on.

"Except for electric current, the rest of the evidence seems to point to the fact that you're a..." I took a deep breath and felt my body shake as I let the breath out. I vaguely wondered at my own sanity. Finally, I blurted out "You're a Vampire!" I quickly rushed on not looking at him or giving him chance to comment, "It's the kind of Vampire I'm unsure about." I was trying to sound business like to cover my nerves. "I need to know...are you a 'Dracula' killer type? Or an 'Edward' needy type? You know...the good bad guy that hates to hurt humans?"

There, I had said it out loud. I could barely believe I'd done it. I took a deep and somewhat shaky breath and blow it out noisily.

"You can speak now." I refused to look at him, afraid of what I would see.

"You think I'm...a Vampire?" He said incredulously as he sat bolt upright in the bed.

Chameleon

He reached over, gently placed a finger under my chin and lifted my head, until I had no option but to look into his eyes. All I could feel was the buzz from his finger and all I could see was his beautiful, bright blue, mesmerizing eyes.

"I swear to you, I am not a Vampire. They don't exist. They are fiction, something born from myths and folk legends. They are twisted tales, distortions of the truth like Chinese whispers."

"If you are not Vampire, what are you then? Are you even human?" I held my breath.

"Yes, I'm human, well...of a sort. I was once more human though." He said, so helpfully.

I let out the breath I hadn't realised I was holding, as he lowered his hand and settled himself, obviously ready, at last, to explain.

"Are you sure you want to know? There is no going back once you do." He said as his eyes searched my face.

I nodded and trembled, I felt a small panic began to build inside. I knew that this was the moment, the moment that would change my world forever. I also knew that whatever he said next, it would not change how I felt about him. I felt my hands grip the bed covers.

"I am different from you and other humans. You talk of Vampires and, like I said, they are fiction. However, like the saying goes 'there is no smoke without fire'. The legend of the Vampire is actually based on the history of a slightly differently evolved race of humans. The stories are loosely based on these advanced humans who are able to use more of their brain and control their bodies more completely than say, you, for example."

I tilted my head in surprise. It was not the answer I had been expecting. I could feel my excitement growing inside as my fear and panic began to ebb, even though I was not sure where this conversation was going.

"Throughout history there have been thousands of reports of Vampires, evil spirits, the undead, incubus and succubus, monsters and demons. Most of these stories can be filtered down to a few common factors." He began to count them on his fingers, "Number one: the draining of blood, spirit or life force. Number two: extended life or immortality. Number three: a hypnotic effect or control over victims, and finally number four: amazing abilities such as speed, heightened senses and other unusual powers. These are the abilities that my kind and I possess. We call ourselves Chameleons. These 'abilities' are feared by the 'Lights', that's what we call non-Chameleons like you."

I sat with my mouth open waiting for my brain to reconnect and catch up, it did, eventually.

"Okay, so you're saying you're not a Vampire, but what you are, is the even more scary thing behind the legend of the Vampire?" My voice shook with nerves. I was in bed with something more scary than a vampire, panic gripped me as I glanced at the door wondering if I could get to it before he could. I swallowed hard and looked back at him.

"Essentially, yes. Do you want me to continue? I wouldn't blame you for wanting to get out of here at this point."

"Yes...go on." My voice came out weak and shaky.

"Are you sure?" He raised an eyebrow.

"Are...there...more of you...out there?" I said and cuddled up in the covers, I found I had begun to shiver. Was it from the cold air of the room or from fear?

"Yes, many more." He said, watching me carefully. "Basically, we can control our bodies with our minds. We can make our hearts speed up to 400 beats per minute, creating a huge flood of adrenalin, which enables us to move incredibly fast. Or we can move at your 'human' speed, when we're in public. As you know, we have great hearing and it's hard not to react when someone whispers you name across the room." He laughed at

Chameleon

the memory. "But we learn to control ourselves."

I began to relax as he calmly told me about himself. For a brief moment I wondered if he was hypnotizing me to be calmer but I quickly pushed that terrifying thought from my mind and tried to concentrate.

"Like you, we do eat but don't have to do it as often as you because our bodies are a lot more efficient. The same goes for sleep we don't, usually, need very much and can go for a long time without it. Obviously, this..." He stretch out his arms to encompass himself in the bed, "...is an exception."

I changed my position in the bed and sat up with the covers pulled up over my chest. I wasn't quite on the edge of the bed but very near it.

"Are you okay? Have you had enough? He said.

"You might as well tell me everything now, I'll let you know if I'm not okay." I said in the strongest voice I could muster.

He nodded and continued, "We live very long lives, in fact we know of no Chameleon that has died of natural causes, so you could call us immortal. We are born naturally, not 'made' like Vampires in the stories. However, we are born completely human like you. We evolve our abilities as we grow older. It normally happens between the ages of fifteen and twenty five or so. No one yet knows why we evolve, we just do. There is nothing unusual about us when we are human, it seems random." He looked at me hopefully and sat up further with his back against the headboard. "With me, so far?"

"Yes." I said, strangely fascinated. "How came the world doesn't already know about you?"

"We like to keep our existence hidden for various reasons, which I don't want to go into right now. We control our bodies to age like you and then we move away and start again, younger. We can age or grow younger at will but the change is only on the outside. We can change back from, say, seventy to twenty, if we wished. Inside, we don't actually age past our evolution age, depending on when that was, it's different for everyone. This is why, throughout history, there have been stories about bodies not decomposing, saints and miracle type stuff but it's usually a Chameleon that is sleeping until the people who have known them, have died. Not the best way to go and it's a tactic that we no longer use." He paused and took a drink of water. Replacing the glass on the bedside table he turned and then placed his hand on my face and drew himself closer.

I was now starting to get used to the gentle buzz on my skin from his touch and the feel of it excited me and, coupled with being so near to him, the butterflies in my stomach had set up residency again. They momentarily distracted me from his amazing, and yet in some ways scary, story.

"Before I go on, I would like to do something. Just in case I don't get the chance after." He smiled that sexy half smile as he slowly moved closer.

My breath came quicker and my heartbeat went frantic as he gently put his lips on mine for a short but gentle kiss. The buzz from his lips was so small and yet so intense that when he broke away I'd started to breathe rapidly and felt slightly light-headed.

"Are you okay?" He asked, looking worried.

"Uh huh." It was all I could manage. I swallowed loudly, "Do that again." It wasn't a request.

I braced myself. He saw it and laughed.

"You're sure?"

"Yes." I closed my eyes. He was very close, I could feel his warm breath on my skin. Again his lips touched mine but this time they were a little less gentle, as if the last time was a test. I returned the kiss and I could feel the urge to grab him and kiss him passionately grow within me. I started to get more animated in my kiss and I felt the buzz increase as my passion did, I quickly put my arms around his neck and pulled him in closer.

Chameleon

Again, I felt light headed and started to feel strange.

Suddenly, Joshua grabbed my arms and thrust me away from him, gasping.

The sour taste of rejection instantly filled me. Angrily, I blushed and could feel the first prickling of tears behind my eyes. I dug my nails into the covers. If he didn't want me, he sure as hell was not going to see my cry about it. Confusion crossed my face. Did he not feel the same as I did?

"Whoa." He breathed deeply and let his hands drop. "I nearly lost it there." He gently stroked my cheek with his finger.

All my emotional turmoil vanished and a calm spread in me as I realised he felt the same about me as I did him.

"We need to be more careful, at least for a while." He said.

I took a deep breath, "I nearly lost control too. That buzz is rather nice when mixed with a kiss." I smiled hopefully and yet felt a little shy.

"You can feel it?" He looked disappointed.

"Yes, every time you touch me I feel it. Sometimes it's slight, other times it is intense. Is that not good? It sure as hell feels good to me." I smiled.

"No, it's not good. I thought I'd more control over it."

"Okay, now you have to explain that." I said.

He sat back again. "Firstly, though, let me explain what we mean by Lights. We call humans 'Lights' because when we look at them we can see a Light surrounding them. You may have heard of it as an 'Aura'. An aura, in scientific terms, is the electromagnetic field that surrounds the human body. It can also be found surrounding any living organism...so animals, plants and trees have it too."

"Do you have an aura?" I said, vaguely remembering something about this in science lessons.

"Chameleons have auras too but ours don't change with our emotions, like human ones do, they are permanently layered

Edain Duguay

like a rainbow around the Chameleons body. This is often the first sign that a human is evolving into a Chameleon, when their auras change. Humans or Lights have a single colour, which radiates about three to four inches, from the skin outwards. There are many colours and moods, as you can image."

I looked at my forearm and hand but saw nothing.

Joshua watched me and continued, "As for the hypnotic control, it comes from our beauty. All Chameleons are good looking; it automatically draws people to us. It's a natural built-in instinct of humans to want to mate with a perfect member of the opposite sex. Basically, it boils down to the instinct to give your genes the best possible chance to continue the species, hence going for someone we think looks perfect, it's the survival of the fittest instinct." He paused and took a depth breath, as if what he was about to say was very important. "The final factor is of the 'Vampire and blood theme', which ties in with our good looks and...there is no easy way to saying this...Chameleons feed on humans."

Shock filled my body and mind, my thoughts were frozen. Blood rushed around my body so quickly, I felt a little faint. Anger and disappointment raised their ugly heads as I managed to look him in the eye. I must have looked horrified, repulsed even, because he paused and grimaced. So he is a Vampire, I thought.

He nervously and quickly continued as if wanted to get it over with. "Now, when I said we feed off Lights that is exactly what we do. Our minds are more advanced and can control our bodies more, we use a lot of our energy in doing it. So we rebuild it by feeding on humans...by taking their Light or energy."

He watched my reaction very carefully. I tried to keep my face blank, not allowing it to show the turmoil of bewildered emotions I felt inside. Although, I was not sure my efforts were working.

Chameleon

"How...exactly...do you 'feed'?" I tried, unsuccessfully, to keep my voice steady.

"We feed by touch. If we need a boost, we just gently touch a human. It takes just a second and we draw that energy into us, through the skin. It doesn't harm the human and often they don't realise we've done anything. For example: some stranger may just brush past you and say 'excuse me' as they go by, that's often a Chameleon. It is like drinking an espresso for us; it gives us a jolt of energy. However, if we want, we can drain all the energy from a human and kill them very easily. Some of us choose not to do it, but it doesn't mean we can't."

He looked meaningfully at me.

I thought through what he'd said and I felt a relief at the way some Chameleons feed, it wasn't as horrifying as I had first thought. He had said 'us' meaning Joshua didn't kill people, but what about the others. He had also said 'some' choose not kill that meant 'some' choose to. The very thought frightened me beyond measure.

Then a thought occurred to me, a mind bending thought. "The buzz. That's the buzz that you are talking about, isn't it? My energy." I was stunned. "Are you taking...my energy?"

"Actually, yes..." He held up his hands and hastily added, "but it is not what you think, please believe me. You see, I evolved during this summer, when we were in Canada, and I'm new to this. It takes a lot of practice when you first get your abilities, to control them so that you don't drain everyone you touch. Sometimes, I slip up by accident, like the other day when you fell down the steps at school and felt the shock from my hand. That's why we stay away from people when we're new, just in case. As for the buzz you feel every time I touch you, I hoped I was better at controlling it...but obviously not."

"Oh. Wait, back up a bit...you say you can kill us by touch? So it wouldn't show when we died?"

"Exactly, you would not be marked inside or out. Older Chameleons can kill you by touch without you ever feeling a buzz."

"Oh my God! Oxford...the deaths." I said suddenly as my brain put two and two together.

"Yes. It probably was a Chameleon in Oxford. You see, not all Chameleons are like us, refusing to feed on Lights. Some Chameleons call us betrayers of our, 'superior species' because we don't."

"That's horrible." My face crumpled in disgust. "Hang on, who is 'we' and what do you feed on if you don't feed on humans?"

"When I say 'we', I mean my family. We are all Chameleons. My family has been Chameleons for a couple of generations even back to Lord Mathers Danforth Marston II who built our school for his son when he evolved in 1899. Anyway..."

"My school was built...for one of you? Wow. Wait, I thought you said it wasn't genetic."

"It isn't normally, we are an oddity in the Chameleon world." He shrugged. "The school was a tool in those days, exclusively for Chameleons, they used it for two reasons; one was to learn to 'act' human to fool the Lights and the other was to further scientific knowledge, to find out about our species." He said. "Eventually, the school held less interest to Chameleons and my family decided to open it up to all students in the 1950's."

I sat thinking quietly for a while. I looked at him, then around the room and back at him again. "So I'm in the house of generations of Chameleons, surrounded by them and any of them, at any time, could kill me?"

"I'm afraid so but we wouldn't. Do you want to go home now?" He said.

"Don't be daft. Your family has been nice to me so far and you're not scary at all." I grinned at him and moved my hand over his and held it. The vibration was slight but still there. "That feels nice." I said.

He smiled and my heart leapt.

Yes, I'd decided, I was in love with a Chameleon and all that entailed.

Now I knew I really was in trouble.

COUNCIL

We sat quietly for a while, each of us lost in our own thoughts.

"I can't be the first human to hear about you, Chameleons I mean. Surely, there are others who know about you...know what you are?" I said.

"Humans only know a little. It's relatively recently that the concept and theory of auras has been openly known about. The Hindus made the discovery of Chakras many years ago, they say they are the seats of energy where the Light is created in the body. The idea of 'energy vampires' is an old one. Although, humans still have a long way to go to 'know' about Chameleons, they certainly are heading down the right road though. This is actually a problem for us, obviously we don't want to be found out and treated like lab rats."

Joshua's hand tightened on mine and I saw true fear in his face.

"The problem is that some Chameleons are only too happy to kill humans, they see you as an inferior race. These Chameleons are in danger of exposing us, whilst others of my kind hide like fugitives. Recently, we've heard of Chameleons being captured by mercenaries of rogue warfare groups, working for who-knows-what government. They want to use us as weapons." He shook his head in disbelief, "We also have our own leaders, like

Chameleon

a Chameleon government, called The Council of Nine. They try to keep us underground but some Chameleons, like the one in Oxford, are not helping. Mind you, he's no longer a problem." He said with an unhappy look on his face.

"Whoa, hang on." I had to collect my thoughts. "What do you mean by 'no longer a problem'? Was he the one who attacked me?" I was stunned.

"We think so." He paused and took a deep breath, "I should tell you, the only way to kill a Chameleon is to remove their head. This disconnects the brain from the heart, the two parts that have to work together for us to live, just like you, but as you can imagine it's not easy getting near a Chameleon to do it, especially when all they have to do is touch you, to kill you. There is also our speed and acute senses to think about, like I said...it's hard...but not impossible." He looked down at the bed covering with a look of pure shame on his face.

"Did...did you kill him?" I looked at him in shock.

He looked away and said through gritted teeth, "Yes." He took a deep shaky breath, "I tried to save you but I arrived too late. It was all my fault, I thought I could put off telling you everything but then you whispered and I knew it was too late."

I squeezed his hand, not knowing what to say. I felt very small.

He turned back to look at me, "I'm sorry I was late and you had to feel that."

His words took me back to that terrible burning sensation like my skin was on fire all over again. I shuddered at the thought. My killer's words came back to me. "What did he mean when he said that I had called him with a whisper? And that he could claim me?"

"Humans, who know about us or work for us, obviously need to know about our abilities, it's a rule we have. Needless to say, we are very careful with whom we trust. If a human who knows about us, whispers something meant for a Chameleon, they must attach the name of that Chameleon to the whisper. That way, if other Chameleons hear it, they will ignore the call because the human is 'owned' or 'belongs' to the name they call. However, if a whisper is heard with no name attached then some Chameleons think it's an invitation to feed and will track down that whisperer."

"So how do they know a whisper is for them and not some other human. People whisper all the time."

"Exactly. Some of us believe it's just a way to give some Chameleons permission to feed, whilst others say they can tell the difference if the whisper is for another human or not. Personally, I think it's BS and an excuse for some to claim more victims." His face mirrored the disgust in his voice.

"Okay. So if you don't feed, more than the odd touch on humans, what do you feed on?"

"My family, and several others, feed on other living things like animals or plants and trees. My mother loves the energy of plants and trees, my father is an animal lover, if you know what I mean." He smiled, "We have pigs and cattle on the grounds that we raise, butcher and sell the meat. My father is always present when they are 'butchered' by our stock-man and takes his energy by killing the animals chosen for slaughter. Obviously, our stock-man is a trusted human. As for Wil and I, we like a mixture of animals, plants and trees."

"Oh..." That's better than humans, I thought with relief, "So why do others of your kind kill us, humans I mean...why don't they feed like you do?"

"Many think humans are inferior and should be treated like cattle, some even prefer the 'taste' of human energy."

"Urgh." I said and shuddered. "I guess what you and your family does makes sense...but...when you feed on the plants or trees doesn't it kill them like the animals?"

Chameleon

"Actually no, they have a continuous flow of energy, they are like the perfect machine, we take some and they replace it, very clever really. You know, you're taking all this very well." He said.

"Yeah weird, huh? I don't feel frightened. I just know that no one here is going to hurt me. Some of the others you describe are scary though, like the one who attacked me." I looked around the room trying to find the right words. "So...how come I'm alive? Not that I'm unhappy about it, you understand." I grinned at Joshua and he seemed truly relieved that I wasn't running away screaming. When I thought about it for a moment, I couldn't believe it either.

"Well...that was my fault too. I was so incensed by what he'd done to you I lost control and...killed him. I didn't even stop to think about it, I just did it. I didn't drain him. I just...separated...his head." His lip curled in revulsion. "Afterwards...I saw you laid on the rocks below and rushed down to you, but I was too late you had...your energy had...dissipated." He swallowed hard. "I held you, not really understanding that you'd gone, I talked to you, even shouted at you but you just laid there. Your eyes were dead, your skin was cooling. I just wanted you alive, I tried gave you a little jolt of my energy not even daring to hope it would heal you. I wasn't even sure I was sane at that moment for trying but I just had to...when I looked down at you in my arms, I knew I had to try."

He looked at me, the haunting emotions were clear on his face, and I instinctively squeezed his hand. I could have said that maybe he had cured my cold the other day but it seemed unnecessary at this point.

"At first nothing happened. I couldn't bare the crushing pain inside, I couldn't allow myself to believe you were dead and so I tried again and again. Then, when I had almost reached exhaustion point, I gave one last push of my energy through my hand over your heart, I thought I could hear your heart beat restart but the minute it did I was so stunned that I moved my hand away and the glorious sound stopped. I brace myself for what I knew would be my last chance and forced almost all my energy into your heart, it burst into life and you began breathing!" He smiled fully and turned his lovely face towards me. "I couldn't believe it, I didn't dare to let go of you in case your heart stopped again. I knew I couldn't leave you to get help, so I decided to bring you here, but the speed I used to get us here on top of the energy I had already used to keep you heart going, wiped me out. I had no clue if either of us would survive the night. I only just made it through the front door and told my parents what had happened before passing out. The rest you know."

"Wow." It was all I could say. With pure joy and without thinking I leaned over and hugged him hard. "Thank you, you're my own personal hero." I beamed up at him as I lay in his arms, the buzz was like a warm blanket around me.

He stiffened at my touch.

I pulled back a little," What?"

"I'm afraid to hurt you, I couldn't bear to lose you again."

"I trust you, you won't." I cuddled back into his arms and he relaxed around me and held me close.

"Thank you for saving my life...well, actually...saving me from death." I laughed nervously excited to be in his arms.

He laughed, "You're very welcome."

He laid his head on mine and held me close. We stayed cuddled in each other's arms for a while as a peaceful silence settled around us and held us safe.

"I have a question," I looked up at him, "actually, I have a couple."

"Now that's a surprise." He raised an eyebrow and grinned.

"Has it ever been done before, I mean is it a known ability with your people to bring someone back from the dead?"

Chameleon

"Not that I know of, no one has told me, if it is."

"What happened to...him? The man who attacked me? What I mean is, what happened to his body? When you die, do you vanish into ash like the cool Hollywood Vampires or what?"

"Nope, that's all Hollywood. When we die, our energy leaves us and finds its way back into whatever living thing is around it, like plants and trees. Then the body looks and behaves just like a human's dead body. The energy never goes into another Chameleon, no one is exactly sure why though. Unless, of course, we were to drain a Chameleon to the point of death, then it would. As for your attacker, my father said he and Wil took care of it. I'm unsure what they did with his...body...maybe they put it in the incinerator out in the stockyard, which we use for the butchery waste." Joshua cringed at his own words.

I shuddered at the cold way he spoke of the man he had killed and how his family seemed to have destroyed the body. Rather my attacker than me though, I thought grimly.

"It's okay, he can't get to you anymore." Joshua felt my shudder and gently kissed me on the forehead.

Even though I knew he could kill me very easily, I also knew he would never harm me. Just being around him made me feel safe. How odd is that? Either I was crazy or my instincts knew more than my brain. I needed a change in subject, I didn't want to talk about my attacker nor his death anymore. "When did Wil...how do you say it?" I frowned trying to remember.

"Evolve?"

"Yes, that's it. When did Wil evolve?"

"A year ago this coming Christmas, six months before me."

"How long does it normally take for one of you to control your abilities?" A thought was forming in my head.

"It's different for everyone but usually a couple of months, why?"

"I've noticed, at school, that Wil still doesn't touch people...shouldn't he be able to control it by now?"

"Ah, you noticed that, huh? Wil...he...well, Wil had an...incident on the day he got his abilities and doesn't like to...ah...tempt fate again."

"Why, what happened?"

"I think that's something you should ask him, it's his story to tell." Joshua said. "Although, he doesn't like to talk about it much."

"Oh...okay." I said as I heard a deep rumble emanate from Joshua's stomach right next to my ear.

"I think the beast within needs feeding. I thought you didn't have to eat often?"

"We don't, usually, I guess all the excitement sapped more of my energy than I thought. I've never slept so much or been so hungry since I evolved." He laughed now in amazement. "Why don't we go raid the kitchen and see what we can find."

"Are you up to it?" I asked.

"I feel fine now. How about you?"

"I'm fine. Grateful to be alive." I smiled.

He climbed out of bed, headed towards his large antique wardrobe and began searching through his clothes. "Here, I think these will keep you warm. Old houses are full of draughts and that..." he gestured to my long nightgown, "looks like something a grandmother would wear."

Joshua passed me a deep blue sweatshirt and matching trousers, made from fleece. "Oh these will be warm, is there somewhere I can get cleaned up. I think I still have mud in my hair from the waterfall."

"That door over there," he pointed next to the wardrobe, "that's my bathroom, you can shower and change in there."

Closing the door behind me, I looked around. The bathroom was the size of my bedroom at the cottage and full of marble and brass. The large tub had an old fashioned shower head over it and the sink had a large gilt framed mirror above it.

A bathroom royalty would be happy with.

Nice.

I critically examined myself in the mirror. My hair was a mess, although I liked it to look tousled, it wasn't supposed to be quite this wild with bits of mud stuck in it. Removing the night gown, I noticed that I had no bruises or cuts from the fall and crashing onto the rocks. I guessed if I had suffered any injuries, they would have been healed from Joshua's energy by now.

Bonus.

So much had happened recently, it was hard to take everything in. My mind wandered over the events and information that had filled up all the space in my brain since yesterday. I took a shower and dried myself slowly using the big warm towel, my brain was trying to do catch-up on events, swirling images and words floated around. I took a deep calming breath, dressed and headed back into the bedroom to find Joshua sitting patiently on his bed. He had obviously just showered somewhere else and was now wearing black jeans and a dark green t-shirt.

Handsome devil, I all but drooled.

"You look better, Kate." He said.

"I feel much better, thanks. You don't look so bad yourself."

"Why thank you, young lady." Joshua stood and made a gracious bow.

"Oaf." I laughed, "Let's find food before we eat the furniture."

We headed down the wooden panelled corridor walking past the room I'd woken up in and continued until we came to a large ornate staircase leading downwards. Joshua led the way down holding my hand. The now familiar buzz was somehow comforting, especially knowing that it was exactly what had brought me back to life.

The stairs lead down to the main entrance hall, a grand place full of marble flooring and walls covered in mahogany panels. There were rooms leading off in every direction. The size of the house stunned me. I had never been in a home so large. As if he heard my thoughts, Joshua paused to let me look round.

"Most of these rooms we don't use. They're open to the public in the summer until September, then the house is all ours again until May."

"Why open the house up at all? Surely you don't need the money." I said quickly without thinking, "Sorry, that was rude." I blushed at my outburst.

"Nah, it's okay and you're right, we don't need to be open for money reasons. It was part of the will stipulations from my Grandfather when my Father inherited the house." His face looked like he was hiding something.

"What?" I said.

"What, what?" He tried to look innocent but failed, badly.

"What am I missing? You're not telling me something."

"You're getting too good at reading me." He smiled, "I thought you may have worked out who my father is."

"Oh? See, I did miss something."

"Don't worry about it now, I have given you a lot to think about already."

"Hey, no fair. Don't be a tease." I said.

"Let's get food first, okay?"

"Okay. Good idea, my brain works better when I've eaten."

We walked down the long hall and I was able to glance into a few rooms on the way. Among them were a parlour, a dinning room and a library. Finally, we arrived at the kitchen, which was nothing like I expected. Unlike the rest of the house, which was antique and stately, the kitchen was ultra modern with stainless steel appliances and all the modern conveniences.

"Bloody hell, I didn't see that coming." I looked around,

amazed.

The kitchen was huge. The counters were made of dark marble, complimenting the light wood of the cabinets. The centre of the room was marked by an island counter with the sink in one half, the other half was a breakfast counter. There were wall units on three walls, a doorway leading off the kitchen that stood open, revealing a huge pantry. On the far side of the kitchen, under the large window looking out over their lovely garden, sat a dark wooden table with seating for six, three of them were taken by Joshua's brother and his parents.

"There you both are. Feeling better?" Helena rose and came closer but stood a little way away from us.

I realised that she held back on purpose, not wanting to get too close, waiting to see how I'd reacted to the news.

"Yes, we're both feeling much better. I've just been telling Kate about the family." He looked at me.

"I see." Helena said as she looked from me to him and back again, waiting.

It was awkward and I wanted them to know I wasn't frightened. If anything, I was intrigued. "I'm very grateful to you for everything you've done for me." I smiled, hoping she would understand.

Helena's face relaxed and a warm, dazzlingly beautiful smile spread across it. She stepped forward holding her hand out to shake mine.

Shaking hands has never been my thing. I stepped past her hand and quickly gave her a hug, taking her by surprise.

"Oh, thank you, dear." She was obviously quite pleased and hugged me back.

Joshua walked up to the fridge and opened it, "Is there anything we can eat? I've been absolutely starved since I woke up."

A quick movement from the table caught my eye, Daniel looked up sharply from his newspaper and stared at his son surprised, his eyes caught me looking at him, he smiled and went back to reading his paper. I found it odd that all of Joshua's family were in the kitchen when they no longer needed food. I guessed it was an old habit they wanted to keep.

"Why don't you two relax, you've been through at lot and I shall have a look to see what I can find." Helena suggested.

"How are you doing, bro?" Wil asked, as we sat down at the table.

"Not bad, considering. I'll have to feed and on top of that I'm also starving for human food. I think my tank is running on empty." Joshua said.

I smirked at Joshua's description. Being empty of energy to him, literally was like a car without fuel. I was amazed at how relaxed I felt with these people even after everything I'd found out today.

Joshua's father turned to look at me with a curious look on his face, "So how are you taking it all, Kate?"

"I'm fine actually. I was telling Joshua earlier I feel safe here. It's a lot to take in, but I'm getting there. I do have loads of questions, though."

"Well, father has been responsible for the Council's history for many years, so he's the perfect one to answer." Joshua said.

"Actually, you mentioned the Council before..." I turned from Joshua to Daniel, "Who are they?"

"The Council of Nine are our eldest and wisest. They rule our people and make our laws, enforce them and supervise the newly evolved. You do know what that means?" He looked Joshua for confirmation.

Joshua nodded.

"Good. Every newly evolved must attend the Council within their first year, usually once they have found control of their abilities. The Council of Nine will then instruct them in the laws of being a Chameleon."

Chameleon

"Like putting a name to whispers..." I said.

Daniel nodded and looked at his son.

"I've told her most things, but not all." Joshua glanced at Wil.

Wil saw his look and his face turned to stone. He looked very angry.

My stomach dropped, what was he not telling me? What had happened to Wil? I began nibble my lip nervously as a knot of anxiety grew in the pit of my stomach.

"Ah." Daniel said as he looked at each of his sons, he turned to Wil. "Do you want to tell her? She deserves to know, considering she is a trusted human now." He asked.

The words 'trusted human' made me feel strange and yet important in an odd way.

Wil continued to look down at the bike magazine he was reading and fiddle with the edge of the page. "No, father. I don't want to talk about it." His eyes remained firmly fixed on the page.

Daniel laid his hand on his son arm. "I understand, son." He paused for a moment carefully watching his son's face.

I felt sad for him. Whatever had happened, he was not over it and he was still hurt.

The room became utterly silent for a few minutes.

"Here you go you two, eggs, bacon and waffles." Helena said breaking the silence as she placed the food on plates.

Joshua and I said thanks, moved to the breakfast bar to eat.

Daniel and Helena were talking quietly to Wil over at the breakfast table. I didn't know what to say, something was terribly wrong. I couldn't even whisper to Joshua, as I knew they would all hear me. I suspected that this ability was not so much handy but more of a pain.

It was an awkward silence, I felt like a stranger in a private family moment, but I just had to know what was going on. I tried a different tack. "When will the Council want to see you, Joshua? I asked as I ate.

"I have to appear before them at the start of November, with Wil." He looked worried.

There again, something wrong. "What will they do with you?"

"We'll be tested. If we pass we're free to go."

"And if you don't?" My fork stopped mid-way to my mouth.

He looked at me, "Then they decide if we're safe to be out in the world or not."

"Are you serious? They have that much power?" I said forgetting the food on my plate.

"That and more, much more." He replied.

There was no mistaking it, he looked worriedly over at Wil. Had Wil done something wrong?

A thought came to me, "You said you had rules when you become a Chameleon. What are they?" I needed to know more. I needed to know both Joshua and Wil would be safe.

"There are ten. You know about whispers already. Another one and one of the most serious ones, is that we are not allowed to kill one of our own kind." Then he added in a quiet voice, "Ever, no matter what."

I totally and utterly lost my appetite.

Joshua had killed one of his own to save me, a mere human. He had broken their law. Tears came to my eyes in an instant. Angrily, I brushed them away. My throat dried and closed in on its self, I had become momentarily speechless. My heart raced as fear for him clutched me in its icy grasp.

"I don't think any other Chameleons know about his death, Kate." Daniel said, as if hearing my distress, "I think we may have the upper hand, at present."

"What if they do?" I spun round on the kitchen stool, "I've put Joshua in danger because of my own stupidity. Why did I

Chameleon

have to keep pushing to know everything?" Anger and fear rose inside me again, "What about you and Wil? Are you in danger too?" Tears were falling freely down my face now.

"If the Council knew we have destroyed the body and so covered up the crime, then yes we would be punished too." He looked grave.

Horror spread fear through to my very bones as all three sets of eyes at the table looked up at me.

"W-What kind of punishment?" I said.

"If we kill our kind, it is an absolute death sentence. For assisting, perhaps banishment or interment...our form of prison." He replied ominously.

"Death?" I managed to squeak out and staggered to my feet. "Death for...for Joshua?" My brain couldn't take it in. I whirled round to look at him.

He sat poking his fork at his eggs in silence, his face ashen.

"Surely you can explain he was killing me? That he was the killer from Oxford. Look at me." I shouted, panicked.

He looked up with his penetrating blue stare. "Kate, don't you understand? What he did...is what our kind does. We feed on humans. That's how Chameleons live. Just because my family and few others are different, doesn't mean the rest are. To them, I killed a Chameleon for no reason. I'm sorry, but that's how the Council will see it. No matter what I say."

"No." I shook my head. "No, this can't be happening." I looked wildly round to the others, my eyes imploring Joshua's father to do something, anything. I felt sick to my stomach and dizzy.

"Only the five of us know what happened, Kate." Daniel tried to be reassuring.

"How can you be so sure?" I said, "Your kind can hear whispers. How do you know that no one else is listening to this very conversation? Right now?"

"We don't Kate, we just have to hope for the best. What's done is done. We can't change anything now. We can only deal with what comes." He said.

"Don't you care?" I shouted.

Daniel stood but didn't move towards me, "Of course I do, Kate. But I have learnt over the years that things have a way of solving themselves." He said.

Enraged, I said, "This can't be happening." I turned back to Joshua, "You should not have killed him for me. I was dead anyway, by then. You should have left it at that." I spat out and ran from the room. Racing down the hall, I could hear Helena trying to stop Joshua from coming after me.

"Let her be, Joshua. You have sprung a lot on her in such a short time, she needs time to absorb it."

I ran past the massive hall with the stairs, onwards into parts of the house I had not seen. It seemed to go on forever in a blur, as the tears just kept coming. Finally, at the end of the long hallway I found myself in a solarium, the glass room looked out into the gardens. The light rain softly tapped on the glass like fingers tips drumming to a song. I sank into a large armchair and sobbed for a long time.

I cringed as I heard footsteps behind me. I didn't want to talk to Joshua just now and turned more towards the window, away from him.

"You should leave and never come back." Wil said.

I jumped, I'd expected Joshua's voice not his brother's.

"It's not safe around us." He said. "You will die, just like my Claire did." He sank heavily into the chair opposite mine.

I wiped away my tears and looked at him. He looked terrible, his face was full of pain. I was afraid to ask but had to. "Who's Claire?"

He looked down at a silver ring on his finger and began moving it around absentmindedly, "Claire was my girlfriend...last year, when I evolved...we were in Canada for Christmas. We weren't arguing at first..." Wil said. "We were happy, playing in the snow, laughing and kissing. Our friends were there, Rick and his girlfriend Jenny...all of us humans. We were having a snowball fight on the skidoos, driving slowly so the girls could scrape up snowballs and throw them. We got carried away and crashed, I totalled my skidoo. Luckily, we weren't hurt but Rick just wouldn't let up, making stupid remarks about my driving all the time. Finally, I lost my temper and hit him, breaking his nose." A slight sad smile cross his face, "Claire and Jenny started shouting at me. Jenny decided to drive Rick back to town to get his nose looked at and promised to send a ride back for us and the skidoo." Wil looked up and gazed out of the window, his mind lost in his memories.

A great dread was filling up inside of me, I didn't know what to do or say, so I just looked at him.

"We began to fall out about anything and everything. Claire decided to walk back to town and set off on her own, I was very angry at her. I know now that the anger was a symptom of me evolving, but I didn't know that at the time. I ran after her, amazed at my speed but still I didn't get it. I should have known." He roughly rubbed his face with his hands. "I grabbed Claire by the arms and told her she was stupid to walk all the way back, especially on her own. My anger turn to passion, before I knew it I'd started to kiss her, she tried to push me off but I couldn't let go. Without realising what I was doing I was draining her, my passion took over and all I wanted was her Light without even thinking about the girl I loved."

The tears in his eyes tumbled over and rolled down his face as he stared at me.

"She...died in my arms. I...killed...her. I had killed the person I loved the most in this world. I didn't mean too...I had evolved that very moment and had no idea of how to control it." He looked away from me back down to the ring. "So you see, you should leave and never come back. Never see my brother again. We're too dangerous for humans to be around."

For a moment I was so stunned, I didn't know what to say.

"I'm so very sorry, Wil."

"It doesn't change the fact that I killed her." Wil said as he stood up rigidly. "And Joshua will kill you too." He said as he stormed out of the solarium.

Alone again with my thoughts, I wondered if he was right? Would Joshua kill me? Eventually? I couldn't see it but then I doubt Claire believed Wil would kill her either. Would Joshua be safe from the council? Would the rest of his family be safe too? Should I do as Wil suggested and get away from Joshua, from them all?

I had no answers to the hundreds of questions running through my mind.

In a daze, I sat watching the sun setting behind the large trees at the far end of the ornate garden. My life had suddenly changed forever. My mindless everyday worries now seemed so childish and silly, and with what I'd found out over the last couple of hours, my life would never be the same. I was desperately worried about what would happen to Joshua and his family, all because of me. My life with mum and Ally seemed so mundane and pointless compared to the things I knew now. The dangers that were real and out there and unlike the Vampires of books and films, amazingly this stuff was real.

As I watched, the last of the light faded, I managed to find a kind of strange peace within the swirling questions. Daniel had been right. What was done, was done and we couldn't change that now. We had to look ahead and I had to learn as much as I could. There were still many unanswered questions, like why hadn't Wil brought Claire back to life, if Joshua could do it? I wanted to know more about the Council of Nine, who they were

Chameleon

exactly and what weird abilities did they have. I didn't want them harming these good...people, if that's what they were...Joshua's family didn't harm humans intentionally and that meant a lot to me. It's always better to know one's enemy and that's how I thought of the Council now.

We had just over two months left until Joshua and Wil had to appear before the Council, irrelevant of whether they know about my killer. I must find out his name, I decided, just so I can stop calling him my killer. "Why does life get so complicated when you fall in love?" I wondered aloud, as was my usual habit when alone. "Especially, when you fall in love with a Vampire." I grinned to myself with the silliness of that statement.

"I am not a Vampire." His lovely voice spoke quietly from behind me.

I jumped as blood rushed to my face from embarrassment of being overheard, "Yeah, you are." I sighed, "Time to own up to it. Anyway...how long have you been standing there listening?"

"Long enough." I could hear the smile in his voice.

"It's rude to sneak up on someone and listen to their unguarded words." I was mortified because I knew he heard me say I was in love.

Damn it.

"It's also rude to tell someone that they shouldn't have saved your life and killed your murderer...if you know what I mean." He said grimly but with a half hearted laugh at how strange that sentence sounded.

"I'm sorry. I was upset and angry. I'm very grateful, really."

"You're forgiven."

I felt his warm hand on my shoulder, the buzz made my spine tingle and I shivered with delight.

"Are you cold?" He asked and instantly blurred across the room and back again and covered me in a blanket, before I'd even realised he'd taken his hand off my shoulder. Putting his arm around me, he pulled me close.

"So you're in love, huh? Do I know the lucky guy?" He laughed quietly, almost nervously.

"Yes." I replied meekly, half of me was afraid he might not feel the same. On the other hand, he had just brought me back from the dead and condemned himself to a death sentence. What more proof did I need from him? I scolded myself.

He lifted my head with his hand and kissed me gently. Closing his eyes he kissed me again, this time more passionately. The buzzing didn't increase it just stayed at the same level in the background. The feeling must have given him more confidence and he continued to build the passion of the kiss, both of us were gasping as our lips parted. He leaned his head back against the chair and smiled. A blindingly triumphant smile, which told me he was more in control of his abilities each time we touched. He seemed very pleased with himself. It was a nice change, from the last couple of hours, to see him smile properly.

"May I ask you something?"

"I would be amazed if you didn't have more questions." His kissed me once more on my forehead and snuggled up against me. "Shoot."

"If you, somehow, managed to bring me back when I had died why didn't Wil do the same when he...when Claire died?"

"You know about that, huh?" His eyebrows shot up in surprise.

"Yes, Wil came and told me a little while ago. He was trying to scare me off."

"Crap." He said, "I'm sorry about that...he's still rather messed up about it. You didn't listen to him did you?"

"I understand he was trying to be kind but, no, he didn't scare me off." I placed my hand on Joshua's chest, "So why didn't he heal her?"

"As far as we know, I'm the first Chameleon to be able to do

Chameleon

that. We were just discussing it. Father has been doing research for most of the afternoon, so far he hasn't been unable to find any record, of any Chameleon ever bringing a human back to life. However, he said the next time he is at Castrum Lucis, that's the permanent home of the Council, he would have a look in the archive records. However, he did seem pretty sure there was no one else with the same ability. I wish Wil did have it...he could have saved Claire."

"Poor Wil, how awful for him. I now understand why he doesn't like to touch people." I stroked Joshua's chest through his t-shirt. It was warm and hard, I could feel his well-toned muscles underneath. I had to force my mind back to the conversation. "How did he explain her body...when they found them?"

"He was crazy with grief, as you can imagine, but carried her most of the way back to town by himself. Obviously, he couldn't tell them what really happened, so he told them most of it. He said that they had been arguing about the crash and that she had just collapsed in his arms, which is the truth, all be it the edited version. They did the autopsy and decided she died of natural causes and Wil was off the hook. Although Wil blames himself even though he couldn't control the evolution any more than he could stop the sun from shining. Not that he sees it that way."

"I now understand why you were so cautious around me at first." I paused for a moment, "Do you still worry about it?"

"Not as much as I did, it's much easier with you now. I think I have it mostly under control, I just have the slight buzz left to get rid off."

"Do me a favour?" I said as a sly smile spread across my face.

"Sure."

"Don't get rid of that around me, I rather like it. Somehow, I find the vibration relaxing." I smiled shyly.

He laughed, "You're weird. I tell you that I can drain you to death with this power and you still want me to leave a bit of it leaking out when I'm around you...because you 'like' it? You know that could be thought of a little kinky, don't you?" He smiled that naughty smile I love so much.

"Yup." I grinned wickedly.

"Weirdo."

"Vampire." I leapt up out of his grasp and ran down the hall, giggling. I looked for somewhere to hide and suddenly he was stood a couple of inches in front me. "Wow, how the hell did you do that?" I put my hand on his chest again, he wasn't even breathing hard.

"I'm fast."

"Cheat." I teased and quickly kissed him on the lips. "Do you think there is any OJ in that amazing kitchen?

"More than likely. The kitchen is usually fully stocked."

"How come? If you and your family don't need to eat often?"

"Well, we only have to eat occasionally, but we like to eat so it's mostly for pleasure. We miss the tastes of things if we don't, so we always have food in. Also, the staff are allowed to help themselves too."

"It is an amazing kitchen, why would you need such a place?"

"Remember, Wil and I were born human and we had to eat just like you. Also, mother likes to entertain and has many dinner parties, not only does she love to be the hostess but it also makes the Lights think were are a 'normal' family." He laughed and winked at me.

Daniel and Helena were still in the kitchen when we arrived. They looked up from the laptop they were both peering at, smiled and went back to the laptop. It sounded like they were planning a trip. Joshua found some OJ and poured us some, I raised my eyebrow enquiringly as he poured his glass.

"I like the stuff also it's rude to let a guest drink alone."

"That's my son." Helena said proudly without taking her eyes off the screen.

I sipped my juice and watched Joshua's parents make notes about flights and it dawned on me that they could both be really old. In fact, they could be hundreds of years old, "Whoa, I've just got it." I beamed, "Can't believe I didn't see it earlier."

"What have you got and is it catching?" Joshua joked.

Daniel and Helena looked at me expectantly.

I directly looked at Daniel, "You're Mathers Danforth Marston III, whom the school was built for in 1899, aren't you?

NORMALITY

Daniel looked at me with a surprised expression on his face. "Why, yes, I am, Kate. That is very astute of you. How did you know?"

"The portraits. I was looking at the pictures of your family in the library at school and there's an amazing resemblance between Mathers Danforth Marston III and you. Of course, I hadn't met you then but now, I see that it could only be the same person. Also, there were no more pictures of the family after Mathers, which, looking back now, is a big give away. Perhaps you should have them made, only use a bad artist so you don't look like you." I laughed.

"Well done, my dear. Well done indeed." He said.

"How old are you...if you don't mind me asking?"

"I will be..." He looked thoughtful for a moment, "130 this year." He said it like it was nothing at all.

"Well, you look good for your age." I said and I meant it. He looked no older than thirty and as gorgeous as his sons.

"Thank you, my dear." Daniel look pleased at the compliment.

"So you really can control how your body ages?"

"Absolutely. We are lucky in many ways, our bodies never grow too old to have children and on the other hand we can decide not to have children also, we have complete control."

Chameleon

Daniel placed his hand on Helena's.

"May I ask how you two met?" I lent against the island counter top and sipped the juice, wondering what it was like for them in the beginning. Was their story similar to mine and Joshua's?

"It was in the 1934, when I was a professor at Oxford and I was on a research trip for a book I was writing on the flora and fauna indigenous to Canada and we met in the woods near Helena's family home." Daniel looked loving at Helena.

Helena returned the look and continued the story.

"He was poking around in the bushes, I thought he was a depraved stalker." They both laughed. "Then I got a good look at him and realised he wasn't. If you can imagine a typical looking Oxford professor, tweed jacket, wild hair, leaves stuck to his jacket, talking to himself and the plants, while making notes in his little book, not even bothering to look up, definitely not the stalker type. I was nineteen at the time and thought this handsome young professor had to be the best thing I had ever seen." She smiled warmly at him, "I hadn't evolved then, but I did a year later, which was a shock to both of us. When it began Daniel realised what was happening and helped me through it, explaining what he was and what it all meant. It was if we were meant to be together from the start."

"Is anyone else in your family a Chameleon?" I asked her.

"No, not before me, nor after, until, of course, the boys came along."

"Just like any other genetic quirk, evolving into a Chameleon can skip generations, effect everyone or can be an isolated case. We just don't know who will become one of us and who won't, it's impossible to predict." Daniel replied.

"It's lovely that you were there for each other in the beginning though." I finished my drink and placed the glass on the counter. "Joshua?" I asked, "Would you drive me home, please?"

"Oh...yes. Yes, of course." He seemed startled, "You can stay here until your mum gets back tomorrow though, you know."

Helena stood and walked towards me, "You are very welcome to stay with us." She said.

"Is everything alright, Kate?" Daniel asked, a worried look crossed his face.

"I just want to be at home and do some thinking. My world seems to have changed a lot. Thank you for taking me in and looking after me, it was very kind of you." I stepped closer to Helena and gave her another hug to show I was still comfortable around them.

"You will come back and visit us again soon, won't you?" Daniel stood up too.

I nodded.

"Your school bag is in the cloakroom. Wil was able to retrieve it from beside the waterfall... Joshua will show you the way."

On the way out, Joshua popped into one of the rooms and soon reappeared with my backpack and his car keys. He led the way out of the large front doors onto the damp gravel drive. It had become fully dark now but the rain had stopped at last.

The drive back to the cottage was a quiet one, an awkward silence sat stonily between us.

I glanced at Joshua from the corner of my eyes several times but he refused to look at me even once, instead, he just stared out the front and drove. His face showed no emotion at all, his thoughts were very well hidden behind the mask. At last, we pulled up outside my dark and empty home, it didn't exactly look welcoming.

"Would you like me to walk you to the door?" Joshua's unusually monotone voice startled me.

A little shocked at his change of mood, I replied, "No, I can manage." I looked at him but he continued to look out the

Chameleon

windscreen. "Thank you for...well, everything." I said and climbed out of the car and closing the door behind me, I quickly walked up the path. His behaviour was baffling, I wondered if he resented me for putting his family in danger after all. I unlocked the door and stepped into the dark hallway, I clicked on the light and closed the door not daring to look back. I heard him pull away quickly and drive too fast down the lane.

I leant against the door, not sure how to react to the sudden change of mood between us again, how can he go from hot to cold so quickly? I tried to think back over our conversations and couldn't find anything that would have caused this reaction, except of course, confessing that I was in love with him.

Crap.

How stupid can I get? I could have kicked myself. That's it, I thought. I must have scared him off by being some obsessed, crazy girl.

I walked around the cottage closing all the curtains and putting the lights on, so it didn't feel so lonely. There's nothing worse than seeing the dark outside when you are alone inside. I needed a distraction, something 'normal' to take my mind off everything that had happened. I decided to watch a movie, so I made some popcorn and had just snuggled up under a blanket on the sofa when the phone rang. The sound made me jump and curse as the popcorn flew in all directions. I nervously leaned over to grab it from the table, hoping it would be Joshua. The spilled popcorn lay forgotten where it landed.

"Hello?" My voice came out nervous and breathless. Damn it.

"Kate? Oh, thank goodness. I was so worried. Are you alright?" Mum's voice sounded relieved.

My excited heart sank.

"Hi Mum, yes I'm fine. Why?" Did she know I'd died? But how could she?

"I rang last night but there was no answer, I rang several

times into the late hours. Where were you?" She demanded.

My brain kicked into higher gear, I couldn't tell her what had happened. I had barely had the chance to wrap my own head around it. "I stayed at Ally's house last night, her mum cooked me dinner and asked if I wanted to sleep over. It was all very girly." The lie was out of my mouth before I had even thought about it.

"Oh, well, that was nice of her. I will have to thank her next time I see her."

Crap.

"How is the course going?" I asked, changing the subject quickly.

"Alright...I think. Not very exciting though, it's all about legal jargon and contract specifications. Although, I've met a very nice man who is on the course too. He's from one of our other offices in Worcester." She sounded excited.

"Oh," I laughed, "picking up guys on the course now, huh?"

"I don't know about 'picking him up' more like we're bored together and having a laugh. Though, he has asked if he can take me to lunch tomorrow, but I don't know if I should go."

"Why not?" I knew mum was a bit shy of dating. She hadn't had a date since she threw dad out.

"I don't know, maybe I'm just too old to date again."

"Don't be daft, mum. Go and have some fun. It's time you found someone to make you happy."

"Yes, m'am." She laughed, "Next, you'll be telling me to be careful."

I put on a stern voice. "Well, as your daughter I'm telling you to go and have fun, but do be careful, I don't want a brother or sister, is that understood?" I couldn't keep my voice level and just burst out laughing.

"Katy, really." She giggled.

"I miss you, mum."

Chameleon

"I miss you too, hun. I'll be home tomorrow night and driving you nuts again with my nagging."

"You don't nag." I realised just how much I'd been missing her. Even if I couldn't tell her everything that was happening, not having her around was still lonely.

"Thanks, hun. You know how to make an old gal happy. I'd better go, I have some studying to do before tomorrow. I can't believe they're giving us homework."

"Now you know how I feel." I said.

"Yup. Okay, Katy I must go. I'll ring you tomorrow sometime."

"Have fun on your lunch date, I want to know every detail, so take notes."

Mum sighed, "Alright. Take care, love you...bye."

I ended the call, picked up the spilt popcorn and snuggled back down under the blanket to watch my movie. I couldn't help but smile, mum always had a way of cheering me up and it was exactly what I needed today.

That night, my sleep was fitful. It was full of disjointed and weird images of my murder and bright colours swirling in rainbows of colour around people. In the depth of my dreams, I saw Joshua with an evil look on his face drain an old lady of her Light and Helena gleefully did the same with a child, whilst Daniel stood by laughing and Wil sat crying in a corner. I awoke sweating in the pitch black, trembling and deeply shaken. I lay awake until the sky had started to lighten. When I did fall asleep again, it was the deep sleep of the exhausted. Thankfully, there were no more dreams.

I awoke to the sun shining brilliantly through my curtains, I opened one eye and peered at the clock, the red numbers glowed 10.36am. I lay in bed and wondered what I was going to do with myself, I needed to distract myself today. I decided I would paint my room, after all, like I said I would. For the rest of the day, I busied myself with the physical labour of moving furniture and painting. It was a welcome relief from the turmoil of my thoughts with just the rolling on of the paint in a mindless, relaxing repetition. The paint was a lovely olive green colour that reminded me of our family holiday in Greece, the year before mum and dad split up. I had loved Greece, the colours and the sun.

A few hours later, I'd finished and the walls were dry enough to drag the furniture back. It felt good to be doing something normal that didn't come from the pages of some horror book, which is how yesterday had seemed to me. I made myself a late lunch of a tuna salad sandwich and sat eating it in my new room, looking around at my work. I was quite proud of myself. I just had to hang the curtains, put the books back on the shelves and it was finished. Saturday had turned out to be a pretty good day so far. Mum hadn't phoned again, though and I toyed with the idea of ringing her at her hotel but I figured, or rather hoped, she was out on her lunch date. The whole thing with dad had broken her heart and I hated seeing her sad. She, of course tried to hide it, but I spotted it now and then and I hated my dad even more for what he'd done to her and to our family.

The afternoon had become a wonderfully warm for the end of September. I spent it outside, sitting in our small back yard reading a dog-eared copy of Clan of the Cave Bear again. I'd brought the phone out with me just in case mum rang and she did. The course had finished early and she would be home mid afternoon after her date, instead of later that night.

I was still sat in the garden reading when mum arrived home, two hours later. She looked tired but happy.

"So how was the date?" I lounged on a sun chair with my book laying on my chest and my eyes closed, letting the unexpected glow of the afternoon sun soak into my skin.

"Actually, it was very nice." Her voiced sounded excited.

Chameleon

I opened my eyes "Oh? Do tell."

"His name is Nathan Alexander. He's forty but looks barely thirty and very good looking, in the tall, dark and handsome kind of way. He works in one of our law offices in Worcester, as a senior assistant to one of the solicitors. He is widowed and has no children." Her eyes twinkled as she talked about him.

"Was he a gentleman?" I asked, pretending to be a stern parent.

"He most certainly was. We had a lovely meal at one of the top restaurants, with champagne for lunch, no less. I got the feeling he was used to spending his money on the finer things. He was funny, utterly charming and I was very flattered by all the attention. The meal went too quickly and soon we were back at the hotel."

"Oh, here it comes." I pretended to be shocked and then looked at her with an evil grin.

"Kate! Nothing like that happened. You are so cheeky. In fact, he was a total gentleman, like I said. He walked me to my room and kissed me on the cheek before saying goodbye." She looked so very pleased.

"Oh, that's lovely, mum. I'm so happy you had a good time."

"He also asked if he could see me again, perhaps take us both out for a meal." She looked wary as if I she wasn't sure.

"I think that's a great idea. I would love to meet the man who can make you excited about a date." I grinned at her.

"Thanks, Katy. I wasn't sure if you would want to. He's going to ring sometime during the week to see if we are available." She looked so happy.

"He definitely sounds interested in you, mum."

"I know, isn't it great? Who knew I could still pull a good looking guy?" She laughed again and sat back in her chair, putting her feet up.

We spent the rest of the day catching up, mum told me

about her hotel and the other people on her course, I in turn told her all about newly painted room.

I went to bed early that night, but not to sleep. My mind was restless and I was still brooding about how I'd prematurely let Joshua know I was in love with him. I felt that not only had I let myself down but I had taken a step back for girls everywhere. The more I thought about it the more my mind made it seem that, perhaps, the love went only one way even if he did save my life. I sadly watched the moon out of my window and finally managed to drift off into a light sleep, waking every time I heard an owl hoot or a fox bark.

Before long, Saturday had turned into a brooding Sunday followed closely by a miserable Monday with no contact from Joshua. As I got ready for school, my stomach lurched with butterflies, it seemed like forever ago since I was at school and knowing I would see Joshua, my heart didn't know whether to wither in shame or leap about excitedly. As usual, I took the bus to school and sat with Ally in Form, we caught up on the news of the last few days. Obviously, I couldn't tell Ally why I was really off on Friday. I told her I felt ill again on Thursday and went home early and slept through most of Friday. Well, it wasn't a total lie. Joshua didn't arrive in Form and I wondered if he was in school at all.

I got my answer in Physics, he was sitting in his usual place, at the table where he, Ally and I usually sat, looking down at his notes and didn't lift his head when we took our places.

"Hi." I said to him quietly.

"Hello." That monotone voice again, he didn't look up.

Well fine, I thought. If he wants to be an ass, he could do it on his own time.

The lesson was agony. I could feel the miserable clouds coming off both of us, at least we had that in common. Neither of us had anything to say to each other and not another word was

Chameleon

spoken. If this was how he reacted to someone telling him they were in love with him, then I guessed he would be alone for a very long time. I was angry and confused, the 'stay away from me' reaction I had evoked in him seemed odd after what we had been through but if that was how he wanted it, then I didn't have to stay around for him to twist the knife. The way I look at it, if you don't feel the same about someone you should tell them and then stay out of their way. For the rest of the day, I made a point of doing just that and stayed as far away from him as each class would allow.

The following morning Ally asked me what was wrong. How could I tell her the truth? That I had made a fool of myself and told Joshua I was in love with him, when he obviously wasn't in love with me and now hated me for endangering his family and being the reason he was probably under a death sentence. Instead, I told her that Joshua and I had fallen out and I was trying to get over him. She had no reason not to believe me and it was left at that.

The rest of the week continued in the same pattern. I stayed away from him and he gave me the cold shoulder whenever the classes threw us together. I had become desperately miserable and spent most of my time in my room at home, telling Mum I had a lot of homework. I was beginning to think that I would never be happy again and that being in love just hurt too much. Eventually, as the days past, I just ignored the sinking pain in my chest that I got every time I thought of him. It was a cold sharp pain that made me wince and sometimes cry. I sadly vowed to myself not to say I love you first, ever again.

Mum kept asking me if I was okay and I pretended everything was fine while I was around her, but I couldn't sustain it for long and would soon go to my room again to do my 'huge pile' of homework. Mostly, I read or listened to sad music, which made me cry and yet, I still listened to it. I realised I was wallowing in my own grief but nothing could snap me out of it. I kept telling myself to get a grip but I wouldn't listen.

In my haze, I remember mum telling me she had heard from Nathan, he had had to go away on business but would be back in a few weeks and promised to take us all out for a meal then. Apparently, he was missing her and looking forward to seeing her again. Seeing the happiness in her eyes just caused the pain inside me to throb viciously.

I knew I was still in love with Joshua, no matter how hard I tried not to be, because every time I saw him, over those long painful weeks, my heart would betray me and leap in excitement. However, his attitude never changed he was cold and unfriendly, which only managed to make things worse. I missed his lovely smiles so much. He seemed angry and miserable, which baffled me. Surely, if he didn't want anything do with me he should be happy, shouldn't he? I gave him a wide berth and gave up trying to understand him. Instead, I would go back to the way things were in the beginning, pining for him from afar. I tried to remember the fun times we had and his touch but every image in my mind clouded over with his cold, closed in face and averted eyes.

It'd become a routine now to battle my inner excitement and not show anything when he was around. I caught him looking at me angrily a few times, like I had hurt him. He would always turn away whenever our eyes met, causing the pain inside me to throb and hurt even more.

On the Friday, at the end of the fourth week of agony, I realised that today happened to be the start of half term, which meant a whole week off school. Even from afar, the thought of a whole week of not seeing him would make me miserable. I had been so involved in my own drama that I was surprised when mum reminded me that we had a dinner date with Nathan that night. I secretly groaned, I knew I would have to muster up the

Chameleon

energy and fake being cheerful all the way through dinner, but I went along with it because mum was so excited to see him again.

They had agreed to meet in a small rural pub between where Nathan lived in Worcester and our hometown of Shipton-under-Wychwood.

Mum was nervous. She had dressed in her favourite blue cashmere jumper over a dark blue skirt, but her hands were shaking and I had to zip the skirt up for her. As the dutiful daughter, I made a suitable effort, I wore my black trousers with my favourite deep purple blouse and I even wore heels.

Mum fiddled with the car heater settings, I got the feeling that she was stalling because she was so nervous. She took a deep breath and started the engine and at last we set off for the King's Head pub and restaurant, one of us dreading the night, the other eager to be there.

The King's Head was a typical country pub, a two story Victorian building, with rooms upstairs to rent, the pub doubled as a Bed & Breakfast. We pulled into the car park and both took a deep breath, mum smiled nervously at me. I knew she really liked Nathan; she hadn't stopped talking about him for the last couple of weeks. I should be grateful to him really, it meant I didn't have to make much conversation. We climbed out of the car into the chilly night and quickly walked across the damp tarmac to the entrance. A man, looking like mum had described, was waiting at the door, his face lit up when he saw us.

"Nathan." Mum voice shook, just a little. She smiled brilliantly.

"Caroline, how lovely to see you again." He smiled and kissed her on the cheek, then looked at me. "This must be Kate, it's a pleasure to meet you. Your mum speaks very highly of you." He smiled a sincere smile.

I smiled back at him. He was six foot tall, lean and, by how his jacket fitted, he was well built too. Mum had been right, he was very handsome and certainly didn't look forty. He had slightly waving hair that was a warm honey colour, like he had been in the sun most of his life. He had a happy, open face, with sparkling blue/grey eyes. I could see why mum was attracted to him.

"It's nice to meet you, too." I smiled, hoping it reached my eyes.

"Let's get inside where it's warm, shall we?" He opened the door and let us in ahead of him. "I've asked for a table in a quiet corner in the back as I understand they have an Irish band playing later and it won't be so loud there." He led the way through the restaurant.

The restaurant was quiet, small and cosy. The tables were arranged around the large stone fireplace, which was lit with a roaring fire. I noticed there were only two other people in the restaurant, an elderly couple that were talking quietly as they ate.

As we approached our table, I saw a huge bouquet of white lilies on it, mum's favourites. Nathan stepped forward and gave them to mum, who blushed with joy and kissed him on the lips quickly. He looked stunned but also very pleased. I smiled to myself, it was obvious he thought as much of her as she did of him. At least, someone has the chance to be happy, I thought morbidly.

During dinner, mum and Nathan chatted about a variety of topics, like work, and their hobbies. I quietly sat and listened. Eventually, the topic came round to Christmas plans. Nathan apparently flew to Florida for Christmas every year, since being in the UK at that time reminded him too much of his late wife. Mum agreed that she was not looking forward to it either. She didn't explain further, but I got the feeling he already knew that mum and dad had split up at Christmas.

Chameleon

The meal progressed and Nathan briefly pulled his attention away from my mum to ask me a few questions about school and my hobbies. Although I wasn't feeling very talkative, I tried to answer fully and not appear rude for mum's sake. I was itching to escape so I could drop the fake smile I was wearing, it was making my face ache. By the time we got to dessert, the Irish band had started playing in the bar.

"So Kate, do you have your eye on any boys at school?" Nathan smiled, obviously trying to include me in the conversation.

I blushed instantly and mum turned to look at me.

"There is someone I like, actually. But there's no point, he's not interested in me." I took a quick swallow of my orange juice to stall for a moment. I needed to collect myself from the sudden shock of having to talk about Joshua.

"Well, who has been keeping a secret then? You never mentioned him." Mum smiled, her eyebrows raised in surprise.

"Why bother? Like I said...he's not interested." I desperately tried to think of something else to say. I had to change the subject quick before I lost the plot and the tears arrived.

"Ah...well, then the young man obviously doesn't have good taste." Nathan laughed, a little nervously.

I smiled wanly, pretending to be amused, but it was the last thing I wanted to be talking about. Mum seemed to sense my mood and placed a comforting hand on mine.

From the bar I could hear the band start another song, it was quiet good and my head perked up listening to it.

"That band is pretty good." I said, relieved I thought of something to say.

"Yes, they are." Nathan agreed.

"Kate hun, feel free to go and have a listen if you want...while Nathan and I chat."

"Thanks Mum. I think I will, if you don't mind, Nathan?" I said.

"Oh, sure. Go ahead, we'll be right here when you get back."

I headed to the bar, temporarily relieved of my daughterly duties.

The room was full, many had come out for the band. I sat at the end of the bar and listened to the band. They were pretty good and the Bodhran player in particular was wonderful. They even got my foot tapping against the stool leg.

I began to relax. I didn't have to work hard at enjoying the music and there was no one around to look happy for. The music was loud and it stopped me from having to think. It was exactly what I needed. I found myself enthusiastically clapping when they finished their first set. The second the music finished the atmosphere at the bar became hectic again, as everyone returned to their conversations and took the opportunity to get another round of drinks. I thought briefly about going back to mum and Nathan but then thought better of it. I would let them have some more time together.

"Hello, there." A familiar voice said behind me.

I spun round so fast that I almost fell off my stool and looked up into Joshua's face. "Oh...hi..." I blushed. I think I actually trembled in fear and excitement as burst of happiness shot through me.

"You look good." His eyes betrayed a hint of confusion, as well as undeniable attraction.

"Well...thank you." I was thrown by this sudden change in our friendship or lack of it and was unsure of how to talk to him. I decided to stand up, so I could speak to him without twisting my neck.

"You grew." He smiled the big sexy smile.

"Heels."

"Ah...heels too, huh? Nice. So what's the occasion?" He asked as he placed two empty glasses on the bar.

"Mum and I are here with her new boyfriend. I'm giving

Chameleon

them a bit of privacy while the band is on...what about you? What brings you here?" I suddenly wondered who he was with. I glance at him again, trying not to stare.

"Actually, I like to come here especially when they have bands on and I love this band." He placed his order of two cokes with the barmaid.

The pause in our conversation turned into an awkward silence, which was broken by the barmaid bringing him his drinks.

"Well," He looked embarrassed. His glance passed over me and settled somewhere behind me. "I had better go. Enjoy the rest of your evening." He smiled tentatively.

"Okay, I will...and you too." I said. My heart was pounding, I was amazed by how much I still wanted him. I wondered if he had seen me when I came into the bar or if he had no idea I was here. Either way he seemed pleased to see me, which confused me even more. I just couldn't get a handle on how he felt.

I was suddenly curious who he had come with and I watched him pick his way across the room, just as the band came back and settled down to start to play again. My view of him when he sat and whom he was sat with, was now completely hidden by the returning crowd. I kept trying to see round people but if I leaned too far, he would see me looking and that would never do, or worse I would fall off the stool. I ordered another drink and decided to play it cool. If I got to see who he was with then I would see and if I didn't...well, I didn't. I listened to the band play for the next thirty minutes and as they finished and started packing up I decided to go back to mum and Nathan. I glanced over to where I'd seen Joshua go earlier and I spotted him sitting with his back to me, talking avidly with someone. I lingered a moment, just as the person he was with leaned forward to grab the glass of coke on the table and looked directly at me.

She was probably the most beautiful girl I had ever seen,

with thick auburn hair that fell in curls around her face. Her skin was luminous, her features perfect from a distance and I could see her eyes were a deep emerald green. She was very Irish looking, I wondered quickly if she was with the band.

Her utter beauty sank into my heart like talons, making me gasp. There was no way I could I ever compete with her. I staggered away from her view, trying to keep it all together. It is one thing to realise that the man you love doesn't feel the same about you, but another entirely, knowing he had found someone else. I instantly and irrationally hated her.

I had exactly one minute to compose myself before I reached mum and Nathan. I needed to extend that time, I glance around and spotted the washroom just ahead. I quickly ducked in and it was, thankfully, empty and several degrees cooler than the rest of the pub. I leaned on the bathroom counter trying to breathe. It felt like someone was stepping on me and I couldn't get the air to fill my lungs. I looked up into the mirror above the sink. The face looking back at me was pale and tired, with big dark rings under the eyes. This whole love thing is not good for me, I decided and closed my eyes, trying to relax.

With a creak, the door of the washroom opened and my eyes shot open. I could have died on the spot. In walked the lovely girl who had been talking to Joshua. Was she following me? She came to stand next to me in front of the mirror, brushing her hair and then leaning in closer towards the mirror to touch up her lipstick. She did all of this without saying a word, not even looking at me. I put my hands under the cold tap, hoping it would cool me down as a hot, sticky sweat prickled all over my body. I washed and dried my hands, pretending as if I'd used the washroom for a reason other than escape and headed for the door.

"Joshua is a good guy, you know." The red head said, "He never meant to hurt you." Even her voice was smooth and sexy.

"I'm sorry?" I spun round to look at her.

"Joshua...I know he is truly sorry if he hurt you." She said as she straightened her skin-tight, dark green dress.

Weeks of misery boiled over into instant rage, "And who the hell are you, to talk to me about my private life?" My voice shook with anger and could feel my face getting red.

She reeled back and the ferocity of my voice, "I just wanted you to know. I'll leave you be." She picked up her purse and walked out without another word.

I was stunned, fuming. I was in disbelief that his new girlfriend had the nerve to presume she could talk to me about him. More over, I was stunned at the venom in my words and that I'd had the courage to say them. I took a secret glee in my actions. I breathed deeply, tried to relax again and ran my wrist under the cold tap to cool myself down, my anger had made me hot and sticky again. I spent much longer in the washroom than was necessary, as I tried, with little success, to get my self under control. I spent several long minutes doing the breathing exercises from drama class. Finally, taking one last deep breath, I managed to pull myself together enough to make it back to our table.

Mum and Nathan were deep in conversation, which stopped when I arrived.

"Hey, how was the band?" Mum enquired.

"They were great." I said without much enthusiasm.

"Glad you enjoyed it, hun." Mum said, but looked at me pointedly, sensing something was wrong.

"We were just making plans to go out for the day in Oxford next weekend, would you like to join us?" Nathan asked.

"Well..." I looked at Mum, who was looking at me again with a mixture of expectant concern. "Actually, I have a test the week after and I wanted to put in some major studying time. But you two enjoy yourselves."

I watched in a silent daze as mum and Nathan finished their coffee.

"Are you ready to go, Kate?" Mum asked.

"Yup, I am ready when you are." I almost smiled in relief. Almost.

Nathan went to pay the bill at the other end of the room.

"So how did it go?" I asked quietly.

"Very well, hun. Very well, indeed." She looked delighted.

I smiled at her, I was genuinely happy for her. "Great."

"Are you alright, Katy?"

"Yes, fine. Why don't you give me the keys and I'll start the car while you say goodbye." I said.

She handed me the keys with a grateful smile and I headed towards the door passing Nathan at the counter. I stopped briefly to thank him for the lovely dinner.

"It was my pleasure, Kate. I hope to see you again soon."

"I hope so too. Bye." I waved as I walked out into the car park and zipped up my jacket. It really was chilly. I sat in the car with the engine ticking over and I switched on the heater. It was so cold inside the car, I could see my breath and I shivered, pulling my coat closer around me. I tried to stay warm and stuffed my hands in my pockets. I couldn't help thinking about Joshua and how he looked so handsome tonight and how it hadn't taken him long to find someone else. No wonder he'd lost interest in me, I'm so plain compared to her. I mumbled swear words under my breath, it didn't help.

A few minutes later and I saw mum heading my way. She clumsily climbed in, leaned over placing the flowers on the back seat and grinned at me. I guessed he must have kissed her because she had a starry-eyed confused look on her face or she'd drank too much. I didn't remember if she'd even had wine with dinner but she seemed a bit out of it. "Do you want me to drive home? I think you had a glass too much." Thankfully, I was allowed to drive the car on my learner's permit, if a qualified driver was in the car too.

"No, I'm fine. I didn't have any alcohol." She insisted.

"Are you sure?" I couldn't see her face now that the car door had closed and the interior light had gone off.

"Absolutely, I'm fine. Don't worry." She started the car and pulled out of the pub car park. We drove down the quiet country road heading back towards home. Her driving started to get more erratic with every passing minute and it began to scare me.

"Mum!" I shouted as she just narrowly missed another car. "Pull over, now." I had barely got the words out when she veered off the road heading towards a gateway, a field and a very large tree. "Brake!" I shouted as mum passed out and slumped in her seat. The front wheel hit the kerb at an odd angle and the car flipped over smashing into the gate and tree.

For a moment, I couldn't work out what was up and what was down. My vision was blurred and I could feel something running down my face. I figured it was blood by the smell. I realised the car was on a strange angle and we were still strapped in, my belt was the only thing keeping me in place. I looked over at mum whose head was on the steering wheel. To my horror, her eyes were open but without any life in them. She was staring at me with dead eyes.

"MUM!"

I struggled frantically to get my seat belt undone, then, abruptly, it unfastened and I smashed onto the dashboard. My head lay facing mum and her horrible, lifeless face. My vision started to go into dots and fade.

The last thing I saw were mum's dead eyes.

TRUTH

Present day

I opened my eyes and stared at the tiles on the ceiling of my hospital room. I had gone over everything in my head, everything that had happened since I'd met Joshua and his family, but it gave me no more answers and only brought back the pain from missing him so much. I couldn't make sense of the crash, but I really didn't care, as long as mum was safe and now I knew she was. I must have dreamed her death and those eyes. However, a lingering blurred image of Joshua standing outside our overturned car remained.

Thankfully, I had stopped feeling sick and Dr. Davis had promised I could go home this morning, if I hadn't been sick overnight and I hadn't. I was now waiting for mum to bring me some clothes to change into and the doctor to sign me out. I had spent only a couple of days in the hospital but I was looking forward to escaping the bare hospital room and the strange antiseptic smell that always seems to be present in any hospital. I wanted my own bed and the safe, comfy surroundings of home.

I sat reading a magazine a nurse had lent me, when I heard the door open. Looking up, I was amazed to see Joshua standing there, looking even paler than usual.

"May I come in?" He said.

"Sure." I lay the magazine down on my lap.

Chameleon

"How are you feeling?" He stood at the end of my bed, looking nervous and unsure.

My heart pounded mercilessly in my chest as my excitement and my own nervousness built. "I'm okay, just waiting to be signed off and then I'm out of here." I looked at him. There was something odd about him, about the way he wasn't looking at me directly it made him seem a bit edgy.

"Do you mind keeping me company for a bit until mum gets back?" I said.

He smiled fully and visibly relaxed. He walked round to the side of the bed and sat on the chair.

"I wasn't sure you would see me." He said, still avoiding my gaze.

"Why?"

"Because of Tara. She said you seemed very upset with me."

Tara, so that was her name. Just her name grated on me like nails down a chalkboard. "I was upset because she had no right poking her nose in where it doesn't belong."

"I told her not to talk to you, but she insisted." He looked down at his hands.

"I don't see why. What do I have to do with your new girlfriend?" I knew I sounded bitchy but I couldn't help it. The anger was welling up inside me again, I could feel it beginning to prickle my skin.

His head snapped up. "She's not my girlfriend." He looked shocked, "Did you really think I could move on so fast?"

"I...she's not? Oh..." I blushed. The anger suddenly drained away to be replaced by relief, so palpable I could almost taste it.

"No. She's not." He said firmly, "She's a close friend of the family, if you know what I mean. She was just helping me out."

"Oh...I see." So she was a Chameleon. That certainly explained the radiance of her beauty. "What was she helping you out with, exactly?"

"Actually, you." He smiled that half smile.

"Me? Why me? What did I do?" It was my turn to be shocked.

"Can we discuss this later? I don't think this is the right place or time. Maybe when we're somewhere more private, like at your home? Speaking of which, how is your mum?"

"As well as can be expected. I saw you...you know."

"What?" He looked guilty.

"I saw you...I remember now...I was conscious, lying against the dashboard and I saw you through the broken windscreen. I saw your car pull up and you instantly appeared by our car. I remember everything went blank, I think I passed out and then I came around again and I saw you put your hand through the broken window and place it on my mum's back. I could hear you talking to someone and then I passed out again." I looked him in the eyes, "You brought my mum back, didn't you? That is why she can't remember anything, isn't it?" Fear grew in my chest, now I knew why he looked so pale and drawn. "Are you alright? It nearly killed you last time."

"My father was right, you are bright." He said.

"Thank you." I said, the tears welling in my eyes, "Thank you for my mum, I mean. I will never be able to repay you."

"You will never have to." He touched my hand briefly and I felt the familiar buzz. He quickly moved his hand away and looked around the room.

"Who were you talking to outside the car?"

"That was Tara, I was telling her about the last time I had done it, how I had passed out for hours and that she should take me home and tell my parents what had happened. I had already looked at your injuries and was going to heal you but then I saw that your mum was...was more injured...and I could only be sure of healing one of you. I'm sorry."

"What? No, you did the right thing." I lifted up my arm and

Chameleon

wiggled my fingers and I touch the bandage on my forehead, "I'm already on the mend, see?" I grinned, "So...was it like last time? Did it knock you out again?"

"Yes, but it was much easier to wake up this time, having done it once before. It was a much easier struggle to find my way back. My family sat by me talking to me all the time so I could follow their voices. They send their regards, by the way. They are very happy to know everyone is okay."

"That is kind of them, please say thank you for me." I smiled, fondly remembering the Marstons and how nice they were to me.

"How did the crash happen?" He asked.

"Not really sure. I remember mum was acting and looking strange, almost like she had been drinking, but she hadn't. Then she got much worse and passed out, the car flipped over and hit the tree."

"Was she sick?" He asked, looking confused. "Are you sure she wasn't drinking?"

"Yeah, the cops even tested her afterwards and said she was clear."

Before we had chance to talk anymore the door swung open again and my mum walked in. She was surprised to see a young man at my bedside. She looked at him and then at me.

"Hello you two. Am I interrupting something?" She grinned knowingly.

Joshua stood up quickly. "Hello, Mrs. Henson. My name is Joshua Marston. I'm a friend of your daughter's." He stuck his hand out for her to shake.

So we are friends again then, I thought. I'm glad he knows what's going on with us, I wish I did. I was speechless at this continued roller coaster ride of 'us' and gaped at him like an idiot. I realised he was asking my mum to shake his hand...his hand that will buzz. Was he trying to be found out?

Mum took his hand and shook it, without any reaction at all. "Nice to meet you, Joshua." She smiled at him and then moved to the bed to kiss me on the forehead. While her back was to Joshua, she winked at me.

"How are ya feeling, hun?" She asked.

"I'm fine, just waiting for the doc to sign me off."

Mum placed a bag on the bed, "I brought you some clothes to escape in." She grinned.

Joshua quietly laughed. The sound of his laughter after so long, made me feel all warm and gooey inside and mum seemed to notice of my reaction to it. I really needed to get a grip, yet it seemed impossible around him and it was becoming annoying but oddly in a good way. I could see her watching me out of the corner of my eye while I was watching Joshua.

"If it's alright with you, Mrs. Henson? I'll continue my visit with Kate once she's at home?" He looked at my Mum.

"It is not me you should be asking, Joshua. But seeing as you have, yes that's fine by me." She smiled warmly at him.

"That's if you want me to, Kate?" He added a little shyly.

Hell yes. Shut up brain. "Sure...I would like that." I could feel my cheeks getting warmer as my blush spread.

"Okay, I'll see you later then. Nice to meet you, Mrs. Henson." He offered his hand again.

Mum shook it and again I watched for a reaction, but there was nothing. She turned away from him as he left the room.

I was grinning like an idiot.

"Well, then...he was a nice young man. Great manners, handsome, too." She said and started unpacking my clothes. "Is he the one you said wasn't interested?" She continued to empty the bag of clothes onto the bed, without looking up.

"Actually, yes." I tried to keep my voice neutral. I was surprised to see a sly grin mum's face.

"Hmm...I think you've got it wrong, hun. He is obviously

head over heels in love with you."

"He is?" I was amazed and glanced back at the door but it was firmly closed and Joshua had gone.

"Most definitely, without a doubt. I know love when I see it."

"Oh." It was all I could think off to say. This was getting more and more confusing. How could he love me, yet be so cold? Had I misunderstood something? I didn't get it. Mum couldn't be right, could she? It made no sense.

Within the hour I was at home, happily sitting on the sofa snuggled in the blanket, talking to Ally on the phone. It took me several minutes to calm her fears and explain that we were both really okay, before she would hang up and let me eat my dinner. We had stopped in town for mum to get us Fish and Chips on the way. I sat eating mine as the last of the afternoon's light faded into a beautiful purple sunset.

"Hmmm...these are yummy mum, it was such a good idea."

"I know." She grinned but then looked serious as she checked her mobile.

"You alright, mum?"

"Yes, it's just that I've been trying to call Nathan since the accident, but he isn't picking up his mobile. He doesn't know what happened."

"Perhaps his battery died." I offered.

"Maybe. I think I'll try him at work tomorrow. Meantime, I'll have to get the car insurance people to pay up so I can get another car as soon as possible. The rental is costing me a fortune. It never rains but it pours." She sighed and screwed up the empty wrapper of her fish and chips.

"You really like him, don't you?" I said.

"Yes, I do. He makes me laugh and feel like myself again, which is something I've not felt in a long time. Anyway, enough about me, tell me about Joshua." She grinned as she sipped her coffee.

"Really? Do I have to?" I said. What could I tell her? I had no clue what was going on between us or even if anything was going on.

"Absolutely. Spill it girly."

"Okay, okay." I told her who he was and how we'd met, although I glossed over the argument during Theatre Studies. Mum loved that he picked me up in the rain, I think it appealed to her romantic heart. I couldn't tell her I had been to his house or why, but I did say that I had seen his house in passing and that it was huge, his family being peers and all.

"Handsome, rich and in love with you too, huh?" She smirked.

I rolled my eyes, "I don't care about his money, mum."

"I know you don't hun, I was only teasing. So are you looking forward to seeing him again?"

"Yes." I blushed. Was I? Yes, I was. I really was. The excitement and nervousness built again just at the thought of it.

"Good, because he's walking up the path." She said as she stood up and headed for the front door.

"What? Crap." I twisted round to see but he'd already gotten to the door and rung the bell.

"Language. Breathe, hun and smile. He is an eager bunny." She winked as she opened the door, "Well, hello again Joshua, how nice to see you."

"I do hope you don't mind me coming round so soon. I would like to talk to Kate about a few things, if I may?" He looked hopeful.

"Of course I don't mind, come in." She led him into the living room and discreetly took her coffee cup into the kitchen.

"Hi, Kate." He stood by the sofa looking awkward.

"Hi...I didn't expect you tonight." I looked at him and noticed he looked tired.

Mum returned from the kitchen, "Please, Joshua make your-

Chameleon

self at home. I was just about to take a long bath. Would you be kind enough to watch over Kate, until I get back?" She said.

"Of course. I would be pleased to." He took his coat off and laid it on the arm of Mum's chair, opposite me, and sat down.

I looked sternly at mum as she came to kiss me on the cheek. I knew she was forcing us together so we could talk. I decided that my mum was sneaky, but I loved her for it. I watched as she went upstairs without looking back.

"How are you doing?" He asked.

"I'm okay...my ribs really hurt when I move or when I laugh and my wrist aches, but I can't feel the stitches in my forehead." I grinned.

"It's a good thing it's half term this week. At least you have some time to heal before school starts again."

"Yes, I suppose so. Although, it won't be much fun having to sit about, trying not to move too much."

"I could help you, you know." He said.

"Help me, how?" I looked at him and it dawned on me, "You could heal me?" I was amazed that I hadn't thought of it before. "Aren't you still recovering from healing my mum?"

"I'm feeling almost back to normal. I told you I recovered quicker this time." He pushed his hands through his hair, moving it from his eyes. "Well, I could heal you some, not too much to be obvious, like a miracle or something, but I could work on healing the ribs and bruising, so you would be more comfortable. Want to try?"

"Sure, anything that would help me move about a bit easier would really be great."

He rose and came to sit on the sofa next to my feet, which were keeping warm under the blanket.

"I've never directed my energy at something specific before. I kind of just let it flow into you and your mum, so it might take me a couple of goes."

"That's okay, I trust you." I looked in those lovely blue eyes and melted.

He flexed his hands self-consciously and reached out, gently placing his hand on my ribs over my t-shirt. I could feel the vibration from his touch, he closed his eyes and looked like he was concentrating very hard. After a minute or so, his eyes opened and he took his hand away.

"Damn. I'm sorry, I can't seem to direct it to just the ribs and the bruising. It's like trying to catch an eel in the dark, it keeps getting away from me. I have no way of grabbing onto the energy." He looked very disappointed.

"Try again...please. It can't hurt, can it?" I pulled his hand back to my side.

He closed his eyes again and concentrated. I could feel the usual pulse of his energy but then I could also feel a strange warmth in my side.

"Oh my God. I think it's ...working." I said.

His eyes flew open, "It is? How can you tell, does it hurt less?"

"Not yet, but I can feel a warmth that wasn't there before. Keep trying."

"Maybe it would work better directly on your...skin." He said.

I blushed and butterflies danced in my stomach, "Skin to skin, you mean?" I said in barely a whisper.

"Yes." He looked me directly in the eye, no sexy smile nor smug expression, just simple concern in his eyes.

"I... okay." I said trying to swallow. It was only my ribs he was going touch after all.

He pulled back his hand as I carefully lifted my T-shirt so that we could both see the dark purple bruise that covered my lower ribs, it looked huge, about the size of a football, I had many others but this one was the worst. He leaned forward and gently placed his hand on my flesh. His hand was warm against my skin, the vibration and heat was exciting. I had to clench my teeth to stop me from reaching out and kissing him as goose bumps rampaged up and down my spine. This time the warmth came quickly and steadily, the ache in my ribs slowly dissolved.

"Yes. It's definitely working. Hang on, I want to see."

I sucked in air through my teeth when he removed his hand.

"Does it hurt when I touch it?" He withdrew a little.

"Only a little but that isn't the problem." I blushed.

"Oh..." He said and looked into my eyes.

I could see he felt the same about touching as I did. I swallowed hard.

Just at that moment, I remembered he could hear my racing heartbeat and my elevated breathing. I groaned inwardly and looked away from those eyes. He placed his hand back on my skin, the warmth was quickly back again. I found that if I closed my eyes it was much easier to relax and focus on the task at hand.

"Ooh..." I groaned. "That's nice...I can't feel the ache anymore." I looked down at my side and I could actually see the bruise shrinking before my eyes. "Holy cow, look at that."

He quickly opened his eyes again and looked down and continued to make the bruising smaller as we both watched.

"Now, that is cool." He said.

"Wow, nice super hero ability you have there, Mr. Energy Vampire." I said. It was amazing, I couldn't feel any pain at all. A huge surge of gratitude swept threw me "Thank you so much." I threw my arms around him without thinking and hugged him. He returned the hug, but suddenly stiffened and seemed in a hurry to let go.

There was an awkward silence as we pulled away from each other.

"I think we need to talk..." I said in a small voice.

"I agree, in fact that is why I came." He started to stand, as if

Edain Duguay

to head back to the chair.

I caught his hand, "Stay here." For some reason I was terrified of hearing what he had to say and yet excited too.

He hesitated but sat back down.

I took a deep breath, to hell with the consequences, I thought, and told him exactly how I felt. "I'm sorry that I scared you off with my declaration of love. But I think your reaction, ignoring me for the past four weeks, giving me dirty looks and the cold shoulder, is not the most mature way of telling someone you don't feel the same way about them."

Joshua opened his mouth to speak but I held up my finger to him and continued, "Wouldn't it be more simple to say you just aren't interested in a person and then leave them alone?" The words had rushed out before I could stop myself and I was feeling angry again.

He looked at me and was obviously speechless for a moment. "You think I was ignoring you and giving you the cold shoulder?" He said incredulously.

"Absolutely. I even have witnesses." It sounded childish but I just couldn't help it.

He abruptly stood up, walked over to the fireplace where he stood with his back to me. I couldn't see his expression. His shoulders started to shudder. He actually had the nerve to laugh at me? I felt like throwing something at him.

Infuriated, I said. "Are you laughing at me?"

He stopped laughing, turned and saw the anger on my face. He rubbed a hand over his face and sighed deeply.

"I am sorry, I didn't mean to upset you. I wasn't laughing at you. I was laughing at us." He said.

"What? Why?" Again I was confused, I was getting too used to this feeling and really didn't like it.

"I wasn't ignoring you or giving you the cold shoulder...I was upset at myself for having scared you off when you were at my

Chameleon

house. I'd guessed that's what I did when you suddenly wanted to go home and you never spoke a word to me in the car. You went inside like you couldn't get away from me fast enough and at school you stayed as far away from me as possible. I blamed myself for being this..." He gestured to his body, "I thought you wanted nothing to do with me now the truth had sunk in."

"I...you thought...wait...you thought 'I' didn't want anything to do with you because you're a Chameleon?" I said.

He nodded, his face clearly showing the pain he had been inflicting upon himself.

"But...I thought I scared you off, when you'd had time to think about what I said about...being in love...with you." I stumbled through the words.

We looked at each other in amazement. I burst out laughing. I understood now, we had got our wires crossed and utterly confused the issues. A huge sense of relief washed over me as the laughter bubbled out.

He started laughing too, "What idiots."

"What a waste of four weeks." I said, "I was very miserable, thinking you didn't want me."

"I was so miserable my brother was all for dragging you back to the house and forcing us to sit in a locked room until we sorted it out. It took me ages to explain he couldn't do that."

"Well, that's what we get for not talking to each other, I guess."

"Kate, are you sure you don't mind what I am?" He said looking serious again.

"To be honest, I don't care what species you are, Joshua. Although, the thought of having a boyfriend who can hear anything I say to my friends and who having surprise birthday parties for will be a little difficult.' I smiled at him, "Seriously, though, I really want to be with you but are you sure that you want me, when there are very beautiful females of your own kind about?" I was thinking of Tara, of course.

"You really don't get how beautiful you are, do you? Remember, I see all of you, even the light that surrounds you." He sat back down and stroked my cheek. "It's you I want, I know that more now than I did in the beginning." He said and leaned in to kissed me gently on the lips, I responded enthusiastically which resulted in making us both breathless. Eventually, he pulled back just a little but his lips were still very close to mine.

"I love you too." He breathed and again kissed me with a long and lingering kiss this time.

My heart swelled in my chest, the butterflies in my stomach came back in full force and the pain of the last four weeks vanished into thin air. I felt actually happy, a real happiness, not the fake kind that I had being hiding behind lately. I could feel the happiness spreading through me, like a ripple on a pond. He pulled back from our kiss and relaxed on the sofa next to my knees with a look of peace on his face.

It took a moment for my voice to return. "May...I ask a question?"

"Like I could stop you." He smirked.

"Funny guy." I rolled my eyes, "How come mum didn't react to your hand shake?"

"That's an easy one and yet also a bit strange. While we were apart, I started testing my ability to touch without draining. Peter, our stable hand..."

"Your have horses? Wouldn't they shy away from you?" I interrupted.

"Yes, we have horses and no, that's only in the movies." He shook his head.

"Okay, sorry. Carry on."

"Peter is our age, he grew up with us. His father is George, our Stockman. Anyway, he knows all about us and was willing to do some testing with me."

Chameleon

Testing on a human? I was suddenly horrified. I must have looked shocked because he paused.

"Nothing severe, Kate. No need to worry." He looked amused, "I knew you could feel something when I touched you and I wanted to stop that happening, so I could interact with humans as usual. So I experimented by touching Peter's arm and straight away, he said he felt nothing. I was surprised, so I began to gently pull more of his energy out until he said he could feel it. I did the same test on his dad and now I know where my line is, so to speak. When I came to the hospital, I kept my energy at the level where I normally have it around you and I felt your body react to the pulse, so I knew you could still feel it, even though Peter and his dad couldn't. Then your mum came in and I thought I'd try the experiment again, to check if it was the same result."

"That was dangerous." I said.

"Not really, I was prepared to say it was static. You would be surprised how many new Chameleons use that excuse to explain an occasional shock while they find their control. Anyway, she didn't feel it and I knew I hadn't changed anything. Only you feel it and I have no clue why."

"Oh, that is odd." I reached out my hand, touch his and felt the familiar buzz. "Just checking. I still kind of like it though."

"You're so weird."

"Isn't that why you love me?" I said, playfully.

He laughed, "One of the reasons."

We sat holding hands quietly for a while, it was so nice not have to think anymore.

"What are you doing for Halloween?" Joshua asked.

"Is it Halloween already? I seem to have lost track. The last couple of weeks are a blur, what with almost being killed, again." I thought about my plans, "Nothing, actually."

"Well, it's next Saturday and my family is having a fancy

dress party. I was wondering if you would come as my guest?"

"Oh, that sounds great." I looked at him and smiled, "I would love to go with you. Fancy dress, huh? Hey, can I go as a Vampire? Or a Chameleon disguised as a Vampire?" I burst out laughing.

"Sure." He laughed too.

In the back of my mind something clicked into place.

"Wait, aren't you supposed to go before the Council of Nine soon?"

He simply nodded. He looked sombre all of a sudden.

"When?"

"1st November."

"The day after the party? But that's only a week away." I said. A now familiar dread prickled its icy way under my skin and seized my heart.

"Then it's a good reason to make the most of next week." His casual optimism wasn't reaching his eyes.

"Where is the Council taking place, anyway?"

"The Council meets in different locations around the world, for this meeting they've rented an island off the coast of Croatia, near Rovinj."

"Oh," The location meant nothing to me, except that it seemed very far away. "How long will you be away?"

He looked evasive, "That kind of depends on how we do. If everything goes okay, we should be back in two weeks."

Neither of us wanted to contemplate what would happen if it didn't go okay. I looked for something to say. "What do they do with you for those two weeks?"

"The first day, you're presented to the Council by your sponsor or sponsors, in our case it's our parents. Then the next day they teach you about the ten Chameleon laws and test you on them. Finally, you are interred for ten days and then tested in public."

"Interred? I don't like the sound of that word, your father mentioned it before...something about it being your type of prison?" I said.

"Yes." He shuddered, "You are literally buried alive for ten days."

"What? You're not serious?" I sat up, alarmed.

"Very." He said. "They bury us alive with no light and no air. Our bodies go into a shut-down mode, but our minds don't switch off. It's ten days of torture. Our bodies use up all the energy stores we have and being newly evolved, we don't have much to start with. We come out very, very hungry, but not for food, for Light. They then release us into a very public area. If we feed in public, we fail and are taken away."

"Dear God, that's barbaric."

"It's the way things are done." He tried to look brave.

"So, if you don't feed?"

"We are set free and, as long as we abide by the laws, we can go where we like and do what we want, for as long as we live."

"Wait, I thought you were considered 'normal' in the Chameleon world if you did feed?"

"Ah...see, that's the distinction. It might sound cold-blooded to you, but the concern isn't about killing humans, it's about exposing the Chameleon race. Yes, we can feed on Lights as much as we like, but we must never expose the Chameleons for what we are, so feeding without discretion in public is forbidden and breaks one of our most sacred laws."

"And if you do feed?"

"Like I said, we get taken away or redacted, never to be seen again. There are rumours, of course, about what happens to the redacted, but there isn't any solid proof."

"Rumours of what?"

"There are a few stories actually, raging from the newly

evolved being killed...to them becoming slaves for the Nine Councillors and confined to Castrum Lucis, that's the Councils private home."

"Has anyone ever refused? To be tested I mean. Ever refused to go?"

"No, never. If you don't attend a Council within one year of your evolution, they track you down and are even harder on you."

"How could it be even harder?"

"They starve you and then put you in a locked room with all the humans you know and care about."

"God, that's terrible." Tears began to well in my eyes as I looked at Joshua. How could I wait here knowing that he is going through that? I thought.

"At that point, the need to feed far out ways the need to protect. When you're newly evolved, ten days of starvation can make you lose all your humanity."

He wiped a stray tear off my cheek. "It can't be that hard, my parents have survived it and Tara, and there are so many of us around the world who must have gotten through it. It's all about maintaining restraint, even if it is a little bit harsh."

"Harsh is an understatement." I needed to be close to him, to feel him safely next to me. I curled up against him and, with my ribs no longer hurting, I was now able to move around more freely even if my cast did get in the way.

"Do you think you can do this?" I asked quietly.

"I have no choice." He sounded resigned.

Silence descended around us for several moments.

"Is that where the idea of Vampires sleeping in coffins comes from?"

"Maybe, I guess. I don't know."

"How do they know that you are a Chameleon, I mean how do they know to expect you in particular?"

Chameleon

"The Council are very old and very powerful. Some are so sensitive, they can tell when one of us evolves. One, in particular, can feel it. Another gets visions and God knows what else, to find you. There has never been any record of anyone being able to escape them."

"Your people are very scary and so powerful. Once you know about all this, it makes humans appear rather weak and vulnerable, doesn't it?"

"Yes...very much so."

He squeezed my hand, trying to be reassuring but my world had change forever. The only sensible way forward was to know as much as I could.

"So are humans allowed to attend these Councils?" I held my breath.

"You're not coming with us, Kate. Don't even think about it."

"You didn't answer my question."

He sighed, "Yes, Chameleons who come to support the newly evolved may bring their 'claimed' humans, but few do, for obvious reasons."

"Did you say support?"

"Oh yes, welcoming a newly evolved to the community is a big social thing, it happens at the end of the interment with a large ball. Chameleons think of it as a coming of age ceremony...when you pass."

"They bury you alive and then you get a party, if you survive the test?" I couldn't believe it, what a frightening world I had fallen into.

"Yes. It's a different world than the one you are used to, I know. The ones who pass are treated like home coming heroes. They are presented at the Evolution Ball at the end of the two weeks. For their families, it's the first time they get to see who passed and who didn't."

"How awful for the families of those that don't pass."

Edain Duguay

"It doesn't happen that often. Most pass and that is the only thought keeping me going at present."

Joshua went quiet for a few moments looking off into space. He seemed to refocus and he kissed my forehead avoiding the plaster over my stitches. "When do you get these out?" He said, obviously trying to change the subject.

"Next Friday. Just in time for the party on Saturday." I felt I had to talk about normal everyday things too, to take my mind off his testing.

"How would you like to spend the day with me tomorrow?" He asked.

"I would love to." My butterflies fluttered in my stomach.

"I thought I could give you the grand tour of my place. Not just the house, but the grounds, the animals and the gardens. I want to take you to my favourite spot too, I think you'll love it."

"That sounds great, I would love to see the horses and the grounds." I smiled up at him. My eyes gazed around the room and my timetable for school, which sat on the coffee table, caught my eye. It had the crest of the school on the front and the Latin motto. "Do you know what that means, the Latin words under the crest?" I pointed to my book.

Joshua looked over and recognised the image, "Yup, that's an easy one..." he smiled at me, "Semper Vivendus' means 'Always Living."

CLIENTELE

The music pounded as she danced with abandon not seeming to care that she was dancing on her own. Her friend had been bought a drink by some guy and was sitting at the bar with him now. He knew because he had been watching. She was beautiful and she knew it, you could tell by the way she moved and he had been watching her move for the last ten minutes, prolonging the chase.

Of course, he also knew she was grinding her hips for his benefit. She liked him to watch. She kept looking at him out of the corner of her eye, making sure she still had his attention. The women in these places were always the same, a young hot body gyrating on the dance floor in tight clothes and looking for Mr. Right now.

He grinned knowingly.

He checked his reflection in the glass wall behind the bar, he was good looking, and he knew he was just what the ladies loved. He turned back to look at her. She smiled at him, a sexy alluring smile and as if by her command, he stood and made his way to the dance floor without taking his eyes off her body. He reached out and touched her hip with one hand and matched her movements to the tribal beat of the song. He could feel her excitement rise, it was obvious in her brown eyes.

It was the age-old look of lust.

The music was too loud to talk, but their bodies spoke on their behalf. He rubbed himself against her on purpose as they danced and could feel her breathing harder. She brushed her chest against him and he brushed his lips against her cheek. His need for her had become obvious and urgent.

The song flowed into another without much of change in beat. Still dancing, she slid her hand up from his hip to his chest and along his arm, all the while looking him in the eye. A knowing grin appeared on his face as his hand moved into hers, he held it and pulled her slowly off the dance floor. She didn't mind, she wanted this too. Without returning to her friend she followed him straight out of the exit without letting go of his hand.

"In a hurry aren't we, babe?" She asked huskily.

"You know it." He didn't turn back to look at her.

She walked with him out the exit and into the nightclub's car park.

"Which is yours, handsome? I fancy some alone time with you." She said.

He grabbed his keys out of his pocket and confidently pressed unlock. A beep went off in the back of the garage. "It's the red BMW at the back, on the left." He started to walk in that direction quickly, still holding her hand.

They reached the car within moments and she grabbed him, pushing him up against the side of the car and kissed him passionately, undoing his shirt as she did so. She was in a hurry. He responded in kind and soon had her top off and started kissing her throat. He broke free, breathlessly and threw open the back doors of his car as he grabbed her and threw her down on the back seat.

She laughed with delight.

"Let's see that lovely body." She said as she laid back, waiting for him.

"My pleasure." He said as he hurriedly unbuttoned his shirt

revealing a very well toned body underneath. In seconds he stood mostly naked outside the car.

She sat up and grabbed him by his underwear band. The meaning was unmistakable. He climbed onto the back seat and she allowed him to undo her bra and skirt. She dispatched his underwear quickly, once he was fully naked, she roughly pushed him over onto his back.

"Oh, so that's how you like it, huh?" He whispered dreamily.

"Oh, yeah." She replied as she lay on him, kissing him more and more passionately by the second.

He started to return the intensity of her passion but instead found himself feeling drowsy and light-headed. As his mind drifted away from this beautiful woman and their exciting sex, he could swear that he saw a red shimmering light before the blackness hit.

Joshua

Joshua and I pulled up in front of the impressive Elizabethan house, his home Marston Court, at mid morning the next day. The weather was clear, although a little chilly for the last week of October. He came quickly round to the passenger side of his car to help me out, although I wasn't in need of help now, since my ribs no longer hurt. Still, it seemed to please him to be the gentleman and I have to admit I enjoyed the attention.

Joshua had told me his parents were really looking forward to seeing me again and for some unknown reason, I was nervous. Not because of what they were, but because of the misunderstanding between us. I took a deep breath and followed Joshua, hand in hand into the house and down the long corridor towards the kitchen, but this time we took a left and entered the lovely old library.

The walls were floor to ceiling with fitted shelves, piled high with books. Daniel was using a laptop at the large antique desk, which sat majestically in front of the large windows. Opposite him was a huge fireplace that contained a roaring fire, ideal for this chilly October day. In front of the fire, on a comfy looking sofa, Helena sat reading.

"Ah...there she is. Hello again, Kate." Daniel said as he rose from his work.

"It is lovely to see you back here again." Helena said with a

Chameleon

smile of welcome. "How are you and your mother doing? I was so sorry to hear about the accident." She rose and stepped a little closer, looking at my forehead and arm.

"We're both doing well thanks." I gestured to my injuries, "These will heal fast enough." I smiled. It felt like I was meeting them properly for the first time, as Joshua's girlfriend.

Helena surprised me as she stepped forward and gave me a quick hug. "I am so glad you are both alright. Joshua was almost out of his mind for the last few weeks and then you were...injured again..."

"Thanks, mother." Joshua looked stricken with embarrassment.

"You're welcome, son." Helena patted his shoulder, pretending to be serious. "Honesty is always the best course of action, no matter what." She grinned at me.

"I thought I would give Kate a proper tour today, as she didn't get one last time. So we'll see you later." Joshua said.

"Great idea." Daniel smiled and sat back down at his desk.

Joshua took me on a quick tour of the rest of the house, as quick as a tour of a thirty-two roomed house could be. I listened abstractly to Joshua's narration about the house and its history, although I wasn't really interested in which part was built when and by whom. I just loved to listen to Joshua's velvety voice. I do remember seeing a ballroom, a games room. I also saw the wing for the staff quarters and the private movie room. It was all very impressive.

We left the building via the solarium, where I had sat all those weeks ago and confessed my love for Joshua. Today, the sky was bright, clear and crisp. We stepped out through the double glass doors and down the steps into the Elizabethan garden.

The garden was impressive, even though the flowers had finished blooming and many plants had been trimmed back for winter. The garden had been divided into four rectangular quarters, with gravel paths around a large Renaissance fountain featuring a woman holding a jug of water above her head and child with his arms stretched up to it. According to Joshua the fountain was switched off until May, when it would be switched back on again for the public. A dominant element of the garden was the balustrade terrace, which ran along the side nearest the house, and on which were great ornamental features, including spheres and obelisks and the Marston family crest.

I recognised a few plants in the borders like lavender, ivy and, of course, the roses but many others were not so easily identified. Well, to me at least. I knew that in the height of summer, this garden would be absolutely beautiful. We didn't linger long as Joshua led the way through the garden and past a wooden doorway in the old stone wall that bordered it.

"What's in there?" I asked as we passed by.

"That's mother's herb and kitchen garden. It's her favourite place to feed, she's kept all the old herbs, which she says have a different energy than the new hybrids." He smiled.

I could hear several birds singing on this lovely autumn day as we walked down the pathway that lead away from the house. We followed the path for a while until it bent sharply, revealing several farm buildings, including the stables. I could see the horses in a field beyond the buildings. We walked through the stockyard towards the stables, passing various pieces of equipment and the odd tractor, here and there. It looked like a working farm. There were a couple of young men cleaning out the stables, while another older man was tinkering with the engine on a tractor. I could hear women's laughter coming from another building. Everyone seemed happy in their work and comfortable with working for the family. Several people even nodded as we went by or called out hello and smiled.

"Do all these people know...?" I asked as I stepped over a

puddle, left over from a recent rainstorm, and I tried not to frighten the free-range chickens that clucked past.

"Not all, just the ones we deal with the most, like George and his family." Joshua let go of my hand and put his arm around my waist.

"Which one is George?"

"He's the one with his bald head stuck under the hood of the tractor." Joshua laughed, "George likes to fix things rather than spend the money."

Joshua spoke of George like he was a well loved but eccentric uncle.

"The guy with the long brown hair..." Joshua pointed a young man who had his back to us and was busy cleaning out a stall. "That's Peter, George and Rosie's eldest son. The other one is their youngest son Joe."

"Where's their Mum, Rosie was it?" I looked round to see where the female voices I'd heard earlier were coming from.

"Rosie will be in the cheese house over there." He pointed to a small brick building opposite, "They're turning the cheeses today."

"Blimey, cheese too. You guys are quite a farm industry all by yourselves."

"My parents have gained much wealth over the years, but like to run a farm the old fashioned way, by growing and making food for the staff families and the local community. We sell our products in the towns nearby, we sell meat, vegetables, cheese and honey."

"And yet you hardly need to eat any." I laughed.

"Yes, but my parents enjoy doing it. When you live for a long time and hardly sleep, you need hobbies." He grinned. "Think about it, this way they are producing food for humans and for themselves, a sustainable life for all."

"Good point." I said, I couldn't help but be impressed. We

Edain Duguay

walked past the last of the stables and the full view of the horse field opened up before us. There were several horses in the field. The instant we came around the corner into their view, a beautiful Palomino trotted over to the fence excited. It's pale main flowing in the breeze and its warm brown coloured coat looked rich amongst the dark sombre colours of late autumn around it. She was quite tall at about 16 or 17 hands high. Joshua walked over to the fence near the horse and stroked her.

"This is Mia. She's my horse. Mia, this is Kate."

"Oh...she's lovely." I stroked her soft, silky cheek as she nuzzled Joshua, "I adore Palomino's, they're my favourites. They're so different in colouring to other horses, it makes them seem more special somehow."

He looked at me pleased by what I'd said, pulled an apple from his jacket pocket and gave it to Mia. He then pointed out towards the pasture, at another horse, similarly coloured. "Her sister Kia is over there, near the black Arab."

"Oh yes, I see her. She's lovely too." I leaned on the fencing watching the other horses while Joshua stroked Mia.

"Kia's more shy than Mia, but good for first time riders. She's got a very calm temperament. When your wrist is out of the plaster, would you like to go riding with me?" He turned to look at me.

"I would love too." I replied excitedly. It must be great to have your own horses, I thought. I had loved to ride, my dad having taken me riding quite often. How nice it must be to ride whenever you want. There was such a difference in our childhoods.

"I'd like that too." He looked me directly in the eyes, "It's nice to share these things with you." Then he kissed me gently on the lips.

"Joshua?" Called a voice from behind us.

Lost as I was in the kiss, the intrusion made me jump. I

looked round to see a young man, who I presumed to be Peter from the long hair, sauntering towards us with a big smile on his face, carrying a rucksack. Peter was my height with wide shoulders, he was attractive and well tanned.

"Josh, sorry to interrupt." He smiled, his smoky grey eyes seemed to twinkle when he spoke.

"Hey Peter, I'd like to introduce you to Kate."

Peter nodded hello. "So you're Kate," He glanced at Joshua and then back at me, "I've heard a lot about you."

"Hello. Nice to meet you, Peter." I blushed, "I hope it was all good things." I looked at Joshua wondering what he had told his friend about me.

"Of course." He laughed and pulled the rucksack off his shoulder and handed it to Joshua. "Josh, your Mother asked me to bring you this. She thought you might need it where you're going."

"Thanks, Pete." Joshua said.

I got the distinct feeling I was the only one who didn't know where we were going.

"Well, it was nice to meet you, Kate. I'd better be off I've got work to do." He said as he started to walk off.

"And you." I called after him. I couldn't help but notice he looked well built from behind too. I blushed and turned back to Joshua who was quietly laughing.

"Don't worry, he has that effect on girls."

"I'm sure I don't know what you mean." I tried to keep a straight face but failed and burst out laughing. "Is he a Chameleon too?"

"Nope, although he could be one with those looks, huh?"

"Perhaps, but that's okay...I have my own Chameleon." I quickly kissed him on the lips, "What's with the bag?"

"You'll see." Joshua took my hand and started walking down the side of the paddock towards the tree line.

We walked slowly through the lovely old woods, the kind where you could feel the age of the trees. There was a mixture of oak, birch, hazel and ash, as well as several others. There were fallen trees that lent on their neighbours and were covered in thick moss. There were also small pools of water and areas that were swampy. The woods had been allowed to let the wildness of nature take her course. This place was very special, I could instinctively feel it when we entered. We walked hand in hand in silence, as if in reverence for the old wood. We must have walked for about thirty minutes along the rough path. In some places, the way became so narrow that we had to walk in single file. The entire woods felt magical and I loved it.

Eventually, I could hear the sound of rushing water and although I couldn't see the source, I knew it was a waterfall from the thunderous sound. We walked to what looked like the end of a tree line, but there seemed nothing beyond except sky. At last, I saw why. The tree line was on the edge of a deep ravine, which was covered in trees. Joshua looked back at me and smiled.

"Are you feeling brave?" He said.

"Well, that depends on what you want me to do."

"Do you hate heights?"

"No, actually, I don't mind them at all."

He stepped closer to me and whispered, with a playful glint in his eyes, "Do you still trust me?"

"Of course." A nervous tremor began to vibrate through me, I wasn't sure if it was excitement or fear.

"If heights don't bother you, you may want to keep your eyes open for this." He swooped down and scooped me up in his arms.

Before I could protest he took a few steps back and made a run for a gap in the tree line. I clung to him tightly as the trees blurred past. Instantly, we were in the air with the cold wind

Chameleon

rushing past us. He'd leapt from the steep ledge down into the ravine, the ground rapidly rushing towards us. I momentarily panicked, only for Joshua to land perfectly balanced as though he'd simply jumped down a step.

My throat had dried with the excitement and my mind spun. Did he just do what I thought he did? Did he just pick me up and jumped off a cliff? I looked at him in shock, "Holy Cow!"

Joshua gently put me down but still held on to me, "Are you okay? I didn't frighten you, did I?"

"Hell no. That was...amazing. Wow. Do you always do that to get down here?" My brain had decided to be as practical as ever, even if my heart still raced.

He laughed in relief, "It's the quickest and easiest way, just call it the Joshua express. I'm glad you liked it."

"Wow." I said again and looked around me. We were by the pool at the foot of a waterfall with a grove of trees surrounding us. The sun shone directly down on us and reflected off the pool. There was a huge, old willow tree near the edge of the pool partially in the soil and partially in the stones that separated the pool from the grass. It was a natural oasis. The entire place exuded an ancient peace and it was very beautiful. I loved it.

"This is what I wanted to share with you. This is my favourite place, and this..." He held out his hand towards the old willow, "....is Grandmother Willow." He walked closer to the old tree.

"Grandmother Willow?" I wondered aloud at the name.

"Yes, it's what I named her the first day I found her, years ago. Of course, it was a lot harder to get down here when I was human." He said, as he shrugged off the rucksack. He gently led me forward to see the part of the Willow, which had grown out over the water, almost like a natural chair.

"Now, that's cool." I said.

"I used to sit there, listening to the water, wondering if I would ever be a Chameleon like my parents. I wanted so much to be like them and live forever."

I turned and looked at him. "Was it hard growing up as a child of Chameleons?" I asked as I followed him over to the seat and sat down.

"I didn't know until I was twelve. Not hard, no, but I felt that I would miss so much if I had to remain human. A human's life is so short when compared to a Chameleon's. I wanted to live a very long time and see everything in the world." He stared out at the pool that was gently rippling from water crashing into it twenty yards away. "Have you thought about that?" He said, "The fact that our time together will be short?" Sadness crossed his face as he looked directly at me.

"It won't be to me. Anyway, I guess we'll have to make the most of it then won't we." I suggested as I reached out and touched his hand. "You know you have been given a gift, right?"

"A gift?" He was astonished. "Now I'm a Chameleon, there is nothing I wouldn't give to be human again, at least for a while and slow down time to enjoy every moment with you."

"I can't believe you said that. What you have been given is an amazing gift. You've been given the opportunity to travel anywhere, learn anything, do anything, no feeling of time running out, not thinking I have to do this now or I never will, no watching your body grow old and die in front of your eyes. You're very lucky, I wish I was like you and we could spend eternity together." I said.

"You don't know what you are saying." He looked me in the eyes, the blue of his eyes blazing in the sunlight.

"Maybe not, but from a human's perspective, being a Chameleon seems like an amazing gift, one that shouldn't be wasted. Perhaps our time together will be a drop in the ocean of time for you, but not for me." I said.

"Don't get me wrong, I'll treasure every moment we have together. It's just that, right now, I can't imagine my life without

Chameleon

you." He whispered as he closed the gap between us and kissed me.

He pulled away breathlessly but with that half sexy smile that I know so well. "At least it will be interesting exploring that effect." He unleashed a dazzling smile.

I forgot where I was and what I was doing for a second, "Uh huh", was all I could manage to say in reply. I watched him as he unzipped the rucksack and pulled some fruit out and a flask, which he passed to me.

"I think mother was worried I'd forget to feed you." He laughed.

"I guess so." I unscrewed the lid and smelt the contents, "Mushroom soup, lovely. Although, I'm not hungry right now, maybe later."

He took the food back from me, placing it on the ground and pulled out a rug from the bag and spread it out on the seat.

"Do you fancy a swim?" He grinned mischievously.

"Are you joking? It's almost the end of October and I bet that water is freezing." My eyes grew huge and my body got goosebumps at the thought.

"You know what I said about trusting me? Well, this is one of those times."

"Okay, but I have no swimsuit and what about my cast?" I glanced at it worriedly.

"You'll be okay in your t-shirt and underwear. Seriously, just trust me." He stood and pulled out a plastic bag from his pocket and some adhesive tape.

It seemed he'd thought of everything and in moments he'd made my cast airtight. He took off his jacket, his jumper and t-shirt. Then, he removed his boots and trousers.

My heart nearly stopped on the spot, I tried not to gape at his gorgeous body.

"The trick is you have to do it quick." He stood in his boxers and nothing else.

"It's alright for you, you can control your body temperature...what about me?"

"You'll see." He held out his hand.

I took a deep breath. I had trusted him this far hadn't I? Why not a little further? I quickly took off my jacket and jumper. Too quickly, I was standing in my strappy top feeling somewhat shy of myself. I shivered as instant goosebumps rose on my flesh. I looked up at him sceptically as I unfastened my trainers and pulled off my socks, already my teeth were chattering with the cold.

"We'd better be quick, you're already turning blue." He joked.

"Shu-tt-tt-tup." I clenched my chattering teeth. I nervously pulled off my jeans and hopped from one foot to the other, wrapping my arms around myself.

Joshua grabbed my hand and ran for the pool. Strange, I could swear I moved faster than I normally would, when he held my hand. Quickly, the thought was thrust out of my mind as we ran into the freezing pool. The frigid waters made me gasp loudly, but Joshua didn't let go and just kept moving in deeper and deeper. The water was crystal clear and felt oddly warmer at the bottom than the top.

"You can see okay underwater, right?" He asked.

"Y-yes." I shivered, my mind noting that he must have been watching me swim at school.

"Take a deep breath, hold my hand and follow me, okay?"

I nodded and did as he instructed.

Within half a second we were underwater, swimming quickly in the direction of the waterfall but aiming for a dark spot below it. Soon enough we swam directly into the darkness and everything in front of me went black. Swimming in the tunnel was frightening and a feeling of being trapped began to

Chameleon

grow. Joshua swam like he could see his way clearly. My lungs began to burn and I hoped wherever we were going wasn't much further. Within seconds we were heading upwards toward a faint light, finally my head broke the surface. I gasped taking in air that was surprisingly warm, as was the water around me.

I looked round and found we were inside a cave whose only entrance was the hole we had swum through. The water was warm like in a heated pool and the air in the cave felt cosy and warm. I realised I could see and looked around for the light source. Joshua got out of the water and was sitting on a ledge to my right. He began lighting some candles from an oil lamp, which emitted a soft glow and there was a large pile of towels sitting on a blanket. He leaned over the water and held out his hand to help pull me out.

"Wow, this place is amazing." Taking his hand as I climbed out, I accepted a big fluffy towel to wrap myself in. "How come it's so warm in here? And where did the candles and other stuff come from?" I asked as I sat down on the blanket. He's a lot sneakier than I would have thought, romantic too. I could get use to this, I thought.

Joshua eyes sparkled in the candle light, "There's a warm spring that naturally comes up in this cave to the right of the pool. As for the stuff, I brought it here before coming to pick you up this morning…I hope you like it?" He blushed a little and put his arms around me on the outside of my towel, so I was all wrapped up in it. "Feeling warmer?"

"Much." I looked up and leaned in to kiss him softly on the lips, "Thank you…this is lovely."

"You're very welcome." He said breathlessly against my lips. "Glad you trusted me?"

"Absolutely." I laid my head on his chest, truly content.

We sat like that for a long time, neither of us wanting to move away from each other. I was completely relaxed and at last

Edain Duguay

my head and heart were on the same page, a first in this relationship, I reflected. It gave me a surge of happiness that I hadn't known in a long time.

"Fancy another dip?" Joshua finally asked.

"Sure." I dropped the towel, stretched and jumped back in. The temperature of the water was even warmer than the cave, and I could now see steam coming off it. If I'd ever had an image of a perfect date in my head, it would've been this. Although, I could never have thought of something so different and so nice. The romantic glow of the candlelight and a boyfriend who is caring and thoughtful. I loved spending time with someone who makes me feel whole, who is incredibly sexy and whom I can't stop kissing.

Perfect.

Joshua dove in and came up behind me snaking his arms around me and hold me tightly against his body. He kissed from the base of my neck up to my ear. He gently turned me around and I coiled my legs around his making us float as one. He continued to kiss my throat as my breath came faster and faster. There was something so sexy about my arms around his back, the skin feeling silky in the warm water. I tilted my head and began my own trail of kisses over his shoulder and up his neck. His hands caressed my back and he began to groan. I swallowed hard, not sure I wanted to take this any further yet. I nibbled him hard on purpose and pushed away from him.

He began to tickle me and a splash fight ensued. I managed to dunk him a couple of times but through my giggles, I couldn't help thinking that he let me. We played for a long time, splashing, diving and kissing in the water. Once I was completely wrinkled from being in the water so long, we eventually climbed out, dried off and sat on the blanket on the ledge. I noticed Joshua's hands, so smooth compared to my pruned ones. "Why aren't you wrinkled?"

"Because I decided not to be." He said unhelpfully and winked.

"That's how I will be one day, a wrinkled old prune while you will still be young and handsome. That just sucks."

"It's still a long way off, Kate." He sounded resigned.

"I wish you were a Hollywood Vampire and then you could 'make' me." I said wistfully.

"I would do it if I could." He said quietly.

"Really? You would?"

"Yes. I told you, I want to be with you. Does that sound selfish?"

"No. Has anyone ever figured out how and why you evolve? Maybe there's a treatment I can have?" I knew the moment I said it I totally meant it, I was surprised by my own conviction.

"Would you really do that, if there was?" He looked at me directly.

"Absolutely. To live forever, to be strong and healthy, to do all the things you want...who wouldn't want that?" I smiled.

"Sadly, no one has ever been able to figure how or why we evolve." He said.

Talking about Chameleon evolution swiftly brought back the sinking feeling I got, whenever I thought about Joshua's testing. It crossed his mind too; I could see a deep worry in his eyes.

"I think I'm hungry for that soup now." I tried to change the subject.

"Want me to fetch it?" He offered, his happy mood seemingly returned.

"I think I'm wrinkled enough for one day. How about we head back to the house?" I stood and reached out my hand to him.

"Okay, remember, it's going to seem very cold out there, compared to in here." He took my hand as we both jumped back into the warm pool and retraced our way back out of the warm cave into waterfall pool.

The pool really was ice cold. It sapped my breath as we swam upwards, to the point that I was panting as we broke the surface and shivering. The second our feet touch the bottom Joshua took me in his arms and carried me at lightening speed back to Grandmother Willow. He grabbed the blanket and wrapped it around me and I snuggled into it, while he passed me my clothes.

Without asking, Joshua turned his back so I could struggle out of my wet t-shirt and underwear and quickly throw on my jeans, jumper and jacket.

"You can turn around now." I said, loving at his gentlemanly behaviour.

Joshua helped me tie the laces on my trainers and removed the bag off my arm. The cast had survived the underwater adventure better than I had, it wasn't even damp. Soon I was shivering a lot less and he passed me a warm cup of mushroom soup.

"I see now why your mum sent the flask, I must remember to thank her for it." I said as I sipped it, watching coyly as Joshua got dressed. I tried, and mostly managed, to turn my mind from the thoughts of his lovely body to more scientific observations. He was comfortable in the cold and had no goosebumps at all. He was obviously controlling the temperature of his body much more efficiently than I. That was all I had and quickly went back to ogling his chest as he put on his shirt and jacket. I needed a distraction before I started drooling.

At last a rational thought came to me. "One thing...how do we get back up the ravine?" I glance up at the tree line, which was probably 150 feet above me.

"The same way we got down." He grinned as he pulled on his boots and tied them. He finished dressing and repacked the bag.

Chameleon

I had finished the soup and it was happily warming my insides. Zipping up the backpack Joshua slung it over his shoulder and pulled the straps tight.

"Are you ready?"

"Sure...I guess." I said, getting the impression that it was going to be a bumpy ride back.

He saw the uncertainty on my face and picked me up into his arms. "You don't have to look."

"Oh yes I do. I want to know how you're going to do this." I smiled bravely and put my arms around his neck just in case. For a moment I wondered if I should hold my breath, but I didn't really think it would help. Nervously, I nibbled my lip.

Joshua backed up several steps and angled himself to the gap in the trees, the same one we'd used to descend into the ravine. He took a running start, the scenery blurred around us. I felt him suddenly crouch down and push upwards as he ran. We sailed through the air heading directly for the gap. The joy of flying again was incredible, not only did it take my breath away but also blew my mind, a truly awesome experience. Within seconds he landed on his feet, safely up on the ridge above the ravine. He gently placed me back on the ground.

"Wow...you know that's very impressive, right?" I gasped.

"Thanks." He grinned, obviously pleased at my reaction.

Joshua took my hand and led the way back on the trail towards the horses and the farm buildings. The late afternoon was starting to get colder and I pulled my hood up over my wet hair. The sun had started to head steadily to the western horizon and the shadows became deeper and more purple as we walked through the ancient woodland. Quite suddenly, we seemed to burst into the openness near the horse field, at the edge of the wood. It felt almost like being released back into reality.

The stockyard was empty and very quiet. I assumed that everyone had finished for the day and had gone home. We walked back through the Elizabethan garden again and up the steps into the Solarium. As we entered the house and neared the kitchen I could hear several voices.

"Welcome back, how was the picnic? I hope Joshua didn't get you too cold?" Helena looked pleased to see us. "Would you like a hot drink to warm you up?" She offered.

"Yes, that would be great, thanks. Thanks for the yummy soup." I smiled and looked toward the large kitchen table to take a seat. I discovered who's the other voice belonged to. I blushed instantly.

Tara looked me straight in the eye with a wary expression and then smiled.

"Hi, Kate. I'm so glad to see you weren't too badly hurt in the crash. How's your mother?" She was sat next to Wil and they had obviously been reading what looked like a newspaper on the table between them.

"Oh, thanks." I felt terrible at how rude I'd been to her in the washroom at the pub. "Mum's fine, thanks to you two."

"All I did was call for an ambulance and drive Joshua back here. He's the real hero." She grinned at him.

"No need to lay it on so thick, Tara." Wil scowled at her.

"I think there is, he's an exceptional Chameleon and should know it." She said.

"Exceptional? How?" I asked.

I took the hot chocolate from Helena with thanks and went to sit at the table.

"No Chameleon has ever healed a human before, at least not one I've heard of." Tara said.

I glanced at the newspaper they were reading. Wil quickly folded it over, before I could read any of the articles.

I looked back at Tara, who was as stunning as I had first thought. This time, she was wearing tight black jeans and a cream jumper, which showed off her auburn hair and amazing

Chameleon

green eyes.

I wished, not for the first time, that I was beautiful too.

"I am sorry about the way I spoke to you at the pub." I said.

"Hey, no problem. I understand completely. I was sticking my nose in, Joshua roasted me afterwards, anyway." She said with a smile.

"The Irish can't help but stir trouble. It's in their nature." Wil said.

Tara playfully punched him on the arm.

"Oh, so that's your accent. I wondered what it was, but I couldn't figure it out." I said.

"Yes, I'm Irish. Born and evolved in Drogheda, which is a harbour town on the East coast of Ireland."

"When did you evolve?" I asked.

"In 1848, at the age of seventeen."

"Oh...so you're older than Daniel then." I was amazed. They really could hold back the years, she looked no more than eighteen or nineteen.

"Yes, I suppose that's true, but I'm not the eldest by far. Some Chameleons are thousands of years old."

"Thousands?" My mind could not take it in.

"Oh yes. Some members of the Council are very, very old."

Once more reminded about the Council, my heart sank. My worries must have shown on my face.

"Ah...I see Joshua has told you about the Testing. Don't be afraid, he'll do well. They both will. And we'll all be there to support them." She looked at Wil with such tenderness and concern that I suddenly realised she liked him, a lot. Unfortunately, it looked like he had no idea whatsoever.

"Not...all." I replied moodily, sipping my chocolate.

Joshua sat down beside me.

"Don't even think about it, Kate. I won't have you in danger." Joshua sounded utterly determined.

Tara looked between Joshua and I, she then glance at Wil and seemed to make up her mind about something.

"You said that humans go, ones that are claimed. Well, couldn't I be claimed by you or your family?" I asked. Aren't I already? At least by Joshua? I wondered. I was confused again.

"No. Absolutely not." Joshua said.

Helena watched our conversation with interest.

Joshua's harsh tone stung, I felt he was being unfair. "You say you don't want me to be in any danger, but how can you ask me to stay here, knowing that you will be." I said.

"Forget it. You're not coming and that's final." He stared at me furiously.

"Fine." I snapped. Angry that he could make me feel like an unwanted child and had embarrassed me in front of everyone.

There was an uncomfortable silence in the room.

Helena returned to reading her gardening magazine with a somewhat practiced disinterested look on her face. Tara was looking at Joshua with an angry expression, like she wanted to say something but held her tongue. Wil pushed the newspaper to one side, obviously finished with it.

"May I?" I gestured to the newspaper.

Wil looked panicked, he looked at me and then at Tara.

"Are you sure you want to read it?" Tara asked.

"Of course, why shouldn't I?"

"You may not like what you see." She looked at Joshua meaningfully.

"What's going on?" He asked

"Show them, William. It will be alright." Helena said.

Wil picked up the paper, flipped it open and slid it across the table towards us. The headline on the front page stood out:

Seventh Naked 'Victim' Found!

Chameleon

I gasped and read the article aloud, "On Monday, the body of a man was found naked in the back seat of his car in the car park of the Sunrise nightclub, having died of 'natural causes'. The Thames Valley police so far have not released any information on the death. The man, who has not been named, was seen leaving the nightclub on Sunday night with an unknown woman." I swallowed hard. "It goes on to talk about the other deaths by 'natural causes' recently and says the police do not think they are connected." My heart raced and my breathing came hard and fast. There was something very familiar about all the details...and it also meant that there had to be another Chameleon in Oxford openly killing people and making the police and journalists suspicious.

"I thought the guy...that...that killed me...was the serial killer?"

"Sebastian may just have been one of a group." Tara said.

"Sebastian? Was...that his...name? Did you know him?" I shudder ran down my spine, so he had a name at last, I thought.

"Yes, that was his name." She glanced at Joshua, "I met him many years ago. Trust me, there was nothing you could have done, Kate. He was a very experienced killer of Lights, not only did he drain their energy but he enjoyed it. Even gave me the creeps whenever I saw him, which wasn't often."

"Sebastian." I said his name again quietly as though naming my nightmare would help disarm it. It wasn't working.

Joshua reread the story himself, seemingly looking for more information than was there.

"Joshua, I was amazed that you could...well, you know...he was a very talented fighter." She said.

"It was blind luck. He was...distracted." Joshua's face tensed and a muscle in his jaw twitched. "So you think there is a group of them?"

"Unfortunately, yes. Sebastian always like to be a part of a group, ruthless killers who played out sick fantasies before killing Lights, even torturing them when their perverse minds wanted some fun." Tara said disdainfully. "They should be stamped out, they're endangering us all for the fun of the kill."

We all sat in horrified silence.

"Sadly, there are some groups of Chameleons like that wherever you go. The Council seems reluctant to rein them in." Helena said.

"But surely, if they are endangering your hidden world with exposure, shouldn't the Council take action?" I said.

"Only Chameleons know that other Chameleons are doing the killings. Humans have no clue what is going on, so why should they interfere?" She replied.

"How many were in Sebastian's group last time you heard of them, Tara?" Joshua asked.

"Five, including him. Three men; Sebastian, Jonas and Marcus and two women; Clara and Izzy. Jonas is a particularly nasty piece of work. He's the leader."

"Oh no...won't they be looking for Sebastian?" I suddenly realised what this meant. If they knew what had happened to Sebastian, they would come for Joshua to take revenge. A tremor of fear began deep down my spine and sent icy fingers through every part of me. How could Joshua be safe, when there were four other strong Chameleons out there who may or may not know he killed their friend?

"They may be looking for him already or we might get lucky. He was off on his own, so it may take a while for them to realize he's missing. That should buy us some time. If you covered your tracks well, it may not even be an issue." Tara stared at Joshua meaningfully.

"Joshua, just be careful and always check to see if you are being followed." Helena was by his side immediately, "I need to speak to your father." In a blur, she left the room.

Chameleon

"Well, at least there are five of us here at the house, if they do figure anything out." Tara offered helpfully.

"But you just said they're all experienced killers. What hope do you all have?" My voice shook with despair.

"Not much, I admit, but there again we are strong too. I think you and your family will be safe though, Kate. I don't mean to be rude but you aren't of any interest to them. So that's one less thing to worry about. However, I would suggest that you don't see each other alone for a while. If they figure out you're a couple, they'll work it to their advantage." Tara said.

"That's what I'm afraid off." Joshua looked at me, the pain and worry clear in his eyes. "I'm going to take you home." He said.

It wasn't a suggestion.

"I'll come with you. Safety in numbers and all that." Wil said.

"Me too. Can't be too careful." Tara grinned.

Within moments we were in Joshua's car with Tara and Wil in the back. Joshua quickly drove through town. There was a strong undercurrent of tension in the car and not even a single word was spoken during the journey. At my house, Joshua and I climbed out of the car and walked to my front door, while everyone else waited by the car, looking around them.

At the door he pulled me close. "I'm sorry about this." Joshua said in my ear.

"Don't be. If I hadn't whispered that day we wouldn't be in this mess."

"If I had told you about the rules and myself, you wouldn't have whispered in the first place. I think it's best if we don't see each other again until after I've been to Croatia. I think it would be safer that way." His face looked stern, brooking no compromise.

"Are you serious? That's not fair. How will I know what's happening or if you're safe?" I argued. Please don't shut me out again, my heart screamed.

"It's the only way to make sure you aren't caught in the middle of something, by keeping you away from us."

"What about the party on Saturday?" It was a feeble hope, but one I couldn't let go of, if it meant I could see him again.

"My mother will probably cancel it now, no point inviting trouble into the house. I will call you when I get back." That steel tone again.

His kissed me urgently, turned round and walked back to the car without another word, not even a glance.

I couldn't believe it, I was all alone again. The tears fell down my cheeks unchecked as I stood on my doorstep feeling left out. Tara glanced over at me and nodded goodbye before climbing back in the car. Joshua started the engine and drove away quickly, his taillights fading fast as he sped down the lane.

I watched them all leave me behind, just as my dad had.

HEALED

The next few days were a waking nightmare.

During the daylight hours, I wandered around the house, my mind lost in the unending worry and bone chilling fear of the danger to Joshua, which had expanded so quickly and engulfed everything. I couldn't settle into any task, my heart was listless with worry. At one point, I caught mum watching me carefully and occasionally she asked what was wrong. How could I tell her? She even wanted me to get checked by a doctor, but I put her off. I had to go to the hospital at the end of the week to have my stitches out anyway, and that was bad enough. The last thing I wanted was to talk to people and what could I tell a doctor anyway?

I just wanted to curl up in a dark corner and hide from the entire world. At night, I barely slept because of nightmares involving crazed Chameleons chasing after Joshua and burying him alive.

I sat playing with my food at the dinner table on the Thursday evening, when mum sat down with a worried expression on her own face.

"I tried to ring Nathan at his office today." Mum said.

"And?" I looked up at her noticing her face for the first time in the last couple of days. She looked tired and depressed.

"He's away on a business trip apparently. I still haven't spoken to him since the accident." She played with her food too.

"I'm sorry mum, I'm sure he'll get in touch when he returns." I tried to sound hopeful.

She smiled gratefully at me, "I guess."

Suddenly the phone rang, making us both jump. Mum's face was instantly excited and she rushed to the phone, took a deep breath and then answered it. "Hello?" She sounded cheery.

"Oh...yes. Hello." She looked over at me. "Yes, Oh...I see, well that's very kind of you. I'm sure she'll love that." Mum raised an eyebrow.

My heart was in my mouth. Who was she talking to? Why was she looking at me in that strange way?

"Of course, we would be happy to do that, no problem at all." Mum sat down at the table still in the conversation with whoever it was. "Yes, that's fine. Of course...yes. That's fine. No, no, thank you." Mum quickly scribbled a number on an envelope from a pile on the table. "I will talk to Kate about it...yes, I've got it. I'll ring you to confirm. Thank you again and it was very nice to talk to you too, bye." Mum put the phone down and looked at me, amazed.

"What? Who was that?" I could feel the panic building. Was Joshua all right? My heart was beating loudly in my ears.

"That was Joshua's mother, Helena. She asked if we could do her a favour."

"Oh...what?" I had no clue what she might have wanted.

"Apparently, her family are going away for their holiday a littler earlier than expected, and wondered if we would allow Joshua's cousin, Tara, to stay with us until the end of the week, when her flight leaves. She said you had met her at their house and got on really well?" Mum looked surprised because I hadn't mentioned her before.

"Oh...oh...yes, she's nice." Was all I could say. Why would she want to come here and why was she pretending to be his

Chameleon

cousin? I wondered.

"Is that why you are down, hun, because Joshua is going away?"

"Erm...yes." I blushed, not because it was the truth but because mum would think I was such a sap, there was no way she could know the real reason nor the terror behind it, but at least now I had an excuse for my behaviour.

"He's only going on holiday, hun." Mum put her hand on mine. "Anyway, you'll be thrilled to hear that Helena just invited you to join Tara and fly out to their villa in Croatia at the end of the week to spend some time on holiday with them." Mum grinned.

I was speechless. On the one hand, I would see Joshua again and, more importantly, soon, while on the other hand, I would be right in the middle of a Chameleon gathering and being human, that was not a good place to be. A dark dread coiled itself around my innards. I realised that if I were to go, I'd be protected by Joshua's family and Tara and that suddenly seemed safer than here, with no protection at all. After all, Sebastian had found and killed me easily enough when I was alone. I had to be safer with Chameleon friends than just humans, didn't I?

Mum didn't notice my inner turmoil and continued to relay the conversation, "If you want to, you are to fly out with Tara on Sunday. Do you want to go love?"

"I would like that, very much. But wait...what about tickets and money?" I knew mum was broke and the insurance company still hadn't paid her for the car.

"They've offered to pay for your ticket and everything else. All you'll need is your luggage and your passport. It's really very kind of them, they must like you at lot." She said.

I remembered that mum thought I had only met them once. "Wow, that is kind. I guess I made a good impression." I said. I couldn't help wondering if Joshua knew about this...the more I thought about it the more I reasoned he couldn't know. He would never have agreed to it, which would explain why Helena rang and not Joshua.

The mystery deepened.

"Very well then, as long as you behave yourself and be safe. I'll ring Helena back, to let her know you are able to go. Tara should arrive later tonight."

"Oh...okay. Tara can have the sofa bed in my room." I had to force myself to sound happy, all the while feeling very uneasy about the whole arrangement. What were they up to?

"Alright, I'll ring Helena back after dinner. When you've finished, you had better go and make up the bed, oh...and start thinking about what clothes you want to take too." Mum was obviously excited for me.

"I will." I found the thought of seeing Joshua again so soon restored my, non-existent of late, appetite. I was ravenous and finished my plate of food in no time at all.

"Croatia, huh? I hear it's lovely there, bright, sunny and warm. They say that it is getting a lot of tourists back since the end of the war. It'll be much warmer there than here so choose clothes for summer, hun."

I rushed up stairs, so excited and yet cautiously nervous that I could barely think straight and quickly tried to tidy my room. I had really let things go recently, too depressed to clean, apparently. I also found bedding for the sofa bed and set it up for Tara. Tara would be with us for two days before we left. I wondered what we would find to talk about for all that time...I was so lost in my own thoughts that when the doorbell rang, it made me jump. I rushed downstairs, just as mum opened the door. I paused on the stairs, excited and nervous at the same time.

"Mrs. Henson?" Tara said in a nervous teenager way.

"You must be Tara, come in, come in." Mum smiled at her and opened the door wider.

Chameleon

"Yes, that's me, thank you for letting me stay with you and Kate." She smiled sweetly, pulling with seeming effort a large black suitcase into the front room.

Tara was dressed very much like me, in jeans and a baggy sweater and she already looked my approximate age. I was seeing first hand how Chameleons were able to trick humans with their age. There was something creepy and deeply dangerous about the whole thing. They could fool anyone, for any reason. I tried not to frown with my concerns and put on a mask of pleasure at seeing her.

"Hi, Tara." I said.

"Hello again, Kate." She smiled from ear to ear.

Mum closed the door, locking it behind her. "We're very happy to have you here." Mum looked at me as I got to the bottom step of the stairs. "Kate, would you show Tara where everything is and where she will be sleeping?"

"Sure, follow me." I motioned to Tara to follow, I was dying to get her alone so we could talk.

"I'll see you later, Tara. Make yourself at home." Mum smiled.

"Thank you, Mrs. Henson."

"Tara, please call me Caroline and you're very welcome." Mum smiled and headed to the kitchen.

I ran upstairs, Tara following behind me carrying her suitcase, as though it was very heavy. As soon as we got into my room and I closed the door, she threw her suitcase on the sofa bed with no effort at all.

"Tell me everything." I launched myself on my bed and she sat on the sofa opposite.

Tara laughed, "I knew you would be up for it. But remember, Joshua was right, it could be very dangerous for you. You must swear to do as I say, it's the only way to keep you safe. Do you swear?" She lent forward awaiting my answer.

That deep dread swirled through my body again. "I swear." I

said solemnly.

"Good." She smiled.

She relaxed and sat back making herself comfortable. "When we got back from dropping you off last time, we had a huge fight about you..."

"About me?" I asked, more than a little shocked.

"Yes, you. Now, if you would let me explain." She grinned.

"Oh...yes, sorry."

"Very well." She leaned against the sofa arm, "As I said, there was a huge argument between the five of us. Daniel, Helena and I thought you would be much safer around us, instead of being left here on your own. After all, we do not know if Sebastian came after you specifically, or not."

I gasped. "You mean it could have been more than accidental?"

"Well, we really know nothing of why he chose to come to you instead of continuing to hunt in Oxford, do we?"

"Good point." I hadn't even thought about that.

"Well, that was my argument. Joshua's convinced himself that it was a fluke and keeping you away from us would be by the far the safer option. Wil agreed with him and things got a little...heated. In the end, we conceded to Joshua's argument. Later the next day when Helena and I were alone, we were discussing the problem again and decided that we wanted to protect you ourselves. We understood Joshua thought he was doing the best for you, we could see he was worried out of his mind." Tara smiled as she saw me blush.

I shifted on the bed to get more comfy and take attention away from my face.

"You are a trusted human now and should be officially 'claimed' as such, this makes you the family's responsibility. Joshua is too worried about keeping you safe to see that. He is very much in love with you, you know."

Chameleon

"I know." I said quietly.

"I can see that you feel the same." She smiled gently at me. "Ah...love, such a strange emotion." She looked sad as she drifted off into her own thoughts.

"So what did you decide to do?" I prompted.

Her attention snapped back immediately. "We pretended I had some personal business to attend to, before the trip to Croatia and that I would catch a later flight. Meanwhile, Helena phoned your Mum about me staying and the 'holiday'. We figured if I hung back here with you, that you would be safer."

"Thank you." I said, still stunned at the idea.

"You're welcome." Tara paused looking me straight in the eye. "When we get to Croatia, you will be protected by myself, Daniel and Helena. As our flight is later, we will miss the start of the ceremonies, but on the first day it is just the presentation of the newly evolved by their sponsors to the Council, more ceremonial than anything else. However, that evening is their last free time until we see them at the Evolution Ball. You know what I am talking about, right? Joshua did fill you in?"

I nodded, "With all the gruesome details."

"Ah...well, that is probably for the best, you will need to know what is going on. When we arrive, we will go directly to the Presentation Ceremony, even though it will have started, as I said. They will think it odd if we don't. You will be staying in my apartment in the Marston's Villa, as my claimed human, do you understand what that means?"

"I think so. Joshua said it's a human who's trusted by the Chameleons that they work for and knows everything about them."

Tara raised a perfectly shaped eyebrow.

"That would be the polite version. Many Chameleons, the Marston's and myself not included, make use of claimed humans as servants, or in extreme cases, slaves. They are often terrorised and live in fear. Not a pretty picture, I know, but you need to know everything. Some offer themselves in service to us, believing that we are Gods. Others serve out of fear of what we could do to them or their families. So when I tell you to do something in company, never answer back. Always rush to do it, and always, now this is important, always use my name when you speak to me, even in a whisper, have you got that?"

"Ah...yes." I said and sighed. "The whispering problem that's what got us in this mess to start with."

Tara nodded. "One other thing with claimed humans, did you ever see any Vampire movies, where they had the odd human hanging around for other Vampires to 'taste' as a gift to each other?"

I did remember seeing a movie with a young dark haired boy being offered as a special treat. Tara's meaning began to dawn on me. "No...you're not serious?" I said, both my eyebrows rose in shock.

"I am afraid so. It's customary that when I speak to another Chameleon who also has a claimed human, I should 'taste' their human's energy and vice versa." Tara said.

"Oh...my...God."

"Let me show you what they will do, so you are fully prepared, may I?" She held out her hand.

My heart raced in sudden fear.

"O...kay." I placed my trembling hand in hers. At first, I felt nothing but then I began to feel weak, like my sugar level was dropping rapidly. I could feel my legs getting wobbly and I had a strange urge to close my eyes against the dizziness that came in waves. The instant she let go of my hand, I was wide-awake again but felt tired and...well, drained.

"How do you feel?" She looked me in the eye.

"Like an empty bottle." My head felt like it was stuffed with cotton wool and I could feel the beginning of a headache.

"That's what other Chameleons will do when they greet me, they will taste you in the same way. Some will do it for a less time than that and you won't feel so tired. Occasionally, you'll get a Chameleon who likes doing it too much, I wanted you to feel it quite strongly, so you're prepared. You should be back to your old self again soon, although after a few of those, you may find yourself feeling a bit hung over."

The haze began to lift and my attention began to refocus, "I am feeling better already...I think I can handle that."

"Good. Just remember it's normal for them to do this, so you must let them, no matter what. We don't want to draw attention to you, or make them suspect that we aren't telling them the truth, do you understand?"

"Yes." I moved back on my bed and lent against the wall, thinking about this and how it felt. What a strange and very different world they all live in. "May I ask a question?"

"Of course."

"They way you just drained me, it didn't hurt, but when Sebastian attacked me, it burned. Why is that?" I said. It had hurt so much that the thought of it made me bite my lip as I tried not to linger on the memory.

"I've already told you that many Chameleons think they are far superior to humans and some are down right vicious about it. Sebastian, and many others, take a lot of pleasure in making the Lights suffer when they drain them. They create the pain on purpose, for their own enjoyment and some say it makes the energy more potent but we believe that's another lie. I, for one, find it repulsive." She looked disgusted.

"Oh...so he hurt me on purpose?"

"Yes, he could have drained you quickly, simply put you to sleep, before draining you to death."

"Charming guy." I said.

"Yes, he and the rest of that group can be very nasty."

"May I ask what you feed on?"

Tara eyed me suggestively.

I must have looked shocked.

"Just joking." She laughed, "You're not my type. I prefer a mixed diet of animals and vegetation. There are a growing number of us now that prefer to feed this way."

"Phew..." I grinned, "Glad to hear that. So how many Chameleons will be there...on the island?"

"A few hundred."

"What?" I said. I could feel my eyebrows rise up to my hairline again. I swallowed hard.

"A few hundred." She repeated. "This is our yearly get together. We catch up with old friends, welcome the new ones, and have ten days of partying. It's the biggest social event in our year."

"Wouldn't I be safer here, with so many there?" I wondered fearfully.

"Not all will be attending and let's face it, if they want you for some reason, they don't have to use Chameleons to do it, do they? There are plenty of humans who will do anything for us."

"Good point, but wouldn't that mean that the group from Oxford will be there?"

"Yes, more than likely, but that's the beauty of the plan. This way we'll be able to learn more about what they know, based on their reaction to you and they'll be unable to do anything about it."

"I don't understand."

"Did Joshua explain that some Chameleons have special abilities?" She said.

"Yes, something about how they 'know' who is evolving. One of them has visions or something."

"Right well, some Chameleons have other talents. I have a friend, Moira, we're sure to meet her at the gathering, she can

Chameleon

tell when a Chameleon is lying. I'm going to ask her to help us. I knew Sebastian and I've met his companions, I'll speak to them and ask after him, with Moira standing next to me. She'll know if they're telling the truth or not. Their response will be particularly telling, if you are standing next to me too."

"Yeah, that makes sense. What happens if they do know the truth? As a whole, you Chameleons don't have much regard for human life, why wouldn't they just kill me then and there and tell the Council about Joshua?"

"The Council is very particular about who kills whom. Certainly, it would never allow a claimed human to die during the gathering, it would start a war. Think of being a claimed human as immunity from being fed on, you'll be safe, because no Chameleon would dare attacked another's property."

"Okay that's gross...but I now understand why I would be safer there, but what about Joshua? Will he be safe?"

"If Joshua is accused of Sebastian's murder, any claim against him is void while he is interred. If one is made during his interment, the Council have to investigate the matter thoroughly before making a judgement and they have to wait for the interment to be over before they can investigate anything. So he would be safe at least until his testing is over."

"I see." I curled my legs up under me and hugged my knees. "I guess it kind of makes some sense, at least we will come away knowing one way or the other."

"Exactly."

"How hard is the testing?" I asked quietly, peering at her over my knees.

"To be honest, very hard. Imagine yourself locked in a dark place, cold, hungry and alone for so long, that you forget how to hope and then you're released into the warm bright daylight next to a pile of your favourite food. Now multiply that by a hundred and you might just get the smallest notion."

I shuddered. "Will Joshua and his brother make it?"

"Yes, but it will be tough for them. They will, of course, be watching Wil very carefully, they already know what he did to Claire. The Council are prepared for him to fail." She looked worried too.

Images clinked into place, images of Tara looking at Wil at the table in the kitchen, how she leaned in towards him as they read that newspaper and how she sat closer to him than anyone else. I looked at her face now and a realisation burst into my brain.

"You're in love with him, aren't you?"

"Yes." She looked directly at me and her pain was plain to see.

"Does he know?"

She shook her head. "He's still stuck on the memory of Claire and what he did last December."

"I'm sorry." I really felt for her, I'd spent four weeks thinking Joshua didn't want me, which was bad enough, but she had spent the last year knowing Wil didn't even notice her.

"Such is life." She smiled sadly.

With a rapid knock on the door, mum popped her head in, "Do you girls want anything before I take my shower and go to bed?"

"No, thanks, mum."

"No, thank you, Caroline." Tara said.

She smiled at us both, "Kate, I'll be here to pick you up at eleven for the hospital tomorrow morning, okay? Be ready, as I don't want be late. I have to get back to work right after."

"Yep, I'll be ready."

"I'm happy to drive Kate to the hospital, Caroline. It would save you taking time off."

"Are you old enough to drive?" Mum said surprised.

Tara laughed, "I got my license in April."

Chameleon

"Oh...right, well if you're sure?" Mum pushed the door open a little more and stood half in the room and half in the corridor.

"Absolutely. I'd be happy to. Think of it as a thank you for allowing me to stay over." She grinned and tucked her hair behind her ear.

"Well, thanks then. In truth, my boss wasn't happy about me taking a couple of hours off as there is a major meeting tomorrow." Mum turned back to me, "Will you ring me and let me know what the doctor says about your wrist?"

"Of course, straight afterwards." I replied.

"Right then, good night girls, sleep well." Mum left, closing the door behind her.

"Thanks." I said to Tara.

"No problem." Tara lay down over the covers fully clothed.

"Do you sleep? I can't remember if Joshua said you did or not."

"Rarely."

"Oh. What do you normally do at night then?" I asked

"Depends where we are or what we're doing. Generally, night and day is the same thing for us and we keep busy. Tonight, I will do a little reading and perhaps lay here in the dark thinking about the next few days. We have excellent night vision, you know."

I found the thought of her sitting in the dark with her eyes open all night, more than a little creepy. I decided I had to encourage her to read, just so I could get some sleep.

"What are you reading?" I said. Please make it be a thick book, I thought.

Tara whipped out the latest bestseller book on Vampires and smiled sweetly.

I burst into laughter, "That's just too funny."

"I've always loved Vampire stories, what can I say?" She laughed and settled down for the night with her book.

By lunch the next day I was sitting in the hospital with Tara, waiting for the results of my x-rays. I'd already had the stitches taken out of my forehead. I now had a pink curved scar just above my left eyebrow, which they said would fade eventually. It didn't bother me, though, since it reminded me how lucky I was to be alive and have mum safe.

I heard my name being called out by a nurse and we were escorted into the doctor's room.

Dr. Mansford stood looking at my x-ray, on the wall mounted light box behind her desk. She turned round and pushed her glasses up her nose and smiled. Her hair was completely grey, cut short and neat and she had that 'kind Grandma' look, and I liked her instantly.

"Hello, Kate. Please sit down." She glanced at Tara and smiled at her too.

"It seems we will be able to take the cast off today."

"Really? That's quick isn't it? I was told I may get it off in a couple of weeks, maybe more."

"That is the usual way of it but your x-ray shows that the bone is fully knitted together, which is rather quick I must say, but not unheard off. Sometimes the first x-ray is shadowed and the break looks worse than it actually is."

"You can go into the room opposite and a nurse will be along soon to take it off." She said as she sat back down behind her desk, "Here's a leaflet on the physiotherapy exercises you will need to do for the wrist over the next couple of weeks, but you should be fine after that. Just try not to hurt it again, once a bone is broken it's a little weaker afterwards and can break easily a second time." Dr. Mansford smiled and did not seem bothered by my sudden healing.

Within twenty minutes I was out of plaster and we were out of the hospital.

"What shall we do now?" I asked as we climbed back into

Chameleon

Tara's little red sports car.

"How about getting you some lunch, I have been hearing your stomach growl at everyone for the last half an hour."

"Really? You folks do have good hearing."

"You have no clue." She grinned mischievously.

"I'll just let mum know that the hospital freed me and then lunch sounds like a good idea." I pulled out my mobile and dialled her number.

After lunch we went shopping. Tara decided I needed a few new pieces of clothing for the 'holiday'. She explained, with a smirk, that her claimed human would be 'better dressed' and that she would pay for everything. I tried to argue with her, but I soon found out that being a Chameleon also meant you were stubborn too. I have to admit though, not worrying about price tags and just buying what I wanted was a nice change. However, we were careful to not go too overboard as mum would start asking questions if I had a wardrobe that a movie star would be proud of.

The final item of clothing Tara made me choose was a ball gown for the Evolution Ball. It was something I'd never bought before and with Tara's excellent taste, we managed to find something very special. Tara had stared at me wide-eyed when I tried it on and I hoped it would have the same effect on Joshua at the ball.

At home, after dinner, Mum insisted on seeing what we'd purchased and a fashion show ensued. I showed her everything including the ball gown, Tara explained that the Marstons were to attend a local ball with the other wealthy families of the area and I was expected to attend. Mum's eyes bulged when she realised that the ball gown was of a decent quality and before she could say anything Tara swiftly stepped in and explained that she had bought the dress for me, as an early birthday present. Even though my birthday was not until February, mum seemed satisfied with the answer, at least, she looked like she was.

By the time Saturday dawned, I was beside myself with excitement and worry. I couldn't focus and did not know what to do with myself. I lay in bed watching her read, it was her second book and she had almost reached the last page.

"How's the book?"

"Really good, thanks." She read the last page and closed the book. "You look tired. You were tossing a lot in the night. Is everything okay?"

"I'm feeling hyper about tomorrow and I have nothing planned for today, to take my mind off it." I sighed and rolled over to stare at the ceiling.

"I have an idea, if you're feeling brave?" She suggested.

Well, that sounds ominous, I thought. "Why? What do you have in mind?"

"There is a private club for Chameleons called Lumiere in Tewin Wood, just outside Welwyn Garden City, about an hour and a half from here. It won't be full today, as many will be flying out to Croatia, however, there will be some Chameleons there. I think it would be good practice for you and it will use up some spare time. What do you think?"

"A club? What type of club?" I sat up excited and yet my stomach fluttered with fear. This was a test, could I really do this? I wondered.

"You know, like an old fashioned gentleman's club. It has private bar and nightclub, which will obviously be closed. During the day, it's a reading lounge...amongst other things. They serve food too, the Chameleon type." She looked to see how I would react.

I gulped, "I guess it would be a good idea to be around a few Chameleons, before I'm thrown in at the deep end."

"Good lass. We'll just tell your mum we are going out for lunch and a drive. You might want to wear something other

Chameleon

than jeans though, something smarter."

"Like what? I said. I had no clue what claimed humans wore and I was more than a little nervous.

"Don't worry, you'll be fine." Tara said.

She seemed to sense my fear...or hear it. Of course, she could hear my heart race and my breathing get quicker.

"I'll be watching out for you. Just put on something casual but smart. I can help you pick, if you like."

"Okay, thanks." I dove into my wardrobe, pulling clothes out to show them to Tara. Finally, she chose a smart pair of trousers and a simple blouse.

"The place will probably close mid-afternoon so the two Chameleons who run it can travel. Think of it as a test drive. The owners are actually very nice even if they would rather feed on human Light than anything else. I've known them for many years. It will actually make you more believable as my human, if others have seen you with me before we go to Croatia."

"That makes sense." I nibbled my lip nervously as I dressed and tried not to imagine the place I was heading to as some nasty dive full of hungry Chameleons addicted to human energy. All I could think of was a vampire feeding frenzy from some movie.

By late morning we had driven past the Tewin sign and entered the small town. "This seems an odd place to have a club for Chameleons. It's so small and isolated."

"That's exactly why it's here. If it were in London, it would get too much attention. Here, it's quiet. The locals know it's an exclusive, private club and nobody disturbs us."

We drove down narrow winding lanes that were canopied by trees, passing houses that were obviously residences of the rich.

"Wow, these houses are huge." I said.

"Yes, some of them are, it's a wealthy area."

We drove a little further and made a sharp right turn up a

discretely hidden driveway. We followed the road for a couple of minutes until it opened up, showing an expansive lawn stretching out in front of an enormous white Georgian mansion, complete with pillars in the front.

"Wow." I said.

"Impressive, huh?"

"It's definitely not what I was expecting."

"What were you expecting exactly? Some seedy little dive in a back street somewhere with pimps peddling humans?" Tara laughed.

"Well...yeah...actually." I laughed self-consciously.

"When one lives for a long time, one acquires wealth and property. There are very few poor Chameleons and they are only that way because they wish to be." Tara pulled the car up by the large garages. "Now remember what I told you?"

"Got it." I swallowed hard and found my throat was dry from nerves. I had no idea what I would find or if I could get away with this charade.

"Walk round and open my door, and remember to use my name when you speak to me." She smiled encouragingly.

I climbed out of the car, quickly walked round to her side and opened the door as she had asked. It seemed weird, almost funny to be playing such a role, except that I was speechless with fear and anticipation. I took a deep breath to steady my nerves and calm my pulse. I had to remember they could hear everything. Tara got out and I closed the car door behind her. We walked up the path past the huge white pillars towards the large solid looking front doors. Tara nodded for me to open the door. I pulled it hard, thinking it would be heavy, but it glided open and I almost staggered backwards.

I saw Tara hide a smile at my door antics as we walked through the doorway and into the private world of the Chameleons.

Chameleon

The first thing I saw was the huge marble reception desk with a large imposing guard on each side, both dressed in black suits, white shirts and black ties. They stood staring at the front doors with their hands behind their backs, like statues.

"Lady Tara, how lovely to see you today. Welcome back to Lumiere." The receptionist, a beautiful blond woman, recognised Tara immediately and nodded at a server who appeared beside her. "Lady Eleanor and Lord Benjamin will be delighted to see you. This is Samuel, he will be your server today. Please enjoy your visit." She smiled sweetly and remained standing until we had moved away following Samuel.

"This way, your Ladyship." Samuel inclined his head and walked down the corridor.

I glanced at Tara, they had called her 'Lady' Tara, now that was something I hadn't known about.

We were lead into the west wing of the massive building and brought before another large set of doors that were obviously the inner entrance. Again, there stood guard on either side of the door, virtual twins to the ones at reception. The guards opened the doors for Samuel and we followed him in. I tried not to look around like a tourist, instead keeping my head high and pretending that I belonged there. My acting lessons were coming in handy in ways I'd never imagined.

The décor inside was all very refined, which made it all the more creepy, knowing that humans were drained here like long cocktails.

There were several rooms off the wood panelled hallway with none of the doors shut. I was able to see into each room, they had a small discrete bar, a barman and guard by the door. I noticed that some rooms had comfy chairs, others were set up with conference tables, some had chaise lounges, some, I was surprised to see, had big ornate four poster beds with comfy chairs place around them. The beds really rather unnerved me, what sort of club was this? What did they do here? I shuddered to think.

At last, we reached a room at the end of the hall and entered it. The room felt bright and airy with many windows looking out onto gardens. It had a very high ceiling, with an ornate plaster ceiling rose. I tried to take everything in quickly without glancing around too much. Down the entire left side of this room stood a large ornate mahogany bar with several high stools alongside it. Directly opposite the bar was a huge lit fireplace surrounded by overstuffed chairs. I could hear the fire roar and crackle as we stepped into the room.

Samuel led Tara to one of the chairs by the fire and waited for her to sit, I stood behind her chair.

"Is this suitable, your Ladyship?"

"Yes, thank you, Samuel. Can you tell Lord and Lady Barrington I've arrived?"

"Certainly, your Ladyship. Do you wish anything for your Light?"

"Just water."

Samuel inclined his head and quickly walked away.

Tara didn't look at me but held her hand out, gestured for me to come and speak to her. "Fetch yourself a stool and sit out of my way." She said it imperiously, knowing full well every Chameleon could hear her.

I quickly looked around and spotted a low stool at a table nearby and placed it next to Tara's chair but slightly behind, just as she had instructed in the car. I glanced round and for the first time noticed two Chameleons sitting in deep conversation in the corner, both with human attendants. The humans were standing, one on each side of the couple.

The couple were practically luminescent with beauty. Both had long blond hair and the polished looks of movie stars. Their conversation seemed very animated. I couldn't hear what was

Chameleon

being said but they looked like they were arguing. Samuel returned with a glass of water, followed by a young woman approximately my age. Samuel placed the water on the table near me but never even looked at me once.

The girl came forward and spoke in a gentle voice, "A gift from Lord Barrington," She held out her arm, "Lord Barrington apologises for the delay, and says he will be with you in a moment."

I stared at her pale arm covered in freckles and then looked up into her eyes. She seemed completely calm and serene as she held out her arm for Tara to taste.

"Thank you." Tara replied as she brushed her hand slowly down the girl's arm from the elbow to the wrist, where she lingered and then removed her fingers.

The girl turned a little pale and I saw her eyes droop and then spring open again. The instant that Tara had finished, the girl smiled, inclined her head and moved quietly away. I felt a little shocked. I knew I would see this but thinking about it and actually seeing it was entirely different. Tara shot me a quick glance to see how I was doing.

"Tara, darling! How absolutely wonderful to see you again. It has been too long. How are you, my Irish beauty?" The imperious voice of Lord Benjamin Barrington boomed across the room and in a flash he stood by Tara's side.

Tall, dark and handsome didn't really do him justice but it was the best I could think of as I tried to gather my wits and not stare too much, being here had begun to feel like I was attending a major movie award ceremony with all these good-looking Chameleons around me. I tried not to look star struck and not to feel too plain.

"Benjamin." Tara kissed both his cheeks and laughed as he bent to kiss her hand. "How wonderful to see you again. I was just passing through and thought I would say hello."

"Splendid, splendid. I see you have a Light and such a bonnie one too." He cooed.

I knew this was my queue.

I stood up, smiled sweetly and offered my arm.

REALITY

With a blur of speed he was immediately beside me.
Taking my hand he raised it to his mouth placing a gentle kiss on it, while looking me straight in the eye. I could feel him draining my energy but he was kind enough not to make it hurt. Just as I started to feel dizzy, he released my hand and reached up to stroke my cheek.

"Lovely, quite lovely. I must congratulate you, Tara, darling. What a lovely choice you've made at last." His attention turned back to Tara as he sat down opposite her in one of the large chairs. "Where are you staying presently?"

I sat down, a little dazed and tired but proud of myself for remaining calm and was glad that I was no longer of interest to him. I allowed myself to be happy, I had managed to fool him into thinking Tara had claimed me. I started to think that I might be able to go through with this after all.

"Oh, I have been visiting with old friends...the Marstons, you know them, of course?"

"Why, yes. Mathers and his lovely wife Helena, super couple. Shame they're Hippies though, but we can't all be perfect." He smiled in a very supercilious way.

I filed away the name he had called them in my brain. Hippies, huh? I would ask Tara later what he'd meant by it.

"Modern times, Benjamin. Modern times." Tara smiled at

him indulgently. "How is Ella?"

"Very well, thank you. She is just finishing with our VIP guest."

"Oh? And just who have you been entertaining?" Tara sat back and crossed her legs at the ankle, every bit a lady.

"We have had the pleasurable company of Lamia, she's been staying with us for a short while." He smiled, full of himself.

"One of the Council? I am impressed, Benjamin. That certainly explains all the guards." Tara smiled.

One of the Council is here, in this very house...now? I thought, as a burning curiosity raged through me. I had to get a look at her, but how? I glanced over towards the two blond Chameleons who had just received their order from their server, by way of a blond haired young boy about the age of twelve, who stood before them holding out both arms, one for each of them. I tried to swallow but my mouth had dried up. I wanted desperately to run across the room, scoop the child up and run away as far and as fast as possible, but I knew I couldn't and I would have no chance of escape. Instead, I watched mesmerized, unable to show just how truly horrified I was. I struggled to keep my breathing even and my heart rate down. Thank goodness Lord Benjamin realised I was new at being a claimed human, he might not take notice of my reactions knowing this.

The male Chameleon made the boy sit on his knee and held him in his arms, gently letting the boy's head fall back. The female unbuttoned the boy's shirt to his navel, and gently stroked his chest, in, what seemed to me, a very creepy way. I could feel the nausea rising and I swallowed it back down. The male kissed the boy's throat as the woman continued to trail her fingers on his skin. I could see the boy getting paler as his energy was being drained. I wanted desperately to look away but my eyes stared in sick fascination. Within moments their server collected the boy and helped him stagger away. The Chameleons acted as if nothing happened and continued with their conversation, as though they had just sipped a refreshing drink. I repressed a shudder and quickly turned my attention back to Tara, not wanting to look at the monsters anymore.

I had missed what had been said between Lord Benjamin and Tara. Tara rose and began to walk out of the room with Benjamin, I quickly stood and followed behind. They walked slowly back up the hallway, talking. I was a bit too far behind to hear their conversation and wished I had the hearing they all possessed. They paused by the doorway of one room and stood watching whatever was happening within. I soon caught up and stood behind them with a perfect view of a huge bed with seats around it.

This time the room was occupied.

A young couple were on the bed in the throws of passion, whilst six Chameleons stood or sat around the bed watching. I stood staring, blushing at what I saw.

My brain was screaming at me to bolt. Yet I didn't dare move, knowing that I was completely outnumbered by superhuman killers who would not think twice about killing me. I tried not to shake with fear.

As the couple became more engrossed in each other seemingly oblivious to their audience, a female Chameleon with dark haired moved inhumanly fast to the bedside and reached over to the woman and touched her just above the heart, on the breast. To my horror, I realised the victim was a teenager about my age. I watched her life ebb away under the woman's hand and she died right there and then, before my eyes, still in the embrace of her lover. The lover smiled at his audience, like he was proud of his part in the matter.

The Chameleon woman looked up directly at me, her piercing brown eyes looked into mine and she had a slight smile on her lips. She inclined her head at me suggestively, I shuddered and tried to hold back the vomit that had risen to the back of my throat. My instincts were screaming for me to run but pure fear rooted me to the spot. The woman was small and slender with straight, long dark hair, a pale olive complexion with a Grecian looking nose. Indeed, she reminded me of the women I had seen in Greece during family holidays.

Somehow, I managed to maintain composure and feebly said, "Excuse me, Lady Tara, it's time for your appointment." With a supreme effort, I managed to give Tara the pre-arranged signal that we had created, if and when I needed to get out quickly.

"Ah...thank you, Kate. Sorry Benjamin, I have to leave now but please do give my compliments to Lamia and Ella. I am sure I'll have chance to speak to them at the gathering." Tara leaned forward and kissed Benjamin on both cheeks before nodding her farewell to Lamia, who continued to look at us with a thoughtful expression, until she finally looked away.

The sheer removal of her gaze allowed me to breathe at last.

So that was Lamia, one of The Council of Nine. I thought. What a disgusting group they are, if she is anything to go by.

We moved quickly away from the door and back down the hallway, the closer I got to the exit the more I kept seeing the images of the girl alive one minute and dead the next without any regard. The urge to vomit was overwhelming. I clenched my teeth hard and breathed through my nose. Finally, we were out of the door and back into the fresh October air. The cool air helped, but didn't stop my bile rising. I quickly opened the car door for Tara and almost ran around the other side and climbed in.

Tara glanced at me. I knew we were still too close to the other Chameleons to say anything. She quickly turned the car around and raced out of the driveway spraying gravel everywhere. The view through the passenger window blurred as we drove down several country lanes, until we were in a secluded spot and Tara was able to pull over. I leapt from the car and stood gazing out over the fields trying to breathe deeply.

The images just kept coming, I tried to think about something other but it was just too hard to do. Shakily, I stood in the cool breeze and closed my eyes. I let the breeze wash over me and cool me down. I waited for my heart rate to return to normal and gradually took some deep breaths to calm my mind. Tara appeared at my side with my water bottle from the car.

"Are you okay?" She asked.

"Yes...it's just a shock to actually see what some of you do." My voice sound thin and trembled.

"It is quite a different matter to see it, isn't it?" She placed a hand on my shoulder, "It's for the best that you got to see that before we get to Croatia. Not that it will make you immune to the horror, but since you will likely see more and perhaps much worse where we're going, it's best to be prepared. Are you sure you still want to do this?"

"I have no choice really, do I?" I took a sip of the water, "Anyway, if I'm going to be a target for Chameleons I would rather be surrounded by you all and know you have my back. I also really want to be there for Joshua. I have made my mind up." I smiled feebly and climbed back in the car.

Tara joined the traffic on the side road again and we headed home.

Again, the image of the girl dying returned, this time I was able to breath through it. "Why did...she...kill that girl during...sex?" It was difficult to speak about the images in my mind.

"Lamia? She prefers to drain the passionate red energy. Most Chameleons have a favourite type of Light. Her's happens to be the kind you get from someone who is in the midst of lovemaking." Tara indicated and turned onto the main road.

"Oh..." I thought about this for a moment. So what we do

creates different coloured light, how interesting and yet how sick of the Chameleons to exploit it. Another thought occurred to me, "What colour do you prefer?" I asked, not sure I wanted to hear the answer.

"I only take short bursts from humans in emergencies, since I live on other energies, as I told you earlier, but personally, if I had to pick one human energy, I would have to say I prefer the energy of laughter."

"Laughter has a colour?"

"Of course, all emotions do."

I thought about laughter being a colour for a while, as we drove along. What colour would it be? Yellow, no. I would prefer to think of it as purple for some reason. I was going to ask what colour it was, when another question came to mind, "Why did Benjamin call the Marstons 'Hippies'?" I said.

"You caught that, did you?" Tara looked at me quickly and then her eyes were back on the road. "There are three types of Chameleons. Hippies are those that live off plants, trees and animals. You know...tree huggers."

I laughed, imagining them all hugging trees, "How apt...and the other types?"

"Those are Feeders and Bleeders. Feeders are like the ones you saw at the club, the couple in the bar and Lamia. Feeders live off human energy but do it painlessly. Some kill the humans they are feeding from, others drain the human to the point of exhaustion and then let them recuperate."

"And the Bleeders?" Just the name filled me with dread.

"They are the hardcore, very unpleasant types. Bleeders enjoy inflicting pain on their victims."

"Like Sebastian?"

"Yes, you were very lucky."

"Lucky?" I was astonished. I didn't feel lucky. I did die, after all.

Chameleon

"The burning you felt before you died is one of the least painful ways they kill...Joshua will not thank me for telling you, but Bleeders literally like to feel your blood cool as you die. This means they usually..." Tara glanced at me, "...punch their hand into the body cavity of the victim and then drain their energy, all the while feeling the person's life drain away as they hold the heart in their hands."

"Ugh. That's revolting." I paled. I was not sure my mind could handle further horrors.

"It may be, but it's true. Jonas, the leader of the group particularly likes to hold a victims heart in his hands. Some even like to do the whole 'Hollywood Vampire thing' and drink the blood as they drain the energy."

"Oh my God." I could feel the bile rising again, "That makes what I just saw almost...tame...in comparison." My hand flew to my mouth as images tumbled in my brain of imagined horrors.

"Exactly." She said.

I could see Tara watching me again.

"You need to eat." Tara said.

"I'm not hungry."

"That's beside the point. You need to eat, I don't want you to go into shock. Are you cold?" Tara spotted a roadside café just ahead and pulled in.

"No, I'm fine. Honestly, I really have no appetite." Food was definitely the last thing on my mind.

"Never-the-less, you will eat something." Her voice had turned to steel and I knew deep down she was right to make me.

At a plastic table, in the middle of the café, I sat sipping vegetable soup while Tara ate nothing. The soup was actually quite good and it was making me feel better. Tara was right, I did need it.

"So Lamia is one of the Council members, huh? She looked...Greek."

"Yes, she is one of the Nine and she's Macedonian, how did you know?" Tara lifted one eyebrow.

"I've been to Greece for vacations. She just reminded me of the people there."

"Lamia is one of the older Council members, several thousand years old, but not the oldest by far. She has a particular taste for teenage humans. She likes her human victims to be young and impassioned, as you saw." Tara watched me carefully for my reaction.

I grimaced at the thought, such a waste of life.

"You did very well today, you know. Not many claimed humans take it so well on their first time."

"Thank you...I think."

"Just remember that on the Island there will be more of it, although they do tend to save the best for last...at the Evolution Ball. Very few humans are actually killed, since it would be too suspicious to the local authorities. Generally, the Council will ship in Lights for our entertainment, they often gather them from the streets, clean them up and drug them. Most don't even have a clue where they are or what is happened even after they have been returned to your world. I will try to keep you from seeing too much of it."

"Thanks." A deep dread was building again in my stomach and I pushed the last of the soup away. I knew Tara was trying to prepare me, but my mind kept looking over the horrific images I had seen today and even worse, the images I created for myself.

"I think I should take you home. You look like you could use some rest, and you still have some packing to do." She smiled encouragingly.

"You're right, I do." I concentrated on the here-and-now and tried to think about my packing list.

Back in the privacy of my room that evening, my tired and

emotionally wrung mind was elsewhere, on the things to come, on Joshua, on the testing, on Croatia and the hundreds of Chameleons that would be there. I needed a distraction and I looked to Tara for it.

"Tell me about when you evolved."

"It's not very interesting."

I looked at her with a hopefully expression.

"Well, if you insist. I evolved in 1848 at age of seventeen. It was during the time of the potato famine in Ireland. Drogheda, my birthplace, is a harbour town on the East coast. We suffered badly during those days and many folks died of starvation...it was terrible." Tara seemed weighed down with the sadness of the memory. "The landlords threw people out for lack of payment. Around every corner, you would encounter families all skin and bone, as they slowly starved to death on the streets."

"How awful." I cringed at my useless words, I really didn't know what to say. I finished the packing and sat down next to her.

"I lost my younger brothers first and then my mother and finally, my father through starvation and the rampant diseases that accompanied it. I was living on the streets barely surviving, not far from starvation myself. After a while, I began to see a strange light surrounding people, I noticed it was around the ones who were dying. I remember looking down at my own flesh in confusion, thinking it was because I hadn't eaten in such a long time and I'd become delirious, but to my amazement, my own body seemed to have a different shine, it had a faint rainbow colour. I was forced to put it out of my head as madness and tried to stay alive anyway I could. I met a family who were as desperate as I and we tried to look after each other. At first, I didn't understand why I would feel better after a long night huddled together for warmth. Then one very cold night, I held one of the children and in the morning, I found that she had died...in my arms and yet I felt stronger than before."

Tara gazed off into space, seeing the tragic moment played out in her head once again. I watched her in silence, waiting for her to continue.

"I realised, in the end, after several more 'unexplained' deaths, that I was very bad luck to have around and word spread. People began to blame me for the starvation that was decimating the town and at one point I was beaten by outraged locals, who couldn't understand why I was looking healthier and healthier and their children continued to die. Finally, I was accused of witchcraft and driven out of town. I barely made it out alive, I was almost torn to bits by the angry mob. I managed to walk to Dublin and eventually found work as I prostitute. It was in the bawdy house where I met Lord Conway, who was also a Chameleon and recognised me as the same. He helped me, explaining what I was and how I could feed to survive. He became my sponsor and presented me to the Council of Nine. Eventually, I married him and we travelled the world together for many years."

Images of her past floated in my mind, like an old movie. "Wait, you're married?" I said.

"Was married. After a hundred years together we decided to go our separate ways. You'll probably meet Michael on the island."

"Wow." It never ceased to amaze me how young she looked and now to find out she had been married for a hundred years, it was mind blowing. I looked at her face and skin for any sign of the years she had seen, but she really did look my age and positively glowed with youth. "Is your ex-husband a Hippie?"

"No, a Feeder. That was one of our difficulties. When we met we moved to the Americas, but after causing all those deaths in Ireland, I didn't derive much joy from feeding. Many years later, we met Mathers, or rather Daniel as he is now, when he came

Chameleon

out to Canada. He taught me that we could live on other energies, not just human. Michael didn't like that I was denying part of my nature, as he put it, and it became...difficult between us. We are still close friends but have drifted too far apart to be romantically together anymore."

"I can see why that would cause a few problems." I said and realised that Joshua would be considered a 'Hippie', I was truly grateful he was one. I could not be with him if he were any other kind of Chameleon.

"Anyway, I moved to the UK and got back in touch with Daniel who by then had married Helena and they took me in as part of their family. I come back to visit them regularly, especially now."

"I guess that's because of Wil?"

"Yes." She grinned at me.

"Isn't he too young for you?"

"You are thinking in human terms. Admittedly, there is a difference in mental years and life experience but it's different for us, our ways are not yours. Remember, we stop ageing at our biological prime, I estimate that I'm about twenty, so Wil is really only a year younger than me. Anything else we can work on."

I stretched my legs out in front of me and then tucked them underneath as I snuggled into the sofa more. I realised that all the Chameleons I had met were wealthy and peers, except for Sebastian but then I knew virtually nothing about him. "Are all Chameleons wealthy?"

"I wasn't but many are wealthy because we live so long and accumulate wealth. Chameleons come from every walk of life and every country. The evolution into Chameleon seems random. Occasionally, it will run in a family like the Marstons but that's rare and usually Chameleons are not connected to each other. The fact that the Marstons family have been Chameleon for two generations makes them unique, it was one of the reasons why your school focused on the science side of things to investigate the evolution of Chameleons. Did you know that your school was actually built for Chameleons?"

"Yes, Joshua told me....it seems weird, knowing that now, kind of being inside a secret society without knowing about it, but I wouldn't change a thing because I wouldn't have met Joshua." I sighed, "I do miss him..."

"You'll be seeing him tomorrow after he has been presented to the Council. I'll also get to see Wil." She smiled.

"I know." I smiled back at her. "What does your kind think about humans and Chameleons being together?"

"Usually, it's ignored. Obviously, it happens but no one takes much notice. It's viewed as a Chameleon just sowing their wild oats, if you get my meaning. It definitely isn't taken seriously."

"Oh." I thought about it for a moment, "At least it's not considered a taboo and we won't have to hide it."

"True." Tara said, "You look tired and it's getting late. You should get some sleep, we have a big day tomorrow." She lent against the sofa arm.

"I'm not sure I can sleep." I chewed my lip.

"Give it a try. I have a feeling that after today, you'll have no problem falling asleep."

I wasn't so sure, especially knowing the images that were floating around inside my head just behind my eyelids. Tara was right, though and shortly after laying down, I quickly fell to sleep.

I awoke with a start, nervously realising what today would bring. I would, hopefully, get to see Joshua again...and an island full of Chameleons. My stomach flipped with nerves. I glanced around to the sofa bed for Tara and found it empty. I was alone in my room. I put my arm over my eyes to block out the low November sun that managed to sneak around the curtains and into

Chameleon

my room, I silently prayed that everything would be okay.

I delayed going down to breakfast and enjoyed these few moments alone with my thoughts. Today was a big day, certainly the biggest in my life so far and I was glad for some peace and quiet. My mind wandered through all the things I had seen and heard in the last couple of days. I certainly had a better picture of the world according to the Chameleons now, but not one I particularly liked. I was so very pleased that the Marston family and Tara, were not like the others. The others, the Feeders and Bleeders, they truly terrified me.

With a deep sigh, I climbed out of bed and headed downstairs to breakfast. By 9.50am we were all outside loading the suitcases and flight bags into to the boot of Tara's sports car.

"You will drive carefully won't you, Tara?" Mum looked worried and nibbled her lip.

"Of course, Caroline. Don't worry, we'll be fine."

Mum reached over to hug me tightly, "Take care of yourself, hun. I will miss you loads." She managed a brave smile.

"I will, mum and I promise to be good." I hugged her back and held on to her for a moment. I knew she was worried, I could see it in her eyes. It was, after all, the first time I'd travelled out of the country without her.

"Call me when you get to the villa, to let me know you arrived safely." She kissed me on the cheek one last time and let go. "And send me a postcard." She smiled.

"I will. Try to enjoy the peace and quiet while you can." I joked.

We seemed to be staying on the local roads, instead of heading into London to one of the main airports. As we drove down quiet back lanes and out into the countryside, a sudden sense of freedom enveloped me. I'd never before done anything like this, never been on an adventure by myself, if this could be called an adventure. I was unsure of whether to be nervous, happy, excited or terrified, so I went for all of them, which left my stomach a worried pit.

"Where are we flying from?" I realised I'd asked nothing about the actual journey.

"Oxford Airport." She looked out of the windscreen to the clear pale blue November sky. "Looks like we got lucky with the weather, do you fly well?"

"Yes, I find it quite exciting."

The fields and small villages whizzed by as we travelled in silence. I was not really in the mood for talking; my mind tumbled through all the possibilities of what would happen in the next two weeks. I was dying to see Joshua but worried at how angry he would be with me for defying his directions...as if that would stop me, I grinned to myself. I was intrigued to see the Council and the other Chameleons, but I knew if I put a step wrong they could easily kill me. Most of all, I was terrified for Joshua and Wil and their testing, specifically, their interments.

Eventually, we turned off the main road into what looked like a cleaner, more sophisticated airport than the usual ones I had been to. All the planes I could see, were smaller too and I couldn't see any large commercial planes. I wondered if we were at the right airport. We pulled up outside the entrance and instantly, valets appeared to open our doors while a porter retrieved our suitcases.

Tara grinned at me as I looked around us, she took my arm and walked confidently through the doors. The inside of the airport was a lot nicer too. Everything looked shiny, clean and crisp. We breezed through to a lounge, where a uniformed woman took our passports and went to complete our boarding passes. Within moments she returned and handed them over, which appeared to be the extent of the passport control and ticket assignment. The lounge had big soft chairs and everywhere, there were vases of fresh flowers, there was even a free bar. I glanced out the window and immediately realised that I was looking at private jets.

Tara stood watching my expression and burst out laughing, "Try not to look like such a tourist, Kate."

"I'm sorry but I wasn't expecting this." I blushed.

"It's okay, I'm just teasing you. Did you think we would be on a commercial flight?" She sat in one of the comfy looking chairs.

I sat opposite her, "Actually, I hadn't given it much thought." My mind had been too full of other things recently.

A uniformed steward approached us discretely. "Excuse me Lady Conway, my name is Christopher. I will be the concierge for your flight this morning. Your pilot has informed me that you may board now, if you are ready."

Tara nodded and we followed the concierge through the set of doors leading outside and across the few feet of tarmac to a small jet. The Concierge paused at the foot of the steps waiting for us to board. Tara led the way and I followed sheepishly, I still couldn't believe that I was going to be on a private jet.

Christopher followed us up the steps and closed the door behind him.

The interior of the plane was incredible. It was approximately seven-feet wide by about twenty feet, filled with big leather chairs with tables and a long leather sofa. It had a beautiful wooden kitchen area to the front of the plane and a large bathroom area at the back. There were enough seats for over ten passengers.

I was speechless.

"Lovely, isn't it?" Tara made herself comfortable in one of the chairs.

"Yes, it is." I followed and sat opposite her. The seat was the most comfortable aeroplane seat I'd ever sat on and I certainly wouldn't be banging my knees against the seat in front of me on this flight.

"This is what you get when you hang around with the Marstons." She laughed, "Lucky us, huh?"

A man's voice came over the intercom, "Good morning and welcome to Aurora Private Charter. I'm Thomas, your Captain for today. You are travelling this morning in the finest member of our fleet - the Gulfstream G200 - with a typical cruising speed of 530mph. We will be landing in approximately three hours at Pula Airport. The weather is bright and clear, providing for a smooth flight today. Please fasten your seat belts for take off. Thank you and I hope you have a pleasant flight."

We duly fastened our seat-belts and the plane moved onto the tarmac to prepare for take off. We were quickly in the air, a process that was a lot less noisy than I was used to. Shortly, we levelled out and Tara undid her belt, after which I followed suit. I imagined that this was how a famous actress would travel and decided I would have my own private jet one day.

"Would you like any refreshments, Lady Conway?" Christopher had snuck up on us again.

"No thank you, Christopher." She smiled at him and turned to me, "You should have some lunch though, Kate."

Christopher looked at me "Miss? Would you like to see the menu?"

"Yes, please." I blushed not comfortable with the attention. He handed me the menu and I quickly flicked through and ordered a sandwich, Christopher vanished again.

"You're enjoying this aren't you?" Tara's lips pulled up into a sly smile.

"Absolutely."

"That sandwich you ordered just happens to be one of my favourites."

"Isn't it odd that you have favourites when... " I lowered my voice, "...you don't need to eat?"

"No, I may not need to eat often, but when I do, I have my

Chameleon

favourite foods. You don't need to lower your voice by the way. Aurora, the company that owns the plane, is owned by a Chameleon and all employees are trusted humans."

"Blimey, you'll be telling me next that Chameleons are high up in government too." I joked.

Tara simply looked at me and smiled sweetly.

"No! I was joking...really? Who?"

"That is not for me to say, but I can tell you that several Chameleons are power hungry and tend to go for the big jobs. You will recognise many of them on the island. Of course, you must remember that it would be a grave mistake to talk about them to any one outside the world of Chameleons. They have several ways of tracking down talkers and silencing them, permanently, if you know what I mean." She said, her face showed the seriousness of her words.

"Oh, I'll keep quiet, don't worry. Let's face it, who would believe me anyway?" I said.

"You would be surprised actually, there are many people out there that would pay a lot to get more information on us. However, that is beside the point. Ah...here's your lunch."

Christopher placed the exquisite meal before me, more of a work of art than a sandwich. "Bon Appetit, Miss."

"Thank you." I manage to say it just in time before he disappeared again.

The flight passed quickly as I ate my lunch and we chatted. For a while I sat watching the clouds out of the window, everything felt like a dream and I was very tempted to pinch myself whenever I looked around the cabin.

We arrived at Pula just under the estimated time of three hours and I thanked Christopher as he escorted us off the plane onto the tarmac. It was a beautiful day in Croatia, bright blue cloudless sky and comfortably warm. I breathed in the air, it was different to the air in the UK, and somehow, it felt cleaner and fresher. Christopher passed our passports to an official who stood waiting, the official quickly checked our details and handed them back. Christopher then nodded to the nearby driver, who stood on the tarmac next to a large black Mercedes. Then, with a stately Bon Voyage, he returned our passports and climbed back up the steps, disappearing back into the jet.

The driver stepped forward, he wore the now usual uniform of a dark suit and tie, he reminded me of the guards at the private club.

"Lady Conway, Miss Henson." He nodded at us both, "I will be your driver this afternoon, my name is David. If you need anything, please let me know." He opened the vehicle's door, we both climbed in and he shut the door behind us. David loaded our bags in the trunk and within moments we were pulling out of the airport. We drove through lovely countryside and alongside the Mediterranean Sea, the views out of the window towards the sea were spectacular.

"It's lovely here." I said.

"Yes, it is. Wait until you see the town of Rovinj. It's quite beautiful and the buildings are a wonderful mixture of Romanesque, Renaissance and Baroque architecture. There are also a lot of the less glamorous, traditional stone houses with red tiled roofs spread all along the coast line. I find those very beautiful too."

"You have been here before?" I turned to look at her in surprise.

"Oh, yes, several years ago. In 1989, just before the War which broke out in 1991. This area was part of Yugoslavia then, not called Croatia as it is now. I have travelled at lot since I evolved, of course, but there are still many places I want to see."

I watched as the scenery flowed by in glorious colour and we sat in a companionable silence. The landscape was full of rocky outcrops, bushes and trees, the usual and beautiful, Mediterra-

Chameleon

nean landscape. It was strangely comforting, something familiar from my childhood memories of family holidays.

The drive took about forty minutes and at last we pulled into the city of Rovinj. Tara had understated the beauty of the city. The streets were narrow, twisting gradually upwards toward a radiant white church at the top of the hill around which the town was constructed. The church's white spire pointed majestically up into the blue sky. The town buildings cluttered busily around the church, their multicoloured walls contrasting against the church's white. It really was breathtaking.

"Wow." I said.

"See what I mean about the houses?"

"Oh yes." I couldn't tear my eyes away. The town looked so colourful and bright with houses several stories high clustered along the narrow cobbled streets. This beautiful place seemed to be at odds in my mind with the horrors I would find on the nearby island.

We drove down to the marina and around it, until we were as near to the pier as our driver could get us. The now familiar feeling of dread crept around my body and into my soul anew. We climbed out of the car into the warm afternoon sun and I felt the warm breeze, coming off the Mediterranean Sea, on my skin. I looked around, behind me were the bright houses and the safety of the town of Rovinj, before me was the pier, which reached out into the beautiful blue of the sea, and opposite were the green trees of a small island.

I swallowed hard. "Is that where we're going...Lady Tara?" I asked, suddenly remembering the rules she had taught me.

"Yes, that's St. Catherine's Island or as it is known in Croatian 'Otok sv. Katarina'."

"It looks nice." It truly did, but it made my skin prickle with dread of what was hiding there.

David, our driver, passed our bags to a porter, who had

walked up from the end of the pier. The porter was flanked by two guards who were similarly dressed as all the others that worked for the Chameleons. I could also see two more guards down at the end of the pier, in front of a small passenger boat.

I eyed the guards nervously and Tara saw me looking at them.

Tara spoke quietly, "The Council of Nine have rented the Island from the owners for the duration and have brought in all their own staff. The human guards are here and in several other strategic places, to ensure our privacy." She smiled and walked towards the end of the pier and the small boat.

I followed behind her as was proper, the porter and guards followed me. We stepped down into the boat and were soon rushing over the water toward the small, wooden pier on the opposite bank. The trip took only five minutes but as I stepped onto the island, I felt like I'd entered an entirely different world.

Chameleon

Reunion

Wherever I looked there were rocky outcrops disappearing into the sea, tall pine trees and bushes, with brick and cobbled pathways leading off into the trees. The porter silently led the way up the path from the little pier. I was relieved to see that the two fierce looking guards remained at the pier.

There appeared to be no official roads, only pathways and trees. Occasionally, we walked past little sub-tropical gardens and I could hear the cicada's vibrating in the afternoon heat. The sky was bright blue and a gentle breeze kept the heat of the sun to a pleasant warmth. If I hadn't known the island was inhabited by Chameleons, I would have said it was paradise.

"Lady Tara, how many guests are expected again?" I said.

"Not sure, but there are usually about three hundred, including the newly evolved."

She looked at me and smiled in encouragement. I swallowed hard and tried to stay positive. At last, the wooded pathway opened into a small courtyard in front of a white three-storey building, which glowed brightly in the sunlight. We entered the Hotel Katarina and the porter lead us to the reception desk to sign in. The reception was silent and virtually empty apart from the porter and the receptionist. I guessed everyone was at the gathering of the Council and the presentation of the newly evolved. Tara had mentioned it would have started by the time we arrived on the island.

"Can you have the porter take our bags to our room, I wish to go directly to the Council meeting." Tara said.

"Certainly, m'am." The tall black man behind the counter replied. "Please follow me."

He led the way through a lounge and down a corridor to a large doorway, he opened the door and stepped back.

Tara nodded in thanks and we quietly entered into a large room. It was packed with Chameleons of all races and descriptions. It was interesting to see that not all Chameleons subscribed to the 'thin is beautiful' idea. In fact, some were very rounded indeed, but all of them radiated an unearthly beauty.

At the far end of the room nine Chameleons sat on ornate chairs in long, deep red, hooded robes, obviously, the Council of Nine. The room was very modern in style and the ornate, old-fashioned chairs stood out like thrones, which I guess was the point.

I glanced along the nine-seated Councillors and recognised Lamia immediately. I also noticed to the left side of the Council was a row of seven young adults dressed in long, plain black robes, the newly evolved. They stood on their own, without any of their sponsors. One of the newly evolved, a girl who had been stood in front of the Council when we arrived, walked back to join the others. My heart stopped as I recognised Joshua standing next to her looking brave but pale in his long black robe, his eyes were glued to the Council members.

"Joshua Marston." A deep voice called out.

Joshua stepped forward and stood with his back to the seated audience facing the Council.

"Joshua's sponsors are his parents; Lord Mathers Marston III and Lady Helena Marston." The deep voice announced as Joshua's parents stood up in the front row.

I looked around for the source of the voice but couldn't spot

Chameleon

the speaker.

"Do you, Mathers and Helena, proclaim that Joshua is ready to be tested?" The Councillor in the middle spoke. He was very handsome with long black hair and dark eyes rimmed with Kohl. He had the face of an Egyptian god, beautiful and terrifying. His voice was quiet yet filled the entire room.

"We do." They said in unison.

"Joshua Marston, at dawn tomorrow you will be taken to be tested on our laws, thereafter, if you are successful, you will be interred for ten days. Do you understand what is expected from you?"

"I do." Joshua's voice rang out with, surprisingly, no hint of nerves.

The Councillor nodded and Joshua returned to the line.

I glanced along the line and recognised Wil who had already been questioned according to his position in the line up..

"Xing Chang." The voice called.

Looking round and spotted where the deep voice came from, a man stood to the far right of the Council, next to the audience. He was a tall man with long dark hair and beard, he looked particularly scary.

"Who is that, Lady Tara?" I whispered and pointed at the large man.

"Oh, that's Grigori. He's in charge of the newly evolved during their testing."

"He certainly looks like a Grigori, very Russian. Was he named after Rasputin?" I joked quietly.

Tara turned to look me in the eye, "No, that is Grigori Yefimovich Rasputin."

"What?" I looked at him again and back at Tara, "Really? The Rasputin?"

Tara nodded grinning.

"Oh my God...I...I guess that's why they had problems killing him." I stared at the big man that was supposed to have been stabbed, poisoned, shot, beaten and drowned. He looked very much alive to me.

I looked back towards the Council. They had seemingly finished with the newly evolved and the Egyptian looking Councillor was now making the closing address.

"Who is the Chameleon that is talking now, Lady Tara?"

"That is Ramy, he is the Council Leader and one of the eldest Chameleons."

"Ramy? Is he Egyptian? He looks it." I wondered quietly.

"He is, yes. Ramy is short for Ramses II." She winked.

"Are you serious?" I looked between Ramy and Tara and back again as was becoming my habit of amazement. Was the entirety of influential historical figures in this room? My mind had trouble comprehending who I was looking at.

"Yes. He's the Egyptian Pharaoh Ramses II, also known as Ramses the Great or the Undead, due to a long lifespan. Now you know why." She spoke softly. "He evolved in 1319 BCE, I think. Daniel will know for sure, he knows all about the Council members, being the Council's Chief Archivist."

I looked back at Ramy, amazed that I was looking at an actual Pharaoh from ancient Egypt. He was giving the last instructions to the young Chameleons about to face their trials.

"You have one night left to prepare yourselves and learn what you can from your sponsors before dawn, when you will be collected by Grigori. If you pass the final test, you will be reunited with your sponsors at the Evolution Ball. If you fail, tonight will be the last time you will see your sponsors and loved ones. May you do well."

The audience stood and applauded as the ceremony came to an end. Quickly, I remembered I was about to come face to face with Joshua and he was going to be furious with me for coming here. I swallowed hard. My mouth had dried up completely and the butterflies had made a hostile take-over of my stomach. At first I couldn't see him, as all the sponsors surged forward, surrounding the newly evolved and proudly embracing them. I couldn't help but feel it was very strange, how happy these people were to put their loved ones through such a gruesome ordeal.

Tara and I stayed at the back of the room and waited. Tara didn't seem overly concerned about Joshua's reaction, but I was very nervous.

The crowd started to move past us, toward the exit to our right. My heart jumped as I spotted Joshua across the room. He was talking to his father and brother. He hadn't seen me and I was able to just watch him quietly for a moment. It had only been a week since I had last seen him, but it seemed much longer. And, although I obviously hadn't forgotten what he looked like, seeing him again reminded me of just how handsome he was, even while surrounded by the most beautiful people I have ever seen. A warmth spread through my body at the pleasure of seeing him again, the type of warmth that made the knees weak but the heart strong. I really had missed him a lot.

Unexpectedly, Helena stood before us, "Come with me, quickly." She headed out of the door with some urgency and we followed without a word. We followed her through the main front door and out across the gardens. We eventually found ourselves entering a luxury apartment building to the east of the main hotel building.

Helena closed the door behind us, then without a pause for breath, she rushed over to me and hugged me. "It is good to see you safe, Kate."

I hugged her back, worried by her concern...was Joshua in danger? "Thank you, is everything alright? Why the hurry?" I stepped back to look at her face.

"I rushed to get you here before Joshua saw you. I know my

son, and how he will react when he sees you. I didn't want it to happen in a room full of our kind. Also, I wanted to let you know there are rumours that a Chameleon has been murdered in England and the Council is investigating."

I gasped as an urgent feeling of alarm spread throughout my body making my skin prickle.

"Do they know who and where?" Tara asked.

"No, that's all we know. We have no idea when they found out about it or who told them." Helena took a deep breath, and turned her attention back to me. "Obviously, we are all very worried but I'm still glad we brought you here, at least you are protected as a claimed human. You see, if they find out who was involved then any loved one would be used as leverage, they can't do that if you're claimed.

"I knew this was a good idea." Tara said.

"I just hope Joshua thinks it is." I nibbled my lip nervously.

"Joshua is very worried about everything, especially you. Please forgive him if he says things in anger when he sees you, you must know that he really doesn't mean any of them." She smiled, trying to be a comfort. "They will be here soon, I suggest you both go and wait for them in the lounge." Helena nodded towards a room down the corridor.

Tara and I walked down the white, tiled hallway into the large living room which was furnished with plush, sand coloured sofas and bright rustic rugs that covered most of the white tiled floor. A large fireplace took up most of one wall and opposite it was a wall filled with huge French doors that looked out over a private beach and a turquoise ocean. It was truly a special place and I couldn't help but feel at home here, despite the danger around us.

Tara went to sit on one of the sofas but I was increasingly agitated and paced the floor, eventually walking over to the window. I stood looking out over the sea, not really seeing it.

Chameleon

What if he is so angry he sends me away? This sudden thought filled me with dismay. What if he has decided he no longer wants to see me, ever? The minutes ticked by unbearably slowly.

My heart lurched as I heard the door open and I began to worry my lip again. I simply couldn't turn to face the door, I was rooted to the spot.

"There you are, mother. We were wondering where you vanished to." Wil said.

"I had something to attend to, any more news?"

"Nothing we haven't already heard." Daniel replied.

"Well, that's good news then...we have visitors, by the way. They're in the lounge." Helena said.

I could hear Helena's footsteps as she walked on the tiles of the hallway towards us and the muted silence of the others behind her.

This was it, the moment I had been looking forward to with equal parts of dread and joy.

"Tara, you made it, Helena said you might come today." Daniel was first into the room and happily welcomed her.

"Hey, Tara." Wil sounded pleased at least.

There was suddenly a frosty silence in the room. I took a deep breath and turned around. All I could see was Joshua's pale, taught face looking at me. He looked both terrified and incredibly angry.

"Kate, how wonderful to have you safely here, my dear." Daniel crossed the room in seconds and hugged me. "Don't look so worried, he will get over it." He whispered quickly in my ear.

I couldn't answer, my mouth had become too dry and all I could manage was a small smile. My eyes never left Joshua, whose eyes were burning into me. Suddenly, the silence exploded with his angry voice but it wasn't directed at me.

"Tara, what the hell are you doing bringing her here?" Joshua said.

"You need to calm down, Joshua, I have a very good reason to bring her." Tara stood and her small frame seemed to grow, her red hair flaming. "You know very well, if anyone was after her or you or wanted to hurt you, by hurting her...it would have been a perfect time to get to her while you are under the ground and the rest of us are here, leaving her unprotected."

"But bringing her here? To surround her with hundreds of Chameleons who could take her life just for the fun of it? Just like that." He snapped his fingers. He looked incredulous at her.

"Do you really think I would bring her here with no plan in mind? You really don't know me well enough yet, do you?" Tara sighed.

"He has a point, Tara. This isn't exactly a place of restraint, you know." Wil said as he nodded at me with a cavalier smile and threw himself down on a chair.

Will Joshua ever forgive me or Tara for bringing me here, more importantly, was it a mistake? No, deep down I didn't think it was. Her idea made sense, even to me.

"What plan?" Growled Joshua, he had not moved even one inch further into the room.

"Kate is here as my claimed human."

Joshua's eyebrows rose.

"I have been training her for the last few days." Tara stared back at him in a challenge.

"That wouldn't work unless others had seen her with you before you got here. They will just think she's food." He spat the word out, but his rage seemed to be dissipating a bit. Perhaps he was beginning to see the validity of the plan.

"Others...have...seen me." My words were out before I knew it.

Joshua turned his full glare on me, "What?"

"I took her to Lumiere on Saturday as my claimed human, she met Lord Benjamin and even Councillor Lamia. She fitted

Chameleon

in very well." Tara looked rather proud of herself.

"You took her to Lumiere? Are you bloody crazy? That place is a killing house for humans. What the hell were you thinking?" He fumed.

"She has a right to know what she is involved in. Besides, I took her on Saturday lunch on purpose, I knew it would be almost empty and I was right. She did see a few things, but nothing she couldn't handle, and more importantly, Chameleons got to see her as my property. She is officially safe here now." Tara face broke into a triumphant smile.

"Tara is correct, Joshua. Kate is far more safe now than she has ever been." Daniel said.

Joshua looked at his father. "She may be safer now, but I still don't like it. She must not be left alone at anytime."

My anger grew. I felt like a child and all the grown ups were deciding my life, without including me in the conversation.

"Wait a minute." My voice shook but I was determined to say my piece, "This is my life and I do not need you to decide it for me."

"Kate," Joshua shook his head and lowered his voice, "you don't know what you are talking about."

I stepped forward into the middle of the room, remembered some of the scenes I'd witnessed at Lumiere and Sebastian's face as he killed me. "Actually, I do...I know quite a lot, including some minor details like the Bleeders...that you decided I didn't need to know about."

Joshua shot Tara a dark look and then looked back at me abashed. "Kate..."

"No, you listen to me now." I was shaking with anger, "I have seen some pretty brutal things recently, including my own and my mum's deaths and now I know about things far worse than that. I know that if someone puts the details together about the dead Chameleon, which is bound to happen, they will know about my murder and why I'm not dead. My life is already at risk and I have every right to be where I want, with as much safety as I can get, whether you like it or not." I took a deep breath, feeling better. "I'm going outside to sit on the beach just there in plain view and if you don't like it...well, that's just your tough luck because I'm here as Tara's claimed human and staying. So bloody well get used to it." I whirled round and marched through the French doors and ran down the stone path to the beach in front.

Breathless with surprise at my own anger, I sat on the low wall under the shade of a pine tree and looked out at the beach and the sea. My mind was buzzing as I remembered Joshua's astonished face and the quick image of Helena's amused look as I stormed out. I took several deep breaths and flipped off my sandals, resting my feet on the cool sand in the shade of the tree. I felt a bit better for being able to vent like that, but I was unsure of how Joshua would take it. He had never seen me that angry. It was our first real fight.

Several minutes later I heard the French door slide open behind me and close again. I didn't turn round and continued to look out over the lovely calming ocean.

"It is good to see you." Joshua's voice was quiet and subdued. He paused on the path leading to the beach.

"You too." I said. A rush of relief flowed though me, knowing he had missed me and was trying to be nice.

"May I sit with you?"

"I guess."

Joshua sat down on the low wall. "I'm sorry for how I acted back there."

"I should hope so." I said curtly. Then I turned to look at him and saw that he looked sad and worried. Not angry anymore, which disarmed me.

"I am glad you are here, really. I understand the plan now

Chameleon

and I see you're safer with my family. Tara was right to bring you, even if I didn't believe it at first. This way, no matter what happens, no Chameleon can touch you."

I searched his face for signs that he believed what he was saying and I could see it was true.

He glanced at my arm. "I haven't seen you since your cast was taken off, I guess it wasn't broken then." He said.

"No. It was, but then someone with superpowers healed it for me." I smiled at him ruefully.

"I did?" He looked down, touched my wrist gently and I felt the familiar tingle.

"I missed you." He said quickly.

"I missed you too."

"Do you still feel it...the buzz, I mean?" He asked.

"Oh yes, that never goes." I said as I looked down at the sand and pushed it around with my toes. "Are you nervous about tomorrow?"

"Not really...not anymore, there's nothing left to prepare for now. I just have to get on with it. The waiting is the hardest, I just want to get it over with."

"I'm sure we could keep ourselves occupied until dawn." I grinned shyly.

"Really?" He smiled suggestively and lifted an eyebrow.

I could hear my heart beat faster and I knew he could hear it too. "How is Wil?" I had to change to subject before my mind and heart gave my body ideas or visa versa.

"He's okay, I think he's more nervous about the testing than I am, but is now happily distracted by Tara's arrival."

"Really? I didn't think he was interested in her, neither does Tara." I blushed, as I knew I had said too much.

"Are you joking? He couldn't be more into her, isn't it obvious?" He looked at me in surprise.

"Apparently not. I can't say anymore though, Tara will kill

me." I said.

Joshua laughed, such a warm sensual sound that melted my bones.

"He's totally in love with her but thinks he's too young, so he keeps it to himself, well...himself and me. He's always talking about her when she's not around." Joshua released that full sexy smile.

I tried to breath but seemed to have forgotten how right at that moment. I could so easily get lost in that smile.

"We could end everyone's misery and play cupid or something." I said.

"We'd better do it quick. They only have until dawn." He became suddenly serious again. "That's if...."

"Do you think he will fail the testing?" I nibbled my lip in worry.

"No one really knows how any one of us will react after interment...that's the whole point of the testing."

"Then we'd better think of something quick." I said, hoping to lift his mood. It worked.

"Right. Why don't we do a 'Beatrice and Benedick'?" Joshua burst into laughter.

"A what?"

"It's just like Much Ado About Nothing, where the friends get Beatrice and Benedick together."

I laughed too, "But we don't have incriminating notes of their love for each other, like they had in the story. What can we use as evidence?"

"Well, at least our couple isn't in denial about their love for each other. They just don't realise the feelings are returned. All we have to do is get them to admit their feelings to each other and let nature take its course."

"That might work. I'll go and have a word with Tara, you can arrange things with Wil." I jumped up and picked up my shoes.

Joshua reached out and grabbed my arm. "Hold on, I've wanted to do this for the last week."

He stood and placed his hands on each side of my face and gently pulled me towards him. I closed my eyes as I felt his lips touch and the buzz mingled with my rising passion. I threw my arms around his neck and pulled his mouth down harder on mine. All too quickly, we were apart and breathless.

"Well, that's as yummy as I remember." I said.

"Could you look any more lustful?" Joshua laughed.

"That's your fault, that vibration...it...does things..." I blushed. "I'm off to find Tara." Before I lose the plot again, I thought to myself. "Where shall I send her?"

"Tell her to go to the north beach and I'll tell Wil to do the same." He reluctantly let go of my hand.

I walked back inside the villa to find Helena reading in the lounge alone.

"Ah...Kate...is everything alright, my dear?" She smiled as she laid her book on her lap.

"Oh yes, thanks." I grinned sheepishly, remembering the scene I'd made earlier. "Do you know where Tara is?"

"She went upstairs to your apartment. If you go through the kitchen, which is the first left, the apartment is up the stairs off the adjoining dining room."

"Thanks." I walked back into the hallway and followed her directions.

The apartment was very similar to the one below and had its own living area, with kitchen and dining room. I could hear Tara humming away to herself and followed the sound until I found her in one of the bedrooms, hanging up clothes.

"Hey." I said.

"Hi, how did things go with Joshua? Is he still being difficult?"

"Nah, he's fine. I think he just needed time to realise that your plan is a good one."

"I knew he would see sense, eventually." She smiled "Your room is that one opposite." She pointed across the hall, "Your bags are already in there. Check out the view." She turned back to hang the dress she held in her hands.

"I have a message for you." I sat on the giant bed.

"Oh?"

"From Wil."

That stopped her, "Really? What is it?" She sat down next to me on the bed.

"He wants you to meet him at the north beach." I smiled.

"Why?" She frowned.

"I dunno, but I did overhear him tell Joshua that he was going to ask you for a moonlight walk. Sounds very romantic to me." It was just a small lie. No harm done, I told myself.

She looked stunned, then frowned again. "Are you sure?"

"Yup, I think he wants to spend some time with you tonight before the testing begins. Looks like this is your chance."

Her face showed surprise, hope and amazement, the warring emotions battled for supremacy. Hope won. "Oh...I..."

"Don't tell me you're nervous now? And at your age." I burst into laughter.

Tara laughed, "Gods, what am I going to wear?"

"You cliché." I rolled my eyes.

"Sorry, but you know what I mean."

"Look, he doesn't know that you know, if you know what I mean. So try something casual."

"Wait, the North beach is nudist. So I'll just go in a towel, pretending I'm just out for a swim." Tara's eyes suddenly took on a wicked gleam.

I swallowed hard. "Oh my, it's a nudist beach?" Joshua had kept that quiet, I wondered if he even knew that. "Are you serious about the towel?"

"Hell yeah. Don't worry, Kate...you will find that Chameleons are far less inhibited about their bodies than humans are." Tara began to get undressed.

"Well, that would be because you're all so damned perfect, I guess."

"Could be." Tara vanished into the bathroom.

"I'll see you later, have fun." I called through the door.

I thought ruefully that Wil didn't know what he was in for and, admittedly, I was also a little bit jealous about the ease of their fledgling relationship. With a sigh, I walked across the hall into my room. The room was light and airy and the view really was spectacular from the balcony. I walked over to the railing and looked out over the ocean. I closed my eyes and breathed in the salty air.

I turned to leave and saw a flash of a blue towel go past my doorway and I knew Tara was on her way to meet Wil. I thought briefly of them together, it must be nice to be so physically confident and not have to worry about shocking people.

Not quite as brave as Tara, I decided to change into my bikini, wrapped a sarong around my waist and headed downstairs, with the intention of going for a swim in the private cove, once I'd had a chance to speak to Daniel. Walking back through the kitchen I could hear voices deep in serious conversation in the living room. Hesitant to disturb them, I decided to have a look for something to eat as a delaying tactic. I opened the fridge wondering if there would be any food in there or not, seeing as the Marstons didn't need it.

To my surprise, the fridge was fully stocked to the point of brimming over. Obviously, Helena had planned ahead. The very thought that she had kindly bought food just for me made me feel warm with gratitude, it was nice to belong to a bigger family than just mum and I, for a change. Thinking of mum made me realise that I missed her already and hadn't phoned her yet. I

Edain Duguay

quickly picked up the receiver in the kitchen and dialled home to calm her fears.

I hung up knowing I'd made mum happier and returned to my search for food. I helped myself to a big bowl of salad with cold meat and cheese and poured myself a large glass of OJ. Sitting at the breakfast bar, I ate my dinner in peace and quiet, which made a nice change from the last few days.

I had almost finished when I heard the apartment door close and voices heading to the kitchen.

"Oh good, glad to see you found some food, my dear." Helena gently touched me on the shoulder as she walked by and sat on one of the kitchen stools next to me. I realised that I felt no buzz when Helena touched me, nothing at all. This thought distracted me for a moment and I quickly remembered what she had said to me.

"Yes, the food is great. Thanks for stocking up for me. I'd wondered about food, but obviously shouldn't have." I smiled as I munched on happily.

"You're most welcome, my dear. Truthfully, I'm still so used to getting food in for the boys, I haven't yet got out of the habit." She smiled warmly, "Talking of the boys, have you seen them or Tara?"

"Joshua went to talk to Wil and Tara went for a swim."

"Ah..." She said.

Just then, Daniel came into the kitchen and leaned against the work surface nearby. "How are you enjoying your stay so far?"

"It's lovely, thanks. It's very kind of you both to bring me out here and pay for me." I said.

"You are most welcome, Kate. It's good for Joshua to share things with someone his own age and as a trusted human you will get to share in many things." Daniel smiled mischievously.

I looked at him enquiringly but he only smiled back.

Now was a good time to get a few answers, I decided. I turned to Daniel. "May I ask a couple of questions?"

"Certainly, Kate. Proceed." He said.

"Could you tell me who the Council of Nine are? I know about Ramy and Grigori...." I said and sat back on the stool.

"Well, Grigori is not actually part of the Council, he just works for them. He can be a nasty piece of work, I suggest you stay away from him as much as possible. Do you know what a Bleeder is?"

I swallowed hard and I nodded. I simply could not hide my deep feeling of revulsion.

"I see you do, Grigori is a Bleeder."

I fought back a shudder.

"And Ramy...what is he?"

"He is a Feeder."

"What about the others? Who and what are they?" I felt an urgent need to know everything about them.

"The Council is made up of four males and five females. The males are: Ramy, Macc Óc...he is Irish and a Feeder. Vetala is from India and is a Bleeder, and then there is Marduk who is Babylonian and a Hippie like us. The females are: Lamia, whom you've met, I understand. She is from Macedonian and is a Feeder. Empusa who is also from Greece and a Feeder; Lamia and Empusa are very close friends. The other Feeder is Chi who is from Colombia in South America. Loo, another Bleeder, is from the Caribbean and finally Lilitu from Mesopotamia, who is a Hippie. She is the eldest of our present Council members."

"I know from school that Mesopotamia hasn't been around for a very long time. So how old are we talking?" I said.

"We believe Lilitu dates back to 4000 BCE, but it's hard to pin down her evolved date. The rest are anywhere between 3500 to 800 years old, approximately. There is no date of when Vetala evolved, he just always seems to have been around, according to

Hindu writings. So he could possibly be older than Lilitu."

"So compared to them, you're all very young?" I looked at both Helena and Daniel.

"Indeed." Daniel said.

"Absolutely." Helena said, "We are mere children to many Chameleons."

"There are many here on the island much, much older than us." Daniel said.

While this news sunk in, I stood and took my now empty plate to the sink and wash it along with my glass and cutlery.

"I meant to ask, you seemed to have gotten your cast off quickly. Was it not as badly injured as they thought?" Helena said.

"Well, the doctor couldn't understand how it had healed so fast, so she presumed it hadn't been as bad as they had first thought, perhaps just a shadow on the original x-ray."

"You don't think that is so?" Daniel asked.

"No. I know exactly why it healed. Joshua healed it."

"Joshua did that?" Daniel was amazed.

"Yes. When he visited me, the night I came home from hospital. He was just trying to reduce the pain by healing my ribs, which he did. It was amazing to see the bruises shrink. But I guess he healed me a bit too much and the wrist mended as well."

Daniel looked very concerned, "That was dangerous. The boy must learn some discretion."

"He tried not to heal me so much that it would gain attention and well, the doctor explained it away, which was lucky for us."

"Yes, very lucky. He needs to be more careful." Helena sounded worried.

I nodded in agreement. I looked from one to the other, worried that I had gotten Joshua in trouble. Perhaps I shouldn't

Chameleon

have told them. "From what I understand, Joshua has an unusual gift for a Chameleon, is that right?" I asked.

Daniel nodded, "Yes, no other Chameleon has demonstrated any healing power, as far as we know. There are some who can sense things like Moira, who can sense lies and Empusa who can tell where the newly evolved are. However, these are rare cases and nothing as 'hands on' and direct as the power Joshua has. He needs to be more discrete when using it though, it may draw unwanted attention to him from quarters that don't have his best interests in mind."

"You mean governments and the military?" I said.

"No, I'm talking about certain factions within the Chameleons, those who don't like the hold the Council has over us and want to be more free."

"Like Jonas' group that Sebastian belonged to?" I said. Worry building inside me again.

"Yes. Joshua could be a very useful tool in a battle between Chameleons. To have a Chameleon that could heal human troops, making them a renewable resource, would be a huge advantage."

"Should we be talking about this? I mean, can't other Chameleons hear us?"

"We are relatively safe here. One of our laws dictates that when we gather in a large group, over-hearing is not allowed and is punishable by death. We have to have some privacy. Anyone caught using information they could only have gotten by over-hearing, disappear very quickly. We have learnt over the years to block out unwanted sounds and it is almost second nature during our gatherings." Daniel said.

"Well, that's a relief because I find it a bit creepy." Talking about the world of the Chameleons made me realise just how truly different I was from them.

"Do you find us very odd, Kate?" Helena asked.

"Odd? Not really. Some of you are very scary and not nice, others seem nice but I wouldn't want to upset them either, if you know what I mean." I laughed nervously, "Your family however, seem almost normal."

"You mean almost human." Joshua's voice interrupted from behind me.

I spun round to find him standing just a couple of inches behind me. I hadn't heard him approach.

"Yes, almost...human." I said.

Moonlight

There was a slightly awkward pause and I tried to think of something to say. "I was just about to go for a swim, do you want to join me?" I said.

"Sure, I'll be with you in a moment." He said.

In a blur, he vanished and was back before I could count to three. He wore swim shorts and an open shirt and was bare footed. Together, we walked out of the Villa and down the pathway to the small private beach.

We stopped a few feet from the sea, I untied my sarong and let it drop to the sand.

Joshua was about to remove his shirt when he saw what I was wearing and stopped mid movement.

"It's rude to stare." I said shyly, not really knowing what to do with my hands.

"Yes, it is, very, and I would never do something like that." He said with a naughty smile, while continuing to stare.

"Stop it." I blushed.

He removed his shirt and it was the third time I'd seen him with this small amount of clothing on and must say that I enjoyed the view immensely. His broad muscular shoulders, rolled down to his trim waist creating a wonderful v-shape. I thought it best to make conversation so I didn't stand there with my mouth open, drooling.

"How come Chameleons are so pale, if they can control everything their bodies do? Surely, it would be safer to be a normal human colour wouldn't it?" I asked.

"We do have control over the colour of our skin and can darken it at will but the problem comes when we need to feed, at which time we go pale again. Rather than always going pale, then dark, then pale again, it seems easier to stay pale and conserve our energy. Humans just presume we aren't sun worshippers and don't even question it." He stretched out his hand towards me, "Now, how about that swim?"

We walked hand in hand down towards the water in the golden early evening light. The sand felt warm beneath my feet and the water was warmer still and very calm. We both dove in and swam further out. I surfaced and looked back at our villa. The building was three floors high and full of glass doors and windows that faced out towards the sea. The bright white colour of the building had mellowed into a cream colour, like butter, as the sun began to head west. Although I could see other buildings on each side of ours, they also had their own beaches and private areas.

Joshua and I swam around and finally ended up in each other's arms in the water. It felt strange to feel so much of his flesh against mine again. Warm memories of our time at the waterfall flooded back to me. The wonderful feeling of the vibration from his energy tingling all over me had become very exciting. Without warning, a sad pain seemed to grow in my chest. I couldn't bare the thought of him failing the test and not having him in my life after today, I held Joshua against me closely, not wanting to let go. We were in enough shallow water to be able put our feet down on the seabed and before long I found myself kissing him with long needy kisses that could easily lead to something else. Something, which for once, I was ready to give to him.

Chameleon

Joshua broke away from the kiss first, "We really need to be more careful."

"Why? Is someone watching?" I looked around nervously. I thought the beach was supposed to be private.

He laughed, "No, Chameleons have affairs with the claimed humans all the time, it's almost expected. No one will look at us twice. No, I mean when we kiss...like...that. I still have to be very careful around you, I could lose control and end up doing what Wil did to Claire...I couldn't live with that."

I saw true fear in his eyes, "I trust you. I know you wouldn't drain me." I said confidently. I couldn't help but feel sorry for him, having seen what his brother went through he must be terrified of making the same mistake.

"Do you? I'm not so sure." He caressed my face with his wet hand, "I often wonder what it would be like to...give in...."

"Maybe when this is all over, we can give it a try?" I blushed.

"Perhaps, I suppose we'll see how my control is after the testing."

I saw his mood darken and wanted to stop him from thinking about it. "Let's get out now. It's starting to get a little chilly." I could feel goosebumps rising on my skin.

"Okay...sorry. I forget you need to stay warm."

We waded back to shore, grabbed our clothes and started to head back to the house. Joshua paused as we got on the stone path leading back.

"Stay here, I'll be back in just a moment." He became a blur again as he rushed into the house.

I turned around and sat under the same tree I'd sat under earlier that day, only now I was looking out over the sea towards the setting sun. There was a definite chill in the air, I began to rub my arms to keep warm and contemplated going inside for my hoodie. A soft kiss landed on my bare shoulder and I felt a warm blanket being wrapped around me.

"Oh, thank you." I said.

"You're very welcome." Joshua replied as he came down to my level and took my hand.

"Where are we going?"

"Not far."

Following him along the small beach, I noticed he had a bag over his shoulder and wondered what he was up to. Finally, we came to a small area of sand with a rock wall at its back and a pre-dug fire pit that was set for a fire. Joshua pulled out another blanket and laid it on the sand between the rock wall and the fire pit.

"I thought you might like to watch the sun go down with me." He smiled but there was an unmistakable sadness in his eyes.

Of course, this might be his last sunset. The thought was too much to bear, so I shut it out and tried really hard to concentrate on the here and now. "What a nice idea." I sat on the blanket still wrapped in the other one. The air was definitely getting colder now that the light had begun to fade.

Joshua put the bag to one side and sat beside me with his arm around me. I could just feel the muted vibration through the blanket. I looked out over the ocean and saw that the sun was almost touching the horizon. We both sat quietly, watching it sinking lower and lower, while the sky turned shades of red, pink, yellow, orange and gold.

"It's beautiful here." I leant my head on his shoulder. Despite the coming horror, in this very moment, I was blissfully happy.

"Not as beautiful as you." Joshua whispered and kissed me on the lips.

Joy surged trough me. My heart missed a beat and raced. I could feel my blood stir at his touch and I relaxed, letting it wash over me. Eventually, we broke from the kiss. I looked into his perfectly blue eyes and scanned his face, taking in all the details. I knew this would be the last time I would see him for eleven days, if he passed the testing. The last time ever, if he didn't. The thought came again unbidden and with it came a wave of despair. Joshua saw my stricken expression and stroked my cheek gently.

"Don't think about it, Kate. Just be here with me, now."

"I'm trying." I said, my voice was no more than a whisper. I cleared my throat giving me a second to collect my thoughts.

I turned back towards the setting sun, trying not to cry. We sat watching the sky darken as the sun, in its inevitable descent, dipped below the horizon. Watching it slide from view left us both quiet and contemplative, it didn't matter though, there was no need for words.

Eventually, all that was left of the sun was a thin slice of violet above the ocean. Joshua rose and lit the fire, which quickly roared into life, since the wood was so dry from the heat of the day. He sat back down next to me and began to empty the bag onto the blanket. He pulled out a small book, an envelope, a dark coloured box, some fruit and a bottle of juice.

"I thought you might get hungry or thirsty." He said.

"Thanks. What are the other things?"

"I have been doing some thinking about you."

"Oh?" My stomach flipped in fear, a terrible feeling of 'the end' brewing inside me. Why would he make me stay away from him this time? I thought desperately, as I swallowed hard and silently prayed I was wrong.

"I want you to have these." He gestured to the three things on the blanket, "The small book is for you to write in, it's a journal. Somewhere to write about us over the next few days or indeed after that if need be, so that one day you can read it again...and...remember us..."

"Joshua...I..." My words died in my throat, I couldn't bear it.

His eyes showed the exact same agony that I was feeling.

He held up a hand, "Please let me finish...it's hard enough." He picked up the envelope, "This is for you, if...if...things don't go to plan. I want you to open it when you get back home. Do you promise me that you will not open it until then?" His face looked solemn and entirely serious.

I nodded unable to stop the tears from welling in my eyes and they began to fall.

He reached over and stroked my tear away gently, "Know that you're in my heart now, Kate. Please remember that, no matter what happens."

"Joshua, please..."

"I want you to have this as well." He held out his hand with the dark coloured rectangle box on it.

I looked from him to the box and back again. Nervously, I reached out my hand and took the box, my hand shaking all the while. It looked like the type of box used for jewellery. I carefully tried to open the box, but it was a little stiff. The hinge gave suddenly and it snapped open and I gasped at the contents. Inside the box was a silver chain with a large piece of amber held in two silver hands, silver earrings to match and the most beautiful silver ring with silver palms overlapping each other, holding another matching piece of beautiful amber. They were exquisite in their detail.

"Oh my God, they're so beautiful." I was staggered. I looked up at him in amazement, "These are lovely but must be worth a fortune. I can't accept them." I became horrified at the thought of taking such a huge gift.

"Too late, they're yours." He smiled, "They belonged to my Grandmother Isabella, my father's mother. My Grandfather gave them to her as an engagement present." He looked at me hopefully.

My heart skipped several beats and then thumped hard against my ribcage.

Chameleon

"I know this is sudden and we've not known each other very long, but meeting you now, before my testing, is the hardest thing. No matter how things go, I wanted you to know how I feel about you. So I'm giving these to you...with the same intent my Grandfather had...you can give me your answer in eleven days."

"Oh my God, Joshua." I threw my arms around him and sobbed into his neck.

He held me in his arms, "It was supposed to make you happy."

"I am happy." I sniffed and pulled back, "Happy and sad." I looked at his lovely face so close to mine. "Thank you." I breathed. A huge joy spread in my heart, pushing away the terrible fear.

"You can thank me with your answer, the next time I see you." He said as he held me close.

Please, please let him come back to me, my mind and heart silently begged the universe.

We lay on the blanket in each other's arms and watched the full moon rise in the sky. The beautiful orb shined moonlight down on us, turning everything to a blue/grey colour. The ocean looked mysteriously deep and black, with silver reflections I noticed as I thought about the gifts and the days ahead. A thought struck me all of a sudden, "How did you know I would be here, for you to give these things to me?" I laid my hand on his chest as my head rested on his shoulder and I looked out to the stars.

"I was going to give them to Tara, to pass onto you, if... " His voice trailed off.

"And when you returned home to me? What would you have done then?" I couldn't help asking. Was it something he was doing only because he didn't think he'd see me again? I wondered.

"The amber would still be yours and the offer would still have been made." He held me closer.

I knew now, that he had planned to do this one way or another. Only then did it dawn on me that he absolutely and utterly, felt the same way about me as I did him. A strange contented warmth spread through me, radiating from my heart out to every extremity of me. I sighed softly and relaxed. At last, I was home. We talked well into the night and the early hours, of anything and everything, trying to fill the huge void that we could both feel coming. We wanted to fill our minds and hearts with each other, before we were forced apart, again. At some point, I drifted off to sleep securely held in his arms. I could feel his warmth and the gentle buzz against me, a deep calmness came over me as I happily drifted off.

I could feel my back was stiff, probably from falling asleep in Joshua's arms and I tried to re-position myself. I reached for Joshua and found nothing. My eyes shot open.

I was in my room at the apartment.

Alone.

Worst of all, there was bright sunshine coming in through the open doorway onto my balcony. It was a long way past dawn and Joshua had already left for his testing. Deep down, I knew he'd brought me back to my bed and had left quietly. An overwhelming feeling of loss spread through me and I quietly sobbed into my pillow for what seemed like hours.

I couldn't help feeling it was incredibly unfair that having found each other, he had to be taken away from me with no way of me knowing what was happening to him nor if I would ever see him again. I cried until I could cry no more. I lay with my eyes closed against the world and reality, wishing it was all a dream and I would wake up at home and everything would be back to normal and Joshua would be human.

I opened my eyes and looked out towards the balcony. I no-

Chameleon

ticed that on the small table, by the bed, lay my three gifts. I lay there for a very long time looking at them, listening to the waves on the shore below. I reached for the book, it's covering of brown leather was soft to the touch and it was obviously hand made. I opened it, turned the flyleaf over to see the first page of creamy white paper had an inscription on it. It was a message from Joshua.

> You hold my heart in your hands.
> Keep it safe, even if I no longer can.
> When you learn to hate me,
> Remember, I will always love you.

The tears ran down my face and splashed onto the page, "Oh Joshua. Are you so sure you'll not be coming back?" I wondered quietly. I clutched the book to my chest and lay looking up at the ceiling, unable to stop the tears as I gasped for breath. A big hole opened up inside me, sending razor blade shards outwards tearing at my heart. I gritted my teeth, determined not to let the sorrow overwhelm me.

Resolutely, I placed the book back on the small table and picked up the velvet case, wiping my tears away I held it against my heart almost like I was trying to fill the empty hollow inside. I climbed out of bed and carried the case with me out onto the balcony. I leant against the wooden railing and looked out to the ocean. It was a perfect blue sea, under a perfect blue sky but the joy and beauty of it didn't reach my heart. I looked down at the case and slowly opened it, once again I was amazed by the beauty of the pieces. The craftsmanship was obvious in the details on the silver hands and the warm, deep glow of the amber was mesmerizing. It looked almost like the hands were holding the Sun.

I touched them gently, reverently, with my fingertips. Remembering their age and their meaning...their meaning then...and now. To spend the rest of my life with Joshua was something that I had only dreamt about but now it was possible if, no, when, he made it to the ball. I decided not to think that he wouldn't. I had to believe he would survive, otherwise all this was pointless. I pushed these ugly thoughts from my mind with great effort. Instead, I sat on one of the balcony chairs and watched the ocean. My mind was lost in the blueness and I was grateful for the peace it brought, if only for a moment.

I jumped when I suddenly felt a hand on my shoulder.

"How are you doing, Kate?" Tara asked as she walked around my chair and sat in the other one.

"Okay, I guess. How about you?" I glanced up at her. She looked perfect as always but there was fear in her eyes.

"Okay, too."

We sat in silence for a while both looking out at the ocean and embracing its hypnotic effect.

I looked at her again, noticing the tightness of her mouth and the corner of her eyes, revealing her worry about Wil. "How did the meeting with Wil go?" I asked, watching her face for a reaction.

Her face suddenly came alive and exploded into a huge smile, "Very well, actually. We are officially courting." She winked at me.

I laughed and she looked surprised, "Courting? Who still uses that word, you mean dating...and that's great." I felt really happy for her.

"Thank you. Of course, we saw through your plan, as soon as we got talking but we decided to forgive you both." She winked.

"Very decent of you." I said.

"How was your evening?"

"Great and horrible...happy and sad."

"Understandable, you've never been through this before. The

boys will be fine, I am sure of it." Her voiced sounded like she was trying to convince herself as well as me.

"They had better be, or I will kill them." A sudden rage rose in me.

"Easy, Kate." Tara said, "You know it's somewhat futile to kill something that is already dead, right?" Tara half laughed and then sighed, realising what she had said.

A distraught silence fell between us, awkward and cold, its tendrils reached out to hold us both in its grasp.

"What's that you're clutching?" Tara voice broke the spell.

"Ah...this is...well...see for yourself." I passed the velvet case over to her.

Tara snapped open the lid and gasped, "Oh, they are lovely." She looked across at me, "You must have had quite a night." She wiggled her eyebrows suggestively.

"Nothing like that, you're so bad." I blushed but I was not totally shocked at what she implied, if I were honest with myself I would have wished for it too. "It's an engagement gift from Joshua...his way of asking me to be his wife."

"My goodness, he really did it? He told me before we left home, that you were all he wanted, but...well, good for him...and you...I think. Did you say yes?" She looked at me while touching the pieces just as I had, gently and with respect.

"I'm to give him his answer at the Evolution Ball."

"That's kind of romantic, if one ignores the whole interment issue and the possible human massacre at the end and...perhaps...disappearing Chameleons. Well, Joshua certainly has a flare for the dramatic, doesn't he?"

I must have looked horrified.

"Come on, you have to admit it is not your usual proposal, now is it?" She grinned.

"I guess not..." I said.

"Don't write him off yet. He is strong, they both are and the testing is easier than you think."

I hoped she was right but I couldn't help thinking that Tara was saying that to make me feel better, which it didn't.

I spent the next few days in a haze, functioning on automatic pilot. After the first terrible night of horrific nightmares involving being buried alive, I had no more dreams at all and very little sleep. I just could not switch off my brain, which of course made me very moody and quick to anger. I avoided Joshua's family as much as I could and sat under, what I now considered my tree, or on my balcony reading various books from the villa. At first nothing would go in, I just kept reading the same lines over and over again. After a few days, I became engrossed in any reading material I could find, from travel brochures to histories about the local areas. The reading temporarily distracted my battered mind and kept the dark thoughts at bay.

Chameleon

Recognition

Saturday, five days before the Evolution Ball, the Council of Nine held a party for all Chameleons present. Claimed humans were expected to attend their Chameleons. Tara had directed me on my tasks for the evening, which were pretty simple. I would ensure I was at her side all evening and I would be expected to allow others to 'taste' me without flinching. The family had decided it was prudent to go, firstly because it was expected and being absent would arouse suspicion, which was the last thing we needed and secondly, we could listen to gossip to see if any more had been learnt about the death of Sebastian.

The four of us, Daniel, Helena, Tara and I, walking behind at a respectful distance, came into the room where the party had already started. The room was full of Chameleons and seemed to be like any other party, with loud music and bright lights and people dancing on the dance floor at one end of the room. At the other end, the quieter folks sat at tables and had more intimate gatherings with friends. The only indication to show that it wasn't a normal party was the lack of buffet food, a staple for every human party but not necessary for a Chameleon one, although there were drinks aplenty. There was also a small table with bottled water by the entrance, presumably for the claimed humans to use.

As instructed, I remained slightly behind Tara, flanked by

Daniel and Helena. Several times they stopped briefly to speak to Chameleons they knew. I recognised at least one of them.

"Lord Benjamin." Tara said as she paused by his table, "Lady Ella, how lovely to see you again."

"Lady Tara, what a pleasure, and Lord and Lady Marston, how wonderful to see you all again." Ella said.

Lady Ella was a petite woman, she had the exotic beauty of a gypsy with jet-black hair and dark eyes. She sprang to her feet to welcome everyone without even giving me a glance. Lord Benjamin rose more sedately and walked around the table to greet us. His eyes never left me, even though he spoke to Tara. My skin crawled it felt like his eyes were devouring me, or at the very least undressing me.

"May I?" He said to Tara without taking his eyes from me.

Without waiting for an answer, he stepped closer and I raised my hand for him. He smiled a sly smile and held my hand gently in his. He didn't taste me right then but instead raised my hands to his lips and I felt that familiar strange pull as he did, I could feel my energy leaving me, but I was unable to move or stop looking into his eyes. All I could see was the look of lust on his face, lust for my energy or my body or both.

"Benjamin, it has been a long time." Daniel voice broke the spell.

Lord Benjamin reluctantly let me go and turned to speak to Daniel.

I saw Helena's hand gripped tightly into a fist at her side. Tara must have spotted it too as she grabbed Helena's arm.

"Let the men talk, Helena. I want to find Moira." Tara whisked us away from Lord Benjamin and Daniel, into the throng of Chameleons.

I had become a little light headed from the small draining and the room spun just a little, as if I'd skipped a couple of meals. I looked around me and realised I was surrounded by killers, hundreds of killers of my kind, of humans. I swallowed hard, trying to regain my composure, just as Tara stopped to talk to a very handsome, tall man.

"Lord Michael Conway, it's good to see you again. How are you?" Tara smiled at the man and stood on her tiptoes to hug him around the neck. She glanced at me and winked.

"I'm very well, Tara. You're looking as gorgeous as ever." The man smiled down at her.

His voice was gentle and soft. He had a Nordic look with long blond hair that was tied back. He was obviously muscular and well proportioned; you could see his chest muscles move under his silk shirt. He also had kind, soft blue eyes. He made me feel safe and I liked him on instinct.

So this was Michael, her ex, I looked at him with new eyes. The red haired Tara and this blond Adonis made a stunning couple. I could see why she was attracted to him. Michael looked at me.

"And whom, may I ask, is this, Tara?" He enquired.

I was amazed, no other Chameleon had ever enquired about me directly.

"This is Kate, my assistant." She smiled sweetly.

"Well, I never thought I would see the day when the lovely Tara had a claimed human." He was astonished and scrutinized me more closely.

"Things change, Michael." Tara managed to keep the same smile on her face.

"Not that much, they don't. I'm sure you'll tell me all about it at some point." He leaned over and hugged her again, "We must get together and talk about that tithe farm in County Durham sometime. Can I come over to see you at your villa later tonight?" He stood up, letting go of her.

I could tell that Tara was tense, her body language had changed the moment he had mentioned the farm, she recovered herself quickly though.

"Of course, Michael. That would be lovely." Tara said quickly, the smile glued to her face.

Anyone that didn't know her would not have spotted it, but I did. I was burning with curiosity but I knew I would have to wait until later, when we could talk more freely.

"Later, then." Michael nodded goodbye, moved through the crowd and quickly disappeared out of sight.

Tara didn't look back at him, but continued through the crowd, heading towards the far wall. She had spotted someone she obviously wanted to talk to and hurriedly walked over to a group who were chatting by the wall. "Moira." Tara called.

A willowy woman with long red hair, turned round and smiled. Although slimmer than Tara and a little taller, they could have been sisters. She had the same red hair and green eyes as Tara, except Moira had freckles on her beautiful face. She obviously loved them or she would have simply made them go away, how interesting, I thought. Her smile was warm and friendly and she instantly closed the gap between her and Tara, throwing her arms around her friend.

"Tara, it has been too long." Moira said in a lovely husky voice.

"Oh, it is good to see you, Moira." Tara hugged her back. "We have so much to catch up on."

"We do, we do." Moira exclaimed.

"Helena, how nice to see you again." Moira smiled and extended her hand.

"And you, Moira." Helena smiled warmly and shook it.

"And who is this, Tara?" Moira wondered as she looked at me.

"This is Kate, my assistant."

"Of course it is." Moira said as she winked at me.

She took my hand as if to taste me, held it for a moment, but

Chameleon

didn't drain me, not even a little bit. She smiled sweetly and let go of my hand.

Tara laughed and began speaking to Moira in depth about the newly evolved, who they were and where they came from. She asked for the sponsors to be pointed out. Moira discreetly showed Tara the sponsors of each. Suddenly, Tara froze and I saw her take a deep breath as she looked across the room at a pair of the sponsors. Again, she quickly recovered her composure.

"Moira, that's Izzy and Marcus. You're sure they are sponsors?" Tara's voice sounded shocked.

"Yes, they are Carlos Stanza's sponsors and Clara and Jonas are Xing Chang's sponsors." Moira's replied.

I knew those names sounded familiar but couldn't place them just at that moment; my mind was still fuzzy from the earlier drain. Without another word, Tara headed towards the couple with Moira, Helena and I following behind.

"Izzy, Marcus. It has been a long time." Tara voice remained normal and cheerful but underneath, you could hear the tightness. Something was not right.

Izzy smiled but her beautiful face did not light up, her lovely long blond hair framed her face and her blue eyes were distant and held no warmth when they looked at Tara. They were cold, like ice. She looked strangely familiar. Had I met her before? I wondered. Marcus had his back to us and he was a mountain of a man. He turned around at the mention of his name and smiled down at Tara.

"Well, now Tara...long time, no see." His smile, like Izzy's, didn't reach his eyes.

Marcus was handsome in a feral kind of way, like a lion watching its prey. His long dark, thick hair had been tied back in a pony tail, his face angular and pointy, his eyes were almost black and very hard to read.

"Yes, it has been a while, hasn't it, Marcus? I hear you are sponsoring one of the newly evolved this year?" Tara enquired.

They looked at each other briefly as if sharing a thought, "Yes, Carlos. Sebastian and I came across him in Peru a few months ago, just as he was evolving." Izzy replied.

"Lucky for him, to have someone around to be with at his evolution, I mean." Tara smiled sweetly.

My heart flipped at the mention of Sebastian. I held my face very still to keep from betraying the turmoil that suddenly flooded me. I remembered then why their names were familiar, Izzy and Marcus were part of the group from Oxford, the ones responsible for the seven deaths...make that eight...including mine. My heart must have beat loudly in my chest as Izzy's eyes flicked to me briefly. She seemed to dismiss me then and her eyes returned to Tara.

"May I?" Izzy said not expecting nor wanting an answer.

Tara had no choice but to allow it.

I held out my hand calmly but in my mind I wanted to scream and run far, far away from these monsters. She took my hand and began to drain me, I could feel a prickle that quickly turned to burning as she glared at me. I had to bite my tongue not to scream out. I refused to give in and glared back at her. I concentrated on creating a barrier between the pain and me and it helped, just a little.

"Where are Jonas and Sebastian? It would be nice to catch up with them too." Tara asked. Her distraction worked brilliantly, Izzy let go of my arm instantly and turned her attention back to Tara.

I could see Helena watching me out of the corner of her eye.

"Jonas is here, but Sebastian is not. He was supposed to meet us in Oxford after he went...on an errand...but he never returned, which is most unusual for him. We have spoken to the Council about it and Empusa says she can't sense him. We be-

Chameleon

lieve he has been killed." The venom was clear in her voice.

I held my composure and gritted my teeth.

"Dead? Are you serious? But who? And how? Perhaps he has just got delayed." Tara played her part well.

"He is not delayed. Empusa was definite that she could no longer feel him, which means only one thing."

"I am sorry to hear that." Tara faked shock, very convincingly.

"Are you?" Marcus asked.

"Of course." Tara faked surprise, "Sebastian and I may not have agreed on many things, but I would not see him dead. Any idea who is responsible? Was it the government or a foreign power?"

"We have an idea who it was. The murderer is someone who does not take our rules seriously and that will be his down fall." Izzy hissed angrily, loud enough for those nearby to hear.

My heart sank, they knew...they knew everything. Oh my God. Izzy's head snapped round to stare at me again, hate filled her eyes. I presumed she could hear my panic, smell my fear. I held my place with the blank expression, but the urge to flee was so intense that I saw myself doing it in my mind's eye, even though I was frozen to the spot.

"You think it's one of us? A Chameleon? My God. Who would be so suicidal?" Tara's amazement was completely believable.

"Yes, we do. Hence the Council is investigating." Marcus replied, looking back at Tara with a smug expression.

"Izzy, you said 'his' downfall, you know who it is?" Helena asked, her face showed a perfect mask of calm.

"We know his name, Lady Marston, but we have been forbidden to speak of it until the Council has investigated our testimony and decided on the best course of action."

"I see." Helena replied, voice utterly calm. She was very much in control, unlike me. My mind was screaming.

Edain Duguay

"If that is the case, I must find Jonas to offer my sympathies and see if I can help in anyway. I'm sure I will see you both again later." Tara turned without waiting for a reply and walked to the quieter end of the room.

As I walked past, I heard Izzy spit out 'Oh, no doubt you will, Hippy." I refused to look at her again and followed Tara and the others as they moved away. My head was spinning with all the new information. They knew about Joshua, and they had already engaged the Council. How did they know?

Once we were away from the loud music, we all stood, shocked, trying to take in the latest information without showing it had affected us. Instantly, from across the room, Daniel was by Helena's side. He could tell in a second that something had happened but could say nothing. In a half dazed state, I glanced out over the hundreds of Chameleons gathered in one room. My mind was so glazed by the news that my eyes were not really seeing the Chameleons before me, almost like I was in a dream. A face stood out in the crowd, someone I recognised. I blinked several times, not believing what I was seeing and then his face vanished into the crowd. I searched around and tilted my head one way and then the another to catch another glimpse. I had to be sure.

"Kate, what is it? You look like you've seen a ghost." Tara asked as she moved to my side.

"I thought I saw...someone..." I looked frantically around.

"Who? Who was it, Kate?" Daniel asked, sounding concerned.

"I...it's not...possible."

"Kate, please what are you talking about, who did you see?" Tara voice was urgent now.

Again I spotted him, "There. It's...it's Nathan, my mum's boyfriend." I pointed across the room to where Nathan was talking to a group of Chameleons.

Chameleon

Tara's eye followed my gaze, "Are you sure? Where? Show me, Kate."

"Over there, by the column to the left of the large flower arrangement. I am absolutely positive it's Nathan...but it can't be...why the hell would he be here?" My brain just couldn't understand it.

"Oh my God." Tara said, stunned.

"What is it?" Daniel insisted, trying to see around the people obstructing his view.

"Nathan...Kate's mum's boyfriend...is Jonas."

"What?" I spun round to look at her.

"You may know him as Nathan, but that is Jonas. Leader of the group in Oxford and one of the nastiest Chameleons to ever have evolved. We have to get Kate out of here, right now, before he sees her." Without another word Tara calmly headed for the exit with us all in tow.

My brain could not comprehend this new fact, on top of the others learnt tonight. I automatically followed them but I didn't see the floor I walked on, or the walls of the corridors we silently walked down. In what seemed like moments, we were inside the villa and I sat on the sofa, stunned and with no recollection of crossing the room. My brain just kept jumping from the images and memories of the night at the pub with mum and Nathan, to seeing him surrounded by Chameleons.

There was a knock at the door. Everyone jumped and stood still for a fraction of second. Helena quickly went to see who it was and came back just as fast with Michael following her. He walked straight over to Tara and sat down next to her. Taking a deep breath, he closed his eyes and he looked like he was concentrating really hard. After several seconds, Michael opened his eyes again. He did not look at anyone else but Tara. I got the distinct impression he wasn't quite over her yet by the way he looked at her right at that moment.

"It's safe. We can talk freely now." He said.

"What do you mean safe? We are surrounded by hundreds of murderous Chameleons with superhuman strength and hearing. How can we possibly be safe?" The words were out of my mouth, before I even knew I wanted to say them. I felt like I had missed a conversation somehow.

However, the others were sitting down, looking a little more relaxed.

Tara took my hand for a moment, to reassure me.

"When Michael evolved he discovered he had a gift, just like Joshua and Moira did. It's not commonly known, however and in fact, the only Chameleons, and now a human, who know about it are in this room, which is how it must remain."

"Okay, what gift?" I asked quietly.

"He can create an area, a sound-proof barrier, which Chameleons can't overhear, kind of like a shield. We are now free to speak without fear of being overheard or caught." Tara explained.

"But I thought it was illegal, one of your laws, not to listen when you gather together." I protested. My mind had finally decided to start thinking again, much to my relief.

Michael clarified, "It is, but some Chameleons still do it. Obviously, they are very careful never to reveal that they overheard something. Anyway, now we are completely safe from listeners."

I sat and thought this over, while Tara reviewed with Michael and Moira everything that had happened, since Joshua had met me. To hear my life explained like some TV drama was very disconcerting and somewhat depressing. I realised Joshua and I had spent very little time together that wasn't consumed by fear or worry. I sat and listened to my life being described to a stranger. It was very surreal. Michael glanced at me several times during the telling, especially after she explained about how Joshua had killed Sebastian and brought me back to life and then again later when he did the same for my mum. A wave of homesickness washed over me as I thought of my mum, I really did miss her. I just hoped she hadn't fallen totally in love with Nathan, or Jonas, as I should now call him.

Damn him.

Moira agreed that through her gift of sensing the truth, she was able to detect that Izzy and the rest of Jonas' group did indeed know that Joshua killed Sebastian. Moira had also discovered that Jonas asked Sebastian to drain a young woman, presumably Kate, although the rest of the group did not know why nor what she looked like. When Sebastian failed to return triumphant, Jonas decided to finish the job himself, hence the car 'accident'. Apparently, Moira heard they had a Chameleon in their group, who is able to see what other Chameleons are doing. It was surmised that the seer had seen Joshua kill Sebastian.

"Is that why Nathan...I mean Jonas...tried to kill my mum and I?"

"Yes, I think so, but I think your mum was just an aside, his target was you all along." Tara said.

I knew then she was right. Nathan had only turned up after Sebastian's death and had gone through mum to get to me. Poor mum, she had been really happy. I thought as I rubbed my eyes, I was starting to feel very tired. I realised that me being the target also explained why she didn't hear from him again after the accident. He had no need to contact her...since he thought she was dead, along with me. "Wait." Everyone looked at me, "Why would Jonas be after me in the first place? It doesn't make sense, I'm just another Light to them."

"That is a very good question, Kate." Daniel interjected, "There doesn't seem to be a good reason for it, except that you are important to Joshua. However, Jonas usually doesn't care about humans, so the question remains...." Daniel sat forward as he spoke. He looked intrigued and worried.

"From what you have told me, I have to agree. No offence, Kate, but why you?" Michael looked at me. "Is there anything missing from what Tara said, something little that we may have overlooked?"

"No, nothing. Nothing I can think of, anyway." I rested my head on my hand as I lent against the arm of the sofa, suddenly feeling exhausted.

"Perhaps you should get some rest, dear." Helena hand touched my arm. "It has been a long, fraught evening and you have been drained a couple of times. You will feel better after a sleep."

"I think I will, but promise to wake me if there is any news, okay?" I looked at Helena and Tara, they both nodded their agreement. I rose and made my way to the doorway, I felt a sudden rush of gratitude towards these people who were putting themselves in danger simply by knowing me. "Thank you all for your help, I know Joshua would appreciate it, if he knew what you were doing. Good night." I staggered through the kitchen with the sounds of the 'good nights' ringing in my ears. The nearer I got to my room, the more tired I realised I was. I could barely find the strength to undress and climb under the covers. Within seconds, I was very deeply asleep.

***

The darkness was absolute, not a chink of light anywhere. The surrounding space was cold and damp, a musty smell of rotting vegetation all around. There was an overwhelming sense of claustrophobia from being confined in such a small space. There was no room to roll over or change position in any way. There was only six inches of space above. The body was closed down, dormant, but the mind was alert and active.

Oh, so very active.

That was the whole idea, the mind tortured and focused on the need to feed. This was the point of the confinement, yet the knowledge of why did not console. The hunger was now upon him, and he felt himself begin to grow weaker as time passed but how much time had passed...he had no idea. It could have been hours or days, there was nothing to mark time's passing in this absolute darkness. Although, judging by his hunger, it had been days, but still it seemed like years, a never-ending nightmare. The only thing he could hang onto were the voices. If he concentrated hard enough, he could hear the voices of those he loved, but every time he did and heard their partial comments, an overwhelming panic came upon him that made him desperate to try to get out and feed.

His sense of self was slipping away, very quickly.

Would he ever get out or would he be in here forever and be turned insane by it, by the darkness, the hunger and the voices. He felt the panic rise again. He kicked and thrashed against the walls of his prison, the hunger driving him to be free, to feed. He had started to become one with the hunger and it frightened him more than anything. How much longer before it took him completely, trees and animals would not suffice or sate the hunger anymore. How much longer before he craved the feel of the energy being taken during passion or worse, how much longer until he had to feel and taste the blood as he fed?

He kicked and hit the wood in a frenzy. His tormented screams that deafened his own ears were blocked from the others above ground by the tons of soil, which lay above the coffin.

Except for one, his beloved, she knew his torment and heard his screams.

***

"Kate, Kate."

I was woken by my own blood-curdling screams as someone grabbed me. I screamed again and pushed them away, afraid of what I would do, afraid of wanting to taste their blood.

"Kate, wake up, it's me, Tara. You were screaming, Kate."

I looked into her eyes as she came into focus and felt her hands on my arms, shaking me. She saw I was awake and instantly held me in her arms.

"It's okay Kate, you're safe now." She said soothingly.

It took me several moments to get my brain back to this reality and shake off the panic of the coffin.

"It was just a dream." She stroked my hair as she held me.

At that moment, everything clicked into place...Izzy, Sebastian, Joshua, the coffin...everything.

I sat bolt upright and Tara let go of me, surprised.

"Is everyone still here?" I asked urgently and glanced out my window, it was almost dawn and the palest of lights was just coming back.

"Yes, they're all downstairs, why?"

"I need to talk to them. Do you think you can make me some tea, while I dress?" I realised I'd been so tired I'd fallen asleep with half my clothes on and they were now sodden with sweat.

"Of course. I'll see you down stairs." Tara stood, looked puzzled and started to walk towards the door then turned back to me, "Are you sure you are alright?"

"No, but I'll live. A hot drink will help." I said grimly.

"One cuppa, coming up." She vanished in a blur.

I changed slowly, allowing my mind to completely wake up. I was astounded by what I had discovered but knew just how important it could be. I made my way back downstairs and into the living room to find everyone still in the same places they were many hours ago, when I had left them. Next to the chair where I had been sitting earlier sat a steaming hot mug of green tea.

"Thanks, Tara."

"No problem." She smiled.

"Are you okay, Kate? We could hear you screaming, was it a nightmare?" Helena looked concerned.

"Yes and no, I will explain in a moment...but first, Michael, is it still safe to talk?"

"Yes, once the protection is up it says up until I take it down, I don't even have to work at maintaining it." He spoke with no hint of ego.

"Okay, let me get through this and then you can all tell me what you think to it. Alright?" I asked and watched as everyone agreed. "Firstly, I want you all to know that Joshua is okay. He is starting to panic and has bouts of hysteria but he's holding his own. Also, he's been able to hear a bit about what has been happening and some of what we have been talking about, although not all, obviously." I waited for the impact of my words to set in, which didn't take long.

There were gasps of shock, disbelief and amazement.

Daniel demanded to know how I know.

They all looked at Moira, who nodded in shock, "Yes, she is telling the truth."

"Wait, there is more." I listened to the profound silence for a moment as I gathered my thoughts. "Since I have known Joshua, I have dreamt of horrible things, of people being murdered by what I now recognise as Chameleons. At first, I thought it was just nightmares from the news articles about the murders in Oxford and, until the party, they were just dreams, and then I met Izzy...you see I recognised her...she was in one of my dreams. She killed the guy in the nightclub car park. It wasn't until I dreamt about Joshua just now, that I finally realised I was dreaming about real things in real time and I then knew that I had recognised Izzy, and Marcus, from my dreams. He had also killed a couple of the victims."

I looked around at the astonished faces, "I think they do have a seer in their group and I think that seer...saw me...seeing them and thought I was a danger. That would explain why Sebastian was sent to kill me, only Joshua foiled their plan by killing him. Jonas must have drained my mum while saying goodbye at the pub and as she began to pass out, she crashed the car. I knew something was wrong with her."

"If what you are saying is true, it still does not explain why they would care if you were able to see what they are doing. Like I said earlier you are just human, not exactly a threat." Michael was the first to reply.

"I know, I have thought about that too. What if the people they are killing were important in some way and they are trying to hide what they are doing?"

"Important, how?" Daniel asked.

I turned to him, "I don't know, it's all I can come up with, though." I said.

"That is an unusual gift you have there, Kate." Moira said.

Everyone looked between her and me.

"I can tell you she is speaking the truth, one hundred percent. She really is having these dreams, seeing these things and is connected to Joshua. Even now during his interment." Moira informed everyone.

"I have never heard of such a thing in a human." Daniel said, amazed, "Even in a Chameleon it would be a phenomenal gift."

I could feel everyone's eyes on me. I blushed and looked down at the mug of hot tea in my hands. I didn't like the sudden attention but it was great to be able to offer something for once.

"We need to get more information about Jonas and what this is all about." Tara said.

"I think Kate is right. Jonas and the others would not be concerned about her unless they fear she knows something or is

Chameleon

about to find out something crucial about their plans." Daniel turned to me. "Is there anything, in any of your dreams, or visions, that might give us a clue?"

"No, nothing. Sadly, I seem to get the dreams or whatever you want to call them, when the event is actually happening. They are not a forewarning, so I am not sure how they can be more helpful...I'm sorry."

"Don't be sorry for such a gift, Kate. It matters not that we do not know ahead of time, what is more important is that we know something more every time. And that is a good thing." Moira smiled.

"True, very true." Agreed Daniel.

"So what now?" I asked.

"Now, we all need to go out and mingle. See if we can find out more about Jonas and friends." Tara suggested.

"May I ask something?" I said.

"Of course, Kate." Helena answered.

"How usual is it for Chameleons to be around humans when they evolve, I mean what are the chances that Jonas and friends were able to sponsor two newly evolve?"

Everyone looked at each other as if they had not thought of it before I had spoken.

"That is a very good question, Kate." Daniel leaned forward in his chair again. "One is possible but two is unusual."

"Izzy said they 'happened' to be there, when Carlos evolved." Tara said.

Moira shifted in her chair, "What if their seer is like Empusa? What if they can see the newly evolved...but before they evolve?"

"Which would mean they could get to them and sponsor them, all the while teaching the newly evolved the ways of Bleeders." Michael screwed up his face in disgust.

"Recruiting the newly evolved but why?" Helena said.

"To create their own army of the faithful?" I said, as a deep dread began to build inside me again. Everyone looked at me.

"The Council need to know about this." Michael said.

"We have no proof, just...a human's dreams." Daniel replied and looked apologetically at me.

"Michael has a point though, Daniel. Perhaps Empusa can help with this, perhaps she can see something else." Tara said.

"If we take this theory to the Council, we confirm Sebastian's murder and condemn Joshua." Helena quietly pointed out.

"All we can do is try to find out more, get some proof if we can and then take it from there. Are we agreed?" Tara asked.

Everyone agreed.

"I will see if I can find Jonas and talk to him. We go way back...having been tested together. Moira, will you come with me? I may have need of your gift." Tara asked as she stood and made to leave.

"Of course." Moira stood and followed Tara out to the hallway.

"What should I do?" I asked as everyone began to move.

"I think you should stay around the villa as much as possible." Said Daniel. "I have a few people I want to talk to as well." He said as he walked out.

"As do I." Michael said as he took his leave, kissing Tara on the cheek when he left.

Tara caught my eyes with a serious gaze. "Kate, I think it is for the best if Jonas doesn't see you at present. Let him think that you are still dead."

"I guess. Do you think it's safe here now though?

"Yes, it's safe here. I will be here most of the day anyway, Kate. You will be just fine." Helena said.

"Thanks." I mumbled, not liking the thought of having to be babysat.

The villa quickly emptied and I was left alone with Helena, who watched me carefully as I walked to the glass doors and looked out at the morning sun on the ocean.

"Kate?"

"Yes?" I looked round towards her.

"Did you see anything of Wil?"

"No, I am sorry I didn't. I only saw Joshua."

"Oh...I just thought I would ask."

"He will be alright...they both will." I tried to sound cheerful.

"I hope so." She rose and collected her book off the small table by the sofa and headed towards me. "I'm going to sit outside and read, would you care to join me?"

"Maybe later. I'm going to make some breakfast, do you need anything?"

"No, thank you. The hunger for food fades over the years. Eventually Chameleons only exist on energy, our elders moved past food many years ago. I find I neither need nor want it very often anymore. The hunger for actual food is much less than when I first evolved." She smiled, opened the glass doors and walked out.

I busied myself making a breakfast of various cold meats, cheeses and bread, with another cup of green tea. I sat at the kitchen counter sipping my tea, thinking about all that has happened over the last night. I couldn't help but feel we were missing something...something big. It eluded me, no matter how long I chased it around my brain. Eventually, I tried to put these thoughts to the back of my mind by recalling the 'vision' of Joshua and what he was going through.

I recalled the paralysing fear he had of himself and what he may do when released. I remembered the feeling as he slipped into crazed hysteria and fought against his confinement. I remembered him trying to listen to our voices. I could almost hear them in my head now, the mumble and murmur filtering through as he tried to listen hard to what was going on around him.

I realised that if I could get closer to him, he would hear me more clearly. I could tell him to keep fighting and that there was only four more days to go. I could tell him about our plans, what we had discovered and about my visions.

I could tell him everything.

I could...if I knew where he was buried.

FOUND

I had a plan.

It was a good plan, but I needed help.

The others had, for the last two days, been talking to their contacts on the island, trying to discreetly gather information about Jonas and his friends. Nothing more had been found out and I had no further dreams. Unfortunately, we had come to a standstill and were no further ahead than a couple of days ago.

On the afternoon of the second day, I was able to get Tara alone on the private beach and knowing we only had two days left before the Evolution Ball, I'd become more than a little desperate to find Joshua and make sure he knew everything that was going on, before he was released from his interment. Tara lay on a towel soaking up the sunshine while listening to her mp3 player. I stood in front of her, blocking the sunshine. She shaded her eyes as she looked up at me, I grinned and sat on the sand next to her.

"How come you're sunbathing?"

"I like to feel the warmth on my skin, why else?" She laughed.

"Most folks do it to get brown, but since you can do that with a thought, it seems kind of odd to me."

"Most 'folks' meaning humans. You are right, of course, I can tan when I like." She looked directly at me and before my very eyes, her skin started to darken until she was a lovely golden colour that sunbathers around the world would die for.

"Wow." I gasped.

"It's nothing. It's so easy, it's boring." Tara smiled as she changed back to her usual pale skin colour.

"Chameleon is such an apt name." I said, amazed at how easy it all seemed to her.

"Isn't it?" Tara laughed, "I actually like the feel of the warm sun on my skin though, it makes me happy. You realise, of course, that it's a form of energy that everyone, even humans, feed on, don't you? Ever noticed how you feel energized and happy after being out in the sun?"

"Oh...yeah, I'd never really thought about it before, you're right...how interesting."

Tara stretched. "How are you doing? Not long to go now." She lay back down on her towel.

"I'm okay, starting to get more nervous as we get nearer to the ball, though."

"That's understandable. I have to admit, so am I." She brushed her hair out of her eyes, it had been moved there by the warm breeze.

I looked at her from under my lashes, gauging her possible reaction to my next question.

"Tara?" I began hesitantly.

"Spit it out, Kate. I know you didn't come here to ask me about sunbathing." Tara sat up and looked directly at me.

"I need your help, yours and Michael's." I continued to explain what I wanted to do by writing it on the pad I'd brought, just in case others were listening. She resisted at first, as it would be dangerous and difficult but after some persuasion she agreed. We'd planned to find Joshua tonight. Although Chameleons don't sleep, the pathways around the island are virtually empty during the evenings, except for a few guests going to one of the many parties that went on all night.

At long last, the daylight faded and Tara and I headed out towards Michael's apartment, under the pretext of going for a walk. Something I was only allowed to do if in the company of a Chameleon, for my own safety and preferably at night when the place was mostly deserted. We had already discussed the plan with Michael earlier, when he had stopped by to talk to Tara. He had tried to talk us out of it but saw reason in the end and he became a willing helper. He was waiting for us as we approached. Without speaking, we started our systematic search of the island. Obviously, there would not be a sign post stating 'Chameleons buried here – stay off the grass' but the island was relatively small with only a few areas where the Council could bury all the newly evolved.

As we walked, I began to hum under my breath.

Tara gave me a stern look as if to say 'shut up'.

"Sorry." I whispered, "Nerves." I mimed zipping a zipper over my mouth and made no further noise.

We followed the cobbled paths around the edge of the island, knowing they wouldn't use the private beaches due to the tide. That only left inland and most of it was covered with small wooded areas, where the pine trees were packed too close together with other shrubbery to allow burials. The only suitable areas left, were few small open spaces and sub-tropical gardens that were dotted about. We casually walked around the island, past many gardens, pretending to stop and chat as one of us quickly checked each area. We had determined that the garden with the burials would be guarded but not so heavily as to attract attention to it. At last, we came to a possible garden, it looked big enough for several graves. There was also a seat at the edge of the garden where a single Chameleon sat reading a book. As per the plan, we walked past and out of view, maintaining that we were out for a walk.

"No, you're wrong." Tara said loudly, "Get your hands off me." She winked at Michael and I, "That's it. I have had enough of this." She stormed off in the direction of the guard.

Michael and I watched through the bushes as Tara sat on the bench next to the guard, fuming and mumbling swear words.

"Is there a problem?" He asked, looking around him.

"Yes, a problem with my ex., humans think 'they' have it bad. Try being married for a hundred of years and then you still can't escape your ex." Tara distracted him by creating conversation about her ex and then more peacefully about the book he was reading. He was obviously warming to her and seemed to think she was interested in him.

Michael and I carefully trod on the ground, which was soft with thousands of pine needles, we climbed through the bushes a good distance behind Tara and the guard. We could see by the moonlight we had the right spot, the flowerbed had been dug up recently and all that was left now was turned over dirt, dry from the heat of the sun. I had no way of knowing where in the flowerbed Joshua was, so I would just have to go for it. I glanced at Michael, who nodded to say the shield was up. Neither the guard, nor anyone else for that matter, would be able to hear me. We had stayed back in the shadows of the trees so we couldn't be seen, and I hoped we would be safe for the next few minutes.

"Will the other ones buried hear me?"

"No, I can direct it so certain Chameleons can hear, while others can't. Only you, me and Joshua will hear this."

I glanced at Tara. She had moved closer to the guard and placed her hand on his leg suggestively. She was good at this, I decided.

I took a deep breath, "Joshua? I know you can hear me and I know you have been trying to hear what is happening. I will explain everything later...after..." I paused not wanting to think about later. "You have just two days left, please be strong, my love. I know you can do this." I swallowed the lump in my throat that threatened to produce tears. "Listen to me, I don't have much time and what I am about to tell you is very important. I saw Nathan, mum's boyfriend, here at a party...only to find out that his real name is Jonas...'the' Jonas. He and his friends know about you killing Sebastian and have gone to the Council, who is said to be investigating. I tell you this not to worry you but to warn you to be very careful and watchful when they release you. I don't know what they're planning." I looked at Michael.

He nodded encouragingly back.

"We have some friends who are checking a theory out, it seems there is a lot more to this than we first thought."

Michael quickly squeezed my arm and I held still in the shadows of the bushes, not daring to breathe. I watched the pathway in front of where Tara and the guard sat. A couple walked past arm in arm, but they were too engrossed in each other to take notice of anyone or anything outside of their little bubble. Within moments they were gone but Tara's spell on the guard was broken and he began to tell her that she should move along and let him read.

"I have to go." I whispered to Joshua, "Please hang in there and know we are doing our best to help you."

"We have to go." Michael said while watching Tara saying goodbye to the guard.

"Okay." I started to move away but paused and turned my head back towards the site of the graves. "I love you."

We quickly moved away and could hear Tara saying goodbye to the guard and walking away. We scrambled out of the bushes and just for safety, we walked around the small island in the opposite direction to the guard and the garden. I felt a kind of elation inside, knowing that I had communicated with Joshua even if the conversation had been one sided. I knew I'd be able to bare the next two days much easier now.

We eventually met up back at Michael's apartment, which looked just as large and as elegant as the Marstons, even though it was only for one person. Tara was waiting for us inside and had sat herself on a kitchen stool. She looked at us with a big smile on her face.

"Mission accomplished, I take it?" She said as she stood to greet us.

"Yes, thank you very much...both of you. I feel better now that Joshua knows what he is walking into."

"You're welcome, Kate. Most of it was actually fun." Michael's eyes slid across to peer at Tara.

I knew which bits he thought weren't much fun knowing how he felt about Tara, I wondered if Tara knew.

"Yes, it was, wasn't it?" Tara laughed. "It's been awhile since I've done anything dangerous, I'd forgotten what a rush of adrenalin one gets."

Michael laughed, "You always did like trouble. Do you remember Istanbul?"

Tara roared with laughter, "Oh yes, I do. Not nearly as much fun as Costa Rica though." She grinned, cheekily.

"I didn't think we would get out of that one alive." Michael laughed hard.

I was beginning to feel like three was a crowd. Oh yeah, I thought, Wil has some major competition, at the same moment, Tara seemed to notice me.

"I had better get Kate back to the villa. Thanks for all your help, as ever, Michael." Tara stood on tiptoe and gently kissed him on the cheek.

"You are always welcome, my lady." Michael made an old fashioned bow and smiled at her.

It reminded me of a similar gesture that Joshua had once shown me, I smiled. I had to admit it, I liked Michael's style.

Chameleon

We arrived back at the Marston villa a few minutes later. I felt tired and emotionally drained from our little excursion, immediately said good night and headed for the shower. Soon, thanks to the hot water, I felt relaxed again and laid in bed looking out the window. I could see the waning moon reflect on the ocean in the distance and hear the sound of the waves on the beach, soon it began to lull me to sleep.

***

The darkness was familiar this time, although it was still completely and utterly disorienting.

An unusual calm had spread, a remembrance of a recent voice that had created a window of hope inside him. He had listened to the words, knew their meaning and understood them. He was not lost to his hunger after all, even though he knew it would come back. He now had a thread to hold onto.

He could feel it rise again, the hunger, the panic of being buried, the fear of what was happening outside and then the desperate need to be in control of the wildness inside. He felt himself slip away into the far back places of his mind as the hunger took over once more. With the hunger came great strength. He had already broken through some of the wooden planks, only to feel the steel box behind it.

His hunger raged and he again began to fight his way out of his confines. He screamed and kicked and punched the walls, clawed at them with his nails. He could feel his fingers bleeding as the nails were torn, he could also feel his body repair the damage over and over again, these actions draining what little energy stores he had left, making his hunger deepen. He continued for hours until he became exhausted and eventually, he felt the hunger begin to fall back and he felt his 'self' come forward again.

His body was almost too weak to fight it off now. When he did manage it, there were only minutes of respite, before the hunger returned again. If it wasn't for the voice, the voice of his beloved, the hunger would have complete control by now.

***

I awoke with tears streaming down my face. As horrible as it was to feel him losing control to his hunger, the fact that he heard me and that it had helped, gave me hope. It also proved that my dreams were definitely a glimpse of reality. I could even feel his emotions and turmoil inside as a result of my earlier words. Sadness and joy once again warred within me but this time they were laced with hope. I lay watching the increasing light as dawn approached, silent tears ran down my face onto the damp patch on my pillow, which steadily spread outwards.

I knew that in about forty hours I would be at the Evolution Ball hoping and praying that Joshua and Wil made it through the testing. I rolled on my back and looked up at the ceiling. Why is it when you want something to come quicker, it seems to take longer? I wondered. As the pale light grew stronger, I tried to remain positive. We had found out nothing further, Tara and Moira were unable to get anything from Jonas, which was not surprising, really.

Shortly after waking, I heard voices downstairs. It sounded like another meeting going on and it made me curious, I leapt out of bed and dressed quickly in shorts and t-shirt, rushing to the bathroom to brush my teeth and my hair, then headed downstairs to find some breakfast and see what the latest news was. I grabbed a glass of OJ, a bowl of cereal and walked into the living room, it seemed that worry hadn't diminished my appetite, if anything it had increased it. Everyone was there, some standing, others pacing. They were all talking loudly at each other at the same time.

"What's going on?" I said as I drank the OJ and walked over to the sofa to sit and eat my cereal. Everyone turned towards me realising I was in the room. None of them spoke. "What? What is it?" My stomach felt like it dropped ten feet through the floor making me breathless.

Daniel stepped forward, he looked very worried. "There has been an announcement from the Council."

Daniel sat down next to Helena and held her hand, she just stared off into space.

Tara came to sit next to me. "The Council have announced they have discovered Sebastian was murdered by a Chameleon and they have that Chameleon in custody. They will be announcing his fate at the Evolution Ball."

My throat lost the ability to speak. I couldn't even remember how to breathe. My mind was screaming 'No'.

I felt Tara's hand on mine, "Kate?"

I looked around the room and realised that everyone looked devastated, the Council had decided and nothing could be done about it now.

It was over.

Everything was over.

Joshua would die.

"Kate?" Tara's voice again.

I could hear her but it was like being underwater, she seemed so far away. Something was slowly curling up and dying inside of me, I could feel it.

I felt myself shake, hands on my arms...shaking me.

My eyes gradually moved to look at her and she came into focus. Instantly, like a switch being turned on, my brain focused.

Tara let go of me as I stared at her. There were no tears, not yet. He was still alive...for a few more hours. "What can we do?

There must be something we can do?" I said, my voice sounded hollow and lifeless.

"There is nothing to do. Our laws are very clear. Joshua killed Sebastian, end of story." Daniel said. His heartbroken voice pierced me like a knife.

"I won't give in, there has to be a way."

Unexpectedly, there was an urgent knocking at the apartment door. It made everyone jump. Moira was the first up and went to answer it.

"Wait...wait! What do you want?" I heard Moira's panicked voice.

A gruff male voice replied, "Out of my way. This is official Council business."

Before anyone could move, a guard stalked into the room flanked by five others. "Everyone stay where you are, we have come for the human...Kate Henson." He looked directly at me, "Come with us."

"Why? Where are you taking her?" Daniel stood up and demanded.

"The Council wants to see her. Someone take one of my men to collect all of the human's belongings."

No one moved.

"Why do you want her belongings, if she is only to meet the Council?" Michael asked suspiciously.

"You can't hurt her she is my Claimed Human, I demand to know what's going on." Tara said.

"You have your orders." He barked.

Daniel stood glaring at the guard who just glared back in return. Helena put a hand on Daniel's arm in warning.

I was unable to talk, the shock of the news and now being seized by guards terrified me beyond what my mind could cope with. I rose on automatic pilot and walked towards the guards. I could feel myself trembling with every step. Strangely, I noticed

Chameleon

I was bare footed and wondered why it mattered.

Without any further discussion, they marched me out of the villa and across into the main building. I was forced along several corridors and down two flights of stairs into a basement. They marched me through many storage areas until we came to a large metal door. One of the guards opened the door and pushed me into the room. Before I could turn round, the door clanged shut behind me and I could hear it being locked from the other side.

I stared at the door for many long minutes, not comprehending. Gradually, I came to my senses and realised just how much danger I was now in. The Council could easily get rid of me if they wanted to, without a trace. My mum would never know the truth. Thoughts of my mum jabbed pains of homesickness in my chest, I gasped and clutched my chest as fear consumed me.

Eventually, I tried to distract myself by looking around at my surroundings. I was in a small storage room, which had been cleared of everything, except a cot with a blanket and a table with two chairs. Opposite the main metal door was another door, wooden this time but no windows. A single bulb hung from the ceiling, dimly lighting the centre of the room, leaving darkness in the corners. I walked over to the wooden door and tried the handle, to my surprise it was unlocked. I slowly pushed the door open with my fingertips, cautious of what might be inside.

It was another small room with a little sink and a toilet, obviously meant for the hotel's human staff. "Well, that's one problem solved." I said out loud and laughed. I couldn't help but notice my voice had a crazed edge to it and I cringed. Was I going mad, already? I wondered. I sat on the cot with my back against the wall and drew my knees up to my chest. I don't know how long I sat there, it felt like many hours, when I stretched out my legs they were stiff and difficult to move.

Finally, the door was unbolted, swung open and banged heavily against the wall, I nearly leapt out of my skin. A man, who was obviously human by the large scar on his left cheek came into the room to place a tray of food and a bottle of water onto the table. He glanced at me and quickly moved away. I looked over at the food and although I had not had breakfast or lunch or... well, who knows how many meals I had missed since being in here, it didn't matter anyway, I wasn't hungry. I stared down at my hands, lost in despair.

"Please, come...eat, drink, Kate. May I call you Kate?"

My head snapped up at the voice and I recognised Ramy at once, standing next to a woman, I recognised her as another Council member. As I watched, Ramy sat on one of the chairs, while the woman stood behind him. The door clanged shut again but this time it wasn't locked. I knew full well that I could not escape, even with the door unlocked or even left wide open. The Chameleons would kill me before I had even moved off the bed.

"Please Kate, do come and join me." His voice was so calm and yet so strong.

I looked between him and the woman, and decided there was no point sitting here sulking. I walked over to the table, sat on the other chair and looked him in the eyes, determined not to show him my fear.

"That's much better." Ramy said with a smile, "I am Ramy and this is Empusa. We are members of the Council of Nine."

"I know who you are." I stated flatly. So that was Empusa, the seer.

"Good, good." He continued, "Now, I want you to tell me about the day that Joshua killed Sebastian, in as much detail as you can, please."

I was shocked that he'd just come out with it like that. The

Chameleon

shock must have shown on my face.

"Yes, we know about it but we want to hear your side of things." He said.

I figured there was nothing for it and I began to tell them what happened on that autumn day just a few weeks ago, although it now seemed a lifetime ago. When I came to the part about me dying, I hesitated but decided to tell I them everything, including Joshua healing me. After all, it was Sebastian that was the bad guy, not Joshua, surely? They listened quietly and I hoped that, just perhaps, the information on his unusual healing ability would save Joshua's life.

"I see." Ramy nodded and gestured to Empusa.

Empusa looked like the archetype of a beautiful Greek woman with long curly dark hair and olive skin. She lent forward and whispered in Ramy's ear and then stood up again. Ramy tapped his fingers on the table a couple of times.

"Empusa tells me she saw you die but in the next instant you were alive again. You say it was Joshua, who did this, who made you live again?"

"Yes, he gave me some of his energy to bring me back to life." I replied.

Ramy stood quickly in one smooth movement. "You will remain here until we decide what to do with you."

The door instantly opened as if a signal had been given, they both left without another word and the heavy door closed behind them. Again, I heard it being locked. I looked down at the food, a cold meat salad with bread and cheese. My stomach turned over in fear and I ignored the food. Instead, I picked up the water bottle and returned to the cot to sip it. I mulled the conversation over in my mind. Obviously, they were surprised by the gift that Joshua had, I could see that on their faces but I could also see interest too, perhaps the information would save him after all. It was the only hope I had.

As the hours passed, I couldn't tell if it was daytime or night time. I wandered around the room several times, looking for cracks in the walls that I could prise with the salad fork, like I had seen it done in the movies. It was the only plan I had, silly though it was, it seemed plausible to me. My mind kept going over everything that had happened over the weeks I had known Joshua, over and over again. Finally, I curled up in a ball on the bed unable to stop my mind from churning everything over. Cold stone fear gripped me with its icy fingers as I wondered what was going to happen to me. Not long after that, I think I began to whimper.

The man with the scar came back, took away the food and replaced it with more. I felt even less hungry than before and only sipped the water. I didn't even get up to walk about anymore, I just lay on the cot, curled up in a ball. Eventually, I fell into a fitful sleep full of doors, I would open one only to find another. I woke up crying and stayed under the blanket, covering my face as it was my only refuge from the light of the light bulb. I had discovered earlier that the switch must have been outside in the corridor.

Again the man came with food. And again, I touched none of it, but I used the delivery of meals to loosely keep track of the hours, this time I didn't even peek out from under the cover. Time became a distorted illusion, as I sat there and my mind was lost to its own wanderings. I barely had the strength to go to the washroom. I could do nothing but wander aimlessly through my fears, alone and terrified.

The door opened for the man again and I groaned. I listened from under my blanket for the usual noise of the man removing the tray and placing another on the table but I heard something different this time, a strange shuffling and a deep growl. I froze, terrified of what they had put in the room with me. It sounded like a wolf. Do wolves live in Croatia? I wondered as I listened hard, I could also make out two sets of footfalls apart from the shuffling.

Suddenly, the door banged shut and locked again.

All I could hear was a low menacing growl.

I didn't move, more precisely, I was frozen to the spot with fear. I reasoned that if the wolf couldn't see me, I might survive. I could hear it moving, sniffing the air. My heart beat loudly in my chest, my brain was suddenly very aware, much more than it had been, even before I was locked in the room. I wondered if I could make it to the bathroom, maybe I could then lock the door, lock the wolf out. Would a locked bathroom door stop a wolf though? Why don't they teach you these things in school? I think I was loosing my mind.

I decided to take a small peek out of the covers so I could determine where the wolf was in relation to the bathroom. I slowly moved the cover back and allowed one eye to peek out. As my fear built, my breathing became louder and more shallow, which made the wolf growl more. I glanced over towards the door where a big burlap bag sat rippling with its contents. They had caught and bagged a wolf, I knew it. Once it was hungry enough, I would be its meal and they would erase my body by having it eaten. The wolf must have smelled me and suddenly was struggling harder in the bag, it was getting more and more aggressive, growling louder and more viciously. I decided my only chance was now, I wanted to make it to the bathroom before it ripped the material and escaped the bag.

The washroom was about ten feet away from my position. With as much power as I could muster I launched myself off the cot but instantly fell to the floor, my legs tangled in the blanket. I kicked and struggled to get out of the blanket just as I heard the first rip of the bag.

The wolf was escaping.

My heart raced insanely in my chest as I finally managed to

kick the last of the blanket off me and jump up, my head swimming from lack of food, making me stagger. I tried to run for the washroom, but it felt like I was running in quicksand. All my actions were slow and my feet seemed not to want to move forward. I gritted my teeth and forced myself onwards, just as I heard a huge rip and a deep-throated growl behind me.

I refused to look back as I reached out for the doorknob. I covered the last two feet quickly and grabbed it. The knob slipped in my sweating hands as panic drove me to open it, knowing it was my last chance. Finally, I managed to turn it, the door flew inwards and carried me with it. I was half way through the doorway when I knew I was not going to make it, I could feel the hot breath of the wolf on my bare legs and a scream began to bubble up in my throat.

Unknown

I screamed so hard my voice broke.

I kicked at the wolf to let me go, all the while keeping my eyes focused on the edge of the door and trying to pull it between us as a barrier. For one millisecond I glanced at the wolf and stopped dead in my tracks.

It wasn't a wolf...it was a person.

Even worse...it was Joshua.

My mind reeled as I looked at him and realised he had no clue who I was. His hunger had taken over. In the split second it took me to realize this, I looked down at my leg with his hand clamped to it. I could feel the once gentle vibration building and beginning to be painful. "Joshua." I said, trying to get his attention.

He didn't even look up, he was utterly focused on my leg.

"JOSHUA!" I screamed at him as the now burning pain became unbearable.

Still nothing.

I had to think fast. I angled my body so that I could get a downward punch on his temple and without thinking about it, my fight instinct took over and I punched him as hard as I could. I heard and felt, a knuckle bone break from the force of the blow and pain shot up my wrist and down my finger.

I gasped in agony.

The punch didn't stop Joshua from draining me but it did make him look up. His hair was matted and stuck to him, his clothes were covered in sweat and soil. His eyes...his eyes were the worst, the love in them was gone so was the anger and any other vestige of human emotion. His eyes were purely feral and dark with insane hunger. Another scream crawled up my throat and burst out as I stared at him in horror. I was deeply afraid of him for the first time in my life. I hated the feeling and it made me very angry. Angry, strong and possibly, very stupid. I grabbed what was left of his shirt, forced him close to me and did the only thing I could think of.

I kissed him.

I harshly forced my mouth on his as the burning pain increased, I threw everything I had into that final kiss. I broke away and whimpered as I felt my life drain away. My eyes never left Joshua's face as he steadily took more and more of my life from me. I could see his eyes becoming more human as he absorbed my energy.

The last thing I saw was his expression of horror at the realisation of what he was doing slowly dawned on him. I hoped that my gamble had paid off as I disappeared into that now familiar blackness. I welcomed it this time, welcomed the relief from the pain and misery. I opened my mind to it and let the blackness engulf me.

I knew time had passed but I was not aware enough to know how much. I felt something cool on my forehead, I tried to open my eyes but they wouldn't work. I tried again, harder and they fluttered open, I wondered if I was in heaven this time. All I could see was the rough stone walls of the basement room. I blinked a couple of times to adjust my eyes to the dim light, bright as it was after complete darkness.

This definitely was not heaven.

I felt something trickle down my cheek and lifted my hand

Chameleon

to brush it away, it appeared to be water. I reached up to my forehead and a wet cloth laid on it, it felt nice as I was strangely hot.

"You might want to leave it there for a while." Joshua said in a quiet, defeated voice.

I sat bolt upright and spun round to see him crouched in the corner with his head on his knees. He was dressed in only his trousers, his feet and upper body bare. I now realised the wet rag must be the remains of his t-shirt. I began to climb stiffly off the cot, with the intention of going to him as the overwhelming relief of seeing him as himself, rushed through me.

"Stay there." He said without lifting his head.

I froze, "Why? What's wrong?" I looked around and listened hard, thinking he heard someone coming to the door. When I heard no sound, I said, "I thought I was dreaming but it really was you. What happened?"

"I killed you." His voice broke with despair and still his head didn't rise.

"What?" I carefully stood up, expecting to be dizzy but found I wasn't, not even a little bit wobbly.

"Please stay there...I'm not sure if I can stop the hunger from coming back...I still need to feed and I refuse to feed off you...ever...again." He looked up at me, a single tear rolled down his cheek, his eyes showed such incredible sadness, it broke my heart just to look at him.

I knew by the look in his eyes the desperation of the hunger had now gone, thanks to my energy, and he was past the worst of it. I walked slowly towards him. "I know you won't hurt me again. I can see it's passed, you've beaten it." I sat down on the floor a couple of feet away from him.

"I'm sorry, I didn't know it was you...I couldn't see or think clearly...all I could see was the energy flowing around you." He looked up at me pleadingly, trying desperately to make me understand. "All I could think of...was getting that energy...no matter what."

"So how come I'm still here? Not that I'm ungrateful, but...how come you brought me back, if all you wanted was the energy?"

"When you punched me I was out of control completely and I was hiding inside, away from the hunger and it was like a dimmer switch being turned on. Slowly at first, I realised that the hunger wasn't all of me, as I'd feared, it was the most of me...but not all. Then you kissed me and I felt your energy properly. It was familiar and it reminded me of when I healed you before."

I moved a little closer.

"I knew who you were and realised what I was doing. I stopped but it was too late, the last of your life was leaving you into me, so I quickly sent as much of it back as I could. This time it was different somehow though, you were unconscious and burning up with a temperature."

I reached over and gently touched his hand. He flinched but didn't move his hand away, I could feel the gentle buzz I loved. "Then what happened?"

"I put you on the cot and tore up my shirt for a cooling cloth...I cleaned myself the best I could in that small sink and I've been sitting here waiting for you to wake up...dreading it."

"Why dreading it?" I asked calmly, never letting go of his hand and slowly getting nearer and nearer to him.

"Because I killed the only person I have ever loved." He cried out in despair. "Don't you get it?"

"And brought me back."

"That's not the point." He said angrily.

"It bloody well is the point. The very fact you stopped and brought me back proves you conquered it. Anyway, it didn't feel the same this time, I'm not sure I actually died. I know how that feels and that wasn't it. Perhaps I just passed out...you didn't kill me."

"I didn't?" He looked astonished.

"You didn't." I smiled and gently put my arms around him.

Joshua stiffly resisted me at first but as my words sank in he held me very close against his chest, not wanting to ever let go. We held each other like this for a long time.

Like so many times before, the door unlocked and in walked the guard. He verified where we were in the room and stepped back out, leaving the door open. Joshua and I stared at each other.

"How interesting." Ramy said from the doorway.

His voice made us both jump and turn to stare at him.

"You are both to be taken to our private apartments to prepare yourselves for the Evolution Ball. You will have no contact with others, except for the newly evolved, until then. Is that understood?"

We nodded.

"Good. Both of your fates will be decided at the ball." Ramy spun round, his long robes flowing in the breeze he caused and walked out.

The door was left open and I could see guards stood outside. We looked at each other again in amazement.

"Can you walk?" I asked.

"Yes, can you?"

"Yes."

We got to our feet and walked slowly to the door. One guard stood back while the other one started to lead the way. We followed slowly behind, as he led us up the staircase to the first floor and to the elevators. The place appeared completely deserted, which gave the building an eerie feeling. Riding up to the tenth floor we were informed that this area was for the successfully evolved only and we were to stay here under guard, until called for.

"Why are they insisting I stay with you?" I asked Joshua as we left the elevator and entered the suite.

"I don't know...what I would like to know is why they put me and you in the same room when they dug me up and not in the market place like the others."

"Hmm...good point." I said, wondering what they were going to do with us at the ball. Fear began to rise inside me again but this time the feeling made me angry, very angry. I was sick of being afraid, I'd been scared for weeks now and I'd had enough. No matter what they did to us, we would deal with it and the consequences. My thoughts became a revelation to me and I began to relax, I felt stronger and more determined than I had in a very long time.

We stood in the hall of the suite and listened, voices came to us from further down. Walking towards them, we found ourselves in a large open plan kitchen and dining area with the newly evolved. Everyone leapt up to welcome Joshua, but the fastest and noisiest was, of course, Wil.

"Josh! You made it, I was worried when I saw you weren't here." He blurred across the room to give his brother a huge bear hug.

"Wil, bloody good to see you, bro." Joshua smiled and hugged his brother back, slapping him on his back. "How did it go?" Joshua asked.

"Not bad, it was much easier than I thought it would be." Wil smiled, "And you?"

"Much harder." Joshua nervously looked at me and then looked away.

Everyone began congratulating Joshua and Wil spotted me.

"Kate, what are you doing here? We're not supposed to see anyone until tonight? Plus...you're...human." He looked puzzled and looked between Joshua and me for an explanation.

Chameleon

Everyone turned to look at me as if I was a special exhibit.

"Long story and not one we have all the answers for...yet." Joshua replied. He turned to the others and said, "This is Kate and she's Lady Tara Conway's claimed human." The others digested this information and immediately lost interest in me.

I was grateful for his quick thinking.

"Where's Carlos?" Joshua asked.

"They told us he didn't make it, apparently he went crazy and started to bleed a woman in the crowd." Wil looked horrified.

"Oh my God, what happened to him?" I asked as I sat down at the breakfast bar.

"No one knows." An oriental girl replied in a haughty voice, looking at me as if I was beneath her.

"That won't make Izzy and Marcus happy." I mumbled.

"Who?" Joshua asked.

"Another long story, I'll fill you in later. I really need to get cleaned up now though. How long do we have before the ball?" I asked Wil.

"About two hours." A pretty blond American girl said from where she sat at the dining table. She smiled at me in a friendly way.

"Thanks." I smiled back at her, "Where can I get cleaned up?" I looked down at myself and realised I'd been in the same clothes for what must have been a couple of days and in a dirty storeroom.

"They put bags in each room, I guess you just have to look for your bag, if you have one." Said Wil, still looking confused.

I got to my feet, thought better of kissing Joshua in front of everyone and headed back down the hall to hopefully find my bags. I need to get away and process everything that had happened and what it all meant, if I could. I knew the Marstons and our friends would be very worried about us all, but there appeared to be no phones in the rooms I passed. I quickly found my belongings sitting on a bed in the third bedroom down the hall. I was pleased to see an en suite bathroom and went through my bags looking for the items I needed. Gratefully, I headed to the bathroom for a very hot, very long soak in the bath.

Once clean and refreshed, I sat on the balcony of the new room looking out over the sea. I was able to relax a little and think about the last forty-eight hours. I had no idea what was coming but I was profoundly pleased to see both Joshua and Wil had survived, so far. A knock at the door brought me out of my thoughts.

"Come in." I called and turned in my seat to see who it was.

"Are you decent?" Wil asked as he crossed the room.

"Sure, come on out." I smiled at him and waved him out to the balcony.

Wil had obviously just showered, he still had wet hair and his t-shirt stuck to him where his body was still damp. He sat in the chair next to mine and looked out over the sea.

"So what can I do for you?" I asked.

"Joshua told me what happened."

"Ah..."

"He is very upset." Wil looked sombre.

"I know. Did he tell you what I told him, about it being different this time? That I'm sure I didn't die, that he didn't actually kill me?"

"Yes, he's not sure he believes you though." Wil shifted in the chair. "I came to talk to you because he told me about the gift he gave you before the testing."

"Oh?" I looked at him and wondered what was coming next.

"He doesn't know I'm here, you understand...he's worried you will feel obligated to give him a reply at the ball, like he asked for. He is worrying himself crazy...if you want him to, he

Chameleon

will withdraw the offer...what with everything that's happened." Wil looked at me pointedly, watching my reaction.

I burst out laughing and by the look on his face, it wasn't quite what he'd expected.

"What's so funny?" His eyes were wide open in surprise.

"Joshua, he is...that's what's funny. He thinks he can find a way out of a marriage proposal just because he tried to kill me." I couldn't help myself from laughing at how ridiculous the situation was. I briefly wondered if I was becoming unhinged.

Wil began to laugh, "Well, when you put it like that." He grinned.

I took on an amused but imperious tone. "You may tell him, in anyway you like, that you are sure I will give him the answer he deserves tonight." I laughed again.

"I knew there was a reason why I liked you." He grinned again. After a reflective pause he asked, "How is Tara?"

"She's fine, worried about you, but fine. She has a lot of faith in you, you know."

A huge smile lit his face up with joy and made him look incredibly handsome. "She does?"

"Yup, I think she'll be very happy to see you tonight."

"And I her. Ten days in a box gives a guy a lot of time to think." Wil stood up, "I had best go and let you get ready. Apparently, there was a message delivered a few minutes ago, to say they will be coming to collect us in about thirty minutes."

"Okay, thanks...I'll see you later, then."

Wil nodded and left the room. I slowly stood up and looked out over the balcony. Unfortunately, I couldn't see the Marston's villa from here. They must be worried sick about Joshua, Wil and I. I couldn't image what they were going through, waiting for the ball tonight.

I decided not to dwell on the ball and all it may or may not bring, instead, I did the only thing I could do, I got ready. I took a great deal of time doing my hair and make up, wanting it to look just right. Lastly, I put on my ball gown. It was a wonderful midnight blue colour with spaghetti straps and a long straight skirt. The top was corseted, while the skirt flowed smoothly downwards. I left my matching shoes for last and searched through my bag until I had found what I was looking for, the velvet jewellery case.

Barefoot, I moved outside onto the balcony again and opened the box in the last of the evenings light. Yet again, the beauty of the pieces amazed me, I touched them gently with my fingertips, and then with a deep sigh I closed the box and held it against my chest. My heart ached as I contemplated our future together. What would it be like to be the wife of a Chameleon? To age and watch him never grow old? My mind wondered aimlessly on all the possibilities until the stark reality hit me with an almost physical blow, there was a very good chance we may not even survive the night. My frustration and anger rose and again it gave me a strength within, which I never knew I possessed.

Time was ticking away quickly, I realised, as I walked back into my room to put on my shoes and I had one last check in the washroom mirror. I heard a knock at the door and the butterflies exploded in my stomach again. "Come in." I called out and took a deep breath, "I won't be a moment." My heart leapt with excitement wondering what Joshua would think of me in my new gown. I took another deep calming breath, straightened my shoulders and bravely stepped out of the bathroom.

Joshua stood in the middle of the room looking the most handsome I had ever seen him. He was dressed in a black dinner jacket and bow tie with a white dress shirt. He looked absolutely gorgeous. I looked up at his face to see total shock on it as he looked back at me.

He appeared speechless.

I started to tremble with him looking at me that way and

saying nothing and began to doubt myself. "Well?" I asked nervously, perhaps I didn't look as good as I felt.

"You are stunning, Kate. Stunning." Joshua's face burst into a massive smile as he took my hand in an old fashioned way and kissed it.

With a quick knock on the door Wil entered the room. "Whoa, you look beautiful, Kate. My brother is a lucky man." He grinned.

"Thank you, Wil." I said, blushing as Joshua put his hand in mine.

"It's time to go, the guards are on their way up." Wil said.

A sombre silence prevailed as we glanced at each other, we all knew tonight would change everything, no matter what happened.

"Are you ready?" Joshua said.

I smoothed down my dress self-consciously, took a deep breath and let it out slowly, then nodded. Hand in hand we headed out of the door and followed Wil down the corridor. We met up with the others in the lounge. They all looked wonderful in their formal wear.

The blond, American young woman who had been nice to me earlier, came over. "Hi, I'm Amanda Carver." She held out her hand.

I shook it and smiled, "Kate Henson, it's nice to meet you." I looked down at her hand in mine but felt no drain on my energy.

She smiled at me.

"May I ask what...you are? I mean, what do you feed on?" I said with a friendly smile.

She laughed, "I'm a Hippie...I like the energy of trees and plants. I refuse to drain humans on principle."

"Glad to hear it." I said, liking her already.

Our conversation was interrupted by a knocking on the

apartment door. The Council's guards had arrived to escort us all to the Evolution Ball. They led us downstairs and through the back corridors of the building until we were at a private entrance to the ballroom. I could hear music being played, something classical and very lovely.

The guard at the front of our group, turned to inform us that when our names were called, we should walk through the door opposite to be presented by the Council. He opened the doorway and stood at the entrance, the noise of the ball reached us from around his large frame. From where we were positioned, I could just see the nine thrones at the end of the ballroom placed on a dais, where the members of the Council were sat and all of them were beautifully dressed in evening wear. The Council watched the dancing Chameleons with a distinct air of authority.

I could see a small part of the room, where some Chameleons were waltzing, each one perfect and beautiful as the flash of colours from their clothing, flowed by.

At last, the piece of music came to an end.

Ramy stood and waited for the room to become quiet.

VERDICT

Ramy looked majestic standing in front of the silenced hall. "My fellow Chameleons, long has it been our tradition to test the new evolved and proudly accept them into our glorious society..." He began.

I turned toward Joshua and watched him, as he watched and listened to Ramy. The very fact that he had made it through the testing, and stood next to me, filled me with utter joy, I was so focused on him that when the first name was called, it made me jump.

"Amanda Carver." The guard said.

Amanda brushed past us towards the open doorway. At the threshold she took a deep breath and walked in with her head held high. A huge roar of cheers and applause went up as she stepped into the room. From where we were stood, I could see her approach the Council. Ramy stood and spoke quietly to her. He smiled gently, gestured for her to turn around and face the audience. The congratulatory applause grew louder as she walked towards the audience and presumably towards her anxiously waiting sponsors, whoever they were. I realised I knew so little about her and yet felt very friendly towards her.

"William Marston." The guard called.

Wil turned around from his position at the front of the line, nodded at us then warily walked into the ballroom. Again, a loud applause and cheers rang out, I could imagine the relief of his parents and Tara as he was presented to the gathering. Without any hindrance from the Council, he walked towards the crowd and was, at last, free from the testing and free to live his life as he wished.

Joshua and I both sighed with relief, it occurred to me that perhaps the Council did not know about Wil and Daniel's involvement in the destruction of Sebastian's body...or they would not have freed Wil. A warm ripple of hope spread through me at the thought. Perhaps there was hope for us all after all.

"Jessica Crow." The guard called. The dark haired Native American girl stepped confidently into the ballroom taking her place amongst her kind to another explosion of applause.

"Alexander Podolski." The guard called.

I looked at the guard and realised that time was running out, it would soon be Joshua's turn...but why was I here?

Alexander walked out to applause, flushed with pride and headed towards the Council. He was greeted and then presented, just as the others had been.

There were just three of us left - myself, Joshua and the oriental girl, who had looked too superior for her own good. She simply refused to look at us, keeping her eye on the guard, waiting her turn with her head tilted at an almost arrogant angle.

It was then that I realised there was an unusually long pause in the proceedings and the ballroom had become strangely quiet.

"Will the sponsors of Carlos Stanza please rise." Rasputin said.

A murmur rippled through the audience.

Ramy rose again from his seat and, in his soft but authoritative voice, broke the silence. "The Council of Nine wish to inform you that Carlos did not pass the interment testing and will not be joining the ranks of Chameleons gathered here today."

Chameleon

He sat back down with no show of emotion at the terrible news he had just delivered, like a judge pronouncing a death sentence.

There was a collective gasp of surprise from the ballroom and a lot of murmuring with a few raised voices, but I couldn't tell who was speaking or what they were saying. Quickly, the crowd grew quiet again though.

I briefly wondered what would or had become of Carlos.

Without further comment the announcements continued.

"Xing Chang." The guard called.

The oriental girl looked at us with a smug smile, pushed past and walked out into the ballroom. A cheer went up and applause erupted, even if it was a little subdued after the recent news.

Joshua and I looked at each other, we were both nervous and tightly held hands. My stomach churned with nerves.

"Joshua Marston." The guard call.

My heart leapt into my mouth and I turned to him.

Joshua kissed me quickly on the mouth and whispered, "I love you." then turned and walked straight into the ballroom.

A terrible dread came over me and filled my heart and mind with its fear. I watched as he approached the Council of Nine while the applause erupted around him. I wished that I were able to see his family and the happiness that would obviously be on their faces, now they knew he had made it through his interment.

Ramy stood, raised a hand and waited for silence.

Joshua was approached by a single guard who took him by the arm and moved him away to one side. The guard remained beside him and continued to hold his arm.

Again the crowd murmured amongst themselves.

My stomach lurched in fear, my palms began to sweat and my breath came in swallow gasps. The now familiar cold clench of fear crawled up my spine. I stepped closer to the doorway, but was held back by the guard. I realised that he was keeping me out of sight. However, I was still able to see Joshua and the Council but not the audience. I held my breath.

The room became deadly silent.

"Will the sponsors of Joshua Marston please step forward." Rasputin said.

Was this it? Was this the end of us all?

I looked behind me and saw an empty corridor leading to an emergency exit, I wondered if I could get Joshua to run towards me. Could we get past this single guard and head down toward the pier? Take the little boat to the mainland, perhaps steal a car and disappear into the wilds of Europe. I knew I was grasping desperately at straws. There was no way, knowing the speed of Chameleons, we would even get to the door. I looked back towards the ballroom and at Joshua, his face looked calm but his fists were clenched. It was the only outward sign he was worried. I began chewing my lip with frustration and nerves.

"The Council of Nine wish to inform you that Joshua has passed the testing and will be joining the ranks of the Chameleons gathered here today." Ramy paused while the applause erupted again.

I managed to breathe in a few sharp breaths.

Ramy held up his elegant, bejewelled hand again. "However..." Ramy interrupted the applause with a booming voice. "He has been accused of a crime...the worst kind of crime imaginable to our kind."

Once again, the audience gasped with shock.

I swore and began to feel dizzy, I staggered against the wall.

Joshua didn't move, he just stared at Ramy.

Ramy waited for the audience grew quiet again.

"Joshua Marston has been accused of murdering Sebastian Doyle. Bring forward his accusers."

Chameleon

I could hear footsteps, echoing loudly in the silence of the ballroom as a person walked across the hall towards the Council. Nathan...I mean Jonas...came into view, walked up to Joshua and stood on the other side of the guard. He looked confident and smug.

Joshua didn't move a muscle.

"Rasputin, please call the witness for the evidence against Joshua." Ramy sat back down in his seat.

"Raffaella DiMarco." Rasputin's deep voice rumbled.

More murmurs from the audience and the click of stilettos on the ballroom floor. I couldn't see where Raffaella stood and I waited anxiously for her 'evidence'.

"Please repeat what you told the Council earlier, Raffaella." Ramy ordered.

"Yes, signor. I..." She spoke nervously with a strong Italian accent. "I saw Joshua run up be'ind Sebastian, while 'e was feeding and with 'is bare 'ands...take Sebastian's 'ead off."

A few Chameleons in the audience shouted in outrage.

Ramy quelled them with a raised hand.

"When you say 'see', do you mean you were there?" Lamia said from her throne.

"No, I see visions."

"So your visions are like Empusa's, would you say?" Lamia asked.

"No, I...I only wish for 'er talents." Raffaella grovelled.

"You are sure it was Joshua Marston?" Ramy asked and gestured toward Joshua with his hand.

"Yes, signor." She said confidently.

"What happened to Sebastian's body?" Ramy asked.

My heart missed a beat. Were Wil and Daniel still in danger after all?

"I did not see, Signor Ramy." Raffaella said meekly.

I managed another painful breath, still clutching to the wall for support. I could hear my heart pounding in my head.

"Whom was Sebastian feeding upon?" Ramy asked.

"What does that have to do with anything?" Jonas burst out angrily. He quickly concealed his anger looking once again serene yet not as smug as before.

"We, the Council, will decide what is pertinent evidence, Jonas." Ramy's voice boomed around the room.

Utter silence descended.

"Answer the question, Raffaella." Lamia said with a voice of cold steel.

"I saw a girl with long dark 'air...is all I know." She replied.

"You may stand down." Ramy dismissed her with an imperious flick of his hand.

"Jonas." Ramy turned to look at him, "What was Sebastian doing in the home town of the Marstons?"

Jonas looked shocked at being questioned. As I watched, I was amazed and alarmed to see his face compose itself into the nice, gentle person I had known as Nathan.

"Sebastian was on a personal errand. He informed me he would be away over night but didn't tell me where he was going nor why." He smiled as if he was having an everyday conversation. "I can't image why this...this abomination to the name Chameleon..." he furiously glared at Joshua, "would have any reason to do something so despicable."

He almost had me fooled, he looked so innocent, so shocked. Then I remembered what Tara had said, about him being the nastiest Chameleon to have ever evolved and I now saw how he was trying to manipulate the Council. I knew instantly I loathed this man and that he had sent Sebastian to kill me, no matter what he was now claiming.

Ramy considered Jonas' words for a moment. "I understand there has been a rash of murdered Lights in Oxford, where you and your associates have been abiding."

"Yes. I believe there has." Jonas replied. His eyes scrutinized Ramy's face.

"It is odd, is it not? That your feeding habits have changed so much?"

"I don't understand." Jonas looked confused.

"You and your associates are Bleeders and yet over the last two years you have also been killing Lights, publicly I might add, as Feeders. How do you account for your change in feeding habits? Have you lost your taste for blood?"

The crowd murmured.

Joshua glanced at Ramy and then at Jonas, not sure what was going on.

I watched Jonas' face, his carefully crafted façade began to crack. He did not look happy at being questioned, not happy at all. I had the distinct feeling that something else was happening here and it wasn't just about Sebastian.

"Account for it? It was not I." Jonas said.

"Jonas, we know it was." Empusa calmly replied, "I saw it."

"Perhaps just a few humans here and there, when there was a need to protect our secret. After all, we must not let the humans know of our presence." He smiled smugly knowing he was using the Council's own laws to help himself.

"Ah...yes...quite true," Ramy nodded, "and yet, Jonas, you have hunted and fed as a Bleeder since you evolved over a hundred years ago and always managed to stay safe from discovery."

"I don't understand what any of this has to do with the murder of Sebastian. I demand the law be upheld and this...boy...be put to death, as our law rightly states." Jonas roared.

I gasped in horror. To fear something in your head is very different to actually hearing it voiced. My mind tried to find a way out for Joshua but I couldn't think of a thing that would help. My panic was almost at the flight level and I found it increasing hard to remain where I was. I wanted to run away and hide, hide until this bad dream ended.

Ramy regarded Jonas, "All in good time, all in good time..." He said, not moved by the outburst. "In answer to your question, the relevance of your answers will be plain to see, once you have answered the question, Jonas."

I could hear the steel in Ramy's voice from where I was stood.

Jonas eyes narrowed as he spoke. "We fancied a change in our diet." He stated simply.

"Ah...a change was it? I see." Nodded Ramy, his long black hair shimmering as he did so.

"Enough of this Ramy, let us proceed." Lamia said impatiently from her throne.

"Yes, yes...my sweet Lamia." Ramy smiled at her indulgently. He reminded me of a kindly Grandfather, quieting an impatient child. Only no Grandfather I'd ever met was as terrifyingly dangerous as this ancient Pharaoh.

"Empusa, would you bless us with information from your visions, my sweet?" Ramy said.

Empusa stood, her hair swinging as she did so. The other members of the Council looked at each other as if this was something unexpected.

"I have seen many things over the last two years, all of which I have shared with Ramy and Lamia." She paused.

The other members of the Councils seemed more alert now.

"I have seen many killings made to look like natural deaths by Jonas and his followers, rather than by their usual Bleeder methods. These killings appeared not to be in a pattern of any sort and they continued to kill other Lights by Bleeding them."

"I can't see how our feeding habits..." Jonas interrupted.

"Silence." Ramy roared as he stood up again.

Jonas fumed but remained silent. He looked around the room and back at Ramy, who glared at him and remained standing. Ramy barely moved his head and the two guards, who were standing against the wall behind Jonas, grasped him with such speed they were a blur. One held a knife to his heart and the other held one to his throat.

Jonas became very still, seething with fury.

Several of Jonas' friends growled and surged forward. I could see guards coming in and lining the walls, they stood silently and watched the crowd.

I remembered the only way to kill a Chameleon was to separate the heart and brain, I glanced back at Jonas and at the two knives. What the hell is going on, why had they grabbed him?

"What is this? I demand to know by what right you hold me?" Jonas said, echoing my thoughts.

"I couldn't see why these unusual killings were happening, until Sebastian killed the human girl, the one that Joshua Marston had tried to defend because of his love for her. It was then that I saw the connection in Sebastian's mind as he did it." Empusa said.

"We have been watching you for a long time, Jonas, and we now know what you have been doing. I only regret we had not understood it earlier." Ramy stated.

"What is this rubbish?" Jonas demanded and struggled against his captors. "There is no connection. We're just feeding like we've always done."

"No, you are not." Ramy replied. "Bring the girl in." He ordered.

My heart lurched as I realised they were talking about me. Joshua's eyes looked over to the doorway and at me, incomprehension on his face.

"In you go." The guard urged gruffly.

I took a deep breath and stepped through the doorway into the ballroom, my heart pounding in my chest. However, I walked out with my head held high, trying not to tremble. I dared only to look at Ramy as I moved across the room towards him. He simply smiled sweetly at me and held out his hand. A few people in the crowd began to clap, as if I were a newly evolved Chameleon who had just being announced, but the applause quickly died away. It was a very uncomfortable moment and I was terrified. I glanced at Joshua and then Jonas, who glared at me with a look of pure hatred.

Taking Ramy's hand I stood next to him.

"I am glad to see your colours are beginning to show at last, my sweet." He smiled at me kindly and turned to face the audience.

Not comprehending what he meant, I looked down at my hands and I couldn't believe what I saw. I had a faint rainbow of colours floating around my skin. He was right, my colours were starting to show. I was changing…or rather, evolving. I was becoming a Chameleon. Oh. My. God. I was evolving. Right then and there, in front of everybody.

I looked across the room to Joshua.

His eyes were wide in surprise. "You're…evolving?!" He said incredulously as a slow smile spread across his lips.

I turned back to look at Ramy. "Is this really happening? Am I dreaming?" My mind could not make sense of it. I looked down at my hands and saw the faint outline grow stronger and become vibrant colours as I watched. I looked up at him and for the first time, ever, I saw the Chameleon rainbow colours that surrounded him.

"Oh my God. You're beautiful. The colours are…." I began to reach out towards him but my arm paused mid air.

"So are you, my sweet." He touched my hand with his and smiled kindly. "This is only the beginning of the evolution, over the next few days you will experience the full change and all the wonders that come with it." He smiled indulgently at me as if he was a family member on a Sunday picnic, not a leader of a council of Chameleons in the middle of a murder trial.

I realised now why he had put me in the basement room, he knew, presumably from Empusa, I was evolving and didn't want anyone else to see it, but why? I looked back towards the audience and saw their Chameleon rainbow colours, they were all so beautiful. I was mesmerized. I spotted the Marstons on the front row, their faces showed the same utter amazement as I felt at my evolution.

"Kate, is the girl that Sebastian killed." Ramy announced.

His voice snapped my mind back to the trial.

The crowd gasped as they looked at me and my now obvious Chameleon colours. Then there attention went to Jonas and I could sense waves of shock and hatred from the crowd.

"As you can all plainly see, Kate is a newly evolved Chameleon. Therefore, as Joshua Marston was defending one of our own from death at the hands of Sebastian Doyle, all charges against Joshua are henceforth dropped." Ramy smiled, a deep and beautiful smile.

A cheer went up from the crowd as Joshua looked at Ramy in amazement, Ramy gestured for him to move over and stand near me. Joshua quickly stepped across the floor to be at my side. He just stood and looked at me, "You're evolving." He said again, quietly this time but equally as astonished as before.

"You're free." I grabbed his hand tightly, never wanting to let go.

We reluctantly turned from each other to watch Ramy and Jonas.

Jonas glowered at us and struggled to get free from his captors, the air around the three men became a blur as they fought. However, the guards managed to hold him.

Several members of the council stood.

"What is the meaning of all this, Ramses?" Demanded a tall muscular black woman.

"What are you doing, Ramy? Have you lost your mind?" The Indian male angrily asked.

"Ah...Loo and Vetala. I think you will find the explanation most interesting." Ramy replied confidently. "Please go on, Empusa dear."

"The connection I saw was that Jonas and his people were killing the newly evolved before they had started to evolve." Empusa explained. "I wasn't completely sure of the meaning until I knew Kate was alive and saw she would evolve."

The crowd exploded in a huge uproar with loud cries of outrage, as Empusa words sunk in. The crowd surged forward angrily and a line of guards quickly appeared before the crowd to restrain them.

All eyes in the room were upon Jonas.

"We have been watching you for the last two years Jonas. Your crimes did not go unseen, I am only saddened by the fact I could not see the connection until recently." Empusa said.

"Jonas Alexander, by the Law of this Council you are sentenced to death for the unspeakable crime of killing thirteen pre-evolved Chameleons." Ramy announced. "Guards, arrest him and his associates."

I looked out into the crowd to see the guards had positioned themselves around every one of Jonas' people. They were stood close to Izzy, Marcus and several others I didn't recognise, though, I wasn't surprised to see Xing included with them. The guards had grabbed all of them.

"Why would you do such a thing, Jonas?" Asked Lamia.

"He wants only the newly evolved Bleeders who will follow him, the rest he kills." The words were out before I realised I'd actually said them.

Everyone turned to look at me and I felt myself blush. I concentrated on not going red and to my surprise felt the flush diminish. Ramy smiled at me, somewhat grimly and nodded.

What I'd said was true.

"Guards, take them away from our sight." He said.

Chaos exploded all around us and I watched as events seemed to happen in slow motion. The guards grabbed their prisoners just as the prisoners turned on them and their fights turned into blurs, until one or the other died.

Jonas made use of the distraction and swiftly turned on the two guards holding him, removing the head of one and then the other with his bare hands. All I saw, in this frozen moment of time, were the knives of the guards clattering on the floor where they'd fallen from their dead hands and then the limp, lifeless bodies falling to the ground with a sickening thud. His sudden strength and agility told me he had been biding his time, waiting for the right moment. I looked at Jonas and realised he was rushing directly towards me, Joshua leapt in front of me as I screamed, terror rooting me to the spot.

Jonas at first seemed to continue to lunge towards me but then suddenly flew in the opposite direction. It took me a moment to realise what had happened, Ramy had stood in front of Joshua and had pushed Jonas back with such force that he'd hit the opposite wall destroying the plaster.

A scream of rage came from my right, I whirled around and saw Izzy heading directly for me, her face a mask of fury, her hair flying out behind her. There was no time to react, she would be on me any second, way before I could move. I saw Michael leap into the air after her, he landed inches away from me with Izzy's head in his hands, her warm blood sprayed up across my arm and onto my chest. I staggered backwards trying to escape it.

With a rainbow blur Loo and Vetala leapt to Jonas' side and helped him fight off the guards now surrounding him.

The remaining Council were herded to the back corner of the ballroom for safety by their personal guards.

In the audience, panic had set in. Chameleons instantly chose sides and it was obvious that trouble had been brewing for a very long time.

Rasputin saw where the Council had been taken and headed across the hall towards them. At first, I thought he was moving to protect them until I saw him reach a Council member and rip his head clean off. He then turned and rushed towards Ramy.

Ramy spun around, surprised to see Rasputin heading for him with a look of pure hatred on his face. Rasputin let out a roar of rage as he closed in. Ramy stood his ground and, as Rasputin got nearer, Marcus charged in too, knocking Ramy over and making him crash into the ornate thrones. Ramy's head smashed against the back wall with a sickening crack.

Rasputin swerved towards me in a blur, he crashed into Joshua sending him flying, scooped me up and hauled me over his shoulder. Without missing a step, he ran over to Jonas and the other Bleeders who were fighting off the few remaining guards.

I yelled out for Joshua in surprise as everything blurred before my eyes. I tried hard not to panic and tried to adjust my eyes and mind to slow everything down. My mind didn't seem to work how it used to, instead of screaming in fear there was a calm feeling spreading throughout my body, creating an astonishing awareness and clarity of thought. I could only presume it was something to do with me being a Chameleon now, that thought disturbed me more than I'd ever imagined it would.

I saw the Marstons and our friends look in my direction for a fraction of a second and then they all burst into life, like a switch had been turned on. They flew across the hall towards us with murder in their eyes. Joshua, Wil and Michael were the first to react and were at the front of the attack.

Marcus and Rasputin, with me still on his shoulder, reached Jonas and several other Chameleons from the crowd who'd joined them, they quickly destroyed the remaining human guards who stood between them and the exit.

Still I felt no fear, just a sense of calm calculation. I knew I would be ready to escape the moment I got the chance. How odd it felt to have such control over my mind.

The last thing I saw was Lamia, as she shouted out orders, telling the remaining guards to follow her as she ran after us.

Recovery

The images of those chasing us bounced in and out of my vision as I was being jostled on Rasputin's shoulder. I tried to struggle free, but I was held with an iron grip. I couldn't see where we were going, only were we'd been. The ballroom and the main building became smaller and all I could see were the stone pathways as we rushed along them. Someone shouted and I could hear fighting in front of us.

I began to think they were going to take me off the island and then it would be hopeless, how would anyone find me? I had no clue what to do and expected to feel a deep dread in the pit of my stomach again, but there was nothing, only calm. How odd it felt.

I looked down the path at those chasing us. The sun was almost setting and the colours of day were changing into twilight, this combined with the rainbows I could see around everyone was incredibly hypnotizing. I concentrated and I could see everyone getting nearer, I could even see the desperate faces of my friends as they chased us. I prayed for help to reach us before it was too late. We came to a sudden halt by the pier. I was thrown roughly into the bottom of the little boat and guarded by Rasputin, just as our pursuers reached us.

Lamia and the guards approached us first, from the left side of the island and immediately began to fight Jonas and his fol-

Chameleon

lowers. Joshua and everyone else were just arriving down the main pathway leading from the hotel. I could see them all fighting with Jonas' supporters, it seemed evenly matched as they blurred in their struggles. I wanted desperately to help.

Rasputin leapt from the boat to join his comrades in the fight.

I looked around, realising for the first time there was only one other person on the boat, the driver and he was obviously human as he had no rainbow colours, just a muddy grey colour hovering around his skin. I did not have time to think about his colour as I spotted a toolbox under one of the seats, luckily the driver was distracted trying frantically to start the boat. I reached in and grabbed the first thing that came to hand, a large wrench. Gripping it tightly in my hand, I walked quietly behind the driver, trying hard not to rock the boat, raised the wrench and brought it crashing down on the back of his head knocking him to the ground unconscious, I hoped.

I checked around me to find that no one had seen me move, they were all preoccupied by the fight.

I noticed Helena was struggling with another female Chameleon, they wrestled and finally Helena got a free hand and punched the woman in the face. I heard the sickening crunch of bone breaking from where I stood a good twenty yards away. The woman, not surprisingly, went down heavily.

I searched the battle for the rest of my friends, all of them were engaged in fights to the death. Each fight was like a choreographed dance, a blur of movement and colours. Chameleon against Chameleon and Chameleon against Human. The images of bodies being torn apart in the bloody struggle terrified me, but it also gave me courage to know they were fighting to stop Jonas and save me. I had to do something to help. I knew that any moment Jonas could jump into the boat and disappear with me forever. God alone knew what would be in store for me if that happened. Grisly images of him holding my heart in his hand, as he drained away my life, flashed before my eyes.

I moved closer to the engine of the boat, with no clue what I was doing but knowing I had to try. I lifted the wooden door that housed the engine and was greeted with the thick fumes of grease and oil. I spotted some wires, grabbed them and yanked. Nothing moved. I tried again, but this time focused all my strength on the task of pulling the wires. Instantly, the wires broke loose and I flew back against the side of the boat, rocking it perilously. I looked at the wires in my hand for a moment and without another thought threw them overboard into the Mediterranean Sea.

My pleasure at doing something, hopefully useful, didn't last long as I felt myself hauled painful up by my hair to face Jonas, eye to eye.

"Ah...Kate, the meddling bitch...at last we meet properly." He laughed, roughly pushed me down on the seat and turned to the steering console.

I leapt up and moved over to the side of the boat to climb out, just as Marcus, Clara, Rasputin and the other two Bleeders from the council, Loo and Vetala, leapt into the boat pushing me back in. I could see Joshua and his family fighting alongside Lamia and the guards but they were just too far to help me.

Jonas paid no attention to them and instead turned the key on the engine.

Nothing happened.

He growled in frustration and turned to glare at me.

I looked at him smugly, "Engine trouble?" I said, surprised at the cocky tone of my voice. I felt that dead calm and strength again, even though I should've been sat trembling in fear.

"Bitch." Jonas turned to his followers, "Release the ropes. Marcus, Grigori grab the oars."

Crap, I hadn't realised there were oars too.

Chameleon

Jonas glanced up at the fighting.

He saw exactly what I did, our side was winning.

Joshua was getting closer. I saw him glance determinedly at me and then punch one of Jonas's human guards in the face, knocking him to the floor.

The boat lurched into movement as Marcus and Rasputin began pulling on the oars and hauled us away from shore. A cry went out as Jonas' followers on land realised they had been abandoned. Most of them, wisely, surrendered quickly and those that didn't died just as quickly. Lamia and the others were rounding up the survivors as I watched my new-found family and friends move further and further away.

Within moments we'd almost reached the pier at the edge of Rovinj town, when Jonas barked out orders to his people instructing them to dispose of the guards on the pier once we landed and to bring the car around immediately. He knew he would not have long to make his escape.

"They will hunt you down, no matter what you do to me." I said bravely, jutting out my chin in defiance.

Jonas grabbed me by the arm and hauled me to my feet. His face was barely an inch from mine as he glared hatefully at me. "You have been a thorn in my side from the start, Kate. You will die by my own hand I swear it but not yet, you have one more use."

"Why not kill her now, boss and get it over with? She's just going to slow us down." Marcus said as he put down the oar.

"Because she is the key, you fool. I hadn't realised just how useful she'll be, until this evening. Now, get the car." Jonas growled.

The Chameleons swarmed off the little boat and overwhelmed the human guards on the pier.

The boat rocked violently and I saw wet bodies flying into the boat from nowhere. I realised Chameleons from the island had swum out after us and leapt from the ocean into the boat, like salmon leaping upstream to spawn. Jonas quickly picked me up and threw me like a sac through the air into the waiting arms of Marcus on the pier. He then turned back to face his attackers and came face to face with Joshua, Wil and Michael. Daniel and Lamia were now already in the boat, fighting the two rogue council members.

I struggled against the hold Marcus had on me, but couldn't get free. "Joshua!" I shouted, hoping he would hear me in the noise that surrounded us.

Joshua managed to free himself from the fight, he leapt from the boat onto the pier, in front of Marcus and I, in one smooth movement. I heard squeals of car tyres as a black BMW screeched to a halt beside us. Rasputin leap out of the driver's side just as two cars of the Croatian Police arrived. Four uniformed officers stepped out of the cars and pulled guns on everyone. Rasputin flew over the bonnet in a blur with the obvious intent to kill them. He had broken two of the officer's necks in an instant. He walked through the hail of bullets from the other two and loomed over them.

Marcus, who had me by the throat, was surprised by the arrival of the police and Joshua took advantage of his distraction and ran at him. Just as Joshua reached him Marcus swung round laughing, as if it was a game.

Jonas was still on the boat and he fought with both Michael and Wil, he smashed Wil into the engine, knocking him senseless. Unfortunately for Jonas, this gave Michael a chance to grab him around the neck. Jonas managed to get out of the throat grip, by pulling back Michael's arm and snapping it at the shoulder. Michael screamed in pain and collapsed, just as Wil got back on his feet. Jonas grabbed Wil and threw him thirty feet away from the boat into the open sea. He managed to slip past Lamia and Daniel who were struggling with Loo and Vetala

Chameleon

in the boat.

Jonas leapt onto the pier and ran for the car.

Rasputin swiftly broke the necks of the last two policemen, he didn't seem to realise he'd been shot several times in the chest. I noticed with a sick fascination as the events whirled around me.

A yell of triumph ripped through the air from the boat as Lamia tore the head off Loo and let her body fall onto the deck and Daniel finally found a way to do the same to Vetala.

Back on the pier, Joshua lunged at Marcus again, as I struggled to get out of his iron grip by twisting away from his body. Joshua's head and chest rammed into Marcus' side and all three of us flew off the pier, we plunged into the warm Mediterranean waters. I was dragged down to the rocky bottom by the weight of Marcus, his arm pressing me against him. I struggled for air as I gulped in the water, my long ball gown weighing me down further, trapping me there as if I was caught in seaweed.

Joshua held on to Marcus and managed to punch him in the face, not an easy thing to do under water. An explosion of bubbles left Marcus' mouth and he released me to grab Joshua, pushing him against a rock trying to hit his head on it.

I was quickly running out of air and panic started to take over. My vision began to go black around the edges, images of my life flashed before me. Images of my mum and dad, together and happy when I was small, of the time in Hyde Park with dad and his girlfriend and her horrible son, of mum and I alone at Christmas, of moving to Shipton-under-Wychwood. I saw faces of those I knew and loved: mum, Joshua, Tara, Wil, Helena, Daniel, Michael, Moira and even Ally from school.

All now lost, never to be seen again.

A sad calmness began to settle inside me as the last of my air left me in small bubbles and I floated down to the sea bed. The calm continued to spread through my new Chameleon body, overriding years of instinct and forcing me to relax. I remembered Joshua telling me that Chameleons didn't need much air to live, it was how they survived during their interment. Without thinking, I opened my mouth as if to draw in the desperately needed air but allowed the water instead. I gasped at the incredible pain in my chest, which only forced in more water. After several long seconds of agony and hoping the end would come quickly, I began to feel my body using the energy of the water to sustain me. I felt the energy ripple through me like ripples on a pond as, my strength began to return and my mind became more and more alert.

I looked over at Joshua just as Marcus struck his face violently with a large rock. I screamed Joshua's name but no sound came out, of course, only water moved out of my mouth. I watched, horrified, as the rock came crashing down again on Joshua's face and I saw his body go limp as his blood swirled and clouded the water around him.

Before I could move, Marcus swam at great speed up to the surface and vanished out of the water. I swam as quickly as I could, in my dress, over to Joshua, his face was more badly damaged than I had feared. It looked crushed, utterly broken and a terrible bloody mess. I grabbed him by the arm and began swimming for the surface, struggling at first with his dead weight. Suddenly, he felt lighter, as though he was swimming to help me, but when I looked down he still wasn't moving and I saw Wil on the other side of him, helping me bring him up.

We broke the surface a little way from the pier. I coughed the liquid up from my lungs and breathed in air again, amazed at how strange it was to feel air expand my lungs where only water had been for the last few minutes. It was almost too easy to change from breathing water to breathing air again. I glanced at Wil who also coughed out the water and then down at Joshua. My breath caught in my throat as I looked at his ruined face.

Chameleon

My gorgeous Joshua would never be gorgeous again. He would be lucky if he could even see again, as one eye socket looked completely smashed inwards. We swam to the pier where Wil climbed out and reached down for him. I held my skirt in one hand and climbed up the ladder to kneel next to Joshua who, thankfully remained unconscious. I couldn't imagine the pain he would be in if awoke.

The fighting had ended and there were bodies everywhere but I saw no sign of Jonas, Marcus and Rasputin, I guessed they had escaped seeing as their car had vanished. Lamia and Daniel were picking up the body and parts, except for the body of the policemen, and placing them into a nearby boat, which had obviously been co-opted as a ferry, since the regular one was unserviceable now.

Michael staggered over to us and sat down on the wooden pier with his back against one of the railings, his arm standing out at a strange angle from the shoulder joint.

Daniel rushed over as soon as he saw us. "How is he?" He asked, the worried look on his face was marred by smears of blood.

"I don't know...we should get him to a hospital." I said looking down at Joshua's ruined face not knowing what to do. "Marcus...he hit him so hard in the face with a rock...a couple of times...oh god, I can see bone in several places." I babbled as tears ran down my face, "Joshua." I whispered desperately.

"Get him, and the rest of you, in that boat and get to the island, now, before the crowd gets nearer or more Police arrive." Lamia instructed.

"I don't know if we should move him." I said, trying to remember what you should do when someone is badly hurt.

"Just do it, quickly." She growled.

A crowd had begun to appear at the opposite end of the pier and they were moving cautiously towards us with flashlights. I hadn't even noticed that the twilight had turned to night. I heard more police sirens in the distance. Wil lifted Joshua and put him in the bottom of the boat next to the gruesome remains of several Chameleons. I tried not to look at the mass of body parts and concentrated on climbing into the boat next to Joshua as Daniel started the engine ready to take us back to the island.

Lamia remained on the pier and called out to us. "Go quickly and keep the lights off. Tell Ramy and the others I need them here to deal with the Police." Lamia said as she turned to face the sirens coming towards the pier.

Within minutes we were climbing out of the boat in front of Helena, Moira and Tara. The remains were quickly unloaded, then Ramy and several others sped off to help Lamia with the authorities.

Helena cried out in shock when she saw Joshua's face as he was carried out of the boat. I realised I was shaking but at that precise moment I couldn't think which of the many traumas I'd witnessed tonight, had caused it.

"Everything will be alright, Kate." Helena said in a calm voice.

I wasn't sure if she was trying to convince me, or herself.

"Let's take him to the ballroom. We can lay him on a table in there." Daniel said as Wil walked down the path carrying Joshua with what seemed like very little effort.

Once inside the ballroom, Joshua was placed on a table.

"Get me tweezers and any alcohol you can find." Daniel said.

Helena and Tara rushed off in a blur to see what they could find, within moments they were back with bottle of brandy and a pair of tweezers.

My anger built at everyone's seemingly unconcerned attitude to Joshua's terrible injuries. "Shouldn't we be on the way to a hospital?" I said through gritted teeth wishing someone would listen to me.

"No need, Kate. We have everything we need here." Michael said.

"No need? Are you all crazy? Joshua needs surgery and probably one hell of a lot of it and he needs it right now!" I said.

"Really, there is no need for such measures, Kate." Daniel said, "Come here and I will show you." He held his hand out for me.

I stepped closer but did not take his hand, anger brewed inside me dangerously. I drew closer to Joshua and cringed at his ruined face.

"Watch, Kate." Daniel used the tweezers to remove a small piece of stone from Joshua's cheek muscle and poured a little of the alcohol onto it.

I watched, incredulous, wondering how any of this was going to help him. It was like living in the middle ages, what next? Leeches?

Even as I watched, some of the edges, separated by the pieces of rock, were knitting together by themselves.

"It's...it's mending." I said.

"You see why we didn't need a hospital?" Daniel said.

"This isn't real...this is..." My mind reeled as I watched Joshua's face slowly knit itself back together, millimetre by millimetre.

"Now you know why we have to be quick about getting the chips of stone out and cleaning the wounds." Daniel said "They will actually get healed over and stay there unless, of course, one cuts them out later. As for the alcohol, it's best to stop any infection now. His body would fight it, of course, but by doing this now he doesn't have to and that energy can be used elsewhere, like healing his face."

"Do you all...I mean do we all...heal like that?" I asked. I heard a loud crack from behind me and I whirled round to see Tara holding Michael's arm. The strange angle at his shoulder joint had gone and his arm looked normal again.

Michael nodded thanks to Tara, who quietly went back to sit with Wil.

I shook my head in disbelief.

"Yes, Kate. All Chameleons heal quickly, unless you separate the head from the body, of course, which kills us completely...as you well know." Daniel explained.

"Does that mean Joshua will look like Joshua again?" I hoped beyond measure it did mean that. I stared down at his face, watching the tissue, muscle and bone knit themselves back together slowly. The deepest wounds were healing first, hiding the exposed bone. It was as horrifying as it was fascinating, my new vision enabled me to look more closely than any normal human eye could. I looked so closely into the wound that I could see the cells as they repaired themselves and came together to recreate his flesh. I became mesmerized by it, by the very details and beauty of it.

His face began to take back the shape I knew and loved. The eye socket seemed to fill out, pushing itself back from the inside out, becoming its proper shape again instead of a huge indent. Joshua's eyelid stitched itself back together leaving fresh new pink skin. The deep cuts on his face began to close until there was nothing left of his injuries other than bright pink scar tissue, which criss-crossed his face, like train tracks at a junction.

I heard his breathing becoming less shallow. I peered at his face looking for any sign of the trauma but there was nothing except the scars, which to my astonishment, were now fading to pale pink. I peered closer and watched as the scar tissue went from pale pink to white and then vanish completely. I could see now, why it's so hard to kill a Chameleon.

Joshua eyes suddenly flew open and he sat bolt upright. He looked round the room like he had no clue where he was.

"Everything is alright son, it's over. You can relax now."

Daniel placed his hand on Joshua's chest and restrained him from getting off the table.

"What happened? Why is everything blurry?" Joshua said.

"You were injured, but you're healing rapidly. Your full sight should return in moments." Daniel said.

"Where is Kate? Did we save her, is she okay?"

I stepped into line of sight of his good eye, "I'm here Joshua." I reached out my hand, placing it on his cheek.

Joshua placed his hand over it and pressed his face against my hand. "Are you alright? Is everyone else alright?"

"Everyone is fine. I'm unharmed, thanks to you...yet again. It's getting to be a habit, you saving me and all." I laughed with relief.

"I will never stop doing it." Joshua sat on the edge of the table and pulled me against him, resting his head on my shoulder.

Helena came and stood next to us, placing her hand on his shoulder. Joshua looked up at her, blinked and smiled. "That's better, I can see you almost properly now mother. The blurriness has nearly gone."

There were loud conversations all around us as the remaining members of the council filed back into the room, including Ramy and Lamia who had just returned from the mainland. There was an acrid smell of smoke and cooking meat in the air, presumably they had torched the bodies of the dead. I shuddered. I could only imagine the amount of bribery and quick talking Lamia and Ramy had to do to keep the events of tonight quiet. I was amazed, yet again, by the power of the Council.

I glanced around at the shattered remains of the ball, bodies and gore sat side by side with strewn chairs and tables. The few Chameleons who had remained were either resting and healing or talking animatedly about the events of the evening.

All of a sudden, I realised I could literally feel everyone around me. I could feel each person's energy near me, like a human can smell the person stood next to them. I noticed that the feeling of energy was very much like a smell, each person was distinctive, like Helena with her flower and tree energy, and Michael with his human feeder energy. Each one utterly different. I wondered briefly if it was normal. No one had mentioned this to me, but then again I guessed there were a lot of things about being a Chameleon I didn't know yet.

"Are you alright?" Joshua asked, seeing for the first time the blood that covered most of my upper body.

I nodded and looked down at the blood covering me. I managed to find my voice, "Yes, I'm okay. It's not mine...it's mostly yours." I moved my hand slowly down my arm, amazed at how quickly the blood had dried on my bare skin and saw again the rainbow colours around my flesh.

"I can't believe it." Joshua reached out as if to touch my arm.

"No, really. I'm not hurt." I said reassuringly.

"No, not that. You, you're evolving." He said, as he looked me in the eye. "Wow."

"I know." I looked down at my hand, "It's so weird to see colour around my hand."

Joshua reached out and took my hand, the two rainbows merged. "Beautiful."

I was suddenly dismayed. There was no vibration in his touch. Nothing.

I let go of his hand. "It's gone." I cried. Saddened at losing it, somehow it had become comforting.

"What's gone?"

"The vibration...I can't feel it any more." I touched him again and first thought there was nothing there, but when I concentrated, I realised that the buzz was still there, however, it was just a lot more subtle...almost like the pull of a magnet. As I brushed my hand over his skin, I could feel the subtle vibration resonating on mine. Finally, I realised what it was, the exchange

Chameleon

of our energies.

"You may not feel it, but I do." His eyes widened in astonishment.

"I can now...wait, you can feel that too?" I looked down at our two hands touching and the rainbow of colours that intertwined there. "A subtle vibration?"

"Yes, I do. That's it exactly...a subtle vibration."

He stared at me with a huge smile on his face.

"Why are you smiling?"

"It's amazing. You're a Chameleon." He grinned, "I will never be able to hurt you again...and nor will anyone else." His face lit up with pure joy, something I had not seen in a long time.

"I hadn't had a chance to think about it." I said. "Why didn't I know what was happening? How come it just came on? Aren't there symptoms...or some warning...before you evolve?"

I needed answers, now that the danger had passed and we were all safe. In fact, I needed to know everything and right now. I could feel the changes inside my body, my organs felt different somehow, I wouldn't be able to explain it if I tried. I just felt different in a subtle way.

"I should have realised...before in the storeroom, you hadn't been eating had you? I saw the untouched plate of food." He said.

I shook my head. "I thought it was just fear not making me hungry, but thinking about it I usually eat when worried. What are the other symptoms?" I asked.

"Well, there's better control over pain, more strength and sometimes a lot of unexplained anger, often a temperature..." He looked at me surprised, "So that explains why you were so warm, after..."

"After you didn't kill me...you didn't, because you couldn't...not that way anyway, as I'd already started to evolve."

"My god, yes, you're right...that makes sense." A look of profound relief washed over him.

I took a deep breath and closed my eyes, trying to feel any differences within me and once again I was able to easily calm my reeling mind. I could think rationally and clearly for the first time in several weeks. I smiled.

"What?" Joshua looked at me.

"I can think really clearly, I tried to calm my mind and it happened instantly."

Joshua laughed, "Welcome to my world."

"I could get used to this part very easily, being a Chameleon is not so bad after all, is it? What about the interment? Will they make me do it now, seeing as I'm here?" I felt cold tendrils of panic creep along my spine as fear filled me again.

"Breathe, Kate. Calm your fears." He said, obviously hearing my change in heart beat.

I closed my eyes again and breathed deeply, willing myself to regain a sense of calm and instantly it returned, I sighed with relief.

"The interment, by our own laws, has to be within a year of evolving, for the very reason that you have to prepare and teach yourself some measure of control. The Council are not allowed to inter anyone so newly evolved as you. They usually only test after six months passed, to give you time to practice. So there is no need to fear them now." Joshua said.

I nodded my understanding as I glanced at the material of Joshua's now torn and bloody shirt. I felt compelled to stare at it, fascinated by the weave of the threads and the colour. The longer I looked, the more my vision zoomed in like before with his wounds, it was like using a telephoto lens. I could see the weft and weave of the pattern and the individual twisted strands that made up each thread. Much to my amazement, I could also see, a slight glow of colour radiating from the fibre.

"Oh," I said, "that is just amazing. The threads in your shirt, I can see them all in detail."

"Ah...your Chameleon vision is starting to show itself. You can see now why some Chameleons can get easily distracted. I once spent hours looking at a dragonfly's wing. You should see that up close." He said.

"Why is there a slight glow in the fibres?" I asked not taking my eyes off it.

"There is energy in everything but it is a very faint in some items, with man-made inanimate objects, especially. With others, like plants and trees, it's quite pronounced."

I managed to tear my eyes away from his shirt to look at him. "So I will see this everywhere?"

"More than likely. It depends how your sight evolves. Everyone is different, some see more than others. It will take a few days for you to fully evolve after which, we'll know better what you can see and what you can't." Joshua said and smiled at me, that deeply sexy smile that melted my bones all over again.

"What? Why are you smiling like that?" I said.

He leaned over and kissed me on the lips, the subtle vibration seemed even better than the buzz I used to feel, it was a thousand times more potent and sexy.

"I guess we have no fear on that score anymore." I smiled a very naughty and suggestive smile.

He actually blushed and I could tell he was thinking the same thing as I was. "I guess not." He laughed.

"Funny, you'd think I'd be tired or hungry after the last few days, but I'm not...I feel...very healthy." I felt like I could easily run a marathon.

"It may take a couple of days before you will need to feed. It's different for everyone." Joshua stood and brushed some loose hair back behind my ear, it had fallen from my now ruined and dripping hairstyle.

"How ya doing, Bro?" Wil said as he appeared suddenly beside us, "Nice Chameleon colours, Kate." Wil's face burst into a massive grin.

"Hi, Wil." I smiled shyly.

He hugged me fiercely, "Welcome to the mad house. This is so cool." He grinned.

"Thank you, I think." I smiled back and realised I'd felt a vibration from Wil too but it was different. "Do you all vibrate?"

"What?" Wil asked looking puzzled. He looked from me to Joshua and back again.

"When I touch you, I feel vibrations through the skin. It's a different vibration for each of you, similar but still slightly different." I explained.

"I have never felt that. Do you feel it, Josh?" Wil asked.

"Only with Kate." He looked at me curiously.

"Really? That's strange." I said.

"After everything that's happened since we met, including you dying and then evolving into a Chameleon, you think that's strange?" Joshua burst into laughter.

"Well, yeah...actually, I do." I couldn't help but laugh too.

Our laughter was interrupted by Tara, Moira and Michael, who were pleased to see Joshua had recovered and amazed to see me in my transformed state. They welcomed me as if I was instantly a part of the family, each one congratulating me. I looked at them, they all had the same rainbow colours floating above their skins, it was fascinating to watch and very beautiful.

"Amazing isn't it, the first time you really see it?" Moira had realised what I was looking at.

"Very, it's so beautiful." I said.

"Wait until you see the humans and watch their colours change as their emotions do, now that is beautiful." She said.

"I saw one, the boat driver...I...knocked him out, and I hope he is okay. His was a muddy grey colour, what does that mean?"

"That's fear, my dear." Daniel said from his seat at the nearby table.

"Oh."

"Hopefully, you will be able to tell which Chameleons are Hippies, Feeders or Bleeders soon." Tara said.

"How?"

"The food they are drawn to have brighter colours in their rainbows. Hippies, for example, have slightly brighter greens and yellows. Whereas the Bleeders are more reds and black, the Feeders have a more balanced colour range." She explained, "Hopefully your sight with develop enough to see the slight differences in the colour levels."

"That's so interesting. I think it could be very usef..." I paused mid word as we were interrupted by people shouting. I glanced over towards the remaining Council members who were having a heated debate at the other end of the room. I could hear them all talking at once like a huge noise in my head. I shook my head as if to shake them out.

"What is it?" Joshua asked.

"They are so loud." I nodded over to the other Chameleons

"No, they are speaking at a normal sound level, it's your hearing it's getting better by the minute, and it'll soon be as good as mine."

I looked at him in despair, "How can you stand this?" I grimaced.

"Focus on one of the voices, anyone's...but just one." He suggested.

I concentrated and immediately all the other voices disappeared and I could only hear a woman talking about despicable traitors. "Okay, that's better...I can just hear one now." It was such a relief.

"Now tune her out, so that there is nothing." Joshua instructed.

I listened to her for a second longer, then thought about a

volume control on a stereo and I mentally turned down the volume, until I couldn't hear her anymore. "Now that is cool. It's lovely and quiet in my head now. Thank you." I smiled at him and stared, again, fascinated by Joshua's rainbow of colours.

"You're welcome." He grinned. "It's much easier to evolve when you have another Chameleon by your side, I was lucky I had my family. Some aren't so lucky." He glanced at his brother who was quietly talking to Tara.

I understood his meaning. "It's hard to think of myself as a Chameleon now, it feels so very strange."

"It can take a bit of getting used to." He squeezed my hand in encouragement.

"I don't feel any different, though. I feel the same...I feel like me." I said, "But more me than before, does that make any sense?"

"What did you expect?" He smiled. "You must have thought about what it would be like, at some point."

"I did, but, I don't know...perhaps...I thought I would feel like a superhuman or even some kind of deadly dangerous...somehow." I laughed nervously, only half joking.

In reality, the fact that I was now both began to sink in.

Beginning

When Ramy returned from the mainland he walked past our small group and over to the body of the Chameleon Rasputin had murdered. He stood still for a moment, looking down at it with sadness. "Prepare Murduk's body to return with us to Castrum Lucis." He ordered the remaining guards.

A few claimed humans, presumably belonging to the Council members, cowered in a small group. I could tell by their aura colour they were afraid, it was the same grey as the boat driver. These were the first humans I'd really looked at since evolving. I felt no draw to them, no kinship any longer. It was strange to know that only a day or so ago I had been one of them and scared almost out of my mind too. A sudden realisation of how fragile they are swept over me. I knew then I would never be able to take a human's life simply to sustain my own.

Wil called jokingly to his brother, "Josh, how's your face? Man, you were ugly, it was grossing me out." He winked at him.

"Thanks, bro. I know I can always count on you to tell me how it is." Joshua laughed and rolled his eyes.

I must have looked horrified, as both Joshua and Wil burst out laughing.

"Ignore those two, Kate." Tara said. "Thank goodness you're safe, we've been so worried."

"I know it's a bit belated but welcome to your new life, Kate."

Daniel said as he moved past us, making his way across the room towards Ramy and the remaining Council members.

I didn't even try to listen to them. I felt kind of numb from everything that had happened today. Today, yesterday, this week, hell the entire month.

"I'm delighted to see you are safe, Kate." Helena smiled as she came to stand by us again.

"I was so worried about you all." I said and looked around at my Chameleon friends, they were all as pleased to see me, as I was to see them. I said to Michael, "Thank you for stopping Izzy and saving my life, I won't forget it." I reached up and kissed him on the cheek.

"You are most welcome." He smiled, a huge and very handsome smile.

He had risked his life to save me, as had all the others. A profound sense of belonging spread through me, I now had a large family. Once again, questions began to turn in my mind, "What I want to know is why Rasputin tried to take me with them and why did he kill that Council member in particular? Murduk, was it?" I looked over at where his dismembered body lay covered with a table cloth, the material now soaking up the blood.

"No clue why they wanted you, Kate, but I think they probably killed Murduk because of his ability." Moira said.

"What ability?"

"He has the power to blind. He can send a field of energy towards someone and all they see is bright white light. He can make it temporary or not. I mean...he could..." Moira looked over at his body too.

"A tactical strike." Michael said, looking in the same direction.

"Looks like it. Smart, if you're trying to escape the Council. There are few on the Council who have abilities and he was the strongest." Moira replied.

Chameleon

Daniel ended his conversation with Ramy and walked back across the room. Not surprisingly, several other Chameleons were jostling for the Councils' attention, demanding to know what was going on and what was to be done about it. Finally, Ramy stepped forward and announced, to those of us remaining, that the Council would reconvene at Castrum Lucis for the funeral of Murduk and the other fallen Chameleons, after which there would be a proclamation. I watched as Ramy quieted many of their fears and gently informed the small crowd that although Jonas, Rasputin and Marcus had escaped, they would be hunted down and destroyed without mercy for their crimes.

Satisfied, people slowly began to leave the room.

"Let's all go back to our villa and get cleaned up." Helena suggested as she took her husband's hand and walked towards the exit.

We quietly filed out of the room. I wondered about Jonas and his companions, where could Chameleons possibly hide from other Chameleons? It seemed a lost cause to even try. As we walked, I looked at Joshua out of the corner of my eye, I realised I could now be with him openly without the possibility of losing him to one terrible death or another. The relief was so profound I could almost taste it and I slipped my arm around his waist as we walked.

By the door of the villa sat three travel bags, Joshua's, Wil's and mine from the 'newly evolved' suite. Presumably, someone had brought them over before all the trouble had started. Grateful for a moment alone, I picked up my bag, went up to my room closing the door firmly behind me and leant against it. I knew I needed to be alone for a while to try to start processing everything. Taking a deep breath and sending the wonderful feeling of calm through my mind, I walked across the room to my washroom and enjoyed a very long bath. I was beginning to feel more like me again instead of the rag doll that had been thrown around from shoulder to boat, to pier, to throat grip and finally into the sea. My body wasn't tired or achy but my mind was and I realised, with astonishment, it would be the only place I would feel weariness from now on. It was going to take some getting used to, being a Chameleon.

Sometime later, refreshed and clean, I made my way back downstairs. Everyone else had also apparently showered and changed too, I sat down next to Joshua on the sofa. They were all subdued and had been going over the events of the evening as I had in my room. It seemed that everything had changed in their world as well as mine and I wondered what all our lives would be like after tonight.

"What will happen now? I mean with the Council." I asked Daniel.

"Well, the Council will regroup, choose new members and rebuild its ranks of guards. I think the large number of Chameleons that sided and fought with Jonas surprised the Council. They have never had an enemy within the Chameleon ranks before, I think this will change many things in the future." Daniel looked serious. "However, the good news is that your mum is safe." He smiled.

I had completely forgotten about my mum over the last couple of hours. "My mum? Oh my god, Jonas. He will try to get to me through my mum again." I sat up panicked.

Daniel held up a hand, "She's alright, Kate. Everything is alright. Ramy mentioned that they sent some Chameleon guards to watch over your mum a couple of days ago when Empusa finally saw you were evolving. She is very safe, please do not worry yourself."

"Oh, thank goodness." I said and sat back.

"I dread to think what Jonas would have done if his plan hadn't been discovered. He would have been able to build an army of Bleeders in secret...but to do what?" Tara said.

Chameleon

"To take over the Council, of course. Jonas is after power and who is more powerful than the Council?" Daniel said.

Everyone nodded their agreement. The Council was more powerful than any government and in the wrong hands there would be chaos. Jonas' reasons were obvious when you had all the information, even to me, new as I was to this world.

"What is Castrum Lucis? I heard Ramy mention it and I'm sure I've heard it before too." I asked.

"Castrum Lucis is the Council's home. It is a private island in Canada, in the middle of Lake Superior, where the Councillors live most of the year. The Chameleon Archive Library is housed there, which is where I work as Principal Archivist. It's also where the Council Chambers are and where they plan the social side of things, like the evolution balls, of course they also deal with disputes and, usually, enforce our laws from there."

"Ramy said there will be a...proclamation? Or something, from them soon." I said.

"Yes. I presume it will be about finding Jonas and his accomplices. It will also probably include future security arrangements for the Council members too." Daniel said.

I nodded, it all made sense after today. Everyone was going to have to be on guard from now onwards.

"How are you doing, by the way?" Daniel asked.

"Me? I'm okay, I think." I looked around at everyone, "It's amazing how quickly I've started to see myself as something other than human. Being a Chameleon really changes things doesn't it?"

"Yes, Kate, it does." Helena said. "Part of the evolution is that the mind simply accepts the change, instead of fighting against it. Many find the transition a surprisingly simple process mentally. However, there is so much more to being a Chameleon than you know." Helena said.

"What about the vibration? Does that ever go?" I said.

Edain Duguay

"What vibration?" Tara asked.

Everyone looked at me.

"You know, the vibration when we touch each other."

"I don't feel anything when I touch a Chameleon, Kate. Does anyone else?" Helena said.

They all shook their heads.

"I get a faint vibration off Kate, but I've never gotten it from anyone else." Joshua said.

"Most interesting indeed." Daniel stood up and walked over to our couch. "May I?" He held out his hand. It reminded me of claimed humans and how they offered themselves to be tasted, the thought repulsed me even more than before, something I'd never have thought possible.

I reached up, touched his hand and I felt the subtle vibration, different yet again to Joshua's or Wil's. As if he was vibrating on a different scale. "Do you feel anything?" I asked.

"No, nothing. Do you?" Daniel looked me directly in the eyes, obviously excited at this new development.

"Yes, subtle but definitely there. It's very slightly different to Wil's and a lot different to Joshua's. It's difficult to describe, but it feels like each of you pulse at different speeds, times and strengths."

"Very interesting." Moira said.

"I can also feel it to a much lesser degree when you stand close to me too." I admitted. "Without touching."

"Really? Well, that is most fascinating." Daniel said and sat back down.

Moira beamed "That's some gift, alright."

"What do you mean?" I said.

"No other Chameleon, I have ever come across, can feel another's energy like that." Daniel said.

"I don't understand, what does it mean? Am I not normal?" I was suddenly worried I wouldn't be the same as them.

Chameleon

"It's a gift, you can tell who is a Chameleon just by standing near them or touching them, you're very fortunate." Moira said.

"Surely you can tell them by their rainbow colours anyway?" I asked confused.

Moira leaned forward in her chair, "Yes, but not all of us see that and you may be able to feel which humans have the Chameleon gene...before they evolve. The only other person that can tell us that is Empusa, and she does it by visions of their actual evolution."

"Oh." It was all I could think of to say.

"Except..." Daniel said.

"Except what?" Michael said.

"Except that Jonas has someone who can see that, too. How else could he find the humans that were going to evolve?" Daniel said.

"Of course, a seer would not only see who was evolving but also what type of Chameleon they would be." Moira answered.

"That makes sense." Wil agreed.

"Talking of visions and seeing as I will only rarely need to sleep, I doubt there'll be any more of them from me." I said. It was actually a comfort knowing this, the visions had not been pleasant.

"You never know with gifts, they have a strange way of evolving too." Moira smiled at me.

I pulled my feet under me on the sofa. "One thing has been bothering me though, why do you think Jonas wanted to take me with him and not kill me? Let's face it, he had several opportunities to kill me today...if he'd wanted." I said. The thought of Jonas reminded me of his words on the boat about how I would be useful.

"Who knows what a crazed Chameleon will do." Tara said.

"When you were with him, did he say anything about it, any reference as to why he wanted you or where they were going for that matter?" Daniel asked.

"I have no idea where they were taking me. I do know that Jonas wanted me alive because he told Marcus. He said I was the 'key' and would be 'useful', but I have no clue what he meant by that." I said.

"The 'key', you say? What an odd phrase to use, a key to what? Hmm...." Daniel said thoughtfully as he put his hand on his chin and leaned on the arm of the chair, "I must say, Kate, you are very lucky he wanted you alive, my dear." He said.

"Yes, very lucky. Especially considering what we know he's truly capable of and I have no doubt we will hear from him again. He is like a bad penny, always turning up." Tara said.

"Tara, you knew Sebastian and Jonas quite well as you all tested together, do you know where he would go to hide?" Daniel asked.

Tara sighed. "No. I know Jonas has a place in Scotland and another in Australia but I'm sure he wouldn't go anywhere near them now, they are too well known." She looked thoughtful, "He must have a secret location, he was always prepared for anything. I mean, just look at tonight, his people were spread out in the crowd and had targets including Murduk and Ramy and I can only imagine who else. I guess Jonas has been planning something along these lines for a long time and tonight was to be ground zero, as it were." Tara said.

"A coup? That makes sense." Michael said.

Moira shifted in her chair, "It is true that he didn't count on Kate being alive, evolving and the Council knowing about it. He presumed she was dead and that was his mistake. Which begs the question, why didn't he know? Why didn't his seer tell him about Kate before tonight and what was going to happen at the ball?

"Another salient point." Daniel said.

"Unless..." I said and paused as I formulated my idea.

Chameleon

"What?" Joshua asked.

"Unless...his seer did see what he was going to do, didn't like what they saw and perhaps kept the truth from him?" I said.

"Possible, but I really wouldn't want to be in the seers shoes right now, if that's the case." Wil said.

"Yeah, not a good place to be." I said.

"We need to know who the seer is, they may be very useful to us and the Council." Daniel said.

"It could be anyone. Whoever it is, they may already be dead, Jonas lost most of his followers tonight." Tara said as she lifted her feet and placed them across Wil's knees. "It may have been Raffaella but she died in the ballroom."

"She did have some ability, but nothing like what she was attesting to. I sensed she was lying at the time but then the trial changed so rapidly I didn't get the chance to report it." Moira said.

"Perhaps the seer is being held prisoner, which also means that after tonight their life is probably forfeit." Michael said.

"It may be that the seer wasn't even here. I mean would you bring your most valuable asset to a fight? Jonas was obviously planning one for tonight." Joshua said.

"Good point, son." Daniel nodded, "The seer may indeed not have been here at all, probably kept somewhere very safe."

We sat in silence, all of us lost in our thoughts.

The idea that this evening was planned beforehand, which meant we had not seen the last of Jonas was a chilling one, especially for me. I got the distinct impression I would be seeing him again one day. I closed my eyes and just lay my head against Joshua's chest. I wished I hadn't, as perfect images of every event from this evening flashed through my mind like a DVD on fast forward. I opened my eyes and gasped involuntarily at the last picture that came into view, the sight of Joshua's ruined face.

"You okay?" Joshua asked.

"Yeah, it's just when I close my eyes, I can see everything that's happened, in perfect detail too."

"That is a result of being a Chameleon. We have perfect recall, and, sadly, it's not always welcome." Michael said with a hint of sadness in his voice as he glanced at Tara, then he looked away quickly.

"I guess it's a good job we don't need to sleep often then, I think I might have nightmares if I slept tonight." I said.

"You will learn to file away much of what you see, so your brain does not get over crowded with images and thoughts, but everything is still there at the back of your mind should you ever need it. Think of it as a type of photographic memory only we get to slow it down and see even more details." Daniel explained.

"I'm sure the ability can be useful in some ways, just not right now." I said.

"You will need to feed tomorrow probably or perhaps the next day." Joshua said, trying to change the subject.

I remembered the conversation I'd had with Tara on the beach. "Will the sun help? Can I feed off it?"

"No, it can revive you a little but you will need to drain some energy from something more substantial and closer. Do you have a preference? What do you crave?" Daniel asked.

Joshua looked at me anxiously.

"Crave?" I frowned. "I don't think...I crave anything. Is that bad?" I felt unsure and insecure. Shouldn't I want to feed? I thought.

"No, that's fine. Probably just a little early yet. Your body stores the energy already in it when you evolve and uses it more efficiently. We will, eventually, need to know what you prefer though, my dear." Daniel said.

"Prefer? Oh...I see. You mean, you want to know what I'll be as in a Hippie, a Feeder or Bleeder?"

"Yes." He said simply, his eyes tightened slightly at their corners in anticipation of my answer.

"You can rest assured I'll definitely not be feeding on humans. Not a chance, not ever. I will never harm something so...fragile."

Joshua visibly relaxed, "Well, that's a relief." He grinned, "Don't get me wrong I would still love you but it would have made things a little difficult."

"I'm not sure I could stand it if you fed off humans either. It must be a hard problem for other couples to get round." I realised what I'd said out loud without thinking, it was what Tara had said about her relationship with Michael, who was a feeder and I glanced discreetly at them both.

"It can be. Relationships between two different types of feeders are tricky and a relationship between a Hippie and a Bleeder is near impossible, I believe." Daniel said.

"Yeah, I guess. It seems I have a lot to learn." I rubbed my face in an odd gesture of fatigue even though I wasn't tired, I looked at my hand contemplating it. There were a few habits that will seem irrelevant and strange now.

"Yes, there is a fair bit to learn, I'm afraid." Daniel said. "The newly evolved are expected to know our history, the laws and the founding of The Council of Nine, alongside the basics of survival and how to feed discreetly, how to survive in dire circumstances and how to fit in with humans. The later being the hardest because you have to control the urge to drain every time you touch someone, even accidentally."

I realised now that becoming a Chameleon was going to take a lot of hard work. "Talking of people, how am I going to do all that when we fly home later today and I have school tomorrow?" I started to feel the panic rise. My heart started to pound and I could feel my blood pressure actually rise.

"Breathe, Kate." Joshua said calmly, squeezing my hand. He'd heard my heart race again.

I closed my eyes and breathed deeply. Within a fraction of a second I could feel the panic drain away, leaving me relaxed and focused again. "That's so useful." I said.

"Yup." Joshua said.

"Really though, what am I going to do? What about mum? What do I tell her?"

"You will have to tell her the truth. There is no way you can hide any of this from her, especially now, when you are vulnerable." Helena said.

"Vulnerable?" I said.

"Yes. You have so much to learn and control, even though you don't know it yet. How can you hide from her that you don't sleep, only eat rarely and don't age. Those are things a mother of a teenager will notice and although she may think you are on drugs to start with, that idea will not last long nor explain everything." Helena said.

"But tell her everything? What if she runs away screaming?" I half-heartedly laughed, however, it wasn't funny.

"Now you know how I felt when I first told you." Joshua said.

"Having met your mum, I think she is strong enough to cope with the truth, plus hiding it from her would be a nightmare." Tara said.

Wil nodded in agreement.

"I think honesty is best when the person can be trusted. I would suggest you confide in her. Would it help if I was there when you do?" Helena offered.

"No, but thanks" I said, grateful for the kind offer.

Helena nodded, "It's probably for the best."

I nodded. "What about school?" I asked.

"Yes, that's a problem. At least I had the summer to gain some control so I wasn't too dangerous." Joshua said.

"School is a little harder to sort though." Wil said, "You've only just started the term."

"I know." I said.

"Why don't you restart after Christmas?" Tara suggested. "That should be enough time to get some control."

"It would be hard for her to catch up and she would need a believable excuse for her absence." Daniel said.

"Why not take a year off? A lot of students do that, anyway...that won't be unusual." Wil suggested.

"A year?" I was shocked, "Is there a need for a whole year?"

"Not for getting control and learning what you need to know, no...but for the humans to accept it as normal, something someone your age would do, then yes. The idea has possibilities." Daniel said.

"You have to remember it's just a year, Kate. Your life is so much longer now, a year is a mere drop in the ocean. You can spend many lifetimes studying anything you like." Helena said.

A year off, made sense I supposed. I'd never even considered it when I was living my human life. It shocked me to think like that, to think of everything that went before was a different life. "Using the 'year out' idea might work...I'll discuss it with mum and see what she thinks too...once I have explained everything else and if she's not locked me up in a mental hospital." I said, deeply disturbed by the thought.

Joshua hugged me closer in reassurance.

I glanced at my watch out of habit, it was 4am. I felt mentally tired from the day but my body felt vibrant and awake. The realisation of not sleeping began to sink in. "Perhaps I will miss sleeping more than I first thought. I have no idea what I'll do to fill the time."

Everyone chuckled knowingly, except Joshua, he looked at me sheepishly. Eventually, when the conversation moved on to who would be best to fill the council spaces, I tuned out voices and watched Joshua's face in silence. I could see he was hiding something from me. My ever improving eyesight could see the tiny muscles and their involuntary movements in his face that proved he was not telling me everything. Those movements gave him away as much as if he'd just told a lie.

"Fancy a last walk on the beach?" Joshua whispered.

"Sure, I'd love too."

We slipped out of the villa, virtually unnoticed by the others. Joshua closed the sliding glass door behind us with a small click. I heard it, but was too lost to other sensations. My newly evolved state gave me a much greater appreciation of our surroundings. I stood looking around me at anything and everything in the pre-dawn pale light.

"Oh my." I said.

"Amazing isn't it?" Joshua stood next to me on the deck.

"I never imagined..." I was awestruck. Everything was different and yet the same. My eyes stared at the fir tree next to the deck, the one I usually sat under appreciating the shade, I watched as its aura pulsed in a beautiful shade of dark green. I reached out to touch it.

"Wait."

"What?" I pulled my hand back quickly and turned to look at him.

"There are things you need to know first, before you try to absorb energy. Also, there are some things I want to talk to you about." Joshua held out his hand, "Walk with me?"

I looked down into his up turned palm and watched the rainbow colours swirl around it. "Sure." I said, a little absentmindedly and I heard him chuckle.

"That is if you can tear yourself away from the colours."

"Oh, yeah. Sorry." I smiled sheepishly. Someday, I would get used to this, but not today.

We walked down the beach hand in hand. The sand was cool

Chameleon

on my bare feet and it was a rosy cream colour in the pre-dawn light. Joshua didn't seem eager to talk even though I could sense he wanted to.

"So what do you do at night time that you were not willing to let everyone else know about?" I asked.

He stopped mid step, "How did you...?"

"Aha. I knew you were hiding something, do you lead a double life? Or is it something I really don't want to know about?" I said. Maybe I shouldn't have asked the question.

He laughed and looked embarrassed but quickly stopped the blush from developing on his face.

"C'mon, I promise I won't laugh."

"Well, if you insist. Just remember, it was your idea, right?" He said.

"Right."

He lowered his eyes. "I do read at night a fair bit but mostly...I watch." He said shyly, raising his eyes again to look at me meaningfully.

"Watch what?"

"You."

"Me?" I raised an eyebrow, "What do you mean, you watch me? Watch me do what?"

"I watch you do...well, almost everything." He stopped speaking and looked somewhat ashamed. "You have to understand it was before...before you evolved, when you were human and breakable." He reached out and touched my face with his fingers, "I watched over you most nights. I sat on your lawn chair and watched your house when you slept or stood in the bushes in your garden watching you when you were awake. I even watched you paint you bedroom, I was sitting in a tree a block away...I just wanted to make sure you were safe. It was why Tara and I followed you to the pub the night of the accident." Joshua looked at me sheepishly, obviously afraid of what I would say.

And he should have been.

I was horrified at the thought of being watched without knowing it but it was also rather funny and I burst out laughing.

It was not the reaction he had expected and he looked confused.

"So you are trying to tell me that not only are you a vampire but you are also a stalker? Your life sounds like a bad movie." I laughed even harder.

His face broke into a smile of relief. "I was just trying to keep you safe."

"You're such a weirdo." I laughed and kissed him on the nose, "Good job I love you, isn't it?"

"Yes, I love you too." He smiled and put his arm around my shoulders as we walked along the beach in companionable silence until we came to the fire pit where we had shared his last night before being tested. Joshua once again built the fire and lit it. He seemed a little subdued.

I sat on the damp sand watching him, his face darkly silhouetted against the pale pre-dawn light shinning off the water behind him. I had no clue what he was thinking but I knew he was deep in thought. It was a pleasure to watch him doing such a simple task. He was unusually graceful, it seemed to be a Chameleon trait. Was I graceful now? I wondered.

My fingers played in the cool sand and when I looked carefully at it, it seemed different somehow. I scooped up a handful and looked closer. The poor light didn't help but I could swear that it was glowing...kind of.

"Freaky, isn't it?" Joshua sat down next to me and looked at the sand in my hand.

"So it is glowing slightly, it's not just the bad lighting?" I said.

"Nope, you're seeing the energy of the sand. Sand is an inanimate object and doesn't have an aura, its energy is, well, sand coloured, just as rocks are rock colour and bricks are brick colour. They still have a residual energy from the components that make them up but not an aura as such."

I looked around me at the rocks and stones on the edge of the beach, it was true, there was a faint energy field around everything and it was the same colour as the object. "Fascinating..." I peered ever more closely at the sand.

He gazed out toward the horizon for several minutes, seemingly staring into space.

"Okay, fess up. What's on your mind?"

"What?" Joshua turned his head to look at me.

"What did you want to talk to me about?"

"Just stuff on being a Chameleon..." Joshua avoided my eyes and looked away.

"And? That's not all, it is?" I reached out and put my hand on his arm, "Joshua you can tell me anything, what's bothering you?"

"Not so much bothering...more curious." He turned and looked back at me.

"Tell me." I said quietly.

"Well...I was wondering...why it was a...No. I mean, I understand if that's how you feel but I need to hear it from you." He said quietly.

"A...no? No to what?" I frowned not understanding what he was saying.

"The proposal."

Of course, the proposal. Everything clicked into place. I hadn't even thought of it since before the ball. I felt somewhat guilty now. I could feel myself blush and decided not to bother hiding it. I hadn't worn the jewellery at the Evolution Ball, which means he thinks I said no. I watched his face as I a drew breath to answer him and saw him cringe slightly as if bracing for bad news.

"Well, I didn't think it was an appropriate time to reply...seeing as either of us could have died at any second." I said.

"So...it wasn't a no?" His eyes widen in hope.

"Nope, not a no. Just a 'lets see if we are alive first' kind of pause." I said.

"Oh...I see." Joshua lifted his hand and stroked my cheek with the back of his fingers.

A ripple of pleasure from his touch swept through me, causing delicious goosebumps.

"And now that we're alive?" He held my face in his hands, just inches from his face.

My breath came quickly as I tried to formulate my answer. "In truth, I've not really had a chance to think about it with everything that's happened today."

"You can take as long as you need. Just know I'm here for as long as you want me."

Joshua leaned in closer and kissed me fully on the lips. A breathless and needy kiss that caused my heart to speed up and now, with my new hearing, I could hear how loud and fast his heart was beating too. I snuggled into his arms with my head resting on his chest in contentment.

As the sky lightened, I spotted the sun rising over the horizon. "Oh." I said and leapt up, standing fully in its rays. I was speechless as I watched the dawning glory that was the sun, life giver to the planet and all upon it. The normal pale colours during dawn were changed with my new eyes into the most glorious explosion of colours from pink to deep gold. Each shade was so much stronger, deeper and more throbbing with life and energy than I'd ever dreamt. It was so full of vibrant colour I felt stunned and speechless as tears of pure joy ran down my cheeks.

My body vibrated with the energy from the sun's rays, I could feel the warmth soaking into my bones. It made my skin pulsate and tingle with energy. I touched my arm in the

Chameleon

sunlight, it felt like I'd been sunbathing all day, it had that warm glowing flesh feeling. I watched the rainbow that surrounded my flesh ripple in the sunlight, like waves. Awestruck, I looked over towards Joshua who was also stood in the glorious light.

He was even more beautiful than usual with the light of the sun on him and his rainbow aura rippling like mine. My heart beat faster and swelled with pride as I realised this amazing man loved me and wanted to be with me forever. Happiness flowed through me, just as the energy of the sun did.

We stood quietly for a long time watching and absorbing the energy of the sun, until finally I spoke. "So, now what?"

"Now," Joshua said and smiled, then held me close, "we teach you how to be a Chameleon."

The next instalment of 'The Chameleon Sagas':

Castrum Lucis

Coming soon

Find out what happens to Kate when she returns to her old life with her new abilities. Will everything go smoothly? More importantly, what will Kate become, a Hippy, a Feeder or a Bleeder? What will happen at Castrum Lucis and will she succeed at her own testing and interment?

Jonas and some of his followers escaped, where are they and what are they plotting next?

All these questions and many more will be answered in Castrum Lucis, Book II of The Chameleon Sagas.

Castrum Lucis

In the home of the Council, anything can happen.

MORE TITLES FROM EDAIN DUGUAY

The Witchlets of Witches Brew
(YA fiction)
Published by Wyrdwood Publications 2013

All Edain Duguay's books can be found at
Wyrdwood Publications.com
and
Edain Duguay.com

About Wyrdwood Publications

Wyrdwood Publications is a small eco-friendly publishing house, founded in 2006.

As an independent book publisher, based solely on the Internet, we have a responsible 'green attitude' to the publishing of our books.

For EVERY 'Green Leaves' book we sell, a tree will be planted!

This book is a 'Green Leaves' book and we thank you for helping us to plant trees in a deforested area of the world.

Go to our Green Leaves Policy page on our website, for more details on how we are incorporating green ideas into our publication business and helping to make a difference to the environment we live in.

CPSIA information can be obtained at www.ICGtesting.com
Printed in the USA
LVOW01s0848180714

394659LV00004B/9/P